Distant
Lover

Other Titles by Gloria Mallette

The Honey Well

Promises to Keep

Weeping Willows Dance

Shades of Jade

When We Practice to Deceive

GLORIA MALLETTE

Distant Lover

KENSINGTON PUBLISHING CORP.
http://www.kensingtonbooks.com

DAFINA BOOKS are published by

Kensington Publishing Corp.
850 Third Avenue
New York, NY 10022

All Kensington titles, imprints and distributed lines are available at special quantity discounts for bulk purchases for sales promotion, premiums, fund-raising, educational or institutional use.

Special book excerpts or customized printings can also be created to fit specific needs. For details, write or phone the office of the Kensington Special Sales Manager: Kensington Publishing Corp., 850 Third Avenue, New York, NY 10022., Attn. Special Sales Department. Phone: 1-800-221-2647.

Dafina Books and the Dafina logo Reg. U.S. Pat. & TM Off.

ISBN 0-7582-0470-1

First Hardcover Printing: October 2004
First Trade Paperback Printing: September 2005
10 9 8 7 6 5 4 3 2 1

Printed in the United States of America

ACKNOWLEDGMENTS

First and foremost, I thank the Lord for once again blessing me with a story to tell, and for giving me an audience interested in reading it.

Much love to my husband, Arnold, for journeying with me on this literary path of highs and lows. Arnold, your patience is, at times, greater than mine—thank you for being the calm one.

Much love to my son, Jared, for trying his best to give me time alone to write—try harder next time, little one.

I humbly acknowledge my editor, Karen Thomas, for once again allowing me to write a story as dictated by my characters and not by a set of rules or formula. As well, a nod of appreciation to my agent, Stacey Glick of Dystel Literary Management, for being proactive in my career; and a special thank-you to Jessica McLean, the national sales representative of Kensington Books, for her selfless encouragement and enthusiasm. In addition, I must thank publicist Peggy Hicks of Tricom for always finding the time to talk and for her expertise in marketing titles by African-American authors.

Much love and appreciation to Trust Graham and Richlieu Dennis of Nubian Heritage of Brooklyn, Queens, and Harlem, New York. You've always believed in me and you've always supported me. You are forever in my heart. Thank you for a fabulous book release party. You're the best. And to David D. Wright of The Orature Repertory Radio Theatre Group, thank you for coming through for me. Aixa Kendrick and Keisha Monique Booker, you ladies were superb.

A heartfelt hug to so many reviewers and book clubs who have always been fair and open-minded when reviewing my titles.

Last but most certainly not least, I tip my hat to the readers, the book clubs, the bookstore owners and managers, and the book vendors all across the country. Without you, my books would not be read. Bless you.

DISTANT LOVER

Yesterday I dreamed of you.
Today I yearn for you.
Every time I ache for the touch of you,
I'm reminded how distant I am from you.
Time and space has long intruded,
my love for you years ago rooted.
You are my distant lover,
you are the desire I cannot savor.
You are my distant lover,
my fantasy, my lover of favor.

—Gloria Mallette

1

Hordes of people—some strolling, some shopping, others hurrying about their own personal business—were rudely brushing past Tandi Belson, irritating her, making her move out of each square foot of sidewalk she claimed while she waited for Brent. She couldn't get mad at Brent. He was only four minutes late. She was the one who was early—twenty-seven minutes early. Of course, if Brent was allowed to come to her house to see her like other girls' boyfriends, she would not have had to sneak and meet him on the corner of Jamaica Avenue and 164th Street, one of the busiest commercial street corners in Jamaica, Queens, on a Saturday afternoon, when she was supposed to be bowling with her girlfriends up on Hillside Avenue. If her father had an inkling, he'd put a dog collar around her neck and let her out only when school was in session. Her father didn't like Brent and the truth was, grumpy old Glynn Belson didn't like her either. But that was all right. His disliking her didn't bother Tandi, at least not anymore.

All that mattered to Tandi was that she had Brent and that they were in love. And it *was* love, although puppy love is what Aunt Gert called it; a hot ass is what her father called it. Of course, neither was right. She wasn't a starry-eyed kid, and she wasn't hot to lose her virginity. She was truly in love, and while losing her virginity wasn't uppermost in her mind, she would not hold back nor would she regret it if it were to Brent Rodgers. He was to die for. Sometimes Tandi felt like she couldn't breathe until she could see Brent again, until she could touch him and know that he was real and not a figment of her imagination. Oh, but Brent was very real. Hadn't he, just the day before, behind the bleachers in the school gymnasium, tongued her deep and long while feeling her breasts under her gym shirt, rendering her weak in the knees and moist in a place where she had not yet been touched? Soon though, that's for sure.

Oh, God! There he is! Tandi's heart leaped. Her pulse quickened as she watched Brent's long, muscular legs bring him closer. The funny thing was, she must have seen him walking down the street hundreds of times, yet each and every time she saw him was like seeing him for the very first time. He still took her breath away just as he did to a lot of girls at Francis Lewis High School. She knew of three in particular who would scratch her eyes out to get with Brent, but who could blame them? Brent was all that and more. He was definitely something to look at. The skimpy muscle shirt and mid-thigh shorts he wore exposed his sculptured biceps, his touch-me pecs, and powerful runner's thighs. Brent truly must have been a beautiful baby because he was so fine now—and he was all hers. Tandi couldn't wait to be in his arms, to taste of his lips, to feel his hardness against her softness. Her entire body throbbed with a yearning so strong she trembled. She wanted Brent to—

"Mommy! Are you sleeping in there?"

Tandi's eyes flew open. She yanked her hand from between her thighs. She quickly sat up, splashing her tepid bathwater up against the wall and over the side of the tub onto the floor. "Damn," she whispered, hating that the bath mat was probably soaked, and most likely the rug, too. She looked down at her legs through the clear water. There wasn't a single bubble left.

Knock . . . knock . . . knock.

"Mommy! Can I have some ice cream and cookies?"

Looking at the door, Tandi sighed heavily. Back to reality. She was no longer that carefree seventeen-year-old girl whose every dream and every waking thought was of Brent. She was a wife to Jared Crawford who no longer noticed her, and a mother to Michael Jared who was the light of her life. Secretly, she ached shamelessly for an eighteen-year-old boy from way back in 1984 when the lazy, hazy summer days of her sexual awakening, combined with soulful love songs whet her appetite for Brent and filled her head with erotic fantasies and made her reality even sweeter when he became hers.

"Mommy!"

"What!"

" 'Bout time! Can I have some ice cream and cookies?"

Although the house was quite warm, just the mention of ice cream and knowing that the icy rains that came with the end of January were still falling outside her bathroom window made Tandi shiver in her tepid bathwater.

"Please, Mommy."

"Did you finish your homework?"

"Yeah. Can I have some ice cream and cookies?"

"Michael Jared, you had cookies when you got in from school this afternoon."

"Mommy, that was hours ago, and you only let me have three."

"That's because you ate a whole package of cookies yesterday."

"It was a small pack. Mommy, we got cookies, why can't I eat 'em?"

"Boy . . . Michael Jared, you're wearing me out. Take three more cookies and let me finish my bath in peace." She knew Michael Jared would ignore her and eat darn near the whole package again. But what could she do? He was a growing boy with a big appetite.

"Mommy, one day you gonna drown in there."

"I'm sure you'll break down the door and save your drowning mother, won't you?"

"That's gross! I don't wanna see you in no bathtub. I'd call nine-one-one."

"By that time, I could be dead."

"They'll bring you back, just don't let them see you naked."

Tandi smiled to herself. "Boy, go get your cookies and ice cream before I change my mind."

Michael Jared was her heart, her baby, but he was at the awkward crossroads of still being a little boy and the awakening of his own sexuality. He had a hissy fit when she told him she use to bathe him along with herself, and sometimes along with his father when he was a baby, which wasn't all that long ago, and now that he'd had his first wet dream and, most likely, compared notes with his equally horny finger-playing buddies, nudity and sex went hand in hand despite what she told him to the contrary. Michael Jared thought it gross to even think of her and Jared as either nude or sexual.

Knock . . . knock . . . knock.

She thought Michael Jared had gone. "What?"

"Mommy, can I watch TV?"

"You know the rules."

"Can I, please? I finished my homework. One hour. Please, Mommy."

Tandi wasn't up to a long, drawn-out debate. "Thirty minutes, Michael Jared, and no more. It's almost eight-thirty."

"Thanks!"

Tandi could hear him running down the stairs. "And don't make a mess!"

Whether Michael Jared heard her or not, he'd still leave melted chocolate ice cream spots on the coffee table in the family room and his empty bowl in the sink without a drop of water in it. Too many times she had tried to get him to clean up after himself, but Michael Jared seemed to prefer emulating his father. There wasn't much she could do about Jared—his mama had already raised him—but Michael Jared, he could still be taught. Tandi wasn't about to saddle her future daughter-in-law with a man who expected his woman to do everything for him except for maybe pick his teeth. That is, not if she could help it.

She often wondered what kind of father Brent Rodgers would have made. God, she had to stop doing that. Drawing her legs up, Tandi planted her feet solidly on the bottom of the tub, gripped the sides, and heaved herself up. Water cascaded down her body back into the tub like a waterfall. Deep in thought, she took her time drying herself off. Lately, more and more, Brent was constantly on her mind. If she wasn't comparing Jared to Brent, she was wishing Brent would call or show up at her door. She hadn't seen him in twenty years so she didn't know if he was alive or dead, married or single, or if he was a bum on the street or president of a company. They had only gone together that one unforgettable last year in high school, but she could still feel what it was like to be kissed by him, and, in her mind's eye, she could still see him walking down the street like it was yesterday. The more she thought about Brent, the more she ached to see him, to feel him inside her; for that she blamed Jared. If her life with him was any good—if he hadn't cheated on her and left her doubting her own ability to keep him interested—she wouldn't be dredging up memories of Brent Rodgers and relying on those memories to feed her emotionally anemic love life.

2

Tandi couldn't say she knew the exact moment she felt her marriage was over; she just knew it didn't end all at once. It didn't end three years ago on the day she was cleaning out Jared's closet and found six love letters from a woman named Jackie, stashed in a pair of old sneakers far back in the closet. Her marriage didn't end altogether that same evening when the first words out of Jared's mouth were a lie about when the letters were written—before they were married—and that he had kept the letters for sentimental reasons. The letters were not dated so Tandi couldn't dispute him but she didn't believe his lie either, not then, not now. If only she'd ended it then, she wouldn't be reliving the hurt she felt that day.

"Jared, if that's the case, why did you hide the letters in your sneakers way in the back of the closet?"

Jared cursed himself for keeping the letters that were spread out on the dining room table before him. "Because I didn't want you to get the wrong idea like you're getting anyway."

"Actually, the hiding of the letters is what's giving me the wrong idea." Tandi picked up one of the letters and had begun to open the envelope when Jared snatched it from her and hastily gathered the rest.

"That's all right, take them," she said. "I've already read them."

Jared momentarily closed his eyes.

"See, Jared, a liar is always caught. You would not have had to hide a letter written before we were married unless you were seeing this woman behind my back when we were going together."

"No. I wasn't seeing her behind your back."

"So when were you seeing her?" She had put him on the spot. His eyes were moving rapidly.

"It was . . . it was before we got—"

"Stop lying, Jared. These letters aren't that old. The paper hasn't even faded. You're having an affair."

"No. No, I wouldn't do that to you."

"Stop lying!"

"I'm—"

She tossed the credit card statement at him. It landed on the floor at his feet. Right away Jared saw what it was and was reluctant to pick it up.

"Motels take cash, you know."

She had walked away from Jared then—out of the house, but not out of their marriage. Like now, back then it was a cold day. She had driven to Daina's house, her and Jared's best friend, but Daina wasn't home and neither was Evonne when she called her. In the end, she had driven around Queens through quiet, tree-lined neighborhoods of modest red-brick houses, intermingled with old white-framed houses with no destination in mind, just to end up back in front of her own brick house of crumbling walls. It was then that she realized she really had nowhere to go.

That was three years ago and since then, Tandi felt as if she had been holding on to her marriage by her fingertips. For a little while there, she had been hoping and praying she and Jared could get back some of their early magic, but that had all been for naught. She and Jared had grown so far apart they had become ex-lovers, ex-friends, nearly strangers in their own home. While she spent most of her time there, Jared was spending all of his time away from it. Working, he claimed. The truth was, he did work long, hard hours, which he faulted for his exhaustion. He had stopped making love to her, he said, because he was always tired. Tandi didn't buy that. Not after she found the letters, not after knowing that Jared used to make love to her at least three days a week even after he'd worked a full day.

The truth was, Jared was no longer interested in her, and she had been too blind to see it. There had been a slew of months that added up to years of first acceptance of Jared's excuses as to why he was too tired to make love to her or too busy to be with her until she got to where she didn't care if he came home or not. She was always irritable, and her irritability intensified the moment Jared walked in the door. Now, she felt trapped—trapped in a cycle of domestic mediocrity and endless days without passion for life or love. Tandi knew she didn't always feel that way; she used to love taking care of her home and her man, that was her life.

That's why she knew she didn't simply wake up one morning and wish Jared would cease to exist; it really was more subtle than that. Over time, little things that didn't seem so important snuck up on her and became overwhelmingly irritating: Jared's dirty socks dropped and left so carelessly on the bedroom floor for her to pick up; the way he left the soap drowning in the dish so that when she touched it, it was repulsively soft and slimy; his chewing with his mouth open, nauseating her; and smacking his food loud enough to be heard a room away. It really wasn't worth it to continually nag him about those things, but she did anyway. Jared's response was his usual blank look and an offhanded "What's the big deal," which only irritated Tandi more. Looking back, Jared was doing the same things and worse thirteen years ago, but then she overlooked them. Now, they were driving her out of her mind.

While Tandi's feelings about her marriage had not soured all at once, it seemed to her that Jared appeared to show his age all at once. She didn't know when stray hairs started growing like vines out of his nose and ears or when sprigs of gray popped up in his moustache. Nor could she recall when his once tight washboard stomach softened a bit. True, he was six years older than she and none of that should have bothered her when her hips had spread a good eight inches since she had Michael Jared eleven years ago, and no matter how many crunches she did, her stomach still wasn't as flat as it was when she was a seventeen-year-old and proud to wear the halter tops and midriff blouses that her father hated. The truth was, her belly button was never going to see the light of day again. And, worse yet, fine lines were beginning to appear around her mouth, reminding her that her thirty-seven years were marking her.

It was times like these Tandi wondered what her mother might have looked like if she had lived. Then she'd know what to expect down the line when her passable good looks morphed into a mask of wrinkles and tired old worry lines. Unfortunately, the one picture she had of her mother was a faded old Polaroid taken when her mother was fifteen years old, and that she had only seen once. Her father said her mother had been shy about taking photos, but it was hard to believe that after a five-year marriage just one picture of her mother existed. She wanted to ask her father if she resembled her mother, if she was like her in any way, but he didn't like her or her brother, Glynn, bringing her up. Maybe their mother's passing was too painful for him still, and being a man—not supposed to cry—perhaps he had never dealt fully with his loss. Who knows? As for herself, Tandi wished her mother were alive so that she could talk to her about Jared. A more experienced voice was what she needed to help her deal with the ending of her marriage. This wasn't something she wanted to share with just anyone, not even her closest friends, Evonne and Daina— especially Daina—who wanted her to be with Jared until she drew her last breath. But Evonne's bored expression whenever she complained about Jared said clearly that she was sick of hearing the same old tales of woe.

Evonne would say, "You and Jared have been taking each other for granted for so long, you've lost your spontaneity. You're too comfort- able with each other, which leads to disinterest, and the pity of it is, you have a lifestyle that most single women, including me, would die for."

Isn't it funny how people on the outside looking in salivate over another's life? If only for even a day, they could live the life of the one they envy. Their minds would be changed. Neither Evonne nor Daina understood completely what she was going through and what she was feeling—unloved and trapped. Daina, who had introduced her to Jared in the first place, had advised her once to get herself a lover on the side and keep Jared as the meal ticket, just as she had done with her husband, Herb. Daina was convinced Herb had a lover on the side himself. Personally, Tandi didn't see why she needed that headache. It would only compound her problems.

When she told Evonne what Daina had suggested, Evonne bitched, "Daina's a tramp. I know you're not going to listen to her."

"Believe me, I don't need to complicate my life any more than it is."

"Tandi, I don't get you. Jared's one in a million. You should be happy you got a hardworking man, and not some bum laying up on you watching television all day and hitting you up for cigarette and beer money. Stop bitching, girl, and count yourself lucky."

It wasn't very often but there were moments when Tandi felt bad about griping about her life with Jared, but she couldn't help it. After all, this Jared wasn't the man she fell in love with, not by a long shot.

This Jared didn't talk to her late into the night about his day, his plans, their life—all of which used to ignite her desire for him. This Jared had lost his passion for her and she had lost hers for him. They were more like roommates than man and wife. Maybe she picked and nagged at the little things and started arguments with him in an attempt to put some fire under his ass, but nary a spark would take, not even a wisp of smoke would materialize. If anything, Jared withdrew from her more. Rarely did he argue back, choosing instead to lock his eyes on the television or an invisible spot on the wall. Mostly, he'd get up and go off into another room, away from her mouth, which was how they started sleeping in separate rooms. Last night was the last straw though. Jared went to sleep on her when she was trying to talk him into taking two weeks off in July so they could take a cruise to Barcelona, a place she always wanted to go. She thought she'd give it one last try to see if they could find their way back, but when he fell asleep on the living room sofa, he could not have angered her more. While Jared slept, Tandi had sat up all night planning her divorce and wondering where Brent Rodgers was.

3

Before Jared's foot touched down on the second step at the top of the stairs, he was, once again, aware that the smell of bacon or breakfast sausage was conspicuously missing. What was different this time was that even the aroma of fresh-brewed coffee was absent. Apparently, Tandi hadn't even made coffee for herself. Jared continued down the stairs knowing that, yet again, he was going to have to stop at the restaurant down the street from his office.

"Morning, MJ."

Michael Jared looked up from his bowl of oatmeal. "Hey, Dad. You're late."

"I know. I overslept." Jared stood behind the chair he'd normally be sitting in eating his breakfast. He glanced over at Tandi at the counter, her back to him. "Morning, Tandi. I didn't mean to fall asleep on you last night. I was beat."

Silently sucking her teeth, Tandi slid Michael Jared's bologna-and-cheese sandwich into a plastic sandwich bag and zipped it shut. She didn't bother to turn around. There was nothing she had to say to Jared about last night or any night. It was her tomorrows without him in her life she wanted to talk about—that is when Michael Jared wasn't around.

Michael Jared looked up again at Jared and shrugged.

In response, Jared shrugged. He glanced at the back of Tandi's head as she went about her business of packing MJ's lunch. He was used to the silent treatment. He turned back to MJ. "Hey, man, want me to drop you off this morning?"

"Can I ride up front?"

"Yep."

"All right!"

"Then finish up." Jared sauntered over to the refrigerator and took out the container of orange juice. It felt light. He shook it. It was almost empty. "Tandi, would you like some juice?"

Still not turning around, she grumbled, "No." She wanted to punch him.

Who was Jared fooling? All of a sudden he had time to drive ten blocks out of his way to drop Michael Jared off despite the fact that he was already late. How magnanimous of him to volunteer to do what he often called "her job." That's another thing she hated about him. If she had asked—no, begged—him to take Michael Jared to school, he would not have hesitated to say no, but because he was trying to get back into her good graces, he was graciously volunteering, and making himself look good in Michael Jared's eyes to boot. Oh, how she wanted to be a bitch and tell him to not do her any favors, but she'd come off looking like the bad guy. If having his father take him to school made Michael Jared happy, she wouldn't spoil it for him, although she hated that big-ass SUV Jared insisted on buying. It was like a truck and Jared drove much too fast in it.

Michael Jared, on the other hand, liked riding high, fast, and hard. He complained that her mid-sized four-cylinder sedan was a whimp car, no power. Most days when she dropped him off, he'd bolt from the car almost before she even came to a full stop. If he had his way, he would get out of the car blocks from school and walk the rest of the way. Of course she knew he didn't want his friends to see that his mother still drove him to school, but that was just too bad. Time would come soon enough when she'd have to let him go it alone. Then, as life would have it, when his butt gets grown, he'll probably be begging her for a ride or even for her car. For now, she'd continue to take him to school. It was about her own peace of mind and her need to know he was safe. Still, she dreaded the day he turned eighteen and got his first car, as Jared had promised him. Already, behind her back, he had been teaching Michael Jared how to drive on the rare occasion he spent time with him—a precious few Saturday afternoons after work. She knew that was a father-son thing and didn't interfere, but just the same, she dreaded the day that was sure to come.

While slowly pouring himself less than a half glass of juice, Jared watched Tandi stubbornly avoid looking at him.

Michael Jared scooped up his cinnamon-sprinkled oatmeal with more enthusiasm and slurped down the last few spoonfuls. He jumped up from the table and was about to sprint out of the kitchen.

"Get back here, mister." Tandi opened the dishwasher door and pulled the tray out.

"Oh," Michael Jared said. He quickly picked up his bowl and half-empty glass of orange juice. For a second he couldn't decide if he wanted to drink the juice or empty it down the sink. One piercing look from Tandi, he turned the glass up to his mouth and began gulping down the juice, some of it dribbling over the side of the glass from the corner of his mouth onto his white oversized T-shirt.

"Look at what you're doing," Tandi said.

Michael Jared looked down at his shirt. "Aww, man."

"Go change," Jared said. He put the empty juice container back into the refrigerator.

Tandi cut her eyes at Jared. It annoyed her that he was playing daddy. "Put on that blue sweater I hung on your doorknob last night," she said to Michael Jared.

Michael Jared quickly placed his bowl, glass, and spoon into the dishwasher.

Tandi shook her head. In his eagerness to be driven to school in Jared's jeep, Michael Jared forgot to give her a hard time about telling him what to wear. He hadn't readily agreed to wear anything she told him to wear since he was eight years old.

Michael Jared raced out of the room, leaving Tandi alone with Jared. She turned back to the counter.

Jared quietly sipped on his juice while watching Tandi. His eyes traveled down from the back of her head to her butt. Inside, he smiled. Tandi had a butt worth smiling about—firm, curvaceous, and definitely a handful. He would have palmed it except she'd only snap at him about last night or say she wasn't in the mood; always an excuse to keep him from touching her the few times he had the inclination, which wasn't too often. He was usually too tired when he got in from work to even spell the word *sex*. Of course, it didn't help that Tandi was mired in one long sour funk that never lifted for anyone but MJ. Tandi was a good mother, and up until the time she found out he had cheated on her, she had been a good wife. He could not have asked for better, which was why he wished he could close up the office and take her on that cruise she so wanted. He owed her that and more for cheating on her.

His affair had been the biggest mistake of his life. It had happened more than a handful of times, but it had been with one woman, Jackie McBride. Jackie had been a client—a good-paying, repeat client—for years. And for years he had ignored her come-ons—getting up close to him to talk, wearing low-cut blouses and short-behind skirts whenever she came into the office, and holding his gaze longer than it was comfortable. As enticing a temptation as Jackie was, he had held strong. Besides, his secretary, Marci, and his paralegal, Raoul, were always around. That is until Jackie scheduled an appointment for four-thirty in the afternoon and then called at five o'clock to say she was stuck in traffic and begged him to please wait for her, that the matter couldn't wait. He knew it could, but he waited anyway. Marci and Raoul left at five-thirty. Jackie showed up at six.

Jackie signed the will he had prepared and instead of pulling out her checkbook, she pulled out a cigarette. She lit it, but she didn't smoke it for long. While talking, she let it burn itself out. Then like a cat, she slinked around his desk and sat up on it in front of him.

"It's hot in here," she said. She unbuttoned her trench coat and slowly slipped it off her shoulders, exposing the red satin bra and bikini panties she wore, and nothing more.

Guiltily, Jared glanced at Tandi. Even now he felt himself getting an erection from the memory. Jackie had opened her thighs wide and pulled the crotch of her panties aside so he could see her nakedness. When she slipped her own finger inside of herself, mesmerized, he watched as Jackie gyrated her hips and moved her finger in and out of her wet, glistening hole, filling his nose with her scent. He forgot his vows. He forgot he was in his office. He rose up in between Jackie's thighs and—

Slam! Tandi slammed the cabinet door, snapping Jared's head from between Jackie's thighs. Under the table, he tried to push himself down without being noticed. Tandi wasn't looking at him, but he felt like she knew he had been caught up in the memories of his affair. He hated that he had cheated on Tandi. Even while he was screwing Jackie, he hated what he was doing. When it started, he thought he'd hit it just that one time, but one time became two and before he realized it, he couldn't stop himself. And it wasn't that it was better with

Jackie. It was different, it was illicit. It was when Tandi found the letters that he forced himself to end it. He had begged Tandi to forgive him and while she had not left, she had pulled away from him. Her ardent kisses, her loving embraces, and her good-natured chattiness had morphed into an irritably angry sullenness. The silence was killing him.

Jared knew how to get Tandi's tongue wagging. "I forgot to tell you. Your brother came into my office yesterday to ask me about an old insurance policy of your father's."

Tandi's response would have been "Who cares?" if she were speaking to Jared. Instead, hoping he'd get the hint she didn't care, she went about picking up bread crumbs, one crumb at a time, with her fingertip. These days she wasn't speaking to Glynn either. He was the one who got along so well with their father, but he always left it to her to go see about him.

Jared refused to give up. "Glynn said he was going out of town for a few weeks."

Tandi mashed a crumb into the counter. "He couldn't call and tell me himself?" She snatched a single paper towel off the roll hanging under the cabinet.

"He said he didn't have time. He asked me to tell you to look in on your father."

Tandi spritzed the paper towel with water and angrily swiped it once across the counter toward the sink. She finally turned to Jared. "What about Leah? Is she going with him?"

"He didn't say. He said he'll call you before he leaves at the end of the week."

"Oh, how big of him. Where's he going?"

"Chicago. He said on business."

"Damnit." She balled the paper towel up and threw it into the open garbage container against the wall. "I am tired of taking care of that crotchety old man. I don't like him, and he certainly doesn't like me."

It was a dirty way to get her talking, but it worked. "Tandi, I don't see how he doesn't like you. You're the one who's there for him whether Glynn's in town or not."

"He doesn't see it that way, the old bastard. Yesterday, after I got back from shopping for him, he said he didn't like the way the pork chops I bought looked. Claimed they were too pale. He wanted me to take them back."

"Did you?"

"Do I look like I took them back? No one takes meat back to the store unless it's spoiled."

"So what did you do?"

"I told Daddy to take them back himself or get Glynn to do it. The whole thing was ridiculous, especially since he's not supposed to be eating pork. His high blood pressure is the reason he had to retire early in the first place."

"So why did you buy them?"

She looked at him coldly. "Because, Jared, I get tired of hearing his mouth."

"Well," Jared said calmly, "why don't you let him run his own errands?"

Tandi put her hands on her hips. "Do you ever listen to anything I say?"

Jared felt his stomach tighten, but he was cool.

"I told you. My father goes wherever he wants, except into a supermarket, which is where he chooses not to go. That old man, who is only sixty-two, is not an invalid, and he wouldn't be sick if he followed his doctor's orders and stopped smoking."

"I know you're not buying him cigarettes, Tandi, so how does he get them?"

"Probably from his little old wrinkled girlfriend down the street who he says is not his girlfriend, but he's been going with her for at least nine years that I know of."

"Who?"

Tandi looked at him like he should know.

"Oh. You mean Miss Iona?"

"Who else?"

"Tandi, give the old girl some credit. She must really like your father. She's hung in there."

"Jared, Miss Iona is a haggard old lady trying to get her hooks into a crusty old man with a pension. And as far as I'm concerned, they deserve each other."

Jared never realized how bitter Tandi was about her father seeing Miss Iona. "You don't like her much, huh?"

"I don't like nor dislike her. I just know that she's going to give my father a heart attack and herself, too, if she's not careful. She shouldn't be smoking either, much less trying to do what I caught them doing in his bedroom last week. That old man is going to have a heart attack."

"Maybe not," Jared said doubtfully. "His heart seems to be strong enough for sex."

"Yeah, well, I wish his heart was strong enough to let him take care of his own errands. It's not fair that he does what he wants and I'm the one who has to take care of him and chauffeur him back and forth to the doctor when he's sick. I'm tired of it."

"Tandi, you know I'd help out if I could, but you know I am not going near the man after he called me an ambulance chaser."

"Yeah, right." She knew Jared would not help her no matter what. "Where would you possibly find the time?"

Jared ignored the sarcasm. "Look, Tandi, don't go over there so often anymore. Make Glynn go."

"If it were as simple as that, I would have stopped going a long time ago. If I stopped, Glynn would never go over there. Like you, he's too busy. Then when I do go, I'd find a mummified body two pounds from being a skeleton. I know my father. Just to be ornery, he'd starve himself to death before he'd go out and shop for himself, just to make me feel guilty."

"What about Miss Iona? Can't she shop for him when she shops for herself?"

"He won't let her buy his food or cook for him because he says women get men through their stomachs, and he doesn't want her getting too comfortable. She might want to move in."

Jared kept trying. "Tandi, if he's starving, he just might let her."

"Wanna bet?" she asked irritably. "He'd rather keep using me, but I have a surprise for him. From now on, he'll have to cook for himself because I'm not going to do it anymore."

"That's what I'm talking about, and don't let him put a guilt trip on you."

"Let? Jared, you keep thinking that I'm allowing my father to fuck with me." Tandi glanced at the door, hoping Michael Jared hadn't heard her curse. She saw that Jared, too, glanced at the door.

"I didn't say you allowed anything," he said.

"Maybe not directly, but you keep intimating it, and you know what I've gone through with my father."

"Yes, I—"

"I don't have to keep telling you."

"No. I was just saying—"

"Jared, what all this comes down to is that my father hasn't done a damn thing for me since I was eighteen years old, and, needless to say, I haven't asked him for anything since then. He's my father so I try to do right by him, but all I'll ever want from him is for him to tell me where my mother is buried."

"Yeah, it's not right that he has never given you that information."

"He says he doesn't know. I think he's lying. He won't tell me because he doesn't want Glynn—who couldn't give a damn—or me going to her grave site."

"I never understood that."

She sucked her teeth. "Jared, I told you before. He hates her for walking out on us and leaving him for another man."

"Maybe he's still hurting."

"I don't believe that for a minute. A man who has an iceberg for a heart can't be hurt."

"You'd be surprised how hurt he could get."

"I doubt it. If my father had a heart, he would not have kept me and Glynn away from our mother after she left him."

"Maybe he feels guilty about that." Tandi's angry glare made Jared feel uneasy. "What's wrong?" he asked.

"Why are you always defending my father?"

"I'm not. I'm just trying to help you understand why your father acts the way he does. Your mother was killed in a car accident two years after she left him."

"And?"

"Your father had to feel guilty about not letting you see her."

"I doubt it."

"Tandi, guilt can make a man really bitter."

She wasn't willing to let her father off that easily. "Jared, my father was born bitter. If anything, my mother leaving him and her death hardened his soul even more. In his bitterness, he made my life miserable, and chances are, he made her life miserable. I will never forgive him for that. I hate him." She realized this was the first time she said that out loud. She'd always felt that way, and she'd always talked about her anger with him, but she'd never said in fact that she hated him. It felt cathartic. "I'll always hate him."

4

From the pained look in Tandi's eyes, Jared knew she was close to crying. And he had brought her to that point. A vein in her neck was pulsating, her chest was heaving. He had baited her and gotten her to
talk. He just hadn't intended to get her this upset. Her rage even surprised him. As calm as he was trying to be on the outside, his insides
were wound as tight as a spool of fishing wire. On top of being tense
about Tandi's anger with him, he was now worried about how angry
she was with her father and Glynn whom he had used to bait her into
talking. Jared knew Tandi's pain, he knew her heartaches, and he
knew all too well the deep dislike she had for her father. It was an old
story, never ending and never resolved. He knew Tandi yearned for
the love of a mother she had never known, and it made her needy for
him to be around when he couldn't. When they first met, and every so
often when she ached for the familial closeness of her father and
brother, which eluded her, she talked about her mother's death, her father's coldness, and Glynn's masking of his emotions. Tandi talked
about how she used to wish it had been her father who died and not
her mother. Thinking about what he had just done, Jared would not
have been surprised if Tandi was wishing the same for him.

"It just isn't fair," Tandi said, feeling drained of any energy she
might have had upon awakening earlier. "Glynn should look after
Daddy. Glynn is his favorite. He's the one who's gonna get the house
and what little money Daddy leaves behind."

"You don't know that for sure."

"I most certainly do. If you'll remember, my father had Glynn's name put on the deed along with his own years ago. Which is why I'm sure Glynn will get his money, but I don't care about that. I don't want anything of Daddy's, which is all the more reason why Glynn and Leah should be over there checking on him."

"The way I see it, Tandi, if you stop, they'll have to do more."

"I wouldn't count on it. Glynn and Leah's big-time careers keep them so busy they don't even have time to raise their own children. They have a live-in housekeeper slash nanny. I hate the way Leah throws that up in my face."

Jared had no doubt he had lost control of the ball. Tandi was beginning to pace. He had to do something to calm her down. Maybe she'd let him hold her. Standing, he'd taken a single step away from his chair when Tandi seemed to sense what he was about to do. She turned her back to him and went through the motion of busily wiping down the counter—again.

Jared got the message. He stayed where he was. "Your father should get a housekeeper. Isn't that what he needs?"

"What he really needs is to move out of that big-ass house and get a studio or a one-bedroom apartment."

"That's an option. Why don't you talk to Glynn about it?"

"I already have. The bottom line? Daddy won't move and Glynn won't make him. And as far as a housekeeper is concerned, Daddy said he doesn't want a stranger in his house snooping in his things or his business."

"Get someone anyway, Tandi. Eventually, he'll get used to it."

Tandi faced Jared. "If my father doesn't want a housekeeper, he won't pay for one, and I am not about to, and Glynn won't do anything Daddy doesn't want him to do."

"Then you don't have anything to lose. Don't go over there anymore. Besides, whenever you spend time over there, you come home upset. You should just stop going, period."

"You're right. I need to put an end to being used there, and here, too."

This was where Jared's unreadable trial face worked in his favor. He didn't blink, he didn't frown, he didn't let Tandi see she had blindsided him and left him speechless.

Sidling over to the sink, Tandi again turned her back to Jared. He was no different from Glynn or her father. They were all using her.

"Tandi, I'm not using you."

"Oh no, you wouldn't think so—you're the user."

Jared shot up from the table. "It's too damn early for this. I have to get to work. What's taking that boy so long?"

Turning on the water, Tandi rinsed the pot she had cooked the oatmeal in and placed it upside down in the dishwasher. She had been wanting to say that to Jared for a long time.

At the bottom of the stairs, Jared shouted, "MJ, get a move on!"

Damn. He had hoped talking about Tandi's father would take her mind off why she was angry with him. Instead he had dug a deeper hole for himself. The situation had gone from bad to disastrous and he didn't know what to do to reverse it. Going back into the kitchen, he saw Tandi was about to close the dishwasher door. That's when he remembered his juice glass. He scooped it up, and reaching around Tandi—touching her on the arm—went to put it in the dishwasher. Tandi quickly stepped an arm's distance away from Jared.

"Damn," he said. "Tandi, is it like that? I can't touch you?"

She said nothing.

Jared went ahead and placed his glass upside down on the rack alongside MJ's. "Are things that bad between us?"

She felt it had to be said, and she did with a cold, unflinching stare.

"What do you want me to do, Tandi? Will getting away, going on vacation, make you feel any better?"

"Not anymore."

That hole was getting deeper and harder for Jared to climb out of, but he wasn't about to give up. "Look, you already know that July and August are slow months in the courts, but I still have cases on the docket. I haven't told you, but I'm planning on hiring an additional attorney and a secretary. I can get a lot done this summer if I don't close the office. If I do, come September, I'll be running in place trying to catch up. But next year—"

"Forget it." She went back to packing Michael Jared's lunch bag with an orange soda, three vanilla cream cookies, and an apple.

"Tandi, just because I can't go on the cruise doesn't mean you can't. Take whatever money you need from the savings account. Take MJ and go. Have a good time."

She cut her eyes at him. "In other words, you're telling me to take my pubertal eleven-year-old son along as my escort. Need I remind you, Jared, that this is an adult cruise, couples, as in husbands and wives, boyfriends and girlfriends? So, while other couples are hugged up and gazing at a picturesque sunset from the deck of the ship, am I supposed to be tucking in my son and doing the same for myself with a boring book as my sole companion?"

"Damn, Tandi, I—"

"I said, forget it," she said, flipping her hand at him. "Obviously, you don't understand that I, and most women for that matter, whether they travel with their children or not, would rather have a man, a lover to wrap themselves around."

"This is bullshit!" He'd had enough. "Tandi, most women would be glad to have a man who opens his wallet and tells his wife she can travel around the world."

"In that case, I'd rather be a single woman. I'd rather enjoy myself on the cruise without guilt or a gold band."

"What the hell does that mean?"

"Do I have to spell it out for you?"

"Damn right."

"I'm ready," Michael Jared announced, coming back into the kitchen.

Tandi glanced over at Michael Jared standing in the doorway. His backpack, loaded with books, was draped over his left shoulder. There was that worried look in his eyes as he looked from her to Jared.

Jared took a set of keys from his pants pocket. "Here," he said to Michael Jared. "Unlock my truck and put the key in the ignition."

"Oh, boy!" Michael Jared eagerly took the keys from Jared's hand. He turned on his heels to leave.

"Jared, I don't want him to put the key in the ignition."

"Mommy!"

"He can do that. He's not gonna turn the engine over—right, MJ?"

"I'm not stupid, Mommy. I'm not gonna start the truck."

Tandi hated this. She hated being the bad guy. "Fine. I'm out of it."

Michael Jared again started to leave.

"Did you forget something?" Tandi asked.

Michael Jared turned back.

Tandi waited expectedly for Michael Jared to kiss her.

"Oh." He hurried to Tandi and kissed her on the cheek. "Ain't I getting too big for this?"

She handed him his lunch bag. "No, and be at the gate at three-ten sharp. Don't make me have to come looking for you."

"Mommy, when you gonna stop treating me like a baby?"

"Get smart with me, it'll be when elephants fly."

Michael Jared had already turned away when he mumbled, "Dumbo already did."

"I heard that, smart mouth."

Watching the two of them, Jared could not have smiled if he wanted to. He was worried about what Tandi had intimated. He waited until MJ raced out of the room and he heard the front door slam.

"Spell it out."

Tandi grabbed a sponge. She began swiping quickly across the length of the already clean counter. "I want a divorce."

"Because I can't go on a damn cruise with you, you want a divorce?"

From where she stood at the end of the counter, Tandi tossed the sponge into the sink. She watched it bounce off the side of the sink back onto the counter. "If it were just about the cruise, Jared, we wouldn't have a problem."

"What is our problem, Tandi? Tell me so I'll know."

"You, Jared. You're the problem. You don't give a damn about anything but yourself and your little law practice."

"That *little law practice* keeps our bank account fat and us in this house."

"Jared, our bank account won't disappear if you brought in less money, and this house? You're rarely in it. Michael Jared and I practically live here alone. And you know something else? You probably have more passion arguing a case than you ever did fucking me in bed."

If a sledgehammer had slammed him in the chest, Jared could not have taken the blow better than Tandi's harsh words. He looked at her just as hard as she was looking at him. "You're going for the jugular, I see. Maybe if I could get past your whining and complaining, I could fuck you with some passion."

Tandi's glare was unrelenting. "All the passion in the world wouldn't give you a leg up on fucking." They scowled bitterly at each other. Until that moment, Tandi hadn't realized how much she hated Jared. No, there was no saving this marriage. She wanted out.

"That isn't what you used to say."

"I was lying."

Damn, how did we get to this point? I'm a lawyer for Christ's sake. I'm supposed to be calm under pressure. "Tandi, what're we doing? We need to calm down. We're saying things that may be difficult to take back.

Why can't you understand that I work hard for you and MJ? Hell, I'm tired when I get home. Any other woman would understand and appreciate what I'm doing."

"Then you should be with any other woman but this one. Why don't you go to the woman you had the affair with?"

Jared knew it was coming, and still it was hard to take. "Say what you want, but I won't let you take me into that argument again. I made a mistake, I've paid for it, and I'm done paying for it. This argument isn't about that anyway. This is about you wanting to control me."

"Again you're wrong. I don't give a damn about you."

Damn, that hurt. "If that's the case, what the hell are you bitching about? Would it make you happy if I close down my practice and stay home with you?"

"I don't want you to do a damn thing except give me a divorce."

Beeep! Beeep!

Tandi glanced toward the front of the house. "I told you I don't like him being in that big-ass truck alone, but oh no, just to show me, you gave him the keys anyway."

Jared decided to not take the bait. Every word he uttered was furthering the argument. "This is crazy."

A part of Tandi wanted to rail against Jared with all the rage she'd held inside for the past three years, but she didn't think it was worth it anymore. What she didn't say before meant nothing now.

"I don't want Michael Jared to be late for school, and I have to get to work," she said, starting out of the kitchen. "I'm contacting a lawyer today."

"So just like that, I'm supposed to give you a divorce and have no say in it."

Tandi stopped at the door. "Oh, and Jared, I'm sure you won't miss us, you have such a busy life. And since you haven't had much to say about anything around here in years anyway, I'd appreciate it if you'd find someplace else to live."

"This is my house. I pay the mortgage. I pay all the bills. If you wanna leave, go ahead, but MJ stays."

Beeep! Beeep!

"Oh no. Michael Jared goes where I go. You never have time for him except for a Saturday afternoon when you take him into your office and even then your attention is on your work. I will not have my son here throughout the week by himself while you're at work."

"After school, MJ can come to me at my office."

"I don't think so. My son will be with me. You can still see him once a week. I have no problem with that, and since you haven't had a problem with it all these years, I'm sure the court will see it that way, too. By the way, you can have this damn house. I don't want it."

Beeep! Beeep! Beeep!

Tandi barely had time to step back out of the way before Jared pushed past her in the doorway and snatched his suit jacket off the banister in the hall. He went to the front door and yanked it open. "Lay off that damn horn!" He looked back at Tandi. "If you wanna leave, leave. My son? He stays."

"We'll see about that."

"That, we will." Strangely, Jared was suddenly calm. What was he worried about? He was a lawyer. He knew how to fight for what he wanted and besides, Tandi would never take MJ and leave. She had nowhere to go. Slipping his coat on over his jacket, he chuckled low and dry.

Jared's chuckling made Tandi nervous. What he might be thinking worried her.

"Tandida, I love you, but don't mistake my love for weakness. I'm not one you wanna try."

"Is that a threat?"

Jared stepped outside and slammed the door behind him, leaving Tandi's question unanswered. That really galled her. Was she supposed to be scared? Well, she wasn't in the least. Jared's threats were just like his promises, empty. He took the news just as she expected he would, heartlessly. If he'd gotten excited and started ranting and screaming, "Baby, I love you!" or "Hell no!" it might have been out of character for him, but she might have felt like he cared a little bit. It was ironic that he said he wasn't weak, when that's exactly what he was. He never argued, he always let her have her way, and he let her make all the decisions about how they spent his money and how she raised their son. She had grown tired of having to make all the decisions. Sometimes, most times, she wanted him to tell her what to do, or even what he wanted. Why did she have to decide what food he put in his belly 365 days a year? Or even when it was time for him to have new underwear?

If Jared was planning to give her a hard way to go in divorcing him because of the house, he was wasting his time. It wasn't her dream house anyway. She'd gladly leave it and him behind; she could make it without him. On her job, she could ask for more listings and work full time. With her savings, she could get a nice little apartment for herself and Michael Jared. No court would give Jared custody with his work schedule.

Feeling a little nervous but certainly not regretful of her decision, Tandi flipped off the kitchen light switch. She had thrown down the gauntlet. It was on her to be at the ready.

5

Tandi switched the telephone to her left ear. Evonne was annoying her, but that was to be expected. She knew she would get no sympathy from Evonne, but she had to talk to someone, and Daina was in Africa, a continent away, hopefully enjoying herself. It wouldn't be fair to lay her and Jared's troubles at Daina's feet. Yet, keeping what she was about to do inside had made her tense and edgy all day. She had no choice but to call Evonne.

"Tandi, I think you should think about this before you do something you'll regret."

"Believe me, I won't regret this. I've had enough."

"But Jared is a good man. Tandi, I know he loves you. I hope you're not making a mistake."

"Excuse me, Evonne, but Jared made the mistake. He didn't seem to love me when he had that affair."

"An affair is about sex, not about love, Tandi, so I'm sure Jared didn't love the woman he had the affair with."

"So that makes it okay?"

"No, but he didn't leave you for the other woman. So—"

"Evonne, I'm not stupid. I know what Jared did and so does he. He cheated. He broke our vows. He ruined this marriage. He killed the love I had for him. I want out. I'm sick of him. I feel used, and I certainly feel unloved. It's over."

"Tandi, listen to me. Maybe you should be trying to do something to breathe new life into your marriage."

"I'd need a hyperbaric chamber for that."

"Then, hell, go get one because you can save this marriage."

"I don't want to, and I wish you'd stop trying to convince me to."

"Okay, what about Michael Jared? Have you thought about how this will affect him?"

"He'll be fine." Feeling quite irritable, Tandi switched the telephone to her right ear. "Look, I have to get off this phone."

"Okay, but Tandi, I'm here for you if you need—"

"Wait. I need a favor."

"Sure, what?"

"My agency only sells houses. Would you check your listings for an apartment? A two-bedroom, preferably in Queens Village. I don't want to have to pull Michael Jared out of his school."

"Are you sure about this?"

"Yes." Tandi heard the key click in the front door. "I'll talk to you tomorrow."

Hanging up the telephone, Tandi quickly picked up the *Essence* magazine from her lap and began to flip through it.

"Thanks, Dad!" she heard Michael Jared say enthusiastically from his bedroom two rooms away.

She could hear Jared talking, but she couldn't make out what he was saying. She waited. He was taking longer than he'd ever taken in Michael Jared's room.

She waited. After a minute Jared appeared in the doorway. The soft carpeting in the hallway had cushioned his footfalls. She saw him there, though she never lifted her eyes off the magazine. In his hand Jared held a huge bouquet of red roses. She tried not to show her surprise.

Jared carried the roses to Tandi who was sitting on the chaise longue and laid them humbly across her lap.

Tandi pretended to be seriously engrossed in her magazine—the words were a blur. She stubbornly refused to acknowledge the fragrant red roses jetting out to the left of the magazine. From what she could see, they were beautiful and plump. Her eyes misted. These were the first roses Jared had bought her in years without being reminded that it was her birthday, anniversary, or Valentine's Day. He didn't bring roses or even weeds after she'd found out about his affair. Unfortunately, these roses were delivered years too late.

Jared continued to stand over Tandi, his arms hanging at his sides, his mind empty of anything clever that would break the ice. "How was your day?" was all he could come up with.

Tandi made herself look up. The hardness of this morning was gone from Jared's eyes. A sad, repentant gaze lingered there, but she wasn't moved.

"Tandi, I'm sorry for whatever it is you think I haven't done to make you happy."

She pushed the roses off her lap onto the floor. "You don't get it, do you?"

Jared watched his seventy-two dollars fall to the floor. "I guess I don't. I can't seem to do a damn thing to please you."

"Oh, there was a time when you could've. When I asked you to go to counseling with me, when I *needed* you to go to counseling with me."

Huffing, Jared shook his head. Was she never going to let him live that one down? The fact that he had not gone into counseling with Tandi was always a sore spot with her. The first meeting he had tried to make, but he couldn't get away from work. After Tandi bitched at him for missing the session, he stubbornly refused to go at all while she continued alone. In hindsight, maybe he was wrong, but hell, how was he to know that then?

"Tell me, Jared, when was the last time you took me out to dinner, to a movie, or to a play?"

He didn't try to guess because he didn't know. "When have I had time?"

"That's my point exactly. You should have made the time. Can you tell me when was the last time you kissed me or even brought me a single rose just because you loved me?"

Jared couldn't ignore the spray of red roses wrapped in lavender-and-white wrapping paper laying on the floor like cast-off garbage. He bought them because he didn't know how else to say he was sorry for not being more attentive, more loving. Apparently, that's not the message Tandi got. He swiped the roses up off the floor and lay them on the brass-trimmed trunk at the foot of the bed.

"Okay, Tandi, let's talk," he said. "First off, I don't want this marriage to end. What do I—"

"You're late. The end of this marriage didn't happen overnight. It's been a long time coming. You've just been too busy to see it."

Jared sat on the trunk next to the thorny roses, unknowingly sitting on two of them. He leaped up and began rubbing his pricked behind.

"Damnit, Tandi. I'm sick of this. I tell you what. You want me to cut my hours? I'll cut my hours. I'll work part-time. Will that make you happy?"

"Go ahead, Jared, be a smart ass. You're just giving me more to be pissed off about."

"Lately, when haven't you been pissed off about something?"

"If you," she lowered her voice, "had fucked me once in a while, maybe I wouldn't've had anything to be pissed off about."

Those words were as prickly as the thorns he'd sat on. "I'm forty-three years old. I work hard. I don't have the sexual energy of a pimply-faced, pussy-begging teenage boy."

"Then you need to buy yourself some Viagra."

Jared felt his face drop. Tandi had hit him right where it hurt. In truth, since he'd had the affair with Jackie, he hadn't had any desire to have sex—except when he thought about that first time with Jackie. That day was branded on his brain and was a part of his sexual fantasy. The downside was that he'd feel guilty every time he thought about it and that's when he had a problem getting it up for Tandi. He had been telling himself he was tired and he had a lot on his mind, but if he had to admit anything to himself, he probably had some sort of psychological impotence that Viagra wouldn't have any effect on.

Tandi was pleased with herself. It was obvious by the devastated look on Jared's face that her words hit the mark as intended. "This morning you called me Tandida. Damnit, Jared, that's what my father calls me, and I've always known that he didn't love me."

Jared rushed to the partially opened bedroom door. He stuck his head out into the hallway and looked down toward MJ's room. He could hear the play by play of the pro basketball game he'd bought for MJ to play on his PlayStation. MJ was into his game so, hopefully, he hadn't heard any part of their discussion. Jared shoved the door closed.

Tandi was glad Jared closed the door, but she resolved to keep her voice low anyway. She didn't want Michael Jared to hear what they were talking about any more than Jared did. It was going to be upsetting to him as it was when she moved him away from Jared. No need to turn his life upside down before then.

"Now you're questioning whether I ever loved you?" Jared asked, going back to the trunk. This time, he stood and planted one foot on top of the plush, royal-blue velveteen cushion laying on top.

"Get your foot off my cushion."

"You need to grow up."

"Fuck you."

"See, that's what I mean. We're not kids, Tandi. We—at least I do— have adult responsibilities that don't permit me to lay around on my ass all damn day."

"You're dirtying my cushion."

Defiantly, Jared ground his shoe into the velveteen.

"Who needs to grow up?" She rolled her eyes away from Jared over to the clock on the nightstand. It was nine o'clock. "That's it. I'm done."

But Jared wasn't done. "Doesn't anything I've done in thirteen years count for anything?"

"My son, Michael Jared, counts for something. He's the best thing to come out of this marriage."

"And I've taken care of both of you."

"Oh, sure. You've been a good provider—financially. Emotionally? You flunk. We could have been gerbils and you wouldn't've noticed."

Jared's foot hit the floor with a sudden thump. "What the hell does that mean?"

"It means there is nothing more that matters between us, and I'm tired of talking." Tandi picked up her magazine again and opened it.

Jared snatched the magazine out of Tandi's hand and flung it across the room. It landed with a clatter on Tandi's dresser, knocking over her perfume bottles.

"That was smart." She swung her legs over the side of the chaise longue although she continued to sit.

Jared didn't care about the mess he'd made. He didn't care—his money probably bought everything on the dresser anyway. "I don't get this. If I were running the streets, gambling away my money, beating up on you, or cheating on you, I could understand this."

"Then you do understand. You cheated on me."

"Goddamnit! That wasn't yesterday. What are you gonna do? Beat me over the head with that for the rest of my life?"

She quickly stood. "Don't yell at me! If you don't like it being brought up, then you shouldn't've done it. I—"

"How many times do I have to tell you that I'm sorry?"

"Never again because I don't give a damn anymore." Tandi went to the dresser and snatched the magazine off her perfume. "What you don't understand, Jared, is that there are other reasons for a marriage to end. If you cared about something other than your practice and yourself, you might know that." She set her bottles upright.

"Damnit, Tandi! You're not making a damn bit of sense."

She smirked. "Not to you."

"Not to anybody. I've put just as much into this marriage as you have. And, damn right, I've been a good provider," he said, again pacing angrily between the trunk and the door. "You don't even have to spend the chump change you earn."

Tandi felt her cheeks warm. "Well, that chump change keeps me from spending your money on lipstick and tampons, but since you're talking dollars and cents, Jared, what I do for you isn't measured in dollars and cents, and that's the problem. You don't think what I do is just as valuable as what you do to earn the dollars that you put into this house."

"Goddamnit, Tandi! I'm tired of you saying I don't appreciate you. No, I don't grovel at your feet and kiss your ass every day, but that doesn't mean I don't appreciate what you do around here."

Tandi's pulse was racing. "Let me shock you, Jared. I don't need you to kiss my ass. You wouldn't know how anyway."

"That's not what you used to say."

"Oh? How long ago was that? Three years? By the way, Jared, whose ass are you kissing these days?"

"Stop it, goddamnit! I'm not seeing anyone."

"And I'm supposed to believe that?"

"Believe what you want, Tandi, but think about this: Maybe if you didn't bitch so much about what I'm not doing and stop trying to control everything, I might want to fuck you once in a while."

"Go to hell! You couldn't fu—"

Suddenly the door was pushed open and Michael Jared stood in the doorway. With worried eyes he looked from Tandi to Jared.

Jared glared at him. "Boy! What did I tell you about knocking when that damn door is closed?"

"Don't you yell at him!" Tandi rushed to Michael Jared. She put her arms around him protectively.

"What y'all fighting about?"

"Go to your room!" Jared ordered.

"Don't you yell at my son!"

Michael Jared's eyes welled as he stared at Jared.

"I said, go to your room—now!"

Turning abruptly, Michael Jared raced down the hall to his room, slamming his bedroom door.

Tandi wanted to go after her son, but turned on Jared instead. "You've gone too far!"

"And don't be slamming my damn door!" Jared yelled, rushing past Tandi to the door. He slammed it shut and abruptly turned back on Tandi, startling her.

Jared's eyes were ablaze. He was too close. Tandi backed up. She had never feared being hit by Jared before, but she did now. The question was, what was she prepared to do if he did?

"This is between you and me, Jared. Don't you dare take it out on my son."

Jared quipped, *"Our* son, babe."

"Then you'd better treat him better than that, or I promise you, you'll—"

"Are you threatening me with my son?" Jared felt his insides grow cold. He felt his chest tighten around his heart.

Tandi looked at him hard and long. That scornfully cold look from this morning was back. Yes, it was over. Turning away, she went to the trunk and looked down at the roses. Their beauty was marred by the hands that had brought them to her. She contemptuously shoved them back onto the floor.

Angrily working his jaw, Jared ached to grab Tandi and shake some sense into her. He didn't care about the roses. They could be thrown down the sewer for all he cared. What bothered him was how angry he was. He had never been this angry with Tandi before. He wanted to grab her and shake her until not another contentious word came out of her mouth.

Tandi again folded her arms tightly across her chest as she sat on the trunk. She crossed her legs. She and Jared held each other's scornful glare, each wanting the other to leave before cutting words made it impossible to turn back, but neither had anywhere to go. For the first time Jared felt he had truly lost Tandi, but he wasn't about to take the blame for all that went wrong.

"I didn't think I was a bad husband. If you're saying because I don't stay home and hold your hand to make you feel like you matter or jump on top of you every night like a horny dog, then I'm guilty. But the way I see it, Tandi, whatever the hell you're bitching about doesn't have a damn thing to do with me. That's something in your screwed-up head."

"Fuck you, Jared. If anyone is screwed up, it's you."

"That's real intelligent, Tandi. I haven't cursed you. Maybe you need to get yourself a real job or do more with your own life so you don't need me up your ass day and night to make you feel fulfilled. Isn't that what you women want these days, fulfillment?"

"Go to hell, Jared! I hate you."

Tandi's hate was clear in the sneer on her lips and in the glare in her eyes. "I have no great love for you either."

"Hey, then we can end this now. I don't have to spend another night under the same roof with you."

He knew that she meant it, but what was he supposed to do? He couldn't lock her up to keep her and he couldn't talk sense to her because she wasn't listening. The more they talked, the worse things got, and he didn't know how it got so bad.

Jared threw his hands up in resignation. "Hey, you're calling the shots. Do what you have to, but I'm not leaving. I've worked my ass to the bone to get this house. I'm not moving out."

"Screw you and this house." She bolted across the room to the walk-in closet and pulled open the door. "I don't want any part of it or you."

Jared was miserable, but he wasn't about to let Tandi get the best of him. "Fine. Then get the fuck out!"

6

Earlier in the day, while still at work, the thought of Tandi divorcing him had played like a bass drum in Jared's head, giving him a brutal, pulsating headache. He couldn't believe he told her to get out, but then he couldn't really understand why she was so angry. If he was trifling, if he abused her, if he was miserly, he could understand why she'd want to leave. Admittedly, he knew he spent less than a handful of hours with her in any given week, but there was nothing he could do about that. He had other things to worry about. Besides upcoming cases, for the past few weeks, he had been interviewing young lawyers fresh out of law school as he was planning on hiring at least one to help him expand his practice. It was time. He could no longer handle his growing client list. He had also been looking to hire another secretary to relieve Marci of some of her clerical duties and an office manager would round out the support staff nicely. He hadn't wanted to tell Tandi until everything worked out before he got her hopes up. If it worked out the way he planned, Marci could make his life a whole lot easier and the new attorney could lighten his caseload considerably. Eventually, he could leave work at a decent hour and take time off for vacations.

Until then, what he needed from Tandi was her support, not her ass to kiss. Seven years ago when he took the plunge and opened up his own storefront practice on Parsons Boulevard in Jamaica, Tandi was in his corner one hundred and ten percent. Then, she believed in him. She helped him set up his books, she helped him pull in clients, and she worked the receptionist's desk. She didn't mind his hours then, maybe because she spent some of them with him, often bringing him his dinner and eating with him. Now, he couldn't drag her down to his office with a team of wild horses and the promise of a chest of diamonds. The way he saw it, she no longer shared his dream.

Now she was gone. Tandi and MJ both. Jared had not bothered to beg Tandi to stay. Nothing he could have said would have made a difference. Tandi had made up her mind, she had gone off in a zone, like a bat out of hell, blind and deaf to him, and had stormed around the house packing her and MJ's bags. And poor MJ, he didn't know what was going on. Bewildered, MJ kept looking at him as if to say, "Do something, Dad." Short of snatching Tandi and shaking some sense into her, he didn't know what to do and didn't want to fight it out with her in front of MJ. Feeling helpless, he finally left the house to keep from putting his hands on his wife.

"Hey, man, you been making love to that drink for the past hour."

Jared hadn't paid much attention to the bald-headed, clean shaven, shaggy-browed bartender standing in front of him. "I'm not a drinker."

"Coulda guessed that, my man. If it was a woman or the lack of money making you brood like that, if you was a drinking man, you woulda tossed back ten of those rum and Cokes by now. Which one of them your problem?"

The nosiness of people never ceased to amaze Jared. He glanced around the room. Sitting at the far end of the bar to his right were two men smoking and drinking, deep in conversation. Behind him a man was drinking a beer, his eyes were glued to the television high up on the side wall. Jared looked back at the bartender, who seemed to be waiting for him to answer, like he expected him to answer.

"Hey," the bartender said, lowering his voice, "I ain't trying to get in your business or nothing, but I figured you might wanna talk."

"That's what you figure, huh?"

"Yep. Men who don't drink don't make it a habit of coming in here late on a work night, as cold as it is, unless it's to watch a special sports event on cable, or if they're looking to connect with a naked body to keep them warm. This isn't a sports night, and you don't look like you're looking for a warm body. Am I right?"

Gulping down his drink, Jared grimaced at the bitter taste. He had forgotten that rum and Coke wasn't a smooth drink. It had been a long time since his partying days and even then, he had not been a heavy drinker. That's why he'd ordered a rum and Coke, thinking that the soda would dilute the rum. He plopped the empty glass down on the bar and pushed it toward the bartender, but he shook his head to another drink. Maybe he did need to talk. Tandi had messed up his head on this one.

The bartender persisted. "Man, I'm all ears."

"Okay. Tell me. Why is it that women are so damn emotional?"

The bartender picked up Jared's glass and set it in a pan of soapy water under the bar. "Because women have too much estrogen."

"That simple, huh?"

"Check it out. Men have a gallon of testosterone, a manly hormone, and a drop of estrogen, a woman's emotional hormone. Women have a gallon of estrogen and a drop of testosterone. You don't need a college degree to figure which sex is gonna ride an emotional roller coaster and drive the other crazy."

Jared didn't have to think about that.

"Damn right. A woman can sho 'nuff put a hurtin' on a man with them emotions. Personally, I'd rather go a few rounds with Tyson than deal with a tight ass and a pretty smile when a woman's acting all emotional."

"I can understand that," Jared said. "I feel like I've gone a few rounds myself."

The bartender wiped a ring of water off the bar. "How about you, man? You down for the count or still trying to duck?"

Jared leaned on the bar. "Man, I'm on the ropes trying to figure out what the hell went wrong. I work ten-hour days, five days a week, six hours on Saturday. I'm not running the streets, I'm not sniffing behind women, and I'm not glued to a basketball or football game on my day off. Anything and everything my wife wants, I give to her, without question. And do you know what she said?"

The bartender placed both elbows on top of the bar and leaned toward Jared. "She said, 'You don't love me, you ain't got time for me, and you can't get it up for me.' "

Jared raised his fist, and he and the bartender tapped fist to fist. "Man, I don't get it. My wife likes good things. How am I supposed to get her what she wants without working for it?"

"Die and leave her your insurance."

"Nah, man. My wife isn't like that. She likes to spend money, but she isn't greedy."

"Yeah, but if you were sitting on your ass or making minimum wage, she wouldn't've married you."

"Maybe not, but—"

"Listen, man," the bartender said, "a lot of women marry men who're making minimum wage or sitting back on their ass. I see it all the time in here. Some of them women got fine minds, fine bodies, and they make that long fine money. The kicker? I've seen them bring that money right down here to Daddy on payday."

"Damn, it's like that?"

"Damn right, and do you know why those dudes got it that way?"

"I'm sure I can guess."

"I'll tell you. Those dudes are taking care of business at home. For some women, that's priority."

Jared shifted on his barstool.

"The way I see it," the bartender said, "there are three types of women: the kind who want a man at all costs, the kind who want the money at all costs, and the kind who want both."

Jared nodded.

"Take a woman like your wife. She's type three. She wants all the fine things your fine money can buy, but she wants you, too."

"And she has it all—me and my money." Jared lowered his voice even more. "I'm not gonna lie to you, I did cheat on my wife three years back, but I've been faithful since then. Right now, I just can't spend a lot of time with my wife. I'm working hard. I—"

"Wait a minute. Back up. Did you say you cheated?"

Again, Jared shifted on his barstool. "Yeah, but it's been over, and I thought my wife forgave me."

"Man, women don't forget or forgive a cheating man—ever. That's their ammo for when they wanna kick your ass."

"Yeah, but—"

"You fucked up."

"Tell me something I don't know."

"Les!" one of the two men down at the far end of the bar called to the bartender.

"Back in a minute, partner. I gotta make my money." Les moved swiftly down the length of the bar to the two men.

Jared checked his watch. He wondered if Tandi had actually left the house. He was hoping she had changed her mind and was still at home.

"Like I was saying," Les said, stepping back into the spot he had briefly vacated, "you fucked up. We all do it. It's like second nature to us, but it's a big deal to women, especially to a good woman, and it seems to me like you got yourself a good woman. If it was just your money she wanted, she wouldn't be asking you to spend more time with her."

"Yeah, but I gotta work."

"What's your name, partner?"

"Jared."

"I'm Les. This is my place."

They shook hands.

"Nice," Jared said.

"Thanks. How long you been married, Jared?"

"Thirteen years."

Les set a wineglass in front of Jared. From a small refrigerator under the bar he took a half-full bottle of domestic champagne. "This is on the house," he said, pouring the champagne.

"No, I—"

"Take the drink, man," Les insisted. "Drink to surviving thirteen years with one woman and to your good fortune at having a wife who still wants you. Think about it: Headaches were invented for women who no longer wanna give it up to their husbands."

Jared hadn't looked at it that way. Maybe he was lucky Tandi still wanted him to make love to her. He took a big gulp from his glass. The champagne was cold, but it had long ago lost its tang.

"Check this out," Les said. "What did God invent for a man who no longer wanted the same old stale wife?"

Jared really wasn't interested. He barely blinked.

"A young woman with big tits and a huge ass." Les laughed at his own joke. Jared didn't. "Man, you need to cheer up. I could hook you up with some prime stuff. Make you forget your own name."

"Man, that's not for me. I learn from my mistakes."

"Then you're the kinda guy who needs to be married. Take my advice. Give your wife a little attention, make love to her, and make her holler a little. Maybe a lot. She'll let off steam, she'll be happy until the next time. Just don't make her wait too long for the next time."

Jared couldn't admit to Les that making love to Tandi was a major part of the problem. "That's not it, man."

"I bet you a round of drinks it is," Les wagered. "I know women, and women need a lot of loving. When they're not getting it, that's when they're not happy. That's when they start looking around. How old are you? Forty, forty-five?"

"Somewhere in there."

"See, that might be the problem. I'm fifty-two myself. When I got in my forties, I started losing that drive, you know what I mean?"

Jared didn't care to hear about another man's problems with getting it up. "I gotta be going."

"Hold up," Les said, putting his hand on Jared's arm. "See, that's why we men have problems—we don't talk. I ain't talking about that bragging crap we did in the locker room back when we was kids. I'm talking about the real deal. Women? They talk about everything. If a woman hasn't had but one man in her whole life, she knows how other men do it because women tell one another those intimate things. Women talk about sex everywhere they go. They sho 'nuff talk about it in here. Some of the stuff they say you wouldn't believe. They're hornier than we are. Man, they talk about sex on the job, in the grocery store, and you know when they go to the bathroom together when they're out in public? They're telling on each other's man then. I believe they tell each other stuff in church, too. That's how come they're always giggling at the minister."

"Oh, come on," Jared said, chuckling.

"It's true. Women know more about what's in our pants than we do, and a handful of them ugly ones probably have never even seen a man with his pants down. If their girlfriends aren't telling 'em, they reading about it in some book on how to make love to a man. In fact, a woman came in here the other night with her girlfriends with a book in her hand. She couldn't put the damn thing down long enough to get her drink on."

"Do you know what she was reading?"

"I found out. I asked. It was *Somebody's Gotta Be On Top* by Mary B. Morrison."

"That's some title," Jared said.

"Man, the woman couldn't stop reading long enough to tell me what the book was about. Said she was at a real good part. Now what do you think she was reading about?"

"Well, if the title is indicative of what the story is about, then—"

"Sex, man! S-E-X. The cover of the book had this woman laying on her back with a blood-red cherry in her ruby-red lips looking like she could take us both on. Yesterday, I had my woman go out and buy the book so I can see what's in it, but she started reading it and won't give it to me."

Jared chuckled. "That book must be hot."

"Women read, man. They're not like us. They don't do much guessing, they go for the facts or read a lot of books with sex in them. What about you, Jared? When was the last time you read a relationship book or talked to a buddy about your problem?"

"I don't have a problem."

"Give up the lie, man," Les whispered, leaning in closer to Jared. "I bet you didn't have a problem getting it up for that woman you had the affair with, but with your wife, you couldn't hold a feather up if it was starched. Man . . ."

Jared glanced sheepishly from one side to the other. He was hoping no one had heard what Les was saying to him.

". . . I talk to a lot of guys who come through here, and I know of what I speak. Nine out of ten, at one time or other, got a problem getting it up."

"That many?"

"Yep. And I've helped most of them."

A skeptical look farrowed Jared's brow.

"I'm serious, man. If you have a problem, you need to go down to the health food store and get yourself some Irish moss. They got it already bottled—it looks and tastes like a vanilla shake. Buying it already made up is kinda expensive though, but you could buy raw Irish moss and boil it up with some milk. It's more potent that way anyhow. Man, pump you right up." Les thrust his fist up and held it strong.

That, Jared was interested in. "So how does it work?" he asked, offhandedly.

"Hell if I know, I ain't no chemist. Something in it makes it work. You drink a couple bottles of that stuff for a few days before getting it on with your wife, she'll have to beat you off top of her with a stick. Bet she won't feel unloved after that."

"How do you know it works? It could be a placebo and you just think it works."

Les drew back and tugged on the waistband of his jeans. "I know it works, I drink it myself. I keep that stuff made up and ready in my refrigerator at home. My woman has never had a complaint. She smiles a hell of a lot. I guarantee you."

"I wouldn't doubt it, Les, but what about Viagra? You ever try it?"

"Why should I give somebody ten dollars a pill when I can make up a gallon of my own hard-on medicine for less than that? I ain't rich."

"Yeah, but Viagra really works."

"Man, I'm sticking with the Irish moss. Pumps me right up, hard as a pipe." Les gave Jared the okay sign with his fingers.

Jared was pensive. It was a hell of a thing, if it worked.

"Look, man, you owe it to your woman to try it."

"Maybe."

"Maybe, my ass. Going without makes a sweet woman bitter, and a bitter woman makes a man's life hell. That's when she starts nagging. That's when she starts sitting around on her ass all day eating candy, watching soap operas and all those busybody wanna-be talk show psychologists. Those shows get a lot of men in trouble, you know."

This time, Jared had to laugh. This guy, know-it-all that he was, was blatantly bold with his barroom psychology but Jared had to admit he wasn't as depressed as he had been when he first came in.

"Your wife put on a lot of weight since you married her?"

"Nah, man, my wife has a good body."

"So she looks good?"

"She's beautiful."

"Well then, man, you'd better get yourself some Irish moss. If you think you have a problem now with your wife, wait till she starts looking at other men and they give her what she needs."

That was something Jared never had to worry about with Tandi and didn't want to think about now. He couldn't imagine her with another man.

"Okay, I see you're skeptical."

"No, it's just that I figure my wife isn't interested in other men or she wouldn't be haranguing me."

"Then give the woman some of your time, man. Women like to have their asses kissed, and when we're chasing 'em, we kiss and suck ass real good. That's what's wrong with us, we take our women for granted. If I were you, I'd work those weekdays just like you doing, but I wouldn't work on Saturday or Sunday. I'd wine and dine my woman."

"But, my practice—"

"Man, keep doing it the way you're doing, your wife is gonna find herself another man to strike up a fire in between her thighs. Before you know it, the only thing you gonna have is your practice."

Jared had to concede that Les could be right.

"I'll tell you something else," Les said. "A lot of the women who come in here by themselves or with their girlfriends, are far from single. And they're not here just to get a drink. They get picked up by dudes ready to give them what their husbands can't or won't."

"You see a lot, don't you?"

"A hell of a lot."

"You married, Les?"

"Nah, man. I've been divorced three times, and I'm running in place trying hard to not get married again."

Jared laughed out loud. "That's deep. Man, I feel like I've been getting marriage counseling from Henry the Eighth."

"Hey, it wasn't my fault none of my marriages worked. My wives were jealous. I gave them plenty of loving and lots of time. They just had a problem with me tending my own bar and talking to women every night."

"Did you meet all your wives here?"

"Yep."

Chuckling, Jared took a final sip of his warm, flat champagne. Then pulling out his billfold, he peeled off a twenty-dollar bill. "Keep the change."

"Class," Les said, taking the money. "I like that. Don't be a stranger. I'd be interested in knowing how you and your woman make out."

Since he didn't feel any better about his problem and alcohol still wasn't his cup of tea, Jared doubted if he'd ever step foot in Les's bar again.

"You take it easy." He shook Les's hand.

"You, too, brother."

All the way to the car Jared thought about what Les had said. Some of it made sense. He was going to look into that Irish moss, and he was going to do his best to give Tandi more time. That is, if she didn't leave him for good. Where would she go, if she did?

7

For almost an hour, Tandi had been driving in circles. She didn't know where to go. If Daina had been home or better still, if she had made it to Daina's house before she left town, she would have gotten Daina's new set of house keys and she would have had a place to stay. Evonne simply didn't have the space in her one-bedroom apartment and neither did Glynn. Michael Jared was slumped down in the passenger seat with his hood pulled low over his face. He was warm because the car's heater was working fine, but still, Tandi had to take him somewhere so that he could get a good night's sleep, and the only place she could think of was a place she had said "never again" about. Her father's house—Sporty's house as she liked to call it. *Never say never* came to mind more than once when she found herself sitting out in front of the last place in the world she wanted to be. It had been eighteen years since she left home, and she had vowed to never come back there to live, but now that she was older, she knew life had a way of making one eat one's words.

Sporty was the only one who had the extra space. He had refused to sell his four-bedroom house after she and Glynn moved out. The house was really underused. Sporty used his bedroom; his den, which was once the dining room; and the kitchen. He said his house was one of the few things he had to show for thirty years of hard work as a telephone lineman. She could only take him at his word that he worked hard. He came home most days smelling of alcohol, though he was always cognizant enough to get on her about not keeping the house clean. While Glynn never lifted a finger to help her, it was he who messed up the house. Glynn was a brat. He was three years older and instead of taking care of her, she had to take care of him, the house, and Sporty. Like she told Jared, the men in her life used her all of her life and here she was out in the cold, dark night with a little boy to take care of.

Why did she have to walk out tonight? Why hadn't she waited until morning? Living with Glynn "Sporty" Belson wasn't easy when she was a child. Sporty had been a tyrant. She had been so afraid of him, she trembled whenever he called her name. The handful of times she dared talk back to Sporty, his vicious backhand soon taught her to keep her mouth shut and do whatever he told her to do, and that was a lot.

Sporty treated her like his own personal handmaiden and Glynn, he treated like his heir apparent. Glynn could do no wrong, while all she did was wrong. If there was a compliment for Glynn, there was a criticism for her. And she took it, absorbed it, and hated Sporty for every single word. She dreamed constantly about one day leaving Sporty and Glynn behind. That hadn't happened. She was still in the same borough—Queens—only minutes away from Sporty who still treated her about the same, but she didn't keep her mouth shut anymore. She bitched right back at him and dared him to touch her. However, nothing Tandi ever said stopped Sporty's vicious tongue, but tonight he was going to have to be civil. She was not going to put up with his ugliness in front of her son. She might have to stay in Sporty's house more than a week until she found an apartment, which was a day longer than Michael Jared had ever been around his grandfather continuously. She wasn't about to let Sporty scare him as he had done her.

"Mommy, I have to go to the bathroom."

Tandi wasn't ready to go inside yet. "Baby, can you hold it a minute?"

Michael Jared answered sleepily, "No, I gotta go, and I wanna go home."

"I know you do, baby, but we can't." She opened the car door.

"Why not?"

"We have to stay here tonight."

Michael Jared looked out the car window. Even in the dark, he recognized Sporty's house. His eyes widened. "I don't wanna stay here."

"Neither do I, but we have to."

"No we don't. We could go home."

Getting out of the car, Tandi felt like a traitor. "Michael Jared, please, can we talk about this tomorrow?"

"But, Mommy—"

"Michael Jared, it's late. Get your backpack." Tandi took both her and Michael Jared's suitcases and started up the dark walkway. She didn't look back at Michael Jared; she knew he would follow. At the door, she set the suitcases on the porch. Her hands froze at her sides as she prayed that Sporty wouldn't be so obnoxiously critical of her for leaving Jared. He would know immediately she had left Jared because she was not going to be able to lie and say she was just visiting when Sporty knew she had not been there that late ever—other than for an emergency for him.

"Mommy, I don't wanna stay here."

Tandi willed her hand to rise. "We'll talk about this tomorrow." She rang the doorbell. She had her own key, but thought it best she not use it. No telling what Sporty would do if she walked in on him at this hour. She looked down at Michael Jared. With the hood on his head, in the darkness, she couldn't clearly see his expression, but she could imagine that he looked like he'd sucked on a lemon.

"Maybe Granddad ain't home."

Tandi rang the bell again. "He's home," she said, knocking at the door. Already Sporty was messing with her. She'd bet her last dollar he was standing in the dark living room behind the blinds peeking out at her and taking in the fact that she had Michael Jared with her. Even during the day he peeked out at people on the street through half-open blinds. He knew something about everything that was going on on the block even without Miss Iona's gossipy confirmation.

"I wanna go home," Michael Jared whined.

The porch light suddenly came on.

Tandi could hear the clicking of the cylinder as Sporty unlocked the door. *Lord, give me strength.*

The door opened. Michael Jared stepped back. Tandi stood her ground although Sporty's six-foot frame dwarfed her. Dressed in a faded red-and-white plaid bathrobe over his pajamas, Sporty stood ramrod straight in the doorway, the scour on his face said what his mouth didn't.

Tandi challenged Sporty's scour with a hard stare. His unyielding black eyes never endeared her to him, and they always made her want to look away. This time she refused. She felt Michael Jared lean against her side.

"What're you doing here this time of night?" Sporty asked gruffly.

"I need to stay here for a few days."

"Why?"

"I gotta go to the bathroom," Michael Jared said urgently behind Tandi. He started to step from one foot to the other.

Sporty squinted at Michael Jared. "I know that's not why you're here."

Michael Jared pushed in front of Tandi. "Granddad, I gotta go to the bathroom."

If he heard Michael Jared, Sporty didn't act like it. He didn't move or invite his grandson in.

"Daddy, are you going to let us in or not?"

"I got company."

"So. We have no intention of going into your bedroom."

Stepping quickly from foot to foot, Michael Jared began pulling his arms out of his backpack loaded with all of his schoolbooks. "I gotta go!"

"Daddy!"

"I ain't stopping him." Sporty stepped aside and let Michael Jared race past him. He dropped his backpack in the middle of the living room floor.

"Boy, don't go near my bedroom!"

"Daddy, please." Tandi carried the suitcases into the house. "Michael Jared is no more interested in what's going on in your bedroom than I am."

"That's what you say now because you wanna get your foot in the door"—Sporty closed and locked the door—"but you know you always got something to say about my business."

Tandi dropped the suitcases to the floor. "I'm tired. I can't—no, I won't—get into a debate with you about your business or whom you're sleeping with. My son—your grandson—and I will sleep upstairs, way out of your way."

"Just don't say nothing about me having company. This is my house, I do what I want."

"Believe me, we won't be staying long in your house." She picked up the suitcases again and started toward the stairs in the back of the house.

"What are you doing here anyhow? Where's your husband?"

Tandi glimpsed Michael Jared coming back from the bathroom. "I have to put my son to bed. Michael Jared, pick up your backpack. We're sleeping upstairs."

"Mommy, I—"

"Honey, it's late. Please, just pick up your bag."

"I wanna know how long you're planning to stay," Sporty said.

Michael Jared waited for Tandi to answer. He held on to the strap of his bag, but the bag itself still sat on the floor.

Tandi fixed her eyes on Sporty but said to Michael Jared, "Honey, why don't you go on upstairs. I'll be right up."

Michael Jared started dragging his bag behind him. Stopping, he turned around. "Are the lights on up there?"

"You scared of the dark, boy?"

"No, I just wanna know if the lights are on."

"I'm coming with you," Tandi said, changing her mind. "Daddy, I'll talk to you in the morning."

"See that you do. I don't like people just showing up on my doorstep."

"I'm not *people*, Daddy. I'm your daughter."

Tandi stomped off toward the back of the house with Michael Jared close on her heels. They passed Sporty's bedroom door, which was slightly ajar. Someone was in his bed, but Tandi couldn't tell who it was, though she figured it couldn't be anyone but Miss Iona. Who else would sleep with such a crotchety old bastard?

"And don't make any noise over my head!"

Tandi smirked. She should probably be telling him to not make any noise period. How she hated Jared at this moment. It was his fault she was here at all. If he had lived up to his promise of being the best husband in the world, she would not have to close her eyes in this God-awful house. She would not have to subject her son to an old man with a lifelong thorn stuck in his foot.

8

By the time Michael Jared blacked out from sheer frustration in Glynn's dusty childhood bed, it was well past midnight. Until Michael Jared closed his eyes, he whined about wanting to sleep in his own bed in his own house. He didn't like Glynn's bed, he didn't like Glynn's room, he didn't like Sporty's house, and mostly, he didn't like Sporty, the only grandfather he had, but Tandi couldn't fault him for that. She didn't like him either. When Michael Jared finally fell asleep, he at least slept through the night—unlike Tandi. The mustiness of her old room from being closed up so long bothered her, clogging up her sinuses. Not even the slightly open window letting in cold air, freezing her to the bone, made her breathing any easier. She had opened one of the windows about an inch in Glynn's room and could only hope that Michael Jared wasn't freezing and was breathing okay. Tandi lay awake in her narrow single bed, listening to decades old settling wood creaking and popping throughout the house, wondering whether Jared was the least bit worried about where she was, and worrying herself about how long she'd have to stay in Sporty's house.

She dozed on and off, waking every time the house made another eerie sound. She was restless to the point of feeling achy from laying down. She was anxious for it to be six o'clock in the morning so that she could be up and about settling her business. Besides it still being dark out, the only other thing that kept her in bed was the bare wooden floor and the fact that her bedroom was right above Sporty's. If she walked around, he would surely hear her. When she was a teenager, he used to shout up the stairs, "What you doing up there? You trying to come through the ceiling?" Back then, she was barefooted or had on socks. She wouldn't dare walk around that way now, the dust balls on the floor were so big they could have been tumbleweed rolling down an old deserted dusty town in a western movie. Over the years, she never considered it her job to clean Sporty's house, certainly not upstairs where no one ventured. What little she did, she did in the kitchen, and that was only because she cooked in there.

At the first light of dawn, Tandi got up and tried to take a quick shower but had to wait ten minutes until the rusty water ran clear through the pipes. Once dressed, she then cajoled a bad-tempered, slow-moving Michael Jared up and dressed for school and, together, they both tiptoed gingerly down the back stairs to the kitchen.

"I don't want nothin' to eat," Michael Jared said.

Tandi was disheartened by the bags under her child's sad eyes. She didn't want him hurt by her decision to leave Jared, but leaving him behind was not an option, not when she felt he would be hurt either way and neglected to boot with Jared.

"Honey, I'm sorry you had a bad night, but we'll be in our own home real soon."

He perked up. "We're going home?"

Tandi realized her blunder. As much as she hated to dash her child's hopes, she had to. "We're not going back to your father's house. We're going to get our own place, an apartment."

"I don't wanna go to no apartment, I wanna go home."

"We can't."

"How come?"

Tandi busied herself with looking for oatmeal.

"Mommy, isn't Dad's house our house?"

"Not anymore."

"But he didn't say it wasn't our house. He said he wasn't leaving because he had worked hard to get it."

Michael Jared had overheard much more than she thought he had. Surely he heard Jared tell her to get the fuck out. No matter what Jared had said that night, he had made it impossible for her to call it her home ever again. And at his tender age, that was something Michael Jared would not understand.

"Mommy, how come we can't go home?"

"Because," she said, taking the round container of oatmeal down off the shelf, "your father and I haven't been getting along very well. It's best that you and I live apart from him for a while."

"I get along with my dad. I shouldn't have to live apart from him."

Michael Jared was right about that, but was he saying he'd rather be with Jared than her? "Honey, let's sit down," she said, leaving the oatmeal on the counter. They sat at the kitchen table. "I will never keep you from your father. You can see him as often as you like, but you know how busy he is. He may not have time to see you other than on Saturdays."

"I could see him every night if we went back home."

"Yes, but if you remember, he's always so tired when he gets in from work. He needs his rest, and if we're not there to disturb him, he'll get plenty of rest."

"He got his rest with us there. Y'all just mad at each other, but y'all can make up if we go back home."

"Honey, it's not that simple. Look, try not to worry about your dad and me. We'll work something out. You'll still see him, and you and I will have a nice new apartment. You'll have your old friends, and you'll make lots of new friends."

Teary-eyed, Michael Jared's chin began to quiver.

The last thing Tandi wanted to do was hurt her child, but she just couldn't go back, not even for his sake. "Honey, I'm so sorry you're upset," she said, putting her hand on his shoulder. "You know I wouldn't want to see you hurt for anything in the world. It's just that mothers and fathers don't always get along. Sometimes when they can't agree to get along, they have to live apart. Sometimes they have to—"

Michael Jared shot up out of his chair. "Y'all can't divorce!"

"Honey, I didn't say—"

"Mommy, Dad's real good to us. He pays all the bills, he gives you money to buy your clothes and my clothes, he buys me computer games. I don't want y'all to divorce."

Tandi didn't think she could feel any worse. By omission she had forgotten how much Michael Jared loved Jared. No matter how little time Jared spent with him, Michael Jared didn't care as long as he saw him.

"What'll happen to me? Where will I live?"

She eased Michael Jared back into his chair. "Honey, listen to me.

I'm not saying your dad and I are getting a divorce, I'm just saying sometimes that happens. For now, we just need some space, some time out. If your father has time, you can spend weekends with him. I promise. I'll never keep you from being with him."

"Then let me go back home."

Tandi choked back her urge to cry. "You don't wanna be with me?"

"Yes, but I wanna be with Dad, too. I want to be with both of you."

Tandi quickly wiped at the tears that rolled freely down her cheeks.

"Mommy, if we go home," Michael Jared said, "I'll clean up my room without you telling me to ever again. I'll take out the garbage, I'll do all of my homework, I won't make noise—"

"Honey, nothing you did or didn't do has anything to do with this. This is between me and your father."

A stream of tears rolled down Michael Jared's cheeks. "And me, too. We're a family, all of us."

Oh, God. "Honey, that's true, we are a family, and we always will be. Your father and I both love you, and we know you love us, too. I don't want you to think for one minute that you are the cause of us breaking up. If it should happen that we do divorce, we're not divorcing you. Your father is still going to love you the same, if not more, and so am I."

Michael Jared folded his arms on top of the table and dropped his head onto them.

Crouching next to Michael Jared, Tandi put her arm around his shoulders and whispered pleadingly in his ear, "Honey, please, please don't cry. I promise you, I'll make sure your dad spends more time with you, and I'll do everything in my power to make you happy."

"Is he all right?" a woman's voice asked behind Tandi.

Tandi looked back and was aghast. A middle-aged woman she had never seen before was standing in the doorway in a sheer pink negligee showing everything that might have been easier on the eyes decades ago. Her hanging breasts and flabby stomach were not a pretty sight. Tandi glanced down at Michael Jared. He was still absorbed in his despair. Grateful for that, she glared at the woman.

"Oh! Does my attire bother you?"

Michael Jared started to raise his head. Quickly standing, Tandi held his head against her stomach. "What do you think?"

"I don't see why it should, I have nothing to hide. My body is beautiful."

Michael Jared stopped sobbing altogether. He tried to pull free of Tandi's hold.

"One woman's opinion," Tandi said, holding Michael Jared's head. With her free hand, she shielded his eyes.

"Your father likes my body."

Michael Jared pulled on Tandi's hand over his eyes, but her hold was firm.

"Miss, my father likes chitterlings, I don't. Therefore, I would appreciate it if you wouldn't walk around here like that in front of my son, or me either for that matter."

"I think your father should make—"

"Bernice," Sporty said, coming up behind her, "I'll make the coffee. Why don't you go get dressed?"

"Oh, sure, honey bun." Bernice smiled mischievously at Tandi as she turned and brushed catlike up against Sporty as she left the kitchen.

Tandi let Michael Jared up. He looked around for Bernice and was disappointed to see she was gone.

"Daddy, who is that woman?"

"None of your business."

"Excuse me?"

"I don't answer to you, Tandida. This is my house. I do as I damn well please. If you don't like it, go home."

For a fleeting but stifling moment, Tandi was reminded of the day she left Sporty's house. That day, too, he had said, "If you don't like it," but he didn't say go home, he had said, "Leave. Get out."

"You're telling me to get out when you're the one who's wrong? You opened my mail. You have no right to open my mail."

"I have a right to look at anything that comes into my house."

In her hand Tandi held the letter from the Department of Vital Statistics requesting the social security number and the correct date of death for Lorraine Belson. That angered Tandi even more because Sporty wouldn't give her that information.

"No, Daddy, you don't have that right."

"The deed to this house says Glynn R. Belson, Senior, not Tandida Belson."

"Does that mean I'm not entitled to privacy?"

"That's exactly what it means. When you have your own house, then you can set up your own rules."

"Daddy, you can't keep bullying me. You can't tell me to not try and get my mother's death certificate. I have a right to know when she was born and when she died. That's my legal right. And I have a daughter's right to put flowers on her grave. But I can't do that, can I? You've destroyed any evidence of my mother ever having been on this Earth. If you could've, I believe you would have gotten rid of me, too."

The hateful look Sporty fixed on Tandi made her want to sink into a corner and hide.

"You watch what you say to me, girl. You're not so grown that I won't give you a good hard backhand."

Tandi held her tongue. She knew well what it felt like to get slapped in the mouth.

"The next time mail comes into my house about your mother, I'll burn it as sure as I'm standing here."

"You can't do that!"

"I can and I will. If you don't like it, leave. Get out!"

And she did. That same day. It was a whole year before she started coming around again and that was only because Glynn nagged her to death about it. Sporty wasn't very welcoming but he did open the door. In that year she stayed away, Tandi realized that Sporty and Glynn were the only family she had. She quickly learned that a soul without family is as alone as a soul marooned on an island. She didn't question Sporty anymore about her mother, but it was a bone of contention always between them.

9

Just thinking about that long-ago day that she was thrown out of her father's house upset Tandi, but this time she wasn't worried about a backhand slap from Sporty. If anything, she was worried about what she might do to him.

She boldly stepped up to Sporty. "I'm no longer a child. Don't ever talk to me like that again."

If Sporty was intimidated by Tandi's closeness, he didn't show it. "Then stay out of my damn business."

"I am not in your business. I am protecting my son from your exhibitionist of a girlfriend."

"Your son would not've seen a damn thing if you had been in your own house."

"Mommy."

"Unfortunately, we're not in our own house, we're in your house and you're going to respect us whether you like it or not."

"Mommy . . . Mommy, I wanna go home," Michael Jared cried.

Tandi's anger was choking her. She was about to tell Sporty about himself but the anguish in Michael Jared's eyes, in his voice, forced her to put her mouth in check. She softened her tone.

"I'd appreciate it, Daddy, if you'd give me fair warning if you or your company is going to walk around here in the altogether."

"Maybe you should give me fair warning when you and your son are going to be sitting around in my kitchen. And that's another thing, Tandida, don't be changing nothing around in here. I like my kitchen just the way it is."

"Daddy, stop it. I have been cooking in this kitchen practically all of my life, and nothing has been changed around in here since I was three, so stop badgering me."

"Tandida, you always had a smart mouth."

"And so have you."

Michael Jared cried louder.

"I'm still your father, girl," Sporty said, looking sternly at Michael Jared. "What's he crying for?"

"Leave him alone." With her hand, Tandi wiped Michael Jared's tears away. "Honey, go upstairs and wash your face."

"I don't wanna go upstairs. I wanna go home."

"Why don't you take the boy home? He doesn't wanna be here."

Tandi cut her eyes threateningly at Sporty. She thought old age was supposed to mellow a person out. Not in Sporty's case. Old age wasn't doing a damn thing about softening his nasty attitude. He was colder and harder than she had ever known him to be.

"What're you looking at me like that for?"

"Michael Jared," Tandi said soothingly, "honey, please go wash your face. I have to talk to your grandfather."

With a loud, "Humph!" Sporty went over to the stove and picked up his old dented aluminum coffeepot.

"Mommy, I—"

"Please, honey, do it for me."

Angrily pushing his chair back, Michael Jared sprang up and stomped out of the kitchen, mumbling to himself, "I hate it here. I wanna go home."

Tandi's heart ached for her child. It would have been easier on him if she had been able to stay at home. As much as she didn't want to, she might have to let Michael Jared go back to Jared until she could get herself settled in her own place. This dreary old house and this even drearier, bitingly bitter old man were not conducive to an emotionally healthy transition to a new life for either Michael Jared or herself.

Glaring hatefully at Sporty, Tandi watched him fill the coffeepot with water from the tap and then spoon the fresh ground coffee grinds she'd bought just the day before into the strainer. All of her life she had been perplexed by him. She used to wonder why he didn't give her away after her mother died since he never acted like he wanted her, much less loved her. If he loved anyone at all, it was Glynn; at least he didn't yell at Glynn the way he did her. Still, he raised her right along with Glynn, alone, without a woman's gentle touch. He made sure they got an education. He made sure they were clothed and fed, but he did not bother to make sure they had laughter in their home. Sporty was always so grouchy, so stern. He showed neither her nor Glynn any real affection. Tandi couldn't remember ever sitting on Sporty's lap or being carried up in his arms. There was not ever a kiss on the cheek or a tuck in bed at night. Sporty and Glynn always shook hands, and at awkward moments when Sporty should have hugged her, he shook hers, too. The only way she knew he liked Glynn better was when he'd say about his report card, "Keep up the good work." About her report card, he'd say, "I want to see some improvement next time." For the life of her she never understood that. Her report card was always better than Glynn's. Even when she got all A's he'd ask, "Don't they give A pluses?" Nothing she ever did was good enough.

"Daddy, why are you so mean to me? What have I ever done to you?"

Sporty set the coffeepot on the stove with a bang. He turned the burner up high enough for the amber-and-blue flame to dance spiritedly under the coffeepot. Then as an afterthought, he stepped back from the stove and looked down at his right hand. He began flexing it open and closed.

Tandi saw what Sporty was doing, but she was too angry to care that something might be wrong. "Answer me, Daddy. Why are you always so nasty to me. I—"

"If that's what you want to talk about, do us both a favor. Don't." Sporty avoided looking at Tandi as he pulled a pack of cigarettes and a slim plastic lighter from his robe pocket. He lit a cigarette and took a deep, lung-filling drag.

"Have you ever cared about me?"

Sporty tossed both the cigarettes and the lighter onto the counter near the stove. "I got better things to do."

She hated that he could so coldly dismiss her. "Daddy, why is there always a battle being waged between us? When I was a child, did I throw up on you or wet myself on your pants? I mean, tell me what is it that I've done to make you dislike me so? What?"

"It's too goddamn early in the morning for this, Tandida," Sporty said, angrily stubbing out his cigarette in the bottom of the sink. "We done had this talk a hundred times, and I ain't of a mind to talk about it again."

"Then stop giving me reason to bring it up."

"Don't you have somewhere to go?" Sporty grimaced as he began rubbing his right arm above the elbow. "Don't you have to get your boy to school?"

"What's wrong with your arm?"

"Nothing!"

"Don't bark at me!"

"Then stop questioning me." Sporty reached for his cigarettes.

Oh, how she wished he'd choke on his blasted cigarettes. "I don't get it. Daddy, you act like I'm your worst enemy."

Sporty flicked the cigarette lighter. It didn't light. He flicked it repeatedly.

The coffee began to percolate.

Completely fed up, Tandi hit the table with the side of her fist. "I'm sick of this! Why are you so damn heartless?"

Ignoring Tandi, Sporty stuck the tip of the cigarette in the flame under the coffeepot and bending down to it, his face close to the pot, put his mouth to the cigarette filter and dragged on it until it was lit. Satisfied, he straightened up.

"Tandida, if you're gonna stay in this house, don't be trying to drive me crazy. Is that why you're here? You drive that man of yours out of his mind? Did he put you out?"

She bristled. "You would think that, wouldn't you?"

"He did, didn't he?"

"Daddy, you know what you just told me about your business? The same here. My business is none of yours. The truth is, I hate that I even had to come here. If I knew of a conveniently located hotel, motel, inn, or rental shack in Queens, I'd be in it right now. As soon as I find an apartment—and I hope it's today—I'll be out of your precious house. But of course, if the sight of me sickens you so much, I'll leave now, this minute."

Sporty flicked his cigarette ashes into the sink. "Since when you listen to anything I say?"

If she could only strangle him. Tandi took a deep, thoughtful breath and let it out slowly. She had inhaled the strong nutty aroma of the fresh brewing coffee, but that wasn't the only smell she inhaled. Cigarette smoke was all around her. She fanned at it with her hand. "Daddy, I'm asking you to please be nice or at the very least cordial to Michael Jared while we're here."

"I don't talk bad to that boy," Sporty said, blowing out a big puff of smoke in Tandi's direction.

Tandi fanned at the smoke. "If we have to stay here a week, I'll—"

"You'll be here longer than a week."

"No, we won't. I'll have a place in a few days."

Taking another drag, Sporty turned his head toward the far corner of the room and blew out the smoke. "It's not easy to come by an apartment these days. It took Iona's nephew damn near a year to get an apartment."

"That was him."

"That's gonna be you, too. First you gotta find one, then the landlord has to do a credit check, and then he has to check your bank account, your job, and your personal references."

"Don't worry. If it takes longer than a week, I'll move out anyway."

"Suit yourself." Sporty's cigarette hung from between his lips as he began rubbing his arm again.

"I will," she said, looking down at her watch to keep from looking at what Sporty was doing. If something was wrong, he wouldn't tell her anyway. She started out of the kitchen, but, as usual, couldn't hold her tongue. "Hey, you better leave those cigarettes, that coffee, and your oversexed women alone. You're a prime heart attack candidate."

"I ain't gonna stand for you telling me what to do in my house."

Tandi locked eyes with Sporty. He was looking at her like she was something nasty stuck to the bottom of his shoe. That look was why she didn't care what he did or with whom. She just didn't want to be stuck taking care of him when he got sick.

"Sporty," Bernice called from the bedroom, "hurry up."

"I'm coming."

Tandi shook her head. "Daddy, you're scandalous, but it's your life."

"Damn right." Sporty started from the kitchen.

"Um, before you go, I need to ask you a question."

Sporty turned back. "What for? I thought you knew all the answers."

"Not to this one. How in the world did you, of all people, ever get a nickname like Sporty? You're such a sour person to have such a fun name."

Sporty's father gave him that name as a child when he was the best right fielder in his division's softball team. That was decades ago before disappointments and betrayals stole his hopes and dreams. "My name isn't who I am, who I am is what life has made me. Don't ask me any more questions."

Tandi left the kitchen to keep from going another round with Sporty.

Sporty tossed his cigarette into the sink and turned on the cold water. The sound of the water drowned out the hissing sound of the lit cigarette being extinguished. Shutting off the water, he shook his right arm out to the side then flexed his fingers repeatedly. The numbness would have worried him if it had been his left arm.

"I have to stop letting that woman sleep on my arm."

10

Already Jared's life was different. Usually he woke up each morning with one client or another on his mind and a revelation or two as to what legal precedence he could use to strengthen a case. He was always eager to start his day, always ready to take on a challenge. Not this morning. This morning, because he had been unable to sleep, he had gone into the office at seven o'clock, an hour earlier, and for the first time didn't have a clue as to where to begin. He used to think there were not enough hours in his day to do all the things he needed to do in his practice. Not this day. As much as he had to do, he felt as if he had nothing to do that was more important than speaking with Tandi. Tandi and where she and MJ could be was all he could think about. After a sleepless night, he had no great revelation as to how to make what was wrong between them right. If he had to, he'd find a way to come home earlier, but did not believe for one minute that his being home earlier would solve their problem or make Tandi happy. Her anger at him was deeper than that. He could play dumb and say he didn't understand why, but he'd be lying. He knew Tandi had never gotten over his affair.

That's something he didn't understand. Why didn't Tandi get over it? It was a long time ago. She didn't leave him when it happened. He had never cheated on her again, and actually, he had bent over backward to make it up to her. Still, she brought it up last night, cutting open the wound and pouring pepper into it to remind him of how much he had hurt her.

The door of Jared's office opened. Marci stuck her head in. "You were so quiet, I wasn't sure if you were here or not."

"I've been here a while."

"Geez, Jared, you look awful."

"I didn't sleep too well last night." He hated having to explain himself. "What's up?"

"Mr. Shavers is on line one."

Jared glanced down at his watch. It was 9:10. The last time he had called home was 8:45. He had been hoping Tandi would have come back home that morning.

"Jared, are you going to speak to Mr. Shavers?"

Picking up his pen, Jared began to roll it slowly between his fingers. "I'll call him back later. Tell him I'm waiting to hear from the insurance company."

"Will do." Marci left, pulling the door closed behind her.

Jared immediately picked up the telephone and called home. For the sixth time in the last hour he held the receiver to his ear while Tandi's voice asked that the caller leave a message. He had left messages, six of them. He wondered if she was there listening to him begging her to pick up the phone. This time he wouldn't beg, he would not leave a message. He slammed the phone down and took a minute to let his stomach calm down. It had been tied up in knots ever since last night when he got back home to an empty house after drinking that cheap, flat champagne. He had called Tandi's office and could only leave a message with the answering service. He had called Evonne and left a message at her office for her to call him. Evonne was one of Tandi's closest friends. If anyone knew where Tandi was, Evonne would. He knew Evonne's number because she had given him business cards for her real estate business to pass out to his clients.

"Jared!" Marci screamed.

Startled, Jared rushed out into the outer office. "What? What's wrong?"

Marci was up on her knees on top of her desk pointing across the room. "There's a mouse over there behind the water cooler!"

"A mouse! Damn, Marci, I thought someone had a gun on you or something."

"It's a mouse, Jared. Get it!" Marci couldn't stop looking at the floor on either side of the cooler.

Jared would have loved to see how fast Marci had climbed up on the desk. She wasn't exactly fat, but she wasn't a small woman either. "Marci, get down. You're messing up important papers." He went to the cooler.

"I'm not getting off this desk until you get that mouse out of here."

Jared kicked lightly at the base of the cooler.

Covering her mouth, Marci screeched.

"Marci, that mouse is more afraid of you than you are of him. Get off the desk and call an exterminator. And while you're at it, call *The New York Times* classifieds and run that ad again for a personal injury lawyer."

"But, Jared, suppose that mouse runs up my legs."

"That mouse is long gone. There's probably a hole behind the cooler." Again, he kicked at the base. He didn't expect that the mouse would run from behind it. Mice were smarter than that. They knew how to stay hidden until they figured the coast was clear. He certainly didn't have the inclination or time to wait out a mouse. He had work to do and he wasn't amused that Marci was still perched on top of her desk.

"Marci, since you're planning to work from atop your desk today, it's a good thing the telephone is up there with you. See if you can reach Raoul. Find out if he made it down to the law library. I need that Anderson versus Queens General Hospital brief today." He started back into his office.

"Jared, come on. You can't make me work in here with a mouse running around. I'm afraid of mice."

"Marci, we're in a storefront on Parsons Boulevard. God knows what kind of stores have occupied this site in the last century. Frankly, I'm surprised we haven't seen a whole family of mice before today. And believe me, that little mouse isn't thinking about you. He's looking for a meal. You can't fault a hungry animal for looking for a meal." Again, Jared checked his watch. "If my wife calls, put her through right away." He went on into his office and closed the door.

Before Jared could get to his desk, the intercom buzzed. He hadn't heard the telephone ring so he knew it had to be Marci still acting silly. "Marci, that mouse isn't even thinking about you."

"Mr. Crawford, a Miss Evonne Fulton is here to see you."

Jared was suddenly hopeful. "Send her in." He met Evonne at the door. "Have you heard from Tandi?"

"I talked to her last night, why? Isn't she home?"

Jared glimpsed Marci looking at him. "Let's talk in my office."

Inside the privacy of his office, he continued to stand while Evonne sat. "Tandi walked out last night. She took MJ with her."

"Oh."

"I haven't heard from her. I don't know where she is. I tried her at work, I tried her at home, I called her brother. Nothing. I thought she might be at your place."

"No, she isn't. Like I said, I did speak with her last night, but I think that was before you got home."

"Did she say anything about a divorce?"

Evonne nodded not too eagerly.

"Oh, man." Jared turned away and back again. "Damn. I didn't think she meant it."

"She meant it. She's serious."

The knot in Jared's stomach tightened, cramping him. He abruptly turned on his heels and went to his caseload board on the side wall. Kneading his stomach with his fist, he scanned the board but took in none of what he saw. A divorce was not what he wanted.

"Jared, Tandi probably just needs a little space. She's pretty upset."

He whirled around. "About what? About me doing my job?"

"That, and the fact that you don't make love to her anymore."

He felt like he was punched in the gut. Les the bartender was right. Jared looked away.

"Don't be embarrassed, Jared. Tandi and I are best friends. We talk."

"That's what I hear," he said, slumping down into the chair under the caseload board.

"I also know about the affair you had."

"Damn, you women talk too much. Look, I'm not having an affair now. I don't know how Tandi could think that."

"Because you had one before."

"You can stop reminding me of my past indiscretion."

"Jared, you had to know that Tandi's never forgiven you."

"I know it now."

"Look, I came here to tell you, face-to-face, that you shouldn't take this too hard."

"How should I take it, Evonne? I love Tandi. I want her and MJ home. I'm not having an affair. I told Tandi that I would never do that to her again. I know I messed up before. I was dead wrong, but . . . but I really need to be talking to Tandi about this."

"Yes, you should be, but, Jared, until she's ready to talk, you need to let her work through this by herself. If you hassle her, you'll only push her faster into a divorce. Give her the space she needs. She'll come around. She'll see that you're a good man and come back."

He wasn't sure about that. "If I leave Tandi alone and don't try to get her back, I could lose her for good."

"Jared, trust me. You won't lose Tandi. She's not stupid. She's stubborn, but she's not stupid."

"Meaning?"

"Meaning that Tandi isn't going to walk out on a good man. She'll come around."

He knew how stubborn Tandi could be. "How much time does she need?"

"I guess a few weeks, a month."

"A month?"

"Jared, the more you go after Tandi, the more she'll show you her ass. I guarantee you, you contact Tandi before she contacts you, she'll tell you about yourself in every way but the holy way."

He didn't doubt it. Tandi had gotten her back up against the wall many times over the years, and the more he tried to reason with her, the more she stood her ground. "So what about MJ? I'm not going weeks without seeing him."

"You won't have to. Tandi is supposed to call me tomorrow. I'll talk to her about MJ. If she lets me, I'll pick him up wherever he is and bring him to you for a visit."

"You'd do that for me?"

"Of course I would. Tandi is my girl and I love her to death, but right is right. You should see your son."

"Thanks," he said, feeling a bit better. Jared rubbed his chin then the sides of his face. It felt like coarse sandpaper. Tandi would hate that he hadn't shaved that morning. There was a time when she used to like rubbing her face up against his right after he shaved. When he didn't shave, although he wore a suit every day, he looked like a scruffy lumberjack. Tandi didn't like that look.

"Are you growing a beard?" Evonne asked, crossing her legs.

"I just didn't shave this morning."

"I think you'd look good with a beard."

"Tandi never thought so."

"Well, I think you would. You should try it."

"Nah. I'd look like my grandfather with a beard."

"What's wrong with that?"

"He was old."

"Oh, Jared," Evonne cooed, "you wouldn't look old. I think you'd look quite handsome."

"I don't know."

"Try it. If you don't like it, shave it off."

Jared rubbed his chin. "Maybe. Of course, I'd have to shave it off the minute Tandi comes home."

"Yes, but while she's gone, you're free to do anything you like."

"I guess," he said, feeling the knot tighten again. He didn't want to be free to do anything he liked. "Evonne, would you do something for me?"

"Anything," she said, a little too eagerly.

"When you talk to Tandi, ask her if she'll go out to dinner with me tomorrow night or any night. Anywhere she wants."

"Jared, I'll go you one better. I'll plead with Tandi to go out to dinner with you."

"Thanks. I'm glad she has a good friend like you."

"I consider myself your friend, too, Jared. If you need to talk, anytime, day or night, just call. Do you have my home number?"

"No."

"Here," she said, pulling out a business card from a side pocket in her pocketbook. She quickly jotted down her home telephone number on the back.

Jared took the card.

Checking her wristwatch, Evonne quickly stood. "I'm showing a co-op apartment a few blocks from here."

"Business is good, huh?"

"Not bad. Selling apartments is a kiss-ass business and being on time is a must. Can't keep money waiting."

"How long have you been in real estate?" Jared asked, standing also.

"Going on seven years. I'm thinking about getting more into selling houses, like Tandi."

"Is she doing okay? I mean, selling houses?"

"Oh, you don't know?"

"Tandi doesn't talk much about her job."

"Well, I don't think she much likes real estate anymore. She hasn't had a big sell lately. Actually, I sell more apartments; there's a quicker turnover. People are less likely to move out of a house than an apartment. But the money is better on a house sell. Plus, I've seen houses that I wish I could buy for myself."

The intercom buzzed. Jared quickly answered it.

"Jared, your ten o'clock, Mrs. Peterman, is here."

"Give me a minute." He walked Evonne to the door. "Thanks for coming by."

"I'll call you as soon as I hear from Tandi."

"Thanks," he said. "If it's after seven tonight, try me at home."

"I will," she said, leaving as Mrs. Peterman stood to come into the office.

Jared felt better knowing Evonne would speak to Tandi for him. He had never sat down and talked to Evonne alone before, but he wasn't surprised at how pleasant she was. Tandi had always spoken well of her—a good friend and very professional. Knowing Tandi, she wouldn't have any other kind of friend. She was usually pleasant herself and was once his good friend. If Evonne could get them talking again, it would be the answer to his prayer. Until Daina got back from her trip, he had only Evonne to rely on.

"Good morning, Mrs. Peterman. I have good news for you."

11

A little voice had told Tandi to keep Michael Jared out of school, but she ignored it. She was sure he would be okay. No sooner had she dropped him off; gotten home; packed two more suitcases of clothes, shoes, and personal necessities for them both when the telephone rang. Assuming it was Jared, again, she let the answering machine take the call.

"Mrs. Crawford, this is Mrs. Laird, the principal of I.S. One Eleven. As soon as—"

Tandi snatched the telephone off the receiver and simultaneously switched off the answering machine. "Mrs. Laird, this is Mrs. Crawford."

"Mrs. Crawford, I'm calling about your son, Michael. I would like for you to come to the school to pick him up as soon as possible."

"Is he sick?"

"No. He's been in a fight."

"What? He doesn't fight."

"He did today. Michael's teacher said he wasn't himself all morning. In fact, he had been quite sullen. When Mrs. Augustine stepped out of the classroom for a moment, Michael picked a fight with another boy."

"Oh, God." Tandi knew her child was only venting his anger at her. "I'm sorry. Is my son or the other boy hurt?"

"The fight was broken up right away, but the other child was knocked down."

"But he wasn't hurt?"

"It doesn't appear so."

"Thank God."

"Mrs. Crawford, we've never had any trouble with Michael. Is there a problem at home we should be aware of?"

Tandi hated to have to put her business out in the open, but to keep Michael Jared from being penalized, she had no choice. "My husband and I have recently separated."

"Oh, I see."

Tandi felt like she was sitting on a hot seat. "Michael didn't sleep very well last night."

"I see," Mrs. Laird said again. "Mrs. Crawford, would you like for me to make an appointment for Michael to see the school counselor?"

"It's certainly a good idea, Mrs. Laird, but let me speak to Michael first. I'll be there within a half hour."

"He's sitting outside my office. Please see me first."

"Of course. Is he suspended?"

"It's his first offense, so I'm only sending him home for the day. If he should do this again, however, he will be."

"Mrs. Laird, thank you for understanding, I'll see you shortly."

Oh, God. What had she done? Had she unwittingly messed up Michael Jared's life? She expected he would have problems adjusting, she just didn't think his problems would start immediately. Picking a fight was something Michael Jared never did, especially being a karate student who was taught discipline and control were the most important skills of the art. Not to mention what she had drilled into him about not fighting. How was it that in a twenty-four-hour period he had gone from a well-behaved child to one who picked fights? Tandi could blame no one but herself. She had disrupted Michael Jared's life—taken him from his father, taken him from his home and put him under the roof of the mighty grinch. Maybe she needed to rethink her plans. Maybe she was going to have to leave Michael Jared with his father for a while.

Tandi was about to leave the house. At the front door she stopped and looked back through the house. There was a dull ache in her heart. She closed her eyes so she could feel what was once her home. When she and Jared first moved in, she had stood so. Then she had felt the emptiness of any life force, good or bad. The house lacked warmth. It lacked that lived-in feeling—it had been empty for eight months prior to their buying it. A year later, after their personal essence seeped into the walls, into the floors, into the air; after her furniture and personal touches gave the rooms personality, she had stood at the door many times with her eyes closed, reveling in the homey aura that surrounded her—the delicious smell of her cooking, fresh flowers in season scenting the air, the life force of their bodies. Back then, Jared's desire for her was strong. Her passion for him was equal that of his. Throughout that first year, whenever they were alone, and sometimes when Michael Jared was asleep, they made love in every room. That is, except Michael Jared's—there was something sacrilegious about that. She had much to be grateful for in those days. Her life could not have been better, but like the once supple white orchid that she saved from her wedding bouquet now sandwiched between the pages of her wedding album, her marriage and her home had wilted and dried out. Perhaps that was because neither she nor Jared had been vigilant about nourishing their love for each other.

Standing as she was at that moment, the homey aura that Tandi so enjoyed was no longer strongly felt. Apparently, how one feels about one's home has a lot to do with how one feels about one's partner. Tandi opened her eyes. Somehow she had to make a home elsewhere for herself and Michael Jared, but first, somehow, she had to find the right words to make him feel better.

12

Michael Jared's head was down, his lip was stuck out, his hands were folded in his lap. His slim body was drawn tight. He looked smaller than he was. He was five feet three, not really a big boy, not yet anyway, but Tandi knew he would be one day because of his size nine feet and his long spindlelike fingers. If he did grow tall, he would be taller than Jared, but for now, he was a little boy hurting because of her desperate need to make changes in her life.

Tandi sat next to Michael Jared and lay her arm around his shoulders. "You all right?"

Michael Jared continued to hold his head down.

Bending lower, Tandi tried to look into his eyes. "Honey, are you all right?"

From under his lashes, tears brimmed and rolled down Michael Jared's cheeks.

Tandi lovingly wiped at his tears. "You're not hurt, are you?"

Shaking his head, he sniffled. "You mad at me?"

"Oh, honey, no," she said, drawing him to her. "I know why you're upset. I promise you, soon, everything will be all right."

"Can we go back home?"

She was afraid he'd ask that question. "We'll talk about it."

Michael Jared pulled away. "Mommy, I don't wanna live with Granddad."

"We're not living with Granddad. We're just staying there for a few days."

"I don't wanna stay there a few days. I wanna go home," he said aloud. Tears washed down his cheeks.

Tandi took a tissue from her jacket pocket and dried Michael Jared's face. "We'll see what we can do, okay?"

Several feet away, the school secretary cleared her throat. Tandi could see the secretary wasn't looking at them directly, but she knew she had to be listening—the pen she had in her hand hadn't scribbled a word.

"Is Mrs. Laird in?" Tandi asked.

The secretary looked up. "She was called away. She should be back in about ten minutes."

Tandi stood. "I'm sorry, I can't wait. Tell Mrs. Laird that I was here and I'll call Mrs. Augustine to get Michael's homework assignment."

"Mrs. Crawford, if you'll wait, Mrs. Laird will only be a few minutes more."

"I have to leave." After helping Michael Jared into his jacket, Tandi picked up his backpack and swung it over her left shoulder. Then taking him by the hand, she led him out of the office, down the long shell-colored hallway out of the building. Nothing Mrs. Laird had to say to her would solve her problem or Michael Jared's. As she drove in the opposite direction of what was no longer their home, she glanced at him.

Michael Jared began to squirm in his seat when he saw they weren't going home. He began to cry again.

"Honey, I made you a promise that everything will be all right, and it will."

"It won't be all right if we're not going home."

"Michael Jared, please give me a chance to straighten everything out. I told you, you will be with your father."

"When?"

"Soon. Just give me a chance to work things out with him."

"But you're not gonna be with him, are you?"

Glancing again at him—his eyes glistening with tears, waiting anxiously for her to say yes—Tandi wanted so much to tell him what he wanted to hear. She looked back at the road.

Michael Jared cried pitifully.

"Honey, I'm so sorry. Please don't cry."

Michael Jared's crying wilted Tandi's resolve to stay strong. She felt like crying herself. This was one time she wished she had only herself to worry about. She had no right to separate Michael Jared from his father, not like this.

"Honey, you can stay with your father tonight, if you like."

Michael Jared stopped crying instantly. "I can?"

She nodded.

Michael Jared dried his face with the sleeve of his jacket. "Mommy, what about you?"

"Don't worry about me. I'll be fine," she lied. Losing him was tearing her heart out.

"You gonna stay in that house?"

"Yep."

"But it stinks. It smells old."

"How do you know what old smells like?"

"From that time we went to visit Dad's Aunt Lucie in Virginia before she died. Granddad's house smells like her house."

Tandi had to think about that for a minute. Was Michael Jared saying that Sporty's house smelled like death? At least that's what Aunt Lucie's house smelled like. Sporty's house didn't have the smell of medicine and death. It had the smell of closeness, staleness.

"Mommy, I don't wanna leave you."

"You won't be leaving me. I'll see you first thing in the morning."

"You'll be okay?"

She glimpsed his worried expression. "I'll be fine."

"You won't be scared?"

"No, honey, I won't be scared. I'll be fine." Tandi patted Michael Jared on the thigh. She understood his fear. It wasn't just about the house, it was about Sporty and his nastiness. To tell the truth, she was afraid, but that she would only admit to herself. She was afraid of things that might be said between her and Sporty. Fighting with him was the last thing she needed. That was enough to make her want to cry. To keep from crying, she concentrated on the road ahead. She didn't want to be apart from Michael Jared but if being at home with Jared made him feel better, then that's where he belonged. Not in Sporty's house where no children ever laughed or played. Neither she nor Glynn ever did. Perhaps Michael Jared sensed that. The house always had a sad, dreary feeling about it. At one time the house was painted white throughout, but even the white paint had faded to a dull gray. There were no bright colors anywhere. Michael Jared had been calling the house a haunted house ever since he was six years old when the lights suddenly went out, bathing them in blackness, scaring him to tears. For years, he swore a ghost had turned out the lights. It turned out to be a blown fuse, but it never made a difference to Michael Jared. Lights didn't go out by themselves.

"Mommy," Michael Jared said in a wee little voice.

"Yes, honey."

"I'll stay with you tonight."

Tandi glanced quickly at Michael Jared then into the rearview mirror. Seeing that she was in the clear, she pulled over to the curb and put the car in park. "Honey, it's all right with me if you'd like to stay with your father."

"But you'll be by yourself."

"I'll be okay," she said, stroking his cheek with the back of her hand. "Thank you anyway."

"I'll stay with you, but I wanna talk to Dad."

"Will you be satisfied with just speaking to him?"

He nodded.

"Are you sure?"

He nodded again.

"Okay. You can call him when he gets home, but please don't tell him just yet where we are."

"How come?"

"Because we won't be there long. Tomorrow I'm going out to look for an apartment, then—"

"Mommy!"

"Okay. Why don't we do this one day at a time?"

Michael Jared's bottom lip shot out.

"Honey, please. Just give me a little time."

His lip was still out.

"Please."

Begrudgingly Michael Jared gave in. He pulled in his lip.

"I love you," she said, again stroking his cheek.

He didn't respond to the sentiment.

"I love you more than chocolate nut clusters," she said, trying to get a smile out of him.

It was tiny, but Michael Jared did smile. "I love you more than chocolate chip ice cream."

She tagged him lightly on the arm. "You're sweeter than chocolate chip ice cream."

His smile slowly vanished. "Mommy, I'm sorry for fighting Sean. He's my friend. I don't know why I pushed him."

"It's called transference. You were upset with me for leaving your father and transferred your anger with me to Sean."

"I'm not angry at you."

"Well, I don't want you to be, but I understand if you are. Okay?" Michael Jared nodded.

"I want you to apologize to Sean tomorrow."

He nodded.

"That's my good boy," she said, again stroking his cheek with the back of her hand. "Everything is gonna be all right. I promise. Okay?"

Again he nodded.

Glancing into her sideview mirror, Tandi pulled the car back onto the road. She hoped she hadn't just lied to Michael Jared. She hoped Sporty's surliness and the cold, drab atmosphere she was taking Michael Jared into would not prove to be her worst nightmare come true.

13

The instant Jared stuck his key into the second lock of the front door, he sensed the emptiness that awaited him on the other side. Tandi never locked the second lock until after he was home or if she herself was out. Opening the door, he stepped into a stillness that he had known only once before when Tandi was in the hospital after having MJ. She was gone five days, and each and every one of those days he missed her being home. It was just as it was at the moment, no "hey, babe," no music, and no voices from the television in the living room. Back then he knew she was coming back, and he was happy she was bringing him a son. This time, it was different. Tandi might never come back, and he was afraid she'd take from him the son she had so lovingly put in his arms minutes after he was born.

Jared didn't bother to go into the kitchen. There was no hot meal waiting for him there. He wasn't hungry anyway. He took his time going up the stairs to the bedroom. Right away, the open closet door confirmed his worst fear—Tandi had been there and had taken more clothes.

"Damnit!" He slammed the door shut. He sat down heavily on the side of the bed. Damnit, he didn't work as hard as he did to end up without his family.

Riiing!

Jared lunged for the telephone on the nightstand, snatching it off the hook.

"Hello."

"Hi."

Jared's heart pulsed. "Tandi."

"No, it's me, Evonne."

Jared dropped the telephone away from his ear onto his right thigh. He felt like a kid who didn't get what he wanted most for Christmas— highly disappointed. He pushed his breath out through his mouth as he brought the receiver back up to his ear.

"You there, Jared?"

"Yeah."

"Are you all right?"

"Have you heard from Tandi?"

"Well . . . no, not yet. How're you doing, Jared?"

Jared leaned forward, resting his left elbow on his thigh. As he began to slowly massage his forehead, he wondered why, if Evonne hadn't heard from Tandi, was she calling. There wasn't anything she could tell him. "What's up, Evonne?"

"Nothing really. I was concerned about you. I called to see if you were all right."

"Hey, I'm as solid as a rock."

"Jared, you don't have to pretend with me. I saw you this morning. I saw how upset you were. I know how much you love Tandi."

"Yeah, well, how come she doesn't know that?"

"She knows. I just think Tandi needs a little time to remind herself that she does."

"So what am I supposed to do while she's reminding herself?"

"Wait her out. She'll come back."

"No sweat."

"Jared, I'm not saying it's gonna be easy. In fact, I was thinking . . . Jared, you might need some time to yourself to re-evaluate your relationship with Tandi."

"What for? I know what I want."

"Well, you might need to see if what you and Tandi have together is all that it could be, or even if it's what you want anymore. People do change, you know."

Jared pulled the telephone from his ear again, but this time he peered at it perplexedly. That's why he never liked talking relationship stuff with women. They talked crap that he needed a psychology degree to understand. If what he and Tandi had together wasn't what he wanted, he wouldn't want her back. It was as simple as that. He drew the telephone back to his ear.

"Evonne, I don't need any time to myself. I already know I want Tandi back, and at one time, I liked what we had together just fine. I just have to get us back to that time."

"Jared, there isn't anything you can do to get Tandi back if she doesn't want to come back. You can't make her fall in love with you again, especially if she doesn't trust you."

That wasn't what he wanted to hear. "Evonne, let me talk to you tomorrow."

"Jared, wait. Have you eaten dinner? I was planning on eating out, maybe we—"

"Thanks, but I'm not up for going out tonight."

"We don't have to go out. I could pick up something and bring it over."

"Frankly, Evonne, I don't have much of an appetite. Thanks anyway."

"We don't have to eat. Maybe I could just come by and we can talk. I'm a good listener."

Jared didn't trust himself to be around anyone. His emotions were too raw, and he wasn't about to cry on Evonne's shoulder. "I'm a little beat tonight, Evonne. I think I'll turn in early."

"Will you call me if you need to talk?"

"Sure. You'll call me if you hear from Tandi, right?"

"Of course."

"Don't forget to ask her to go out to dinner with me."

"I won't."

"Thanks. Later." Hanging up, Jared glimpsed the clock. He lay back on the bed. It was only nine o'clock. At work he often wished time would stop so he could get more done. Today, of all days, it felt like the clock stopped altogether. He was exhausted from his work day and from a long sleepless night filled with worry about Tandi and MJ. He wasn't used to worrying about either one of them, mainly because Tandi always had a handle on everything. She took care of MJ, the house, him, their lives. Other than his practice, he never had to concern himself with their day-to-day life. By this hour, he would have had dinner and would be drifting off to sleep while MJ thought of new ways to stay up past his bedtime until Tandi was at her wits' end.

Tandi would threaten, "Boy, if I have to tell you one more time to go to bed, I'm going to come in there and tie you to the bed by your fingers and toes."

MJ always thought that was funny until Tandi got mad enough one night to make good on her threat. She tied one of his wrists to the bed and was trying hard to do likewise to the other when MJ started screaming for him to help him. He went to the doorway and stood with his arms folded, watching MJ kicking out wildly while Tandi tried to grab his free arm.

"I'll go to bed!" MJ cried.

Watching them, he had gotten a good laugh out of it, but as Tandi stormed past him, she said, "Thanks a hell of a lot! You could help me with your son and make my life a hell of a lot easier."

He hadn't thought anything about what she'd said at the time or any time after that, but thinking about it now, she was right. He could have been more involved and given her a break. Maybe if MJ had seen that they both meant business, he might not have given Tandi such a hard time every night. Yeah, he should have done more, but he always had an excuse—he was tired, he had real problems to deal with.

Riiing!

Sitting up quickly, Jared again snatched up the telephone. "Hello!"

"Hi, Dad."

"MJ? Hey, son," he said, relieved, happy, and close to tearing. "Where are you?"

"I can't tell you."

"Why not?" Jared looked at the caller ID box. *Unavailable.* The number was blocked. Damn, Tandi never had the all call blocking feature added to the phone so all callers could be seen on the caller I.D.

"Because Mommy said so."

"I won't come where you are," he said, feeling his throat tighten. "I just wanna know that you're safe where you are."

"I don't feel safe here 'cause—"

"Michael Jared!" Tandi shouted in the background. "Don't say that. You know you're safe here."

Jared's heart started racing. "MJ, let me speak to your mother."

"Mommy, Dad wants to talk to you."

Jared didn't hear Tandi say anything. He hoped she was coming to the telephone. He waited.

"Mommy, here," MJ could be heard saying.

Jared pressed the telephone to his ear, trying to listen for any sounds of Tandi coming to the telephone. What he heard in his ear was the thumping of his own heart.

"Mommy, please talk to him."

The silence was deafening. Jared had to tell himself to not shout out Tandi's name. "MJ," he said softly.

"Mommy, please."

"MJ," Jared said again, though louder.

"Huh?"

"MJ, tell your mother I'm sorry. Tell her I want her to come home."

"She's not here."

"Weren't you just talking to her?"

"She went out the room."

Jared closed his eyes briefly. *Go slow,* he told himself. "MJ, I miss you and your mother."

"I miss you, too. Dad?"

Jared's throat tightened again.

"Dad, I wanna come home."

Jared's nose began to sting. He rubbed his eyes, smearing long overdue tears onto the sides of his face.

"Dad," MJ whispered, "we're at Granddad's."

"Oh, God." Jared felt sick. "MJ, I'm sorry, man." He knew how desperate Tandi had to be to end up at her father's.

"Dad, can you be nice to Mommy so she'll wanna come home?"

"MJ, I'll be super nice. I promise. Tell your mother that I would like to take her out to dinner tomorrow so we can talk."

"Okay."

"And, MJ, tell her I wanna see you. Ask her if I can come by tonight to see you."

"Okay. And, Dad, when you come by, can you bring my computer?"

"I will if I have to, but I hope you and your mother will come back home."

"Me, too."

"Go ask her if I can come by to see you."

"Okay."

Jared heard the receiver being put down on a hard surface. It clanked in his ear, but he didn't dare pull the receiver away. He didn't want to miss a sound. He knew he was hoping against hope, so he began to pray. *Please, God. Please let her talk to me. All I need is a chance.* Like a kid, Jared waited with his fingers crossed.

"Aww, Mommy! Please."

"Michael Jared, did you tell your father where we're staying?"

Jared wished he was there for his son.

"But I want him to—" Michael Jared said softly.

"Boy! Say good night. It's time to get ready for bed."

"But I still wanna talk to my dad."

"Michael Jared, what did I say?"

"Aww, man."

The receiver was bumped on a hard surface. It rattled in Jared's ear. "MJ."

"Dad, I don't wanna sleep here. I hate it here."

The anguish in MJ's voice tore at Jared. He started massaging his head.

"Hang up the phone!" Tandi ordered.

"But, Mommy, Dad wants us to come home. He said he's sorry."

"Michael Jared, for the last time, hang up the darn phone."

"Dad, can't I talk to you a little while longer?"

God, how Jared wanted to defy Tandi. He wanted to tell MJ he could stay on the telephone as long as he wanted and was about to when, thankfully, his better sense kicked in. Wasn't that what Tandi had been talking about—him not backing her up?

"MJ, do like your mother said. Go on, get ready for bed."

"But, Dad, I wanna talk to you."

"MJ, don't give your mother a hard time. I want you to call me tomorrow, okay?"

"But Dad—"

"MJ, if you go to bed now, maybe tomorrow I'll see you."

MJ whined, "But I wanna see you tonight, I don't like it here."

Jared's throat was so tight he had to force himself to swallow to wet it. "MJ, please. For me, please go to bed."

"Okay, but I don't wanna."

"I love you, son."

"I love you, too, Dad."

Tears brimmed. "Tell your mother I love her, too."

"You do love her, don't you, Dad?"

Jared's tears spilled over. "MJ, don't ever think that I don't love you or your mother. I love her very much, and I want her to come home. Will you tell her that for me?"

"Yes."

"Go to bed now, okay."

"Okay."

"Don't forget to call me tomorrow," he said, wiping at his face.

"I won't."

Long after Jared hung up, he continued to look at the telephone. He couldn't believe Tandi had taken his son to live in Sporty's house, the very place she herself had vowed to never live again. God. Jared was still hearing MJ's hurt little voice in his head. MJ was a little boy caught in between a mother who had always been there for him and a father who had not. He had been treating MJ like he was all grown up and didn't need to be coddled by his daddy, but he was wrong. MJ was just a kid, a kid who wanted what all kids wanted—their parents together.

Untying his shoes, Jared took them off and tossed them across the room. Fully clothed still, he lay back on the bed with his hands clasped on top of his stomach. An overwhelming feeling of loneliness covered him like a heavy quilt. He wasn't a stranger to that feeling. He had felt that sad and lonely once before—the day his older brother died. Melvin had died of a drug overdose when he was two weeks shy of turning twenty-two and one day after getting his degree in political science. Melvin was going to be somebody, the whole family knew that. Celebrating with his friends, Melvin had been partying hard that Friday night and set no limits on what he drank, what he popped in his mouth, or on what he inhaled into his lungs. News of his death devastated the family, especially Jared. He had looked up to his big brother and had planned on being just like him.

Jared's tears flowed freely now. He never thought he could feel as badly as he did when Melvin died. He thought nothing could hurt him like that again. Well, he was wrong. He was feeling that same emptiness, that same loneliness, and he was scared—scared that he could end up alone. He had to get Tandi back. Hopefully, since she would not listen to MJ, maybe she'd listen to Evonne and meet him for dinner. Hopefully.

Suddenly his eyelids felt heavy. Letting his body relax, Jared closed his eyes and let himself sink into the vacuum of darkness that embraced him.

14

Michael Jared must have reminded Tandi ten times by the time she drove up in front of his school that she had promised she'd drop him off at Jared's office after school. Before he ran off, his face had lit up like it was Christmas morning, making her feel worse than she did the night before when he started crying after she made him get off the telephone. If Jared only knew how much his son loved him, he might think about reworking his priorities. Simply saying he wanted them to come home and that he loved her wasn't enough. And really, at this point, it meant nothing to her. It was too late. There was no going back for her, but she would not stand in the way of Michael Jared having a relationship with his father—it wasn't too late for them.

Beyond that, what was uppermost in Tandi's mind was finding her own place. She had gone through the real estate section of *The New York Times*, she had made several telephone calls, and had seen two apartments. Neither was right. Either they weren't large enough or in one case, it was in the back of the building—no light, no view. Nothing was more depressing than looking out at a washed-out, red-brick wall twenty feet away or at someone else's back window with a pink or blue bath mat hanging from the windowsill to air out. That view she knew all too well. She and Glynn used to spend many a day being babysat by Aunt Gert in her Brooklyn apartment when Sporty went away or wanted to send them away. Aunt Gert wasn't their real aunt but a friend of Sporty's. For years Aunt Gert lived in a rear fifth-floor apartment facing an array of bath mats, underwear, sneakers, pants, and even containers of milk and juice out on the ledge to keep cold.

Tandi often wondered if people had run out of space in their refrigerators or if that was a way of keeping their own private stash from greedy relatives.

And the underwear? Tandi couldn't understand how a woman could hang her panties out a window for the world to see. Panties were such a private thing. Once when she talked about a pair of obscenely large panties hanging from a clothesline across the way, Aunt Gert said, "One day your panties might be that big and you're not going to want anyone talking about them." That Tandi couldn't imagine, but that did stop her from talking about the different sizes and styles of panties she saw on the clothesline and the kind of women who might wear them. Glynn, on the other hand, got a big kick out of looking at those panties. In fact, he developed a serious panty fetish and a love for big butt women. Throughout junior high and high school, Glynn went after the girls with the big butts whose panty lines showed through their pants. He was proud of his reputation for being an ass man. The little freak lived his fantasy, and as far as Tandi knew, that's why he married Leah. Her wide ass was the biggest thing on her, never mind that she was so obnoxiously self-important. Glynn didn't mind that. He only cared that Leah wore her pants and skirts butt-hugging tight and that her panty lines were as prominent as the lines on the sides of an oversized cantaloupe. If he was true to his nature, Glynn was still buying Leah's panties. He was a pro at that. He used to buy panties for all of his girlfriends.

If Aunt Gert had known how that view through her back window influenced Glynn, she would have painted her windowpanes black and nailed her windows shut. Though she did once smack Glynn upside the head when she overheard him say about a pair of bikini panties, "I'd like to get inside the girl who wears those." The next time they went to Aunt Gert's apartment, she had hung large pots of draping pothos at her windows to keep Glynn back, but he would part them like curtains when she wasn't in the room and look out anyway. Hanging the plants did, however, do the trick for Tandi. She thought they brought floral life to the otherwise drab scene out the back window.

Jared's house may not have been her dream house. It did, however, have a wide open view of a spacious backyard, which Michael Jared played in happily. One day, hopefully soon, she was going to get a house he'd like just as much. Until then, she at least wanted a large bright two-bedroom apartment facing the front of the building.

Sitting alone at a table at The Pancake Hut, Tandi picked at the cold western omelette she'd ordered. She had to think seriously about how much she could afford to pay for rent. Her commissions were respectable but few and far between. Realistically, unless she got a full-time job, she wasn't sure if she could earn enough to pay rent for a pigeon on a ledge. She had enough money saved to get an apartment and furnish it, but after that, she might have a problem. Finding another job was the next order of business. She had never been all that serious about her job. In fact, she didn't much like it, but until she could find something else, she was going to speak to Bob, her boss, about giving her more listings.

As Tandi was beginning to see, getting her life on track wasn't going to be easy. Being the breadwinner while trying to be a full-time mother to Michael Jared was kind of scary. She had no doubt that she could do it—so many women did it every day—it was not having enough money that worried her. Again, Daina came to mind. She really needed to talk to Daina who, with her devil-may-care attitude, would have put everything she was going through in perspective. Sure, Daina would have called her a fool for walking out empty-handed, but Daina would have also understood why she had to leave. Evonne, on the other hand, for the past two days had been pressing her to go back to Jared, and she was tired of hearing it. Until now, Tandi hadn't realized how small her circle of intimate friends was.

Tandi pushed her plate aside. She had four hours to kill before Michael Jared got out of school. Leaving behind a half-eaten omelette, she set out for the supermarket. She needed some ammonia. Her room and Michael Jared's could use some serious cleaning. If she thought they were staying more than a week, the first thing she'd do was paint the dingy white walls and put up banners and posters in Michael Jared's room similar to the ones in his room at Jared's. In lieu of all that, the least she could do was vacuum the carpet, clean the blinds and the windows, and wipe off decades of dust from the furniture.

Unhurriedly pushing her shopping cart, Tandi took her time going up and down the aisles inside Key Food. By the time she got in line at the checkout, she had picked up five pounds of chicken cutlets, a quart of milk, a loaf of whole wheat bread, a two-pound box of rice, frozen carrots, a gallon of ammonia, a can of furniture polish, some air freshener, and a pair of rubber gloves. At least tonight Michael Jared would be able to breathe.

"Tandi? Is that you?"

Tandi looked to the next line at the buxom woman smiling at her. Something about her smile was familiar but she couldn't say she knew who she was.

"I know you know me, Tandi Belson. Kathy Orson. Actually, Kathy Pilgrim Orson. Francis Lewis High School."

Tandi took in the woman's wide hips, large breasts, and round face. A different body, a rounder face, but the same smile. She remembered. "My goodness, Kathy. Hi."

Kathy stepped off her line closer to Tandi. "It took you a minute to recognize me, huh? Hell, I'm twice the size I was in high school."

"But you look great," Tandi said, taking Kathy's hand and holding it. It was but a gentle holding of hands for a brief moment, but it was nice. It was warm like their friendship had been during their junior and senior years. Of course, she remembered Kathy.

"Tandi, you look really great. How have you been?"

The woman in front of Tandi moved up, leaving space for Tandi to put her groceries on the checkout counter. "I'm good." She stepped back on line and began putting her groceries on the counter. "How about you?"

"I'd be lying if I said my life was great, but it's not bad. Hold on," Kathy said, going back to her shopping cart. She pushed it up and began to quickly put her groceries on the counter. She continued talking. "I have three kids, a girl and two boys, and an ex-husband who gives me the blues. When I was with him, he cheated on me; now that we're divorced—four years—he claims he's ready to settle down. Now we're dating. I should marry his ass again just to make his life miserable."

Tandi chuckled. Jared wouldn't know if she was making his life miserable or not. He wouldn't notice. She moved along with the conveyer belt carrying her groceries to the cashier. For a minute she couldn't see Kathy until she also moved closer to her cashier.

"Tandi, are you married? Do you have any children?"

Tandi glanced at the older woman behind her. The woman seemed to be waiting for her to answer. "Married with one son," she said across to Kathy while taking out her wallet. She saw her total ring up. She paid the cashier with two twenty-dollar bills.

"So you still live out here in Queens?" Kathy asked.

"Yep. I live in Queens Village, but my father still has the house in

Hollis." Tandi saw no reason to explain that she was back at her father's.

"I'm in St. Albans now." Kathy paid the cashier. "I'm amazed we haven't run into each other before now."

"Small world, but many roads," Tandi said, accepting her change and helping the cashier bag her groceries.

"Tandi, we should get together sometime to talk about old times."

"I'd like that." Tandi took her two bags of groceries.

Kathy took her four shopping bags. Together they walked out of the store to the parking lot. At Kathy's car, they exchanged telephone numbers. Tandi gave her office number. She went on to her own car and was about to pull out when Kathy pulled up alongside her.

"Tandi, you won't believe this, but your name came up just a few weeks ago."

"Really?"

"Yes. I was at Morton's Restaurant in Manhattan and my ex and I were leaving when I bumped into, of all people, Brent Rodgers."

Tandi's heart fluttered. She couldn't believe it. "Brent Rodgers?"

"Girl, Mr. Fine himself. He's back in New York."

She made herself ask casually, "Where has he been?" But she wanted to ask, *Is he married?*

"He's been living in California. Girl, he's been married and divorced twice."

"Whoa."

"He asked about you."

Again Tandi's heart fluttered.

"He asked if I see you anymore. Of course I told him no because we've been out of touch. He said he would love to see you again."

Tandi's cheeks warmed, yet, it wasn't lost on her that Kathy was the one who told her that Brent liked her when they were in high school.

"I can tell by the look on your face that you wouldn't mind seeing him again. I remember you guys were inseparable. I thought you would eventually get married. What happened?"

"Time and distance, I guess," Tandi said, although at one time she had thought she and Brent would marry also. When he joined the Navy right out of high school, he forgot about her. He stopped writing, he stopped coming to see her on his furloughs. Now she understood why.

"Well, now you're married, which means—"

"My husband and I recently separated," she said quickly.

"Girl, that's fate. You want Brent's telephone number? I have it right here in my daily planner."

Tandi wanted to shout, *Give it to me!* but she quickly suppressed the urge. She didn't want to seem overly eager. Boy, but did it make her feel good to know he had thought of her. "Did you say he's been divorced twice?"

"Hey, maybe Brent was looking for you in his ex-wives."

"Yeah, right." Tandi wouldn't even let herself believe that. "Kathy, I think I need to leave Brent alone."

Kathy opened her pocketbook anyway. "Girl, you know you want his number. Don't be shy."

"Oh, I'm not shy. I'm just cautious. I pass."

"Are you sure? I have it right here," she said, holding up a small leather-bound daily planner.

Tandi shook her head.

"Okay, if you're sure, but I can't believe you've never thought about him."

If Kathy only knew. "Kathy, it was great seeing you again. I'll call you soon," she said, waving as she turned out, leaving Kathy probably wondering why she didn't take Brent's number. Oh, how she wanted that number—even more so knowing he asked about her. The fact that Brent did ask meant that he might have secret desires for her as she had for him. Oh, God. Wouldn't it be a dream come true if she and Brent got together?

Girl, as Daina would say, *get a grip.* Brent was part of her fantasy and not her reality. For the time being, there were complications aplenty in her life. Adding Brent to the equation would only make it worse, especially while she was staying at Sporty's. Sporty would throw a serious fit. He never liked Brent. Not to mention it would be bad timing. Michael Jared wouldn't be able to handle it. He would die if she introduced Brent to him as the man she was seeing.

"Oh, Lord," Tandi said aloud. "Girl, you have got to get a grip. Regress. Just because Brent asked about you does not mean he wants to be with you. That's your fantasy, not his, and before any fantasy can be indulged, you have to take care of your child first and foremost. So get Brent out of your mind. *Poof!*" She flipped an imaginary magic wand. "Be gone."

The wand didn't work. Brent danced around in Tandi's head every minute of the drive back to the house. She wanted so badly to see him, she started fantasizing again. Boy, was she in trouble.

Pulling up in front of the house, Tandi saw, to her surprise, that Sporty was out. She rushed upstairs to her room and changed into a pair of jeans and a T-shirt and went straight to Glynn's old room. Tackling first the old Venetian blinds whose metal slats were covered with dust and dirt, she sneezed twice. They had been closed for so long, the stiff dirty pull string was stuck to the rusty pulley. She pulled on it several times to loosen it. Who else in the world still had Venetian blinds made out of metal slats? No one! Once washed, she saw that the blinds were speckled with rust and yellowed by time; no longer white, but lighter by far than they had been the hour before. Drawing them up, she went at the old wood-framed windows with the same determination to let in as much sunshine as possible.

"I can smell that ammonia all the way down at the front door," Sporty said, gruffly. "What you cleaning for? I thought you weren't planning on staying long."

"Hi, to you, too." Tandi continued to wash the window.

"What you cleaning up in here for?"

"In case you hadn't noticed, it's dirty in here. I don't want my son coming down with some allergy."

"If you take him back home, he won't catch anything from my house."

Tandi stopped wiping. She began to count to ten as she looked up at the mountainous white clouds that filled the sky. It was cold out, as it should be for the end of January, but the sun was shining and the sky was clear and picture postcard blue. New Yorkers had been lucky—very little snow had fallen this winter. A single bird caught Tandi's eye as he alighted on a branch. He didn't stay. He took off like he was in a hurry. When she was a little girl, she often wondered where birds hurried off to. That was something she still hadn't figured out. Turning away from the window, she dropped the large yellow sponge into the bucket sitting on the chair next to her.

"Daddy, I'll be out of here in a few days."

"You going back home?"

For a heartbeat Tandi glared at Sporty before taking up the sponge again. She squeezed the sponge hard, choking every drop of water out of it.

"Wherever I'm going, Daddy, I'll be out of your way. That's all you really want to know, isn't it?"

Sporty frowned. "It's never been easy to talk to you. I'm just gonna say my peace and I'm not gonna say one word more."

"I doubt that," she said under her breath.

"Tandida, I heard you yelling at your boy to get off the phone last night. I guess he must've been talking to his daddy. I heard him crying going up the stairs, so I guess you don't plan on going back home, but I think you oughta. It's best for the boy."

"I know what's—"

"I'm talking," Sporty said, his voice heavy with bass.

Tandi was dumbstruck. No matter how used to her father's harsh ways she was, he could still shut her up in an instant.

"Now, Tandida—"

"No."

"No, what?"

"I told you last night, Daddy, you will not speak to me any way you want."

"I don't know what you're talking about."

"You never do." She turned her back to Sporty and dunked the sponge in the water. Slowly squeezing the water from it, she counted to ten.

"All I'm trying to say is, it's your own business if you don't want to go back home, but you better think about lettin' that boy go back to his daddy."

You old bastard. Tandi squeezed the sponge until her fist was a tight ball and the yellow cellulose fanned out on either side of her fist.

"It's a fact that a man can do about as good as a woman raisin' kids. I know what I'm talking about. That's all I gotta say." Sporty started to leave the room.

Tandi quickly turned around. "It's funny you should say something like that. A lot of women, including myself, would not agree with you."

"You wouldn't, huh? As far as I can see, you and Glynn turned out all right."

"I'm not so sure about that. Glynn could use some therapy."

Sporty lifted his brows. "Why's that? You saying I did something to Glynn? You saying he's crazy?"

"He's no crazier than I am, but he could sure use some help in figuring out why he's so disgustingly selfish and controlling."

Sporty narrowed his gaze. "You saying that's my fault?"

"You spoiled him."

"You always claimed he was spoiled. He used to say the same about you."

"I wasn't the one who got a car at eighteen."

"No, but you got a trip to Hawaii."

"I paid for half of it. I don't remember Glynn paying a cent for his car. And his car cost more than my trip."

"Be careful, Tandida. You sound mighty jealous of Glynn."

"Jealous, I am not, but I see as always you've dismissed anything I had to say as being inconsequential. You've done that all my life."

"You sayin' I treated you bad? That I didn't do right by you?"

Tandi had to pause. What was she doing? How did she get herself suckered into this conversation? Again she dunked the sponge in the bucket of water. She squeezed it hard and watched the water slip out between her fingers.

"Why don't you answer me, Tandida? You sayin' I didn't do right by you?"

"Daddy, we've reopened this scab too many times. It is sadistically redundant."

"Humor me," Sporty said, his voice low and deep. "Tell me how I wronged you."

She chuckled. "I know this game. See, we always play this game your way. You tell me that you did what a lot of men would not have done and how grateful I should be. You'll degrade my mother without mentioning her name and stop me from asking about her. I lose every time because I'll end up tense and angry."

"And you're not tense and angry now, right?"

Tandi dunked the sponge into the bucket, splashing water on herself and the floor. "Let's not play this game."

A little smile crept across Sporty's lips and swiftly faded when Tandi frowned at him. He knew what buttons to push. He knew how far to go and she knew this. She had seen that wicked little half smile and knew that he knew that he had gotten to her. That was the sick little game he played with her as far back as she could remember. When he knew he had her, he'd smile that evil little half smile out of the side of his face and then pull back, satisfied with himself. Even knowing this, she always fell into his trap. When was she ever going to learn?

"Tandida, that ammonia opened up my sinuses. I'm probably gonna get a nasal infection or cold or something."

Tandi glowered at Sporty. She wanted to call him a hard-nosed son of a bitch. She wanted to tell him she didn't need to be in his house, but she couldn't. Instead she busied herself trying to open the second window. It wouldn't bulge. Old paint, dust, and time had glued it shut. With the side of her fist, Tandi tapped all around the frame. Feeling the strain across her chest, she grunted as she pulled on the window with all of her might. It wasn't lost on her that Sporty wasn't making any moves to help her. Finally the window opened with a jerk and cold air washed over Tandi cooling her down. Wasting no time, she took up her sponge and stuck her arm outside the window up to the shoulder, awkwardly bending it around the frame, trying to reach higher to wash away the weathered soot. Water ran down her arm.

"Heating oil cost money, you know."

"Oh, please! How much, Daddy? Just tell me, I'll pay for it."

"I don't want your money."

With the side of her face pressed to the pane, her neck pinched by the wood of the frame, Tandi gritted her teeth and ignored the cold. She widened her strokes, wiping furiously at the dirt and grime.

"You missed a spot to the right." Sporty started out of the room. Under his breath, he said, "Stubborn, just like your mother."

Only after he was gone did Tandi relax and ease up on her strokes. She had heard what he said about her mother. A long time ago she gave up on trying to find out what he meant by that. As much as it goaded her, she wasn't about to dwell on it. It would only aggravate her more. Besides, Sporty always said things like that to get the last jab in. She thought time was supposed to mellow a person. Apparently, in Sporty's case, he wasn't getting any more mellow than a piece of rotting meat forgotten in the bottom of the refrigerator. She'd had enough of him growing up, and as sure as she was breathing, she wasn't about to repeat her childhood and endure his heartlessness, and most definitely, she was certainly not going to have Michael Jared exposed to him any longer than she had to. She tossed the sponge into the bucket. It was time to call Evonne.

15

"*Sorry* I'm late."

Evonne looked up from her menu. "Just ten minutes. I was a little late myself." Evonne closed the menu. "Tandi, you look terrible."

"Tell me something I don't already know," Tandi said, sitting.

"I'm sorry, but you do look awful."

"I haven't had much sleep."

"Obviously." Evonne lay her menu on the table. "Tandi, why are you staying at your father's? You hate the man."

"I had to stay somewhere."

"You could've called me. You could've—"

"Evonne, you don't have the space and you do have a social life. With me and Michael Jared around—"

"Are you ready to order?" the waiter asked, suddenly appearing at Tandi's shoulder. He placed a glass of water in front of her with one hand. In the other he held a small order pad. He pulled a pencil from behind his right ear.

Tandi wasn't hungry. "I'll just have a cappuccino. Light on the cinnamon, please."

"Make that two," Evonne said.

"Anything else?"

"That's it," Evonne said.

The waiter turned abruptly and walked away, hanging his pad over his apron at the waist.

"Tandi, I won't lecture. You know how I feel. But, please, make sure you know what you're doing. You don't want to look back years from now and regret this decision. I always thought you and Jared had something special."

Tandi began pleating the hem of the white tablecloth that rested on her lap. "Maybe we did, before he cheated on me."

The waiter returned with the cappuccinos.

"Tandi, you have got to let go of that. The man said he was sorry when it first happened, and I sorta believe he meant it."

"Sorta?"

"Tandi, neither one of us is a fool. A man can be just as sorry the third time as he is the first time."

"Yes, and we both know that *sorry* is a sorry word."

"True, but you can't stop trusting forever. You'll be miserable. You'll always be suspicious."

"Better suspicious than naive."

"That's a miserable way to live."

"Evonne, that's my point exactly. I've been miserable for the past three years. I did everything but stand on my head to get Jared to look at what we used to have. I hoped and prayed we could get whatever it was back, but he was always too busy. Believe me, I understand what he's trying to do and I was in his corner from the start, but . . . but now I'm so angry with him, I feel like that anger is a part of my being." Tandi lay her hand over her heart. "Evonne, I wear that anger with Jared on my face, and I can feel it stinging my tongue whenever I speak to him or about him. I know Michael Jared sees and feels my anger at his father. This is why I can't be around Jared right now."

"Damn, Tandi, I didn't know you were feeling it that deep. I had been thinking if you could get over what happened and really gave Jared another chance, he might open his eyes."

The urge to cry eased up. "I seriously doubt it. I'm no miracle worker, I can't make a blind man see."

"Tandi, if you feel that badly, maybe you do need to divorce Jared."

She teared. "Look, I'm all messed up here." She dabbed her eyes with her napkin. "Enough about me and my problems, Evonne. What's happening in your life?"

"Nothing." Evonne sipped her cappuccino.

"How's Richard?"

"Richard is fine, but crazy out of his damn mind. Do you know he wanted to go bowling the other night?"

"What's crazy about that?"

"Tandi, really. Do I look like I'm about to put these expensive ass"—
Evonne held her hands flat out for Tandi to see—"diamond-tipped,
one-inch nails inside the germified nail-breaking holes of a bowling
ball?"

Sipping her cappuccino, Tandi chuckled.

"See, that's why Richard is about to be shown the door. He's too
blue collar for me."

"Evonne, Richard is a corporate tax accountant. His collar can't get
any whiter."

"Please," Evonne said, sucking her teeth. "I am not talking about
his profession. I'm talking about his attitude. Richard thinks blue collar. The boy likes to bowl. He likes to hike. He even likes to eat hot
dogs off the street. Yuck."

"Evonne, why're you knocking Richard? He's a good man. Besides,
you and I both have eaten hot dogs from a street vendor when we've
been out shopping all day."

"That was one time and we were in a hurry. Richard does it as a
matter of course. He likes them. He'll pass up a four-star restaurant to
get a dirty dog off some pissy-hand vendor."

Tandi began to laugh.

"What are you laughing at?"

"You. You are too funny. I knew you were snooty, but not this
snooty."

Evonne flipped her hand at Tandi. "Like you aren't."

"Oh, honey, I am so far from snooty."

"You can't prove it by me. Look at the clothes you're wearing."

Tandi glanced down at her gray knit sweater and matching pants.
It didn't cost her much because she caught it at a sixty percent off sale.
"I paid eighty dollars for this, and pray tell, what do clothes have to do
with snootiness?"

"Snooty people don't wear cheap clothes, and you never wear
cheap-looking clothes. And what about your house? I remember when
Jared let you renovate the kitchen and bathrooms because you thought
they were old-fashioned when they were perfectly fine."

Tandi was beginning to feel not too good about the way their conversation was going. "Evonne, I think we need to talk about something else besides me."

Evonne folded her arms and sat back. "Fine. Let's go back to Jared
then."

Tandi was puzzled by the way Evonne was looking at her. Her eyes were hard and unwavering. She looked like she had tasted something bitterly sour. "What's wrong with you, Evonne?"

"Nothing's wrong with me, but as I see it, something's wrong with Jared, and that's because of the problem he has, and that problem is you."

Tandi's mouth dropped open. Was she in the twilight zone?

"That's right, I said it and it's true. You know what you said about Richard being a good man? The same could be said about Jared."

"Wait a minute. Evonne, whose side are you on? Jared cheated on me. I did *not* cheat on him."

"Of course not. You're Little Miss Perfect."

Wham! Where the hell that came from Tandi didn't know, but it certainly knocked the wind out of her. "Perfect? Evonne, is that how you see me?"

"That's how you see yourself, Tandi, and frankly, that's probably how a lot of people see you, including me."

Tandi gasped. Was this girlfriend talk? If it was, she wasn't enjoying it.

Evonne flipped her hand at Tandi. "Child, don't look so scandalized. Being perfect isn't something to be ashamed of. The way I see it, you're perfect and Jared isn't. He's like me. We're imperfect. See, Tandi, I believe we're all entitled to make mistakes, but then the mistakes are either forgotten or forgiven, and we all move on."

"That's easy for you to say. Jared didn't cheat on you."

"No, but—"

"He cheated on *perfect* me."

"Yes, he did. It was an act of an imperfect man. Your husband made a mistake, Tandi. Get over it."

"Evonne, Jared may not have committed an act of treason or hammered the last nail into the palm of Jesus Christ, but he broke his vow to me."

"And he won't be the last man to do that to you or any other woman out there. Look, Tandi, I talked to Jared last night. He's really upset."

"You called him?"

"No, he called me."

That struck Tandi as curious. "He doesn't know your home number."

"He's not stupid, Tandi. All he had to do was look at the caller ID box. I must've called your house a million times—my number isn't blocked. Look, the man needed to talk to someone. I'm your friend, who better to talk to?"

That made sense, but she wished Daina was home for Jared to sound off on.

"Jared sounded terrible, Tandi. He's really upset about you leaving."

"Isn't that just too bad? What did you say, Evonne? Forgive or forget? Well, I'm forgetting about Jared. I've made my decision, and I'll live by it just as Jared is doing."

Tandi threw her napkin onto the table. "Oh, and Evonne, how sweet of you to have all this empathy for Jared. Save it. He doesn't need it. Jared is kinda cold—very little upsets him. My leaving probably hasn't even nicked his emotions—maybe his pride, but not his emotions. If he called you, he was calling about Michael Jared. Him, he cares about."

Evonne picked up her cup. She took a slow, pensive sip and frowned. "This stuff is nasty when it's cold. I may as well drink water." But she didn't. "You're right. Jared did ask about Michael Jared. In fact, he talked mostly about him. What he did say about you was that he didn't blame you for walking out, that he would have done the same thing if he were in your shoes."

For some strange reason, despite what she had said about being angry with Jared, Tandi felt hurt. "That's fine. So if you knew that he said that, why were you trying to make me the bad guy in all of this?"

"Tandi, I love you. I can't stand seeing you messed up like this. Believe me, I was just trying to get you to want your marriage back."

"Don't worry about it. Just leave it alone. As for Michael Jared, Jared can see him this afternoon."

"Does he know where you're staying?"

"My big-mouth son told him last night, but I don't want Jared coming to my father's house. It'll only make things worse over there. They've never gotten along."

"Girl, I wouldn't want your troubles." Evonne took a sip of her water. "Tandi, I owe you an apology. I was hard on you because I care. You were right to leave Jared. I see that now."

Tandi didn't know what to believe. She had no idea that Evonne felt the way she did about her. *Miss Perfect?* No matter what Evonne's reasons were for saying what she did, the feelings were there, and they were critical and damning.

Evonne reached across the table and touched Tandi's hand. "Please don't be mad at me. I was only trying to make sure you were doing the right thing. Like I promised you yesterday, I am going to help you in any way I can."

"Thank you," she said, relenting a bit. "Look, Evonne, I don't want you involved in all of this. I'm sorry Jared bothered you. I'll tell him not to call and annoy you again."

"Oh no," Evonne said, lightly waving her hand. "He didn't annoy me, and actually, I can talk to him for you since you don't wanna see him. Maybe I can get him to understand how much he's hurt you."

"I doubt it, but don't bother with that either. Leave it alone."

"Okay, but you should let me be the go-between because you can't just cut off all communication between you two. You have a son."

That was true.

"Think about it, Tandi. If Jared has an emergency, he knows that I'm the one person you'll always be in touch with besides his pal, Daina, and she's away, right?"

"I don't think we'll have too many emergencies between us."

"You will if Michael Jared is with either of you and he gets hurt."

That was true, too.

"Would you ladies like anything else?" the waiter asked.

"Yes, please," Evonne said cheerfully. "Two more hot cappuccinos. Ours are cold. And, please, bring me a Danish. I'm hungry for something sweet all of a sudden. What about you, Tandi?"

"Nothing."

The waiter left.

"Evonne, can we talk about the apartment? Where is it?"

"One hundred and seventy-second Street, off Hillside Avenue. Two large, beautiful bedrooms on the front. You get the morning sun, and it's bright in there all day. I can show it to you tomorrow. Tandi, you'll love it. I'll help you move in."

"Good, because I'm on a mission. I'm forging ahead with a new life and a hellified new attitude. What I even thought I ever wanted, I'm going after."

16

Tandi did love the apartment—four large rooms all facing the front of the well-kept, clean, half century old building—no brick walls to block her view onto bustling Hillside Avenue. If her car broke down, she had plenty of transportation only minutes away. Tandi wasted no time on second thoughts. She went directly to the manager's office to fill out the application. Mrs. Langhorn assured her she would put a rush on the credit check so that she could be in the apartment within a week—two weeks at the most. From the apartment, Tandi went straight to the bank and had a teller's check for thirty-six hundred dollars drawn up to cover a month's rent and two months' security. When the application approval came, she wanted to be ready. There wasn't much she had to buy in the way of furniture; the bedroom suite in the spare bedroom was hers, as was the set in the dining room. It was her money that had made those purchases and so much more throughout Jared's house, that made it more than a house of brick and plaster. She was going to have to buy furniture for Michael Jared's room, but then it was time he had more grown-up things. His single captain's bed with the attached desk was a mite small for his growing body. He was going to like having a big new bed. It might take a little while, but he would get used to their new life. One day at a time was all it was going to take. Michael Jared was going to be fine, and so was she.

By the time Tandi picked Michael Jared up from school, she was surer than ever that she was on her way to getting her life together. Of course, staying another week or two under Sporty's roof didn't set too well with her, but she could stomach it knowing that the end was only

a week or two away. Michael Jared, however, would think a week or
two an eternity. As it was, this morning he started counting the hours
until he would see Jared. He even promised to do his homework in the
office until Jared was ready to leave. Tandi reminded him of that minutes before she pulled up in front of Jared's office. Thankfully, Jared
was nowhere to be seen.

"I'll pick you up at the house at eight-thirty. If your homework
isn't done, you'll see your father only on the weekend."

"It'll be done." He closed the car door.

"No kiss good-bye?"

Quickly looking around at the few men moving along the sideway,
Michael Jared looked uncertainly at Tandi. He frowned.

"Honey, I've got news for you. Any one of these men, unless they
have an alternative preference, would be glad to have a woman kiss
him in front of the others."

"Yeah, but not their own mothers."

He had her there. "Go on," she said, shooing him away from the
car. "Go see if your father's inside, and don't come home without your
hat."

Michael Jared rolled his eyes comically. "Bye, Mommy."

"Bye, yourself," she said softly, feeling somewhat bruised. Michael
Jared was her all and he was growing up, growing away from her.
Soon she'd have to let him go off alone with his friends; and not too
long after that, he'd have a girlfriend who'd be the all-important
woman in his life, and then he'd go off to college, leaving her alone
with warm memories of the little boy who would forever be her baby
in her heart. One day she'd blink and he'd be married, no longer her
little boy but someone's husband. She was sure that Michael Jared
would love her as his mother no less, but he would need her no more.

"I see him!" Michael Jared yelled from the doorway. "He's in the
back!"

With a quick wave, Tandi hurriedly pulled away. She didn't want
Jared to see her or her him. Besides, she had to get back to the house.
She still had work to do on Glynn's old room.

17

Michael Jared begged to see Jared every day and every day he did. It was the only way Tandi could ease her guilt about spiriting Michael Jared away from his home, from his father, who, though he hadn't been around on the occasion of his every little scraped knee, or for a single spelling bee or for his karate demonstrations or the bestowing of his belts, was still a father Michael Jared loved. There was no doubt that being with Jared was good for him. He finally had the father he deserved and was by birth his right to have. Of course, Jared wasn't exactly Mr. Mom. Michael Jared said Jared usually took him to Burger King for dinner. That would not have been Tandi's choice, but she said nothing because it was safer that they ate out. It seemed that on the second night Jared tried to fry chicken at home, and he burnt the poor bird to a crispy critter and the frying pan to a crusty black greasy relic. The house had filled with smoke and the strong smell of burnt grease. Jared was so disgusted, he threw out the frying pan with the burnt chicken and grease still in it. From then on, they either went for take-out or ate out, which Michael Jared loved. He was smiling again, content to be with his father in the afternoons and his mother in the evenings.

Ironically, Michael Jared was better off now that she and Jared were apart. He spent all day Saturday and most of the day Sunday with Jared, hanging out like Tandi always dreamed they would. When Michael Jared was a baby, they, all three of them, hung out as a family. She couldn't take enough pictures of the two of them. Her favorites being Michael Jared asleep atop Jared's chest, both breathing in unison, just as she and Jared had lain so many times after making love. A part of her longed for those idyllic days again, but the reality was, they were gone. Michael Jared was no longer a baby and could never be as close to Jared in that way again, while Jared had forgotten that she had ever been that close to him. It was one more thing to be angry with him about, another reason to not want to see him.

Of course, after more than a week, Tandi knew she could not continue dropping Michael Jared off at the office or picking him up at the house and getting away clean without having spoken to Jared. She wasn't surprised when she pulled up to the office and found Jared waiting outside. He came to her side of the car, squatting down outside of her raised window. His closeness unnerved her. She refused to look at him. He tapped on the glass.

Michael Jared nudged Tandi. "Dad wants to talk to you."

Although she was looking straight ahead, she knew both Michael Jared and Jared were staring at her, waiting for her to roll down her window. She wasn't ready to be face-to-face with Jared.

"Mommy."

Exhaling loudly, Tandi pressed hard on the button, lowering her window.

"Hey, Dad," Michael Jared said. He leaped from the car and raced around to stand next to Jared on the sidewalk. "Mommy, I'm going inside. I'll see you later."

"Michael Jared—" she said, turning her head to look at Michael Jared and found herself looking into Jared's soulfully sad eyes. Her heart thumped. She forgot what she had been about to say. She quickly turned away. She could feel her hands begin to shake so she clutched the steering wheel tighter.

Jared rested his folded arms on top of the door.

"I know," Michael Jared said. "Don't forget my homework, and get my black high-tops."

"And eat some vegetables, please."

"O-kay." Michael Jared backed away from the car but he kept his eyes on Tandi, even after he went inside the storefront.

"I miss you," Jared said.

"I . . . I have to go." She wanted him to get off the door.

"Did you read my letter?"

No, she had not read the letter he had Michael Jared bring to her the first night. It was still sealed inside the envelope, tucked away in the side of her suitcase. Long after Michael Jared had gone to bed in his spankingly clean room, she had sat on the side of her bed holding the letter, turning it over and over in her hand, not wanting to read it, yet curious about what Jared could possibly have to say to her. If he had made promises, she was not interested as he was not going to be able to live up to them. She had ripped the unopened envelope and letter in half, gone downstairs to the kitchen and thrown it into the garbage container. Minutes later, back in her room, she thought, *Suppose one day I wonder about what he has written?* She had gone back for the letter, which had a dab of grease on one corner of the envelope. Cleaning it off as best she could, she wrapped it, grease stained, inside a paper towel and put it in her suitcase.

"Tandi, I meant everything I said. If you'll give me the chance, I'll—"

"I haven't read your letter. I haven't had time."

That, Jared knew wasn't true. Tandi read all of her mail, including junk mail. Not reading his letter meant she didn't want to talk to him, which was why she wouldn't look at him, but that was all right. It gave him the chance to look at her. He always liked her nose—it was small and slightly rounded. It was a little nose, perfect for a pretty woman, perfect for Tandi.

"I love you, Tandi. I want you to always remember that."

Her hands were hurting from gripping the steering wheel. "Jared, I have to go."

He heard the strain in her voice. "Just listen to me for a minute."

"Oh, you have a minute? When I wanted you to listen to me, you didn't have the time."

"Tandi, I'm trying. Let me try."

Tandi turned her head slightly and glimpsed Michael Jared out of the corner of her eye. As she suspected, his nose was pressed against the glass door. The hope in his eyes was crystal clear, but that same hope was foreign to her.

"In the last three years, Jared, I don't think you ever heard a word I said."

"I'm not gonna lie to you, Tandi. I didn't take everything you expressed concern about to heart. I didn't think—"

"That's just it," she said, looking at him. "You didn't think there was any merit in anything I tried to talk to you about. Nor did you think I mattered."

"That's not true."

Tandi put the car in drive. "I have to go."

"Wait." He stood and held on to the car door as if he could hold the car back from moving. "We need to talk more, Tandi. Can we go out to dinner? Can we—"

"Jared, I can't do this right now."

"Then, let's—"

"Michael Jared is watching us. I don't want him to see me pull off with you still hanging on to the car."

Glancing over his shoulder, Jared saw the worry in MJ's face. "Will you at least think about meeting me for dinner next week?"

Again looking straight ahead, Tandi wouldn't commit herself.

"Okay," Jared said, "just think about it." He stepped back from the car.

Finally able to pull away without causing a scene, Tandi had driven a block before the tears came. She was angry Jared had cornered her like that, but being that close to him confused her. She wanted to slap him, she wanted to kiss him, she wanted to be with him. That wasn't the way she was supposed to be feeling. And later that evening when Michael Jared handed her a second letter, she immediately put it way. She didn't want to know how Jared was feeling or how sorry he was. She didn't want anything he had to say to seep in and make her doubt herself any more than she already did. Her future was ahead of her, not behind her. In a few weeks she would be in her new apartment, well on her way to a new life.

Three days later she saw Jared again, but this time, she had to speak to him. "If it's not a problem, tomorrow morning I would like to go to the house and inventory the furniture and other household things that I bought with my own money. I need them for my apartment."

That knot was back, tighter than ever. "Don't do this."

Tandi fixed her eyes on the center of the steering column. "We don't have to fight over custody of Michael Jared. You can see him as often as you wish. As for money, I need at least two hundred dollars a week for him. I don't need anything for myself, but Michael Jared has expenses that I won't be able to cover right away. He—"

"Tandi, we can work this out. Please—"

"No," she said, shaking her head, "we can't."

"Just tell me what you want me to do. What will make this right?"

She shook her head again. "Nothing."

"But—"

"Jared, I am so angry with you for so many reasons. If I came back and if we didn't resolve our problems, I would only end up hating myself, and you, and I do not want to hate either one of us like that. We have a child to raise."

"So we should talk, and talk and talk until we find a way to work through our problems."

"Jared," she said, no longer afraid to face him, "I'm all talked out. The juncture at which you and I stand is now destined to take us onto different paths. It's been coming for a long time. I need to be away from you in order to go forward. Can't you understand that?"

The lump in Jared's throat was as big as the pain in his heart. Hell no he didn't understand that. He didn't understand when the sadness in her eyes said that she still loved him. It wasn't anger he saw there. When tears beaded up on the rim of her eyelids he knew that he was right. Maybe Evonne was right. Maybe he had to stop pushing.

"Tandi, I haven't been fair to you. I hurt you, you didn't hurt me. You're the one who needs time to sort out your feelings. I'm giving you your space. In the end, if you find there's a chance we can try again, I'm here." Jared tapped the car door once and stood back, freeing Tandi to leave.

Thank God. "I won't be late picking up Michael Jared."

"Good. By the way, don't worry about furniture. I'll buy you new furniture."

"You don't have to do that."

"Just tell me how much you need. As for Michael Jared, you have your own checkbook, take what you need. Just keep records."

"Thank you." For whatever reason he stopped pressuring her, she was grateful. She watched as Jared went off into the storefront. At the door he put his arm around Michael Jared and took him to the back. She had never said Jared wasn't a good man, only that he had cheated on her and that he no longer loved her. In the time since she left him, she had seen more emotional potential in him than she'd seen in a long time. And he proved to be more of a father to Michael Jared than he'd ever been. If she went back to him, Michael Jared stood to lose the father he had gained and for that alone, leaving Jared was worth it.

18

Tandi could not wait to get started on her new life, which was why she was not about to sit back and wait for a new life to find her. She was going after what she wanted her new life to be, and possibly, whom she wanted to be a big part of that life—Brent Rodgers. That possibility was very intriguing to say the least, and for the first time in a very long while, she was excited. Kathy gladly gave her Brent's number—it was his job number at a marketing firm. Tandi dialed it right away.

"Brent Rodgers."

Her heart leaped. His voice was deeper, but it was him. "Hi, Brent Rodgers."

"Who is this?"

"Tandi Craw . . . Tandi Belson."

"Tandi Belson. Baby, it's good to hear your voice. How are you?"

"I'm fine, Brent. How are you?"

"Real good, now that you've called. I was hoping Kathy would bump into you."

Tandi felt like she was dreaming. "Yes, I saw Kathy."

"You sound real good, Tandi. You've been on my mind for quite some time. I'd love to see you."

Tandi smiled like she had won the grand lottery prize.

"Baby, please tell me you're not married."

"Well, I am married, but let's just say my marriage is recently over. I do have a beautiful son, however. And you, Brent? I hear you're twice divorced."

"Guilty."

"Any children?"

"Two girls and a boy. They live with their mothers in California. So, does 'recently over' mean that I can see you?"

Tandi covered her mouth to stifle her excitement.

"Tandi?"

Uncovering her mouth she answered subtly, "Yes to your question."

"How about dinner tonight?"

"Yes . . . no! Not tonight," she said, not wanting to come across as too eager. "How about Friday night?"

"I've been wanting to see you for years. Friday is a very distant two days away."

Oh, she could not have dreamed this any better. "For me, too."

"I wish today was Friday," Brent said, his voice low, throaty, seductive.

Tandi felt like dancing. "Me, too."

"Then let's pretend that it is."

She could do that. "Okay."

"Where can I pick you up?"

Her eyes darted around Sporty's living room. Not here, for sure. "I'll come to you."

"I like that," he said softly. "I have an apartment on Hillside Avenue at One hundred eighty-sixth Street."

Small world. The apartment she hoped to get was just blocks away. "Why don't we meet at a restaurant?"

"That'll do. Let's meet at Franco's on Queens Boulevard. Do you know where it is?"

"Yes."

"Let's make it an early dinner. I was planning on leaving work in another ten minutes or so anyway. If you can get away, let's meet at five-thirty."

She didn't have to pick up Michael Jared until eight-thirty. "Five-thirty is fine."

Tandi barely hung up the telephone before she started giggling uncontrollably. She felt like the young girl of long ago waiting to be held by Brent. She had no doubt that being in his arms again would ease the dull ache in her heart. It was time she lived her fantasy.

19

Over dinner Brent spoke of old times, old feelings, and old dreams. Tandi had eaten very little and couldn't remember what it was she had eaten very little of. Though she did remember, clearly, being held tightly against Brent's hard body and being kissed passionately on the lips when they first met outside the restaurant. She remembered his eyes caressing her face and his hand holding hers ever so gently long after the table had been cleared. Brent ordered another glass of white wine so that they could stay and talk a little while longer. Tandi heard all about his ex-wives and his three children, all of whom he left behind in California; all about his travels; and all about the jobs he'd held over the years in and out of the military. About herself, Tandi spoke extensively only of her pride and joy—Michael Jared—and about her work in real estate. About Jared, she said nothing other than it was hard to talk about all that went wrong, only that it was over.

With nothing else to bring each other up to date on, Brent suggested they leave but Tandi was afraid. The restaurant was safe. Feeling as she did—horny as hell for Brent—she knew once she stepped outside the restaurant, she would meekly follow Brent wherever he led. In her fantasy, that would be into a passionate, no-holds-barred lovemaking fest. Every nerve in her body was afire with anticipation. She would be surprised if Brent wasn't feeling the heat coming off her. Shamelessly, she wanted Brent, and as far as she was concerned, she was free to want him, though she didn't want him to know how badly she wanted him. If she nose-dived into Brent's bed without even a hint of trying to restrain herself, he would surely think her too easy. More importantly, she didn't want her hunger for him to scare him away.

With his arm around Tandi's waist, Brent walked her to her car parked a block away on a dark side street. It was while Brent's arm was around her waist that Tandi became aware that her waist wasn't as small or as firm as it was when she was seventeen. Goodness. What if she and Brent were to become intimate? What if he barfed at the softness around her waist or at the sight of her sagging breasts? What if he got past her body but found making love to her boring?

Since that long-ago day when she and Jared first made love, Tandi had not been with another man, and she and Jared had not made love, serious love, in a very long time. No, she definitely could not go to bed with Brent tonight. She wasn't ready.

Brent squeezed Tandi about the waist. "I like the way you feel." He drew her closer.

"Oh, I've gained so much weight."

"Just the right amount of weight. I always thought you were too skinny."

"You did not," she protested, hitting him playfully.

"I did. I remember I used to be able to put both my hands around your waist. Baby, I used to think you didn't have any ribs."

"I thought you liked me that way."

"No, baby, you liked you that way. I like what's in my arms right now—a woman." Brent began to sensually run his hand up and down Tandi's back, each time getting closer and closer to her behind.

The embers of Tandi's desire were ablaze again. Whatever her misgivings, she wanted to be with Brent. She wanted to—no needed to—be made love to.

"How about us going over to my apartment?"

Oh, God, yes! Visions of Brent making love to her popped into her head, but just as quickly, Michael Jared's face appeared before her eyes. "What time is it?"

Brent checked his watch. "Eight o'clock."

"Darn," she said, slipping out of his arms. "I have to pick up my son."

"Isn't there someone you can call?"

"No. I have to pick up Michael Jared myself."

"Baby, I have plans for us."

Tandi liked the sound of that—plans for us. "But my son—"

Brent kissed her lightly on the lips. "If it wasn't for your kid, I'd kidnap you."

"Believe me, I'd let you," she said, feeling absolutely divine.

Brent kissed Tandi again, this time tonguing her, devouring her.

Forgetting that she was on a public sidewalk, Tandi gave herself over to the kiss she had dreamed so long of.

"Ooo, Mommy, they're kissing," a little girl said, pointing at Tandi and Brent.

"You people should be ashamed of yourselves," the woman said, picking up her pace and practically dragging her daughter behind her.

Embarrassed, Tandi couldn't pull away, Brent held her captive against her car. He pressed his hardness into her. She wanted more. The kiss continued, passionately, exploring, intensifying Tandi's desire. When Brent finally let up enough for her to breathe, he kissed her twice more on the lips before he loosened his hold on her—though not completely.

"You feel so good." He started to grind, stiffly and barely noticeably, his erection into Tandi's stomach.

Right there, in the dark, on a public street, Tandi throbbed and moistened. She couldn't ignore the sweet pulsation between her thighs. She couldn't ignore the tingly hardness of her nipples. She wanted the promise of how Brent was making her feel fulfilled. She wrapped her arms around his neck and pulled him down to her. She parted her legs so that she could feel him against her most private place. This time when they kissed, she matched his gyration, pressing just as hard against him. She began to tremble as her pulse quickened. Every nerve in her body awakened; she started moaning. Then suddenly Brent pulled away.

"Baby. Oh, baby. We need to take care of this," he said, pecking Tandi on the lips.

With her eyes closed, Tandi lay her forehead against Brent's chest. She was totally embarrassed but her body wasn't. Tiny spastic impulses pulsed in her vagina, leaving her divinely weak.

Shaking out his leg, Brent tried to push himself down inside his pants. "Man, I might not be able to walk."

Tandi touched him. His hardness was like a pipe. "Take me to your apartment."

"Are you sure? What about your son?"

Again, Tandi dropped her head onto Brent's chest. "Oh, damn."

Brent kissed Tandi on the top of the head. "I want you to go home with me, but—"

"But?" she asked, surprised.

"But you have to take care of your son. Besides I don't think you're ready for me."

She blinked. What happened? Had she missed something? Hadn't she just engaged in dry fucking right out there on the street? She wasn't ready?

Brent kissed Tandi on the forehead. "Baby, I know how it feels to be just getting out of a relationship. It's pretty painful and, for you, it's still very new. I know you want to sort out your feelings about me and your ex."

"I pretty much know what my feelings are, Brent."

"Baby, when you come to me, I want you to be sure it's me you want."

"Brent, I appreciate you being sensitive to my situation, but I know what I want. My reasons are clearly defined, and my feelings for you are very strong."

"Baby, the feeling is mutual. I'm letting you go tonight because I don't want you to worry about your son. But know this, I want you so bad I can taste it."

He wasn't the only one. Maybe she was moving too fast. "You're right." She drew back when Brent went to kiss her on the mouth. No telling what she would do if they kissed again. "Too dangerous," she said, getting quickly into her car.

"Is tomorrow too soon?" he asked.

"Not soon enough."

"Good. Since you don't want me to call you at your father's, you can call me at my office or at my apartment."

"I'll call you tomorrow afternoon."

"I'll be waiting."

On her way to pick up Michael Jared, Tandi found herself humming a song that she didn't even know the words to. She felt absolutely divine. Settling into her new life was going to be a whole lot of fun.

20

Jared couldn't stop looking at his wedding band. For so long, it had been such a part of him he paid it no mind from one day to the next. With his thumb he twisted the band around his finger. It really was a part of him, but it meant nothing without Tandi. Earlier, if he hadn't walked away from her, he might have brought his fists down on the roof of her car and pound it until she listened to him. Hours later he was still wound so tight emotionally he couldn't concentrate on his work. He left the office much earlier than he had intended and took MJ home. When Tandi came for MJ, he sent MJ out to her. He couldn't face her.

He watched Tandi drive off. He watched her taillights until she turned out of the block. He stood in the doorway for a moment longer staring at the spot where her taillights disappeared and imagined that she'd suddenly appear there again, her mind changed, her love for him strong again. Wishful thinking. The corner remained dark. Giving up, he closed the door on the emptiness of the street only to find himself embraced by the same emptiness inside the house. In his den, he turned on the television and began channel surfing. Nothing held his attention. He tried to play a game of chess against an invisible partner. He was losing.

Buzzzz!

Jared immediately turned off the television and rushed to the front door. His hopes were instantly dashed when he saw it was Evonne standing where he had hoped Tandi would be.

"I saw your lights. I hope you don't mind that I stopped by."

He really did mind, but at the same time, he didn't feel like being alone. "Come in. I'm having a grand ol' time all by my lonesome."

"Jared, you don't have to go through this alone."

He led Evonne into the living room. "Evonne, I appreciate you worrying about me, but you're Tandi's friend. You should—"

"Jared, I'm your friend, too. Tandi is going to be just fine. She knows what she wants. You're the one who needs a friend. If you need to talk, I'm here."

"Have you spoken to Tandi?" he asked, rubbing the back of his neck.

"Yes. She's getting ready to move into her new apartment."

He sat heavily in the armchair.

"Jared, you knew about that, didn't you?"

"Yeah, I knew."

"I have to be honest with you," Evonne said, sitting down on the edge of the coffee table in front of Jared. "Tandi had planned on getting an apartment even before she left you."

Jared slumped against the back of the chair.

Evonne lay her hand on Jared's knee. "I'm sorry, but I thought you needed to know that. Tandi is wrong to be putting you through this."

"I should have listened."

Evonne began to lightly rub Jared's knee. "Don't be so hard on yourself. Tandi owns some blame in all this. She was selfish."

He looked at her curiously. "How could you say that? Tandi—"

"Jared, hear me out," Evonne said, taking her hand off his knee. "You need to open your eyes. Tandi is a very selfish woman."

He was confused. Next to Daina, Evonne was Tandi's best friend. "I don't know if I'd call her—"

"Selfish? Believe me, Jared, Tandi is selfish. You gave her everything her heart desired; she wanted for nothing. I know this. She told me so. What you didn't do was be at her beck and call, which was impossible."

"You understand that, right? I tried to tell Tandi that I had a practice to run, which I literally ran alone up until five years ago."

"Jared, I tried to tell Tandi that myself. I told her she couldn't have everything. Jared, you don't have anything to feel bad about. You gave Tandi a wonderful life."

"I tried to give her everything she wanted."

"Yes, but it wasn't enough. Tandi would have always wanted more, and, to be quite frank, you would have never satisfied her—sexually."

Jared's eyes popped. "What do you mean? I did just fine satisfying Tandi—before."

"Jared, I'm being honest with you. You should not be beating yourself over the head; Tandi isn't. When you stepped out on Tandi, I believe you went looking for the love she wasn't giving you."

"That's not true. I didn't go looking for any such thing. Tandi was giving me everything I needed, I just didn't know it. That affair, literally, just happened. It was sexual tension that itched until it had to be satisfied. That's all it was."

"Oh, I see. But even so, Jared, you could have been with Tandi twenty-four hours a day, seven days a week, and she would have found something to bitch about."

He was dumbstruck. "I don't get this, Evonne. Why're you saying these things about Tandi?"

"Because I want you to see your marriage for what it is."

"And that would be?"

"Over. It's been over for years."

Jared felt like he was being hit between the eyes with a sledgehammer. Words deserted him.

"Jared, whether you realize it or not, Tandi's behavior drove you into that affair. And forgive me if I hurt you with this, but Tandi left because she no longer wanted you. She told me that, many times."

All of his hopes sank like a canoe with a crater-size hole in it.

"Tandi kept throwing that affair in your face because it gave her something to blame you for. Even when she was begging you to spend more time with her, she knew you couldn't. She made demands you couldn't meet, which gave her an excuse to walk out."

Was Evonne right? Had Tandi been looking for an excuse to end their marriage?

"I'm sorry, Jared, but I had to tell you. I didn't think it was right for you to pine for Tandi when she had no intention of ever coming back. In fact, she said it was time you both moved on and find happiness with other people. That's what she's done."

Jared sat forward. "What? She's seeing someone, already?"

Evonne again put her hand on Jared's knee. "Jared, you can't tell Tandi I'm the one who told you, but yes she is seeing someone."

Suddenly standing, Jared began to pace. "Damn! That quick? My God!"

"Jared, you—"

"Damn. She'll be filing for a legal separation, won't she? I can't believe this."

Evonne stood also. "Tandi said—"

"She didn't tell me she was seeing someone."

"Do you really think she would?"

"Who is he? Do you know him?"

"I met him once about six months ago."

"Six months ago? Are you serious? She's been going behind my back for six months?"

Evonne nodded.

Now everything was starting to make sense. Tandi was having an affair of her own. That's why she walked out. That's why she was throwing his affair in his face. That's why she wanted a divorce. Jared sat wearily in the armchair. "I can't believe this. What the hell am I supposed to do?"

"Move on," Evonne said, sitting down on the arm of his chair. "Look, Jared. I know you're hurting, but you'll get through this. You'll be okay."

He didn't see how that was possible. He bent forward, leaning down on his thighs, his hands hanging limply in between.

Evonne began to slowly rub Jared's back. "I know it's hard to accept that it's over between you and Tandi, but with time, you'll be okay."

For the second time that day, Jared felt like crying. "It's my fault. I messed up a long time before Tandi did."

"Jared, listen to me." Evonne leaned into Jared. Her breasts were pressed into Jared's shoulder. Slyly, she rubbed her nipples on him. "Tandi is my friend. I love her dearly. But you have got to ask yourself, do you need a woman who could not only have an ongoing affair behind your back, but walk out on you and take your son from you?"

Jared was numb. He hadn't considered that Tandi was cheating on him, that she had laid all the guilt for their marriage ending on his shoulders alone, that she had another man in her life.

Evonne began massaging the tight muscles in Jared's shoulders. She moved from one shoulder to the other and then both shoulders at the same time. Evonne's hands felt good and although her massaging was beginning to make him feel uneasy, Jared didn't stop her. She began massaging down his back.

"Jared, your muscles are so tight. If you lay down on the sofa, I can get to your back better."

Clearing his throat, he sat back. "No, that's okay. I feel a lot better," he lied. "Evonne, I appreciate you talking some sense into me."

"That's why I came over. I thought you should know the truth."

"Well, Tandi might not like that you told me the truth."

"She knows. I told her I would talk to you."

That made him feel even worse. "I guess she wanted you to get me off her back."

"Well, she just wants you to go on with your life."

"Thank her for me," he said bitterly. "Never mind. I'll thank her myself." He started for the telephone.

"No!" Evonne said, stopping Jared. "Let it go. If you throw this up in Tandi's face, she might try and keep you from seeing Michael Jared. I know you don't want that."

"I don't want MJ in the middle of this. But if Tandi shacks up with the guy she's seeing, I'm going for full custody. Hey," he said, suddenly standing, "I feel like going out. Wanna go for a drink?"

"Sure."

There was a powerful ache in his heart, but a strong, stiff drink would take care of that. Jared grabbed his keys, turned off the lights, and closed the door on thoughts of Tandi.

21

Being pulled gently out of the black abyss of sleep, Jared felt soft hands, feathery light, glide smoothly across his chest, then ever so slowly down past his stomach to his penis. He lay there, his eyes closed, his head swimming, his body feeling as if it was light enough to float. "Tandi," he moaned, throatily, as his senses were aroused and tantalized by her nimble fingers. His breathing quickened, his body began to undulate, his head turned from side to side while his own hand went in search of her most erotic places, places that he knew very well. Far off in the distance, though she was as close to him as his own skin, he heard her panting breathlessly in his ear while her tongue flitted in and out of that same ear. He floated higher. It had been a long time since he had been so aroused. He felt as if he was soaring, like an eagle, free of any earthly hold. In the darkness he rolled on top of Tandi, entering her, taking her completely. In the beginning, and for years, she had always made him feel that way—so alive, so transported. They used to joke that because of their passionate lovemaking that the child they conceived in such fervor would genetically be implanted with the same passion. He wondered if MJ would carry that torch into his lovemaking. He'd be a lucky boy if he did—he'd be just like his daddy. Smiling to himself, Jared soared to even greater heights and burst through the clouds a happy man.

Jared lay spent on top of her. She was breathing just as hard as he as she rubbed his behind with both her hands. Kissing her tenderly, he slurred, "Tandi, I love you so much."

If Tandi returned the declaration in kind, Jared didn't hear her. Sleep drew him back down again into its black abyss where not even dreams penetrate.

22

Tandi considered driving away when she saw Jared's SUV still parked in the driveway, but she had much too much to do. Inventorying the house was the first, most important, chore on her list. Jared knew she was coming—she had told him so—so this could only mean he had waited around to talk to her. This, she didn't need, not after the restless night she'd had. It was just another of her many restless nights, but this time she tossed and turned because she ached to be made love to by Brent. If he could make her feel what she felt last night with their clothes on, damn, what would she feel if she was butt naked and he was inside her? No, she couldn't sleep. She was too hot to sleep.

That look of burning desire she saw in Brent's eyes, she had not seen in Jared's in years. Yet, she had to wonder if it was only sexual gratification she wanted from Brent. Was there more to be had or, in fact, was Brent capable of giving her more? Something had gone wrong in his two marriages that he had to bear some blame for, but how much blame was his? While she already knew what Jared was capable of, the question was, now that he was willing to listen, was he willing to give her what she wanted emotionally? Was she willing to give him another chance when Brent was her dream come true? Wait a minute. Why was she even thinking about second chances? Hadn't she already given Jared a chance? Why was she even confusing herself with these questions?

When she awakened that morning, she was determined to continue walking the path she chose. She decided she would give herself six months to explore her feelings about Brent. If, at the end of that time, she felt there might be a future with him, she would file for divorce from Jared. That she would do, whether Brent was in her life or not.

Not bothering to ring the bell, Tandi let herself in using her own key. If Jared was there and tried to pressure her into talking, she would leave. In the front hall, she stood and listened for sounds of where in the house Jared might be. She heard not a peep. In the living room the drapes were drawn against the daylight, rendering the house eerily dim and still, so still that Tandi could hear the soft whispered humming of the transformer for the doorbell, which sat hidden atop the protruding decorative molding above the door. Turning on the light in the living room, she left the drapes drawn as Jared had.

"Jared."

He didn't answer.

"Jared!" she called louder.

Again, he didn't answer.

Maybe he wasn't home after all. He could have driven his sedan to work, though it was unusual for him to leave his SUV parked outside the garage.

Tandi checked the unopened mail on the hall table. There was a postcard from Daina addressed to her and Jared. "I love it here, but it's not home. Missing you all. Love, Daina." *I miss you, too.* She really did miss Daina and couldn't wait for her to come home. Shuffling through the rest of the mail, Tandi saw none addressed to her specifically. Michael Jared had been bringing her mail to her every night. As to be expected, Jared hadn't opened any of his mail. He rarely did without her pushing him. The mortgage and the utility bills were all due but that wasn't her concern anymore. She started to walk away, but then, thinking better of it, grabbed up the bills. If she didn't take them and pay them, Jared would fall behind and ruin both their credits. She stuffed the envelopes down into her pocketbook and from it took a pen and pad on which to make a list of everything she was taking. No better place to start than the upstairs bedrooms.

At Michael Jared's bedroom doorway Tandi surveyed the room. She would leave his room intact as he would be staying over often enough for it to remain so. His computer she would take, along with most of his clothes. Moving on down the hall, Tandi was surprised to see that her—no, Jared's—bedroom door was closed. Usually, once they were up for the day, the door was always left open, but she was the one who used to leave it that way.

Tandi opened the door wide. This room, too, was dim. Slivers of daylight peeked around the sides of the blinds and through the slightly opened slats. There was just enough light to see that the rumpled covers were piled high on her side of the bed. Usually, she was the hoarder, but she wasn't in bed. Jared was. He was asleep, lying on his back, his naked body exposed down to below his belly button. Tandi was really surprised. Jared never slept late during the week and he certainly never missed a day of work. Concerned, she went to stand over him. Jared was breathing, so he wasn't dead. She took the time to look him over. She used to love running her hands all over his body, feeling him, exciting herself and him. Having naughty thoughts, she lifted the sheet and peeked at his penis. No doubt, he was blessed. Not surprising, Tandi's desire for Jared was not dead, and the urge to touch him was tempting. Lowering the sheet, she stared at his face. He looked peaceful; his lips looked kissable. No, her desire for him was not dead. Bending down to him, she kissed him long and tender until he started to respond, opening his mouth to let her tongue in, sending a foul, nauseating odor of rancid alcohol up into her nostrils.

"Oh!" Tandi pulled back. "Jared!" She poked him in the shoulder. "Jared, wake up. Have you been drinking?"

Groaning, Jared slowly opened his eyes into slits. He grimaced as he tasted his own tongue.

"You smell awful. You've been drinking!"

Jared's eyes stretched wide. "The rush of a splitting headache assaulted him as a wave of queasiness swept over him. He tried to sit up, but his right arm wouldn't move—it was pinned down. Falling back, Jared felt like he was about to heave and have a heart attack at the same time.

"Jared, what's wrong with—" Tandi's eyes were suddenly drawn to the moving covers on the other side of the bed. Her eyes widening, her mouth opening, she stepped back from the bed to the door. She switched on the overhead light.

Seeing the startled look on Tandi's face, Jared stared at the covers moving next to him. He could feel warm flesh moving up against his side. "Oh shit," he said, yanking his arm from under Evonne's head.

He leaped off the bed, pulling the covers off Evonne's face and naked body. That's when it hit him, he was naked, too.

"Oh shit!" Jared quickly snatched up his briefs from the floor alongside the bed, yanking them on.

Tandi dropped the pen and pad. She felt like someone had thrown a bucket of ice cold water over her head. She froze.

"It's not what you think," Jared said. The pain in his head was screaming at him.

"Tandi," Evonne said, sitting up, leaving her nakedness uncovered, "I can explain."

In total disbelief, Tandi began backing toward the door.

Jared reached out for her. "It's not what you think."

Tandi slapped frantically at Jared to keep him from touching her. "What I think is that you and my ex-best friend are the scum of the earth." Disgusted, she ran from the room.

Jared ran behind her. "Tandi!"

Running hard, Tandi rushed headlong down the stairs.

At the front door, Jared caught up with Tandi and grabbed hold of her arm. He spun her around. "Please, listen to me! I was drunk. I thought I was making love to you."

"Liar!" She clawed wildly, digging her nails into his arms, trying to make him let go of her. "I hate you!"

"Tandi, I was hurting so bad, I didn't know what to do. I . . ."

"I don't care!"

". . . I tried to drink my pain away. You know I don't drink."

"I don't care what you were trying to do. Get your filthy hands off me! I hate you!"

"Tandi, please. I didn't know what I was doing."

"I don't care! Let go of me!" She took hold of Jared's middle finger and brutally pulled it back until he let go of her.

Jared ignored the pain in his finger. "Tandi, listen to me. Please, listen to me."

She snatched her pocketbook off the table and seeing the mail, grabbed it out of her bag and threw it on the floor.

"Tandi, Evonne told me you were seeing another man!"

She whirled around and looked him dead in his bloodshot eyes. "That's a goddamn lie!"

"She said you were seeing him for six months, and that's why you wanted a divorce."

"You're stupid, Jared. You believed vicious lies out of the mouth of a snake."

"But she said—"

"Tandi!" Evonne called from midway up the stairs.

Jared and Tandi both looked up at Evonne.

"Evonne, didn't you tell me Tandi was seeing someone?"

Tandi glared up at Evonne, wearing Jared's dark blue Mechanic on Duty T-shirt, which just covered her pubic patch. Tandi's stomach churned, gnawing at her, making her ill. "My, Evonne, I think you're showing a bit more than I need to see."

Evonne tugged on the edge of the T-shirt. "Jared and I were drunk. We made a mistake. Let's sit down and talk about—"

"I trusted you, Evonne. I thought you were my friend."

"I am."

"Didn't you tell me Tandi was seeing another man?" Jared asked.

"That's not what I said, Jared. You must've heard—"

"That's a damn lie!" Jared started for the stairs. "What the hell are you doing?"

Tandi opened the front door.

Jared rushed back to her. "Tandi, she's lying. I got drunk and—"
Slap!

Tandi's open-handed slap caught Jared across the mouth, stinging his lips. Yet, the pain in his head was far worse than the sting of the slap. He grabbed his head with both hands. "Oh, God," he moaned.

"You're both dogs!" Tandi ran from the ugliness of their betrayal.

23

*H*olding on to his throbbing head, Jared stood in front of the open door, unable to move. If it wasn't for the cold, sobering breeze splashing in his face and all over his naked torso, chilling him, confirming that he was wide awake, he'd swear he was in the throes of a crazy nightmare that he just could not wake up from. Awake or asleep, he could not believe what he had done.

"Jared, close the door," Evonne said, walking felinelike down the stairs.

Jared dropped his arms to his sides and continued to look blindly out into the street. Nothing made sense. What hell had he gotten himself caught up in?

Evonne rushed to the door and closed it. Laying her hand on Jared's chest, she stood before him, looking up into his pain-etched face. "Jared, it's not like we did this on purpose."

Jared knocked Evonne's hand away.

"Jared, please don't be upset with me."

He backed away from Evonne. In the living room, he flopped down into the very same armchair he had sat in the night before while he listened to hurtful, vicious lies from Evonne's mouth that drove him to drink. He couldn't believe he had been that gullible. Closing his eyes, he pressed the pulsating veins in his temples with his fingertips, trying to stop them from throbbing.

Evonne eased as close to Jared as she dared. "Jared, what happened between us couldn't be helped. It's not like we planned it. It just happened."

"Nothing just happens," he said, opening his eyes. "You cajoled, you manipulated, and you flat-out fucking lied."

For a stunned moment Evonne sat staring stone-faced at Jared. "We made love, Jared. Was it so bad for you?"

He couldn't believe she asked him that. He looked up at her wearing his T-shirt, wearing it like she'd always worn it. He remembered looking across the table at her the night before in the low lights of the lounge and wondering, why was she being so nice to him? Why was she telling on Tandi? He wondered no more. The reason was boldly in his face, and he couldn't stand to look at her.

Evonne asked again, "Making love to me wasn't so bad, was it? It was great. We made great love."

Jared smirked cynically. "You got it wrong. *We* didn't make love. I fucked and you were my spittoon."

Evonne gasped. "You don't have to talk to me like that."

"Like what? Like you're a whore?"

"Why are you trying to hurt me? I told you the truth about Tandi. Do you think for one minute she would tell you she was seeing someone? She's the one who's lying to you. Yes, Tandi was my best friend, but—"

"Then tell me, Evonne. How did Tandi's best friend end up bare ass in my bed?"

"Alcohol, Jared. We were both drunk."

"Tandi didn't buy that lame-ass excuse, and neither am I."

"But it's the truth."

He looked her dead in the eye. "Who drove us home?"

"I did."

"So, I'm supposed to believe you were sober enough to drive, but not sober enough to stop what happened between us?"

"I drove very carefully."

"So you knew what you were doing?"

"I was drunk, Jared, but not as drunk as you. I can fix this with Tandi, if you want me to. I'll go see her and—"

"And what, Evonne?" he asked, suddenly shooting up out of his chair, sending his head spinning into orbit. He clutched his pounding head as he swayed woozily. "Damn."

Evonne sprang to her feet and reached out to catch him. "Are you all right?"

He pushed her away and stepped even farther away from her himself. "How the hell did we end up screwing?"

"We . . . it just—"

"That's bullshit!"

"Okay. You want the truth? Then hear it. The truth is, Jared, you asked me to make love to you."

Drunk or sober, he had never been attracted to Evonne. He sneered at her. "You're a goddamn liar! If I hadn't been drunk, I would've fucked a dead duck before I would've touched you."

Jared's words struck Evonne's tongue mute. Stunned, she stared at him, unable to say anything that he would believe.

Jared bounded over to the window and yanked on the drapes, pulling one side back to the wall. The sunlight shone brilliantly through the open blinds, sending a sharp pain through his eyes into the top of his head. He squeezed his eyes shut and slammed his hands up against the sides of his head. He wanted to crush his own skull. It was no good to him if he couldn't remember asking Evonne to make love to him. However, he couldn't even remember leaving the lounge or getting home and climbing into bed with her. He did remember making love, but he thought it was Tandi he was with.

Evonne crept over and stood just behind Jared. "Please don't be angry at me."

He moved away. "Go home, Evonne."

"I didn't lie to you, Jared. Tandi had no intention of coming back even before this happened. She—"

"You don't know that."

"But she filed for divorce."

"Then why did she kiss me this morning?"

"She didn't kiss you, I did."

"Stop lying, Evonne! I know Tandi's kiss."

"Do you? Last night when you were making love to me, you called me Tandi."

What he suspected, he was now sure of. "If I called you Tandi, Evonne, why the hell didn't you stop what we were doing?"

"Because you were making love to me, to my body, and it was everything I ever thought it would be. I didn't want you to stop."

Jared could feel the hairs stand on his arms. He knew what he heard, he just couldn't believe it. He had no idea Evonne had the hots for him, and he certainly never made a pass at her.

"You want the real truth, Jared? Can you handle it?"

"Are you capable of telling the truth?"

"Yes, I am." Evonne got closer to Jared. "Yes, I knew what I was doing, and I have no doubt you knew what you were doing and with whom. And, if you'll admit that to yourself, you'll forget about Tandi, just as she's forgotten about you."

The previous night flashed in Jared's mind. Why hadn't he seen what Evonne was doing? Tandi was right about him. He never noticed anything, no matter how up in his face something was. He felt stupid. He watched Evonne come closer.

"And in case you don't remember, Jared. Last night you asked me if I wanted you since Tandi didn't."

Jared couldn't dispute what he couldn't remember, but those words could never have come from his mouth.

"I said yes last night," Evonne said, pressing herself up against Jared's unyielding, ramrod-straight body, "and I'm saying yes now."

Jared grabbed Evonne's upper arms and brusquely shoved her away. She stumbled backward against the coffee table but she kept herself from falling.

"You make me sick. Get out before I forget that I don't hit women."

"Don't be stupid! Tandi doesn't want you." Evonne started back to Jared and again tried to get close to him. "I'm the one who loves you, Jared. Not Tandi."

He couldn't believe this was happening. Disgusted, he shoved Evonne harder, making her sprawl out on the floor. His T-shirt was above her waist, exposing her nakedness, repulsing him. He looked away.

"Evonne, if I have to tell you again to get out, I'll throw you out into the street just as you are."

Beginning to cry, Evonne awkwardly got up off the floor. "Jared, I've loved you for a long time. I can give you what Tandi never could—unconditionally."

"Can your lying, crazy ass give me my son, as he is, raised by Tandi? Can you give me the kind of love I would die to have back? And ask yourself this, Evonne, can you give me a strong enough stomach to ever wanna touch you again?"

Hugging herself, Evonne cried, "Why are you treating me like this? I—"

"Go! Get the fuck out and take that nasty-ass shirt with you."

Evonne ran from the room and up the stairs.

Jared rushed to the foot of the stairs. "If you touch anything in that bedroom, I'll kill you!" The pain in Jared's head didn't bother him anymore. The only thing that did was his fear that Tandi would never forgive him for sleeping with Evonne.

24

Tandi thought maybe if she could scream or even if she could cry, she might feel better. As hard as she tried, she could do neither. She felt as if a plastic bag had been pulled tightly over her face, suffocating her, taking her life's breath. She had driven recklessly back to Sporty's house, with all the windows open, gasping for air, praying she wouldn't have an accident. She had to be around for Michael Jared—that she was cognizant of.

Alone in the house, alone in her room, she had tried to make herself cry. She had clutched her stomach and doubled over, trying to drag the tears out. She had punched her thighs, she had latched on to her hair and pulled it at the roots, hurting herself, trying desperately to feel external pain so that she could cry, but nothing she inflicted upon herself was as painful as seeing Evonne, naked, in her bed next to Jared.

Tandi tried hard to shake that hideous vision out of her head, but it wouldn't leave her. It was as clear as if Evonne and Jared were at that moment in front of her. She couldn't help but imagine Jared had touched Evonne like he used to touch her, that he'd done to Evonne what he hadn't done to her in a very long time. What she wondered was, was this the first time or had they been sneaking around behind her back and laughing in her face? It didn't matter the answer. She hated them both, and they were both deserving of any and all ill will she could wish for them.

What in the world had she ever done to warrant such betrayal? From the time she and Evonne met fifteen years ago while waiting to get their hair done at the salon, Evonne had been like the sister she never had. She thought she could trust Evonne with her life and her husband. When it came to men, be it boyfriend or husband, the thin, invisible line that a sister should never cross, Evonne had obliterated. A long time ago they had talked about never touching each other's man—not out of curiosity, not out of retaliation, not even out of desperation. They made a pact that if either of their men made a pass, they would tell, sparing no details, as their one true pledge to the other was to always remain loyal, always sister-friend to the end, but that was not the way it played out. As she saw it, nothing on Evonne's face said she had been so drunk she didn't know what she was doing, and nothing in her eyes said she was remorseful. Jared said Evonne told him she had been seeing someone. Was that Evonne's lie or Jared's? It was somebody's lie. Had Evonne been secretly coveting Jared all this time? Had she always been waiting for her to leave him so that she could slither into his bed? Just weeks ago, hadn't she said if Jared was put up for adoption someone would be waiting out there to adopt him? Did she mean herself? No wonder Evonne was so eager to give her a helping hand in moving out of his life.

And Jared—at no time did she ever suspect he had any interest in Evonne. When Evonne was over, he usually left the room and on the rare occasion they were all out together, Jared paid no more attention to Evonne than he did to a piece of lint on his pants. In fact, he said of Evonne that she was annoyingly talkative. Had that been his way of throwing her off? If it was, it worked. She never suspected him of being attracted to Evonne. It was the woman, Jackie, he had had the affair with who had preoccupied her, not the woman—the serpent she called friend—who was right under her nose.

No matter how it happened, the bottom line was Jared had cheated on her again. It didn't matter that they were separated. He should have been able to control that tubular piece of flesh and blood between his thighs. He should have waited until her scent no longer lingered in the sheets, until the mattress no longer remembered the outline of her body. He should have waited until she no longer cared. That's why she should have slept with Brent the night before. Maybe then she would not have cared. Well, there was nothing to stop her now. Today, she would know what it was to quench the yearning of her own body. It was her turn to be satisfied.

25

"Glynn, I need a favor. I need you to pick Michael Jared up from school and take him home with you for the night."

"Tandi, I'm at work in Manhattan. I can't leave."

"I know you're at work, Glynn. I called you, remember? I need you to do this for me, like I'm always doing something for you."

"Fine, Tandi, but can't you pick him up yourself and bring him over to the house after Leah or I get home?"

"No, I can't."

"Why not? Are you in the hospital or something? Is this an emergency?"

She was not about to tell Glynn that the emergency was that she be made love to by Brent Rodgers or she would dissolve into an emotional mess. Glynn didn't even know she had left Jared, and she wasn't of a mind to tell him.

"Glynn, I never ask you for anything. In fact, you've been home for more than a week, and you haven't come anywhere near your father to check on him. You've left that all up to me, as usual."

"That's what you know, Miss Know-it-all. I spoke to Dad this morning. I've spoken to him damn near every morning since I've been back."

That didn't surprise Tandi a bit. She was never privy to anything that went on between the two of them. "So, Glynn, was it too much for you to call and let me know you were back in town?"

"I didn't see where it was necessary. Dad told me you left Jared and you were staying there. I saw no reason to come over and check on him."

"You knew about me and Jared? Why didn't you call anyway?"

"Because you didn't tell me yourself," Glynn said. "Tandi, I don't have time for this petty discussion. Dad's home. Ask him to pick up Michael Jared."

"I thought you said you spoke to Dad this morning?"

"I did."

"Then why is it you don't know he went to Atlantic City this morning? He probably won't get back until after ten tonight."

"I guess he forgot to mention he was going."

"Yeah, right. That's because he knew you'd tell him not to go. Look, Glynn, will you please do this for me. Would you pick up your nephew?"

"I can't just up and leave."

"You know damn well you can. You don't punch a clock, Mr. Executive. Should I remind you that I've done things for you that were inconvenient for me at the time?"

"Tandi, I don't have time for this. You're in a nasty mood. You'd better go dig your fangs into Jared. What happened between you two anyway?"

"None of your damn business!" She slammed the receiver down. She picked it up and slammed it down again twice more. "Damn you, Glynn!"

Riiing!

Tandi snatched up the receiver. "What?"

"What the hell's wrong with you?"

Tandi slammed the receiver down again and immediately buried her face in her hands, wanting desperately to cry. She made the plaintive, wailing sounds of crying, but no tears flowed. She felt like there was a plug stuck in her tear ducts as well as in her soul.

Riiing!

She felt trapped in a cage of emotional frustration and betrayal from which she could not break. She felt wired. She could not let Michael Jared see her like this. It would scare him out of his mind.

Riiing!

Glynn had to help her. There was no one else. Aunt Gert passed on ten years ago. Daina would have taken Michael Jared, for sure, if she were in town, and she wasn't due back for two months.

Riiing!

Tandi took a deep breath to try and calm herself. She picked up the telephone.

"Tandi! What the . . ."

"I'm sorry," she said, her voice cracking.

". . . hell's wrong with you? If you think . . ."

"Glynn! Glynn, just hear me out."

". . . I'm going to put up with your shit, you better think again. I . . ."

"Glynn, please! I have no one else to turn to. Please. Will you please do this for me?" she asked as calmly as she could. "I'm begging you."

The phone was silent in her ear.

"Please, Glynn, I need you."

"Tandi, what's wrong? Tell me what the hell is going on."

"I can't right now, Glynn. Please. I just need you to do this for me. I can't entrust my son to anyone but you, and he should see more of his cousins."

"Where's Jared? Did something happen to him?"

"Will you do this for me or not?"

There was a loud silence on the other end of the line, intensifying Tandi's anxiety.

"What time should I pick him up?"

She gasped a soft sigh of relief. "Three-ten. Do you know where his school is?"

"One hundred and thirteenth Avenue?"

"Yes."

"Michael Jared is going to ask questions, Tandi. What should I tell him?"

"Tell him I had to do something for his grandfather. He'll understand that. If he wants to speak to his father, let him, but he cannot see Jared tonight. And I mean that, Glynn. Do not take Michael Jared to his father, no matter how much he begs."

"It's your call, Tandi, but what if he wants to speak to you?"

"I can't tonight," she said, feeling drained. "He'll know something's wrong."

"He'll know that anyway, if he can't speak to you."

"Please, Glynn, just tell him I'll speak to him tomorrow. Tell him I'm all right."

"Whatever you say. I'll leave here at two."

"Thank you. I'll be by first thing tomorrow morning."

"Fine. And, Tandi, you and I will talk tomorrow?"

"I can't promise that, Glynn. It hurts too much."

Glynn was silent. Tandi held the telephone to her ear, waiting for him to say something mean-spirited.

"Okay, Tandi. I don't know what's going on, but I'm here for you."

"Thank you," she said, relieved Glynn was coming through for her. In the state she was in, she didn't want Michael Jared to see her. And actually, she needed more than an evening to work her way through this madness before she saw him again, but she'd take what little time she could get. Maybe being with Brent would give her back her emotional stability. She quickly dialed his number. This time, she would not tread lightly or timidly, she would be the hunter.

"Hello, Brent Rodgers."

"Hi, Brent Rodgers. When was the last time you played hooky?"

26

Jared was numb. He had gotten into his SUV with the intention of going to work, but two hours later he was still sitting in the driveway fingering the tiny gold ankh hanging from his neck, lost in his nightmare, cursing himself for sleeping with Evonne. If he could turn back the hands of time, he would turn it all the way back to Christmas Day thirteen years ago when Tandi gave him the ankh. She said then, "Women get heart-shaped trinkets as symbols of love and since I can't give you a locket, I'm giving you this sign of life, an ankh. It's also a symbol of my eternal love." At that moment he could not imagine their love wouldn't always be strong.

It was 1:45 when he finally went on to work. He didn't know what else to do. Secretly, he was hoping—no, praying—Tandi would show up to drop MJ off. Jared kept praying in his head as he walked into his office. Marci was on the telephone trying to explain his absence. He quietly sat behind his desk and waited for her to finish the call.

"Jared, where have you been? I started to put an APB out on you."

"I'm sorry I'm late."

"Late? Jared, I called your house fifty times. You had a court appearance. Raoul had to go and have the hearing postponed."

"Damn, I forgot."

"You forgot? Jared—"

"Did I get any calls?"

"Of course you did. And two of the lawyers you were supposed to be interviewing were here on time. They left here pretty angry. One guy came in from New Jersey."

"Damn. Call him back. Reschedule. I'll go to him in Jersey. Did Tandi call?"

"No," Marci answered, looking more carefully at Jared. "Where did you sleep last night?"

"Why?"

"Because you don't look like you got any sleep."

Jared rubbed the tight, pulsating spot between his brows.

"You and Tandi are having a hard time, huh?"

"How—"

There was a loud knock on the open door. Marci and Jared both looked at Raoul standing in the doorway.

"We were worried about you," Raoul said.

"I know, I'm sorry. Did you get a continuance?"

"Twenty-four hours. No one was happy, particularly Mr. Hickson."

"I bet. He's been waiting to go to trial for three years. Marci, please call him and offer my apologies and tell him I'll be there tomorrow."

"I've already done that."

He should have guessed that. Marci was always on point.

Raoul placed a folder on Jared's desk. "This is the Kirsch file. I need to go over the hospital report with you. We might have a problem."

"Specifically?"

"It seems the hospital is saying that Mrs. Kirsch's blood was scarred with the hepatitis B marker long before her gall bladder surgery. If that's the case, then we can't claim she got infected blood during that surgery. Hence, the hospital is not liable."

"Then the pre-surgery bloodwork should have picked up on that marker. Mrs. Hirsch contracted hepatitis after the surgery according to her primary doctor." Jared's headache was coming back. The painkiller was wearing off. "Try to get in touch with the doctor's office and see if you can speak with him. If you can't get clarification from him, call me later at home, and I'll get on it."

"Will do."

"Marci, Raoul, I should apologize to both of you. Things are pretty rough at home right now, so forgive me. I'm not exactly myself."

"Is there anything I can do?" Marci offered.

"No . . . no." Jared looked hard at his watch, trying to focus. His headache wasn't letting up. He stood. "I just stopped by to see if everything was okay and to pick up MJ but I don't think he'll be here today."

"Why not?" Marci asked.

"Raoul, you get on that for me. I'll be in touch."

Raoul acknowledged Jared with a nod. He left right away.

"Marci, I have some business to take care of. Take care of things here for me."

"Of course, but your clients—"

"Tell them I'll return their calls tomorrow. Call me at home if something really important comes up."

"And how am I to determine that when everything is *really* important?"

"If no one is on their deathbed, then it's not important." That said, Jared left the office. He trusted Raoul. He was the best paralegal he'd ever had. And, Marci—no one was better. She had been working with him for four years, and this was no time to doubt her abilities.

Outside in his SUV, Jared waited—just in case Tandi brought MJ. He prayed she would.

27

The instant Tandi's body came together with Brent's, she was plunged into the depths of her most rapturous fantasy. She gave herself completely over to Brent when the tip of his tongue first flicked sensuously across her erect nipple and then drew it into his mouth sucking on it, making her moan for more than his mouth. Brent's hand glided lightly down her body until it found Tandi's most needy place. He began fingering her pulsating clitoris, making her gyrate her hips, wanting more than a tease. Moaning for more, she sucked air in through her teeth. She pushed her pelvis up off the bed into Brent's hand until he slipped his finger inside her, exploring her, thrilling her, sending her eyes back in her head. With her muscles she gripped his fingers and pulled on him while pushing up and grinding herself against his hand.

"Baby, you're as ripe as a juicy peach," Brent said, climbing on top of Tandi.

When he entered her, filling her, Tandi's breath caught in her throat. Oh yes. Her fantasy was real. As Brent began to move inside her, Tandi was feeling everything she had dreamed or even imagined. She started to cry, startling Brent.

He stopped moving. "Baby, am I hurting you?"

Shaking her head, she held on to him with her arms and legs, keeping him inside her.

"Then what's wrong?"

Unable to stop crying, she began kissing him fervently, hungrily, trying desperately to erase from her mind the sight of Evonne and

Jared in bed together. She could not understand how such an ugly vision could invade her mind and mar the beauty of Brent making love to her.

With her heart racing, Tandi continued to weep even as her and Brent's bodies continued gliding smoothly in rhythmic, erotic unison. She was weeping not only for the pain that still filled her heart, but also for the ecstasy of the release she had been craving for years. Brent didn't disappoint her. He made love to her more than once and well into the night. They fell apart, arms entwined, legs interlocked, bodies heaving, both satisfied. When he could catch his breath, Brent rolled over and began kissing Tandi's breasts, making her feel both beautiful and desirable. No longer would she have to beg Jared to make love to her. She had Brent.

He rubbed her stomach. "I knew it would be like this."

Tandi agreed with a smile.

"Your husband must be crazy to let you get away."

"My soon-to-be ex is crazy," she said. "He slept with my ex-best friend."

Brent sat halfway up. "You lie."

She shook her head

"When did this happen?"

"When it happened doesn't matter, the fact that it did, does."

"Baby, you don't need friends and family like that. Forget them. Let me take care of you. I would never hurt you like that."

She kissed Brent on the neck then on the chest. "I'm so glad you're back."

"Me, too." He kissed Tandi on the top of the head. "Baby, you said you were moving into your own apartment this weekend. Why don't we move in together?"

She had to think about Michael Jared. What she wanted could not outweigh what was best for him. "I don't know if that's a good idea."

"Why not? You're not with your husband anymore."

"My son hasn't met you yet."

"I can meet him tomorrow. Kids like me. What else?"

"I'm not divorced, Brent. Actually, I'm not even legally separated from my husband."

"So. The divorce is gonna happen, right?"

"Yes."

"You left because he cheated on you, right?"

She nodded. There was no need for explanation.

"I don't see a problem. You're no longer with him. He caused the breakdown of your marriage, right?"

Again she nodded.

"Then you're free. Let's get on with your life."

"That's what I want, but aren't we moving a little fast?"

"Not if you consider the fact that we should have been together since we were teenagers," Brent said. "I say we've moved a little slow."

Yes, she and Brent should have gotten together a long time ago, but it didn't happen, and the truth was, at that moment she was frightened by the prospect of them moving in together so quickly. If she had only herself to worry about, she might seriously consider it. Then again, what if it didn't work out between them? She couldn't put herself or Michael Jared through another breakup so soon.

"Brent, we haven't seen each other in more than twenty years. These two days together have been wonderful and—"

"And the rest of our life will be just as wonderful. I know you don't doubt that."

"Not that I doubt it, I just think we should get to know each other again before we make such a serious commitment. Actually, I think it would be fun to date for a while."

"Baby, dates are for kids. I'm a man who likes having a serious relationship."

"That's good to know," she said, realizing she hadn't given much thought to what it might mean to really be with him. "But, Brent, suppose you don't like that I clip my toenails in bed?"

"Hand them to me, I'll eat 'em."

She slapped him on the arm. "That's disgusting."

"There is nothing disgusting about you, baby. I wanna be with you. I don't want another twenty years to get by us."

Tandi lay down again and nestled up against Brent's strong, warm body. Isn't this what she wanted? "I need a little time to get my son used to the idea. My son is pretty attached to his father, and I don't wanna scare him into not wanting to live with me."

"How about a week?"

"Brent, I need more time than that. I can't put a timetable on my son's well-being."

"Okay, two. That's my final offer," he said, gently massaging Tandi's breasts. "I don't want you to change your mind."

"We'll see," she said, not wanting to be pressured into cementing their relationship before she had time to catch her breath. "How about your children, Brent? Are you close to them?"

"My ex-wives are vindictive. I left them, so they figure they can punish me by keeping my children from me."

"They can't do that legally. Have you filed for visitation?"

"I did for my daughter, but her mother gave me a hard time every time I went to pick her up, so I let it go. I didn't bother to file for my sons. They've already been brainwashed. That's why I moved back to New York—out of sight, out of mind."

"Oh, Brent, I'm so sorry," she said, hugging him. "I think that's awful. You have a right to see your children."

"Tell their mothers that."

"Are you paying child support?" Tandi didn't know what made her ask that question.

"Every payday, but I don't wanna talk about that. Being back with you is the only thing on my mind."

They made love again. This time they were slower, but they were no less passionate. Hungrily, Tandi took all Brent was willing to give. He wanted her to stay the night. She couldn't. She needed to be where Michael Jared could reach her if he had to. As soon as she walked into Sporty's house, she went straight to the telephone in the living room. Her mood was lighter, the tenseness had lifted from her body, and she was well sated. She felt like talking to Michael Jared after all.

"He's sleeping," Glynn said sleepily.

She was a little disappointed. "How is he? Was he upset?"

"Not at all. He and Sean played computer games after they did their homework."

"Did he speak to Jared?"

"No, we couldn't reach him. He wasn't at home or at his office and his cell phone was taking messages."

"I'm not surprised," she said, starting to feel badly again. Jared must have been with Evonne all day. "Glynn, thanks for taking Michael Jared. I'll see you tomorrow."

"Tandi, by the way, your son doesn't want to be called Michael Jared anymore. He wants to be called MJ."

"He said that?"

"Yes."

"Jared is the only one who calls him MJ. I've never particularly liked it."

"Well, just so you know, he does."

"Why has he never told me?"

"Probably because you're his mother and you'd try and talk him out of it."

"I would not."

"Then maybe it's just a male thing. Hey, whatever. He wants to be called MJ."

"MJ, it is," she conceded, though her feelings were hurt. "I'll see you tomorrow."

"By the way, you sound better."

"Yeah, I feel better. Good night." If Glynn only knew how much better she really felt and why, he'd have a fit. He'd find out soon enough about Brent, but this name thing with Michael Jared wanting to be called MJ, that concerned her. Jared had called him that almost from birth, and although she had noticed he responded to it right away, she had continued to call him Michael Jared because she liked the way the two names rolled off her tongue. Perhaps what was bothersome about him wanting to be called MJ was the thought that maybe, subconsciously, he wanted to be with Jared and not her. She could not lose her son to Jared, especially if Jared was going to be with Evonne. There was no way she would allow Evonne to be a part of Michael Jared's life. That was never going to happen. But she had to stop thinking about Evonne and Jared. They were ruining the afterglow of her blissful evening. If they wanted to be together, then so be it. She was going to be with Brent.

Sporty had not gotten back from Atlantic City. She had the house to herself, but she didn't feel like going up to her room. Turning on the television, she stretched out on the sofa and let herself sink into the deep thick cushions. She could rest for now, knowing that her life was looking up right nicely.

28

Jared didn't know why he went back to the bar, but this time he had enough sense to not drink what he couldn't handle. A glass of sparkling club soda was a safe bet after the day he'd had. Tandi didn't show up with MJ. That didn't surprise him. It was the tear that slipped from his eye right out in front of his office that did. He kept his face turned away from the office because he knew Marci was watching him sitting out there waiting for Tandi. By four o'clock he knew for sure Tandi wasn't coming and since he couldn't handle being at work with Marci's questioning eyes on him, he pulled off when more tears threatened. He found himself on the Southern State Parkway headed out to Long Island with no particular destination in mind, just a long, endless drive to clear his head and to be alone with his thoughts. He didn't think his life could get any worse, yet he didn't think he'd ever find a way to make it better. Damn. It would be his luck that after having problems with getting it up for Tandi he would get drunk and get it up with Evonne with no problem—that is that he knew of. He had gone and bought the Irish moss like Les the bartender had suggested but he hadn't touched it—it was still sitting unopened in the refrigerator. It was his bad luck that his nature, when it least needed to, would rise on its own without any urging from him. What a cruel joke.

It was late when he got back to Queens Village, but there was no reason to go home. He ended up back at Les's Bar, the place of his total undoing.

Les stood in front of Jared, his hands resting on the bar. "Going it alone tonight?"

"I should have gone it alone last night."

"You didn't seem like you were hurtin' none. Your wife made sure of that."

"That wasn't my wife."

"Man, you coulda fooled me. That babe was on you like white on rice, like stripes on a zebra. Man, the way you talked about your wife, I thought it was her."

Jared shook his head solemnly.

Leaning in closer, his elbows on the bar, Les whispered, "Couldn't get it together with your old lady?"

"Never got a chance."

"Man, you know how women are. They play hard to get when they're mad. They want you to crawl on your hands and knees until your bones poke through. Didn't your daddy ever give you lessons in crawling?"

Jared chuckled sourly. "No, but I tell you, after what happened this morning, I'd crawl on my belly if my wife would even consider talking to me."

"What happened this morning?"

Jared pulled back. "You're mighty nosy, aren't you?"

Les laughed. "When it comes to my customers, I like to say, I'm sympathetically curious. Talk to me, brother. I might be able to help."

"No one can help me with this."

"Give me a chance. Marriages are my speciality. What happened this morning?"

Les's eyes reminded Jared of a dog hungrily watching his master prepare to hand him his dinner. The only thing Les wasn't doing was letting his tongue hang out.

"C'mon, man, talk."

Jared did feel like talking. "That woman you saw me with last night was my wife's best friend."

"You didn't."

He barely moved his head, but he nodded.

"Did you get caught?"

Jared barely blinked.

"Aww, man," Les said, pushing away from the bar. He raised his hands to his head and quickly dropped them. "You're not supposed to get caught."

Jared glanced from one end of the bar to the other. No one was looking at him, but a woman was looking at Les. "C'mon, man. Hold it down."

Les lowered his voice. "Boy, you should be beat over the head with a stupid stick."

"Why don't you tell me something I don't know." Jared was annoyed with himself for opening his big mouth. That's all he needed was to be told how stupid he was. He pulled three singles from his wallet and tossed them onto the bar. He stood.

Les pushed the bills back toward Jared. "Hold on. Don't be so hasty. I just didn't expect that from you, especially knowing how you feel about your wife. Sit down."

Only because he still didn't want to go home, Jared climbed back on the stool and immediately drank his club soda. He brought the glass down hard on the bar and pushed it aside.

"That's rough, man," Les said sympathetically. "You drank a lot last night. I knew you wasn't a drinker but I thought you had it under control."

"Control, my ass. I was blind drunk. I didn't even see it coming."

"The girlfriend ate you alive, huh?"

"Man, I can kick my own ass."

"Your wife isn't hearing a thing you say, is she?"

"Not a word."

Les took Jared's glass and put it in a pan under the bar. "I know a guy who was caught by his wife, not one time, not two times, but three times. Mind you, he wasn't drunk, he knew what he was doing."

"Is his wife still with him?"

"Nope. She left him after the third time but he didn't care. He always had a woman waiting in the wings. He used to say, 'Man, if your wife ever catch you in bed with another woman, deny, deny, deny. And if she don't believe you, recruit a spare.' "

That irritated Jared. "That's dumb. How does anyone deny something like that when he's caught with his pants down?"

"That dude? Easy. He told me once if he got caught on top of his own mother, he'd go to his grave denying it."

"A real asshole," Jared said. "Man, don't tell me anything else that idiot said, but I do wanna know how he got his wife to forgive him after the first two times."

"Hell, man, he said he kissed her ass every which way but the wrong way. And I can tell you, he had some big-ass lips, so you know he did some big-ass kissing. That dude had the kind of lips that cover the whole top of a beer can and half the label down the side when he turns the can up to his mouth. Now that was a sight to behold."

Jared wasn't amused. He didn't crack a smile.

Les sucked air through his front teeth. "Man, you'd ruin a stag party."

Jared still didn't react.

"Anyway," Les said flatly, "the short of it is, the dude's wife forgave him. A year later he got caught again but those lips weren't hitting on a damn thing. He said his wife tried to scratch his eyeballs out."

"I never thought I'd say this," Jared said, "but he's one dude his wife should have castrated."

"Ouch," Les said, frowning. "Man, castration for infidelity will never get my vote. That's extreme cruelty and inhumane punishment. I'd rather you cut off my head."

"That's—"

"You know what head I mean."

Jared began chuckling softly at first then a little louder. Though he was laughing on the outside, inside, he was miserable. Ironically, he was in a way sentencing himself for what he'd done to Tandi. No way did he want to lose his manhood, but at that awful moment when he saw the devastated look in her eyes, he might have complied as humbly as any candidate of eunuch school. He had never been so ashamed.

"Jared, man, go see your wife."

He shook his head. "She won't let me near her."

"Then call her."

"I don't think—"

"Don't think, man. Just do it. Women love that sort of thing. Do you want her back?"

Jared lowered his eyes. He was close to tearing again. Damn, he was messed up. He hadn't cried this much since his brother died and before that, never as a man.

"Well, do you?"

"Yeah," he said, looking up again.

"Then call her and beg like a man looking down the barrel of a shotgun. I mean if you think about it, you are begging for your life."

He nodded pensively.

Les reached back and picked up the cordless telephone on the shelf. "It's on the house."

Jared started to take the telephone but realized he would have no privacy. Les would want to listen to every word, and he wasn't into begging in front of an audience.

"I have my cell phone out in my car."

"I'm on your side, brother. I feel your pain."

"Thanks." Jared lightly thumped fists with Les.

"Let me know how it goes. I'm not closing up until midnight."

On the way out the door, Jared raised his thumb, thanking Les, but Les's advice wasn't enough. He was going to say a little prayer before calling Tandi.

29

In the hazy dawning of her awakening, Tandi could hear Sporty saying, "I don't know, Jared. You know how stubborn Tandida is. I've never been able to talk sense into her myself."

Wide awake, Tandi sat up and looked across the living room to the étagère where the telephone usually sat. It was not there and neither was Sporty anywhere to be seen. The telephone cord lay on the floor snaking its way through the archway of the living room out into the hallway, disappearing somewhere down the hall. Tandi hadn't heard the telephone ring but she was certain Jared, who had to have found out she was at Sporty's from Michael Jared, must have called because Sporty would not have called him. They hadn't spoken in years. The last time was five years ago when Jared told Sporty he didn't like the way he spoke to her. The two of them argued. Jared was kicked out of Sporty's house never to step foot in there again. The fact that they were speaking now could only mean that neither meant her any good.

"Come over and talk to her yourself. I—"

"No!" Tandi bolted off the sofa. She sprinted out into the hallway.

Sporty stood halfway down the hall holding the telephone base in his left hand and the receiver to his ear. He stared at her.

"I don't want him coming here."

"Let me talk to her," Jared said.

Sporty held the receiver out to Tandi. "Tell him yourself."

"Hang up the phone, Daddy."

"This is my phone. You don't tell me what to do."

"I said, hang up the damn phone! I don't wanna speak to Jared, and I most certainly do not want to see him."

"Tell him yourself."

"Daddy, this is not your call. I will not speak to Jared, and you should not be speaking to him either."

"You don't tell me who I should or should not be speaking to. This is my damn house and my damn telephone. I'll speak to anyone I damn well please, and I will have anyone I want in my house, including Jared Crawford."

"You must really hate me."

Sporty brought the receiver back to his ear. "Jared, Tandida got her ass up on her shoulders about something. With her nasty attitude, I can see why you had to put her out."

"Mr. Belson, I did not put Tandi out."

Tandi glared at Sporty. "You're a vicious old man."

"Girl, don't make me draw back my hand."

Jared shouted, "Mr. Belson, what're you doing?"

The last time Sporty threatened to hit her, Tandi had just graduated high school and even back then, although he intimidated her, he had to know she wouldn't stand still for him putting his hand on her. Her anger at him, then and now, gave her the strength to stand strong. She stared him down, daring him to hit her.

Sporty saw that Tandi wasn't afraid. "I'm your father, girl. You give me my due!"

"Mr. Belson! Mr. Belson, leave her alone!"

Tandi felt strong. "Have you ever given me my due, Daddy? You have always treated me worse than any bum on the street. You're a hateful, bitter old man." She watched Sporty's eyes shrink into tiny brown peas right before her eyes. She wondered if he was thinking about hitting her with the receiver he gripped so tightly.

Listening on the line, Jared felt helpless. He could not believe he had made things even worse for Tandi.

Sporty wasn't backing down. "It's because of you that I'm bitter."

"Blame me, as usual. Aren't you getting sick and tired of that same old song? This is why you don't deserve my respect."

"That's the thanks I get for raising another man's bastard."

Tandi gasped. She felt the blood drain from her face.

"Goddamnit, Mr. Belson!" Jared screamed. "What the hell are you saying?"

"Don't be cussing at me, boy! I ain't nobody to play with."

Tandi was livid. She struggled to understand what Sporty had just said. *That's the thanks I get for raising another man's bastard.* As mean as Sporty had always been to her, and as often as she wished he wasn't her father, strangely, she was not the least bit happy to hear him finally say she was some other man's child.

"You're a vicious old bastard!" Jared shouted into Sporty's ear.

"Go to hell!" Sporty slammed the receiver down onto the base. He pushed roughly past Tandi, knocking her against the wall. He carried the telephone back into the living room.

Tandi was in shock. She couldn't rebound quickly enough to do anything about Sporty pushing her. An overly strong, pungent smell of cigarettes mingled with the dense air of anger was left in Sporty's wake, reminding her he had spent his day in a smoke-filled casino throwing his money away. Her mouth slowly closed as her mind kept playing the word *bastard* over and over in her head. Nothing had ever given her such pause, not even seeing Jared and Evonne. Was he saying he was not her father because he was angry? Or was it simply the truth? She had always questioned it, but was it true? Maybe that's why he never treated her like his child, why he never loved her like she was his child.

Riiing!

Sporty snatched up the receiver. "Go to hell!" He slammed it down again.

The abrupt jingle and crashing sound of the telephone startled Tandi. She turned toward the living room.

"I don't have to put up with your nasty mouth," Sporty said angrily. "This is my house!"

Tandi blocked Sporty from leaving the living room.

"Get out of my way!"

"No. We have some talking to do."

"I don't have—"

"First! Not one more time do you have to remind me this is your damn house. That fact has been pounded into my head as far back as I can remember, and so has the fact that I've never felt like I was your child. I'm not, am I?"

"Get the hell out of my face!" Sporty shouted, abruptly stalking across the room away from Tandi. He began to anxiously pat his shirt then his pants pockets, searching for his cigarettes.

When she was a little girl, that booming voice used to scare Tandi to death, making her hide in a corner of her room, the one place Sporty gave her privacy. He rarely entered, which was curious since he always ranted that every nook and cranny of the house was his.

Sporty found his cigarettes in his shirt pocket, where they always were. Tapping out a lone cigarette, he jammed it in between his lips then shoved the pack back down into his pocket. He began searching for his lighter.

That booming voice no longer put fear in Tandi's heart. She found herself not running to her room, but running at him, and when she got to him, she grabbed onto his arm and snatched him with all of her might around to face her.

"*Am I* your daughter?"

The unlit cigarette dropped out of Sporty's mouth onto the floor at his feet. He abruptly shook Tandi off him. She was forced to back up.

"You're out of your damn mind!" He bent down to pick up his cigarette and almost fell forward onto his face but his left arm shot awkwardly out in front of him. His hand hit the floor and he caught himself. He fell hard and clumsily onto his right knee, which made him grunt.

Seeing Sporty fall to the floor was startling, but Tandi didn't care that he was on the floor. "Tell me, old man. Am . . . I . . . your daughter?"

Sporty was trying to pick up his cigarette with his right hand. He touched it but he was having trouble grasping it—his fingers wouldn't bend.

Tandi saw that Sporty seemed to not be able to pick up his cigarette. "What's wrong with your hand?"

"Ain't a damn thing wrong with my hand!" he snapped, dropping down onto his other knee.

Sporty's face looked strained; the veins in his face and neck had popped out. "Then if there's nothing wrong, get up off the floor," she said, wanting to not be concerned but she was.

"You're driving me goddamn crazy!"

"Then tell me the damn truth, and I'll leave you the hell alone."

"Get . . . away . . . from . . . me." Sporty was suddenly sounding out of breath. Down on all fours, he grimaced as he grabbed the cigarette with his left hand and placed it deep in between his forefinger and second finger of his right hand. Straining, he got clumsily up onto his left knee then straining even more, pushed himself unsteadily up off the floor.

As angry as she was with him, Tandi could see something was drastically wrong. "You better sit down."

"Leave . . . me alone."

"You got it. Why don't you fall on your damn face? I don't care."

The cigarette dropped from in between Sporty's fingers to the floor again. He didn't seem to notice. He was intent on leaving the room. Again he pushed past Tandi, this time with not as much force as he seemed to be favoring his right leg.

"Get . . . out . . . my house."

"Not until you explain what you meant about me being some bastard's child," she said, knowing he was heading for his bedroom where he could lock her out. She pushed ahead of Sporty into his bedroom before he could close the door.

"Get . . . out," he said, breathing laboredly.

"I am tired of your nastiness and your innuendos about my mother, about me. I want to hear you say it once and for all that you are not my father."

Holding on to the doorknob with his left hand, Sporty slumped against the door. "Get . . . out . . . my . . . room," he said weakly.

Before her startled eyes, Tandi watched the right side of Sporty's face—his mouth, his cheek—droop. Still she persisted. "Am I your daughter, goddamnit?"

"You're . . . your . . . mother's . . . daughter!"

"Why can't you just say it?"

Suddenly, Sporty dropped down to the floor like his legs had been shot from under him, collapsing onto his face.

"Daddy!" Tandi dropped down onto her knees alongside Sporty. She pulled him over onto his back. His eyes were wide and glazed as he gasped for air. Quickly unbuttoning his shirt, she tried pulling it and his undershirt away from his neck.

"Daddy! Daddy, can you hear me?"

Sporty slowly lifted his left hand about a half foot off the floor and strained to lift it even higher but it suddenly plopped down to his side. He struggled to breathe.

There was a look of sheer glazed terror in Sporty's eyes. Tandi shook him. "Oh, God! Daddy, what's wrong?"

"I . . . can't . . . move," he slurred.

"Oh, God."

Tandi looked around for the telephone. She crawled hurriedly over to the nightstand, and grabbing the telephone, pulled it crashing down onto the floor. Her fingers trembled as she jabbed buttons for 911. It rang. It rang.

"Come on!"

It rang.

"Nine-one-one, what's your emergency?"

"My father collapsed! He can't move! I need an ambulance! Send an ambulance!"

"Miss, please calm down. What's the address?"

"One ninety-four dash twenty-three, One hundred twelfth Avenue in Hollis. It's the fifth house on the block."

"Is your father breathing?"

Tandi crawled quickly back over to Sporty. "Yes, but with difficulty. Hurry!"

"Is he conscious?"

"Yes."

"Did you find him this way?"

Tandi started to touch Sporty's forehead. She quickly drew her hand back. "It just happened. Is the ambulance coming?"

"EMS is on the way. Miss, what is your father's name?"

Sporty's breathing came in raspy gasps.

"Glynn Belson, Senior. Hurry!" she said, tossing the receiver behind her. "Daddy, they're coming."

Sporty's eyes were open, though they appeared to not see. The right side of his face was frozen into a droopy mask almost like his features had melted like hot wax.

"Daddy, can you hear me? Are you hurting anywhere?"

Sporty's gasping stopped cold.

Sporty's silence scared Tandi. She couldn't tell if he was breathing or not. She put her ear to his chest but she wasn't sure if she heard his heart beat or her own, as hers was thumping in her own ears.

"Oh, God, help me." Tandi positioned one hand on top of the other over Sporty's heart and timidly pushed down. Feeling no give, she moved down a little. She knew she was supposed to be doing something with his nose and his mouth, but what? She put her hand on his nose and squeezed it. A soft whoosh of air escaped from his mouth. She quickly let go of his nose. He was breathing, thank God.

The far-away sound of a siren began drawing near. Tandi hurried to the front door and flung it open as the ambulance pulled up in front of the house.

"Please hurry!" She was relieved she was no longer alone with Sporty. It was her fault he had collapsed. In hindsight, if she had stayed the night with Brent, this would not have happened. A flood of tears gushed from her when the paramedics entered and she pointed the way to Sporty's bedroom down the hall. She stayed out on the stoop, her head back, her shoulders shaking, crying in the night to the full moon above.

30

Jared didn't know what he'd find when he got to Sporty's house. What he feared most was finding Tandi even more devastated than she was after finding him and Evonne together, if that were possible, and it was possible if her argument with Sporty got nastier after he got off the telephone. He should have known better than to listen to Les and call the house. He should have known better than to speak even one word to Sporty Belson. In his desperation to speak to Tandi, he had really messed up, and he saw that the minute he pulled onto 112th Avenue and saw a police car and two ambulances parked outside of Sporty's house. They were closing the door. Double parking, Jared leaped from his SUV and ran to the ambulance. He reached for the door handle.

"Sir," an EMS officer said, "don't open that door."

Jared yanked open the door anyway.

"Hey!" The EMS officer knocked Jared's hand away.

Jared saw only Tandi. She was sitting on the side of the stretcher staring down at Sporty. "What happened? Are you all right?"

Tandi's blank, shell-shocked gaze was Jared's answer.

The EMS officer tried to close the door in Jared's face. "Mister, we have to get this patient to the hospital. Get back."

"That's my wife," Jared explained.

"Then meet her at Jamaica Hospital."

"Tandi, I'll meet you at the hospital."

"No," she said softly.

"You shouldn't be alone. Where's MJ?"

"He's with Glynn."

"I'll meet you at the hospital," he said again.

"No."

"Tandi—"

"Let's go!" the paramedic working on Sporty shouted to the driver.

A police officer came up, and taking a firm hold on Jared's arm, led him away from the ambulance. The EMS officer then slammed the ambulance door, sending it on its way, its sirens blaring, its emergency lights flashing wildly.

Jared stood in the gutter watching the ambulance speed away.

"Go home, mister," the police officer said.

"What happened to Mr. Belson?"

"Looks like a stroke."

"Is he alive?"

The police officer began walking away. "Check with the hospital."

Jared looked at the house. It looked locked up. There was nothing for him to do. At a time like this, when Tandi needed him, she didn't want him near her. MJ was going to need him and, in time, he hoped Tandi would also.

31

If a bird had broken its wing, if a cat or dog had broken its leg, if Michael Jared or any child was sick and tubes and wires snaked from his weak little body to cold metal and plastic machines forecasting the state of his health in monotonous beeps and flashing numbers and degrees, Tandi's heart would ache. But to witness the downfall of a bitter, contentious old man, Tandi could only stand in awe that such a mighty beast could be brought down at all by something other than the swift sling of a machete or a blast from a well-aimed gun. But it was a stroke, a cerebral thrombosis, Sporty's doctor said, that had stricken Sporty, and although he lay hooked up to all kinds of machines monitoring his heart and giving him his life's breath, Tandi could feel no pity for him. She tried to tell herself that it was fear and maybe even guilt she was feeling, but the truth was, she was feeling absolute disdain for her father.

Although Tandi didn't speak about her feelings to anyone, she was sure Sporty knew. The angry glint in his eyes said so. He couldn't speak, he couldn't move any part of the right side of his body, but his eyes moved and spoke loud and clear, "You did this to me." Doctor Weitzman said no one was to blame but Sporty himself. He explained to both her and Glynn that with Sporty's high blood pressure, his heavy smoking, his drinking, and his consumption of fatty foods, that he was hell bent on having either a stroke or a heart attack. Whether he had been sitting and watching television or dancing a jig, he was going down. He had been warned time and again, and time and again

Sporty told Doctor Weitzman to kiss his ass. He had said more than once, "I don't wanna live if I can't enjoy living."

Well, he almost got his wish—and so had Tandi. Before Sporty's collapse, after he said those horrible words to her—*That's the thanks I get for raising another man's bastard*—she had wished him dead. Was that it all these years? Had Sporty treated her with such malice because she wasn't his? If she wasn't, then why did he raise her? More importantly, who was her father?

Again Tandi was of two minds. She wanted Sporty to die for making her life so miserable, yet, she also needed him to live. He was the only one who had the answers Glynn disputed even existed. She hadn't told Glynn immediately about what happened, just that Sporty was upset when he got home. Three days later, he wanted to know what he had been upset about.

"Are you crazy? Of course you're his daughter. No wonder he had a stroke."

"Glynn, you heard what the doctor said. Daddy didn't have a stroke because of what I asked him, he had a stroke because of his lifestyle."

"Tandi, arguing with him didn't help, especially when you were already upset yourself."

"That's right, Glynn, put it all on me." She went back to dusting the étagère.

"Neither one of you know how to back down."

"He's the one who said I was another man's bastard."

"I'm sure Dad said that out of anger. He probably got tired of you asking him if he was your father."

"That's not how it happened."

"Maybe not this time, but you have asked—many times."

"Damn right. Glynn, you know he's never treated us the same."

"Damnit, Tandi. Would you please stop this? I'm sick of hearing this. Think about it. How would you feel if MJ asked Jared if he was his father?"

"Michael Jared looks like his father. I, on the other hand, look nothing like mine."

"Tandi, how do you sound?"

"I don't care how I sound, Glynn. I want answers!"

Glynn flopped down into Sporty's recliner. "This is insane. You probably look like our mother." He pushed the chair into the reclining position, raising his legs.

"How do you know? Have you seen a clear enough picture of our mother to say that I do?"

"No, but—"

"Well, don't you think that's strange?"

"Tandi, I don't have to see a picture to know you probably look like our mother."

"Probably, again. Tell me, Glynn, do you remember that big black steamer trunk up in the attic that always had a padlock on it?"

"Yeah, and?"

"It's still up there—locked."

"Why were you in the attic in the first place?"

"I stored my suitcases there, which I have the right to do," she said irritably. "Anyway, I've searched for the key to the trunk. I can't find one. Isn't that strange?"

"No."

"God!" Tandi threw the dust rag on top of the television. "Try to give a damn, Glynn."

"About what? Your fixation?"

"No, about a trunk that has been padlocked for decades, that Daddy won't even open to appease his own sense of nostalgia."

"You don't know that he never opened that trunk."

"I do know. There's layers of undisturbed dust on it an inch thick. He's never wanted us to touch it, and he himself won't touch it. Why?"

Glynn slammed his fist down on the arm of the chair. "Goddamnit, Tandi. I'm tired of hearing about that trunk. You've been harassing Dad for years about that damn trunk. I'm telling you, you have got to stop this."

She couldn't. "Glynn, suppose Daddy killed our mother and stuffed her body in that trunk?"

"You're losing your mind," Glynn said, pushing the recliner up right.

"But suppose—"

"Tandi, you're calling our father a murderer! He didn't kill our mother, and her body's not up in that damn trunk in the attic."

Tandi sucked her teeth. "Well, he could've. That trunk is certainly large enough to hold a body. It's mighty strange that Daddy forbade us from ever touching that damn thing."

"That's because your ass was always so nosy. But, Tandi, I saw our mother the last day she was here, remember? I told you that. She left. I saw her leave. She never came back."

"Just because you didn't see her come back, don't—"

"My God, Tandi! Why are you so desperately trying to pin a murder on our father? Why—"

"Okay! So she's not up in the attic. Suppose the trunk is filled with her things? We could find out who she was."

"Tandi, leave the damn trunk alone. Nothing you find out now will make a difference in your life."

"You don't know that."

"What will a picture do for you, Tandi? Not a damn thing. Besides, if there were pictures, Dad probably burned them when our so-called mother walked out on us, and I don't blame him. She didn't care enough about us to take us with her or come back to see us. The hell with her." Glynn flipped his hand as if to ward off thoughts of their mother.

On the rare occasion she and Glynn discussed their mother, Tandi always got tense. She felt like a ton of bricks rested on her chest. Glynn hated their mother as much as Sporty did, although he had never known her for himself. He had learned to hate her at Sporty's knee, a place she had never sat. Admittedly, she had a little hate in her for her mother, also. Not so much for her but for what she had done—walked out on them and left them to be raised by a hateful man, then for her mother to die, leaving them forever, was what she hated most.

"Tandi, when Dad comes home, you better not make him worse off than he is by bringing up this crap."

"I better not?"

"I mean it."

"What are you gonna do to me, Glynn? Put me in a headlock like you did when we were kids whenever I didn't do what you wanted me to? Or, are you gonna tell Daddy on me? Oooo. I'm so afraid."

"Tandi, what's wrong with you?"

"You really wanna know? It's you. It's Daddy. It's Jared. And . . . and . . . forget it." She almost said Brent because he was proving to be no different. Plus, Glynn didn't need to know Brent was back in her life. He would spit bullets. He never liked Brent, said he was a loser. The fact was, Glynn was the loser. In high school, he had lost the two hundred meter race to Brent, a freshman, more than once. He'd hated Brent ever since.

"Well, sis, it seems to me, you're blaming every man in your life for your troubles."

"That's because you're all bleeding me dry."

"Stop being so melodramatic. Everyone isn't beating up on poor Tandi."

"You know, Glynn, you have never stood by me unconditionally. You've never—"

"That's bull. Who do you think got Dad to let you go away on that ski trip to Aspen with your friends even after you stole my keys and backed my car into the side of the house? Dad wanted to kill you for that. Remember?"

"Okay, okay. That one time you—"

"More than that one time. How about the time you got sick in school from smoking and drinking that cheap liquor? Who took care of you?"

"I said okay. Maybe you were there for me a few times."

"Wow, a whole big two times, huh, Tandi? I guess it would hurt you to admit that I've always been there for you. Maybe if you let go of some of your anger at Dad, then you might see that I've been a good brother to you."

Tandi had to wonder if Glynn was right. Could her anger at Sporty have clouded her perception of Glynn? Growing up, he really hadn't been a bad brother.

"But, Glynn, you've never taken me seriously about my real concerns about Dad or anything that really bothered me."

"Tandi, you're talking like you're the only one who has problems. Have you ever asked me about my life? I'm not tiptoeing through any goddamn tulips on easy street."

Okay, so he had her again. No, she hadn't asked Glynn about his life because he seemed to always have it together. "Glynn, I've never seen you harried or indecisive or financially in need. Your house is always in order, and you always look so put together. I never thought for a minute you had problems."

"How wrong you are, sis. If you ever gave me the time of day, you might know what my life is really like."

"That's not fair, Glynn. After you married Leah, it was you who didn't have time for me. Leah and Leah's family became your family."

"That's not completely true. Yes, Leah's family is my family, but so are you and Jared and MJ. The question is, why haven't we found time to be a family?"

"According to you, you're always busy. You—"

"Tandi! We're going in circles. We're back to blaming each other."

"That's easiest, isn't it? Look, Glynn, I need a break. I need to get away from my life."

Glynn threw up his hands. "Fine. Do that. Run away. Then you'll be exactly like our mother."

"I didn't say a damn thing about running away!"

"Oh, my mistake. I wasn't sure what I heard, Tandi. I just wanted to make sure you weren't talking about running off and leaving your son behind."

Tandi thrust her fists on her hips. "How dare you say that! I'm nothing like our mother. I would never leave my son!"

"See that you don't."

"Glynn!" Tandi's arms slammed to her sides.

"Calm down. I didn't say you'd do what she did."

"Well, I don't even want you to insinuate it." Tandi went to the front window and looked out. It had rained earlier as it had done on and off all week, and now the grass in the front yard looked greener, taller, but the warmth of spring was still weeks away. Shaking out her arms as if to release the pressure, Tandi then rolled her head from side to side, stretching out the tightness in her neck.

"Glynn, have we ever seen eye to eye on anything when it came to talking about our parents?"

"Yes. We both agree that we wish our mother hadn't left us."

He was right about that. How different would their life have been?

"What's going on in your life, Tandi, now that you've left Jared? Are you seeing someone?"

"Why?"

"Just asking. Although, in my opinion, I think you should work things out with Jared. He's a good man. I always liked him."

"Then you get with him."

"Don't get cute. Are you seeing someone? Who is he?"

"None of your business."

"That's all right, little sis. I'll meet the new man in your life sooner or later, just don't walk in the door with Brent Rodgers."

Tandi's eyes almost popped out of her head. "What?"

"I know you didn't forget that bum. You were stupid over him. The guy was a total dog."

"He was not!" She couldn't believe Glynn pulled Brent's name out of thin air like that. "What about the tramps you went out with who Daddy had no problem with."

"They weren't his daughters."

"It makes a difference? You were his son, Glynn. But never mind that. You told Daddy on me when I tried to climb out of my bedroom window to go meet up with Brent."

"That's because you almost broke your neck trying to lower yourself with an electrical extension cord tied around the leg of your bed. It wasn't long enough or strong enough. If I hadn't been out back emptying the garbage, you would have fallen and broken your stupid neck."

"I could have made it."

"That's not the way it looked to me."

"Well, Glynn, thanks to you, I couldn't go out for a month, and I had to stay in my room without a television the whole time."

"You're still mad about that?"

"What do you think?"

"C'mon, Tandi." Glynn stood. "I probably saved you from being raped that night. Brent had a bad rep."

"Says you."

"All the guys knew about Brent—old bang 'em and hurt 'em Brent. The girls who had some sense stayed away from him. You, you were a kid. You were so naive."

There was that word again. Did everyone in the world think she was naive? What Glynn said about Brent, she knew nothing about. In high school, he never forced himself on her.

"In case you hadn't noticed, Glynn, I'm far from naive now. I can take care of myself."

"Well, just in case you can't, sis, I'm always here for you. Now, can we still agree that you'll stay here until Dad gets a little better and the home health aide settles in?"

"I've been thinking," she said casually. "Iona Lewis has been visiting Daddy almost every day. Why don't we talk to her about moving in?"

"Hell, no! Dad would have another stroke."

"I don't see why. He's been going with her for years. He hasn't stopped her from visiting."

"But he doesn't want her to move in, and in fact, he doesn't wanna see her anymore. He told me he knows she only wants to marry him for his pension."

"So," she said, knowing Glynn wouldn't want Iona Lewis getting her hands on Sporty's house or bank accounts. "The woman deserves something for going with a scorpion all these years. She should move in."

"No, Tandi. Dad is our responsibility. One of us has to be here."

"That one being me, of course."

"Do I have to tell you again that I can't."

"Then understand this, Glynn. I'm staying because my apartment hasn't come through yet. I'm also staying out of the goodness of my heart and because you won't. But I'm warning you, I have no patience for that old man anymore. He better not pluck my last nerve."

"Man, Tandi, I don't know why you hate him so."

"Man, Glynn, I don't know why you love him so."

Checkmate. They stood looking at each other, neither willing to explain as their reasons would never sway the other.

"Okay, sis, I have to get going. Give your brother some love."

That mushy feeling Tandi got every time she hugged Michael Jared and thought about how much she loved him, she got when Glynn kissed her on the cheek and wrapped his arms around her, hugging her tightly. She kissed and hugged him just as tightly. When they pulled apart, both their eyes glistened.

"Love you, sis." Glynn headed for the door. "Okay. The hospital bed should be here in a week. I'll come over to help get Dad's bedroom ready."

Tandi retrieved the dust rag from atop the television. "I can't wait."

"Oh, by the way. Dad will be coming home in a hospital wheelchair. I ordered one of those motorized chairs. He'll be able to operate it with a switch on the armrest with his good hand."

A weak feeling crept up Tandi's legs to her knees. She sat down on the sofa.

"I also ordered everything else the doctor suggested: the bedpan, the walker—"

"Just make sure the health aide is here the day he comes home." Tandi cringed at the thought of having to empty Sporty's bedpan.

"She'll be here."

"And make sure there's a health aide scheduled for the evening hours."

"There will be," Glynn said, opening the door. "Tandi, I want you to take care of yourself."

"I'm fine, Glynn."

"No, you're not. I've never seen you so on edge."

"I said, I'm fine."

"Okay," Glynn said, not convinced. "Anyway, I'm gonna help you with Dad, don't worry, but if it's your breakup with Jared that's still upsetting you, you have got to get yourself straight with him, one way or the other. Do you want me to talk to him?"

"Hell no. Glynn, I don't want you to go anywhere near Jared. I don't even want you talking to him."

"Wait a minute, Tandi. I'm not gonna stop talking to the man—I'm not a kid taking sides. I won't talk to Jared about you, because whatever's going on, that's between you and him, but I'm not gonna stop talking to Jared, man to man. Like I said before, I like him. He's all right with me. Look, I'll call you tomorrow."

Tandi hated to admit it, but Glynn was right. Just as it was for Michael Jared, she had no right to sever the relationship that Glynn and Jared had. This wasn't his battle. Tandi slumped back against the sofa cushion. She really was exhausted. She couldn't remember the last time she had spoken this long with Glynn. Maybe she needed to do that more often. Besides Michael Jared, Glynn was her only family. As far as she was concerned, Sporty was a question mark.

Glynn stepped out onto the stoop and almost bumped into Evonne.

"Hi, Glynn. Remember me?"

Tandi snapped to attention.

"Sure, Evonne. It's been a long time, but I'd never forget you. You're looking good."

"So are you."

"Tandi's inside."

Tandi made a mad dash for the door to try and lock it before Evonne could step inside. She didn't make it. Evonne was already inside. She was dressed in a blood-red blazer and a short black skirt, looking every bit the viper she was.

32

"Tandi, I have to explain what happened."

"You can't. What you did is inexplicable."

"I know, and I'm sorry." Evonne pushed the door closed, the lock clicked when it caught.

"You weren't acting like you were so sorry the morning I caught you in bed with Jared. In fact, you had a disgustingly smug look on your face, like you had gotten over on me."

"That wasn't smugness, that was shock, and I wasn't trying to get anything over on you."

"Not from my vantage point, Evonne. You seemed to be quite satisfied with what you had done."

"Well, I wasn't. I couldn't believe what Jared and I had done."

"Yeah, right."

"Tandi, I know you hate me, but we've been through so much together. I would never, purposely, do anything to hurt you. I was drunk. That night was a mistake." Evonne pressed her fingers to her forehead. She closed her eyes as tears squeezed between her lashes.

Tandi back-flipped her hand. "Cut the drama. I'm not buying it."

Evonne's tears dried up. "Tandi, I truly hate what happened, but I was trying to be a friend."

"Gosh, Evonne, I don't know if I can stand having a friend like you. Why don't you get the hell outta here before I lose my *snootiness* and kick your ass." Tandi fixed as threatening a glare as she could muster on Evonne. She really did want to kick Evonne's ass, but she just couldn't see herself clawing and shrieking like some mud wrestler over a man who'd cheated on her a second time and in her own bed no less. Tandi went to the door. She yanked it open.

The tears that filled Evonne's eyes this time were real. "Ah, c'mon, Tandi. You know I wouldn't, purposely, do anything to hurt you. You—"

"Just leave, Evonne! I don't ever wanna see you again."

Evonne turned away from the door. She wiped her eyes. "You didn't say that last year when you neglected to draw up and have your client sign that Property Condition Disclosure Statement before he left town . . ."

Tandi's grip on the doorknob tightened. "Digging deep, aren't you?"

". . . If I recall, you were *soo* happy to see me after you called me, all hysterical, because the buyer had signed the contract of sale, and sin of sins, the lawyer realized there was no Property Condition Disclosure Statement in the folder. That's a legal, binding document, but you know that, don't you, Tandi? The whole deal could have fallen through and worst of all, that lawyer could have reported you and your agency to the Department of State's Division of Licensing Services. You were clearly in violation of Article 462, sweetie, which every seasoned broker and salesperson in the State of New York knows like the back of their hand. You and your agency could have lost your license if it wasn't for me."

"Couldn't wait to remind me of that, huh?"

"Actually, I'm reminding you of how good a friend I've been. I put my own career on the line by drawing up that bogus disclosure statement and forging that man's signature, and getting it to you before that meeting ended. I did that for you, Tandi, and that's been our little secret. I bet your precious Jared doesn't even know about it. You wouldn't want him or anyone to know you did anything illegal, would you?"

Tandi closed the door. She had been desperate that day. She had forgotten the disclosure statement and with her client, the seller, being out of town, and herself being stuck in the meeting with the buyers and their lawyer, she had no way of getting a statement drawn up. She had excused herself from the meeting under the pretense that she was calling her office to have the document, which she said she had on file, brought over. Instead she had called Evonne on her cell phone and asked her what to do. It had been Evonne's idea to draw up the disclosure statement as well as to sign it. Tandi knew it was wrong, but there was too much at stake, and no one was ever the wiser. Looking back on it now, she was ashamed of what she had done, but what choice did she have?

Evonne unbuttoned her blazer. "After all I did for you, you can't give me five minutes to explain what happened between me and Jared?"

Folding her arms, Tandi leaned back against the door. "That's just it, Evonne, what you did for me was business. What you did with Jared was personal."

"Perhaps, but what happened with Jared wasn't planned. When Jared called and asked me to come over, I went because he said he needed someone to talk to."

"And I'm supposed to believe it was you he needed, right?"

"He said he needed to talk to someone who could give him insight into what you were feeling. Tandi, I swear, I tried to get him to understand why you left, and I was trying get him to see what he had to do to get you back."

"So you climbed in bed with him to show him what to do?"

"Damn, Tandi, it wasn't like that. We talked for a long time. It was late, and I guess Jared didn't want to be in the house alone. He suggested we go out to some bar he knew."

"Jared doesn't go to bars."

"He wanted to go that night. I went along just in case he drank too much. And, Tandi, if you're honest with yourself, no matter how angry you were with Jared, you would not have wanted him to drive drunk."

"Now that's interesting. I would not have wanted you sleeping with him either, but that didn't stop you but a second." Tandi stepped away from the door. "Evonne, let me tell you why what you're saying doesn't make sense. In all the years I've been with Jared, I have never seen him drunk. He's a social drinker. He doesn't drink to get drunk."

"He did that night. I was there. If I hadn't been there, no telling what could've happened to him."

At that, Tandi couldn't help chuckling cynically. "If he were as drunk as you say, he might've slept in his car or in the gutter, but he didn't have to, did he? Not when my best friend, Evonne, was there to watch over him."

Evonne sucked her teeth.

"You're such a kind, considerate friend, Evonne."

"That's exactly right, Tandi. I proved that to you a year ago, and I proved it with Jared."

"Oh my God. You actually believe that?"

"It's the truth. Where I went wrong was, I started to drink, too, and maybe I drank a little too much."

Tandi began to pace. "Evonne, I really don't wanna hear any more of this. Please leave."

Evonne sat. "Not until I tell you my side. Not until you hear the whole story."

"I don't care about your side."

"Jared was drunk, I was drunk," Evonne said, ignoring Tandi. "I had a hard time getting him into the house. He fell out in your front yard. I couldn't leave him there."

"So correct me if I'm wrong, Evonne. Wasn't it a lot easier to let Jared fall asleep on the sofa on the first floor, than it was to get him up a flight of stairs to the second floor?"

Evonne was stumped. She stared blankly at Tandi.

"I thought so."

"I thought I was doing the right thing. I was trying to be—"

"Yes, I know. You were trying to be a good friend."

Evonne brought her fist down hard on the arm of the chair. "You're not being fair!"

"Fair? Excuse the hell out of me, but do I have to remind you, Evonne, that you screwed *my* husband? Why the hell am I supposed to be fair to you? Am I supposed to be patting you on the back, congratulating you? I think the hell not! From what I hear, you lied on me."

Evonne yanked her oversized silk scarf from around her jacket collar. "I lied on you? What about your soon-to-be ex-husband? He wouldn't lie to you, right? Well, let me tell you something I was trying not to tell you."

"More drama. Save it. I don't need it." Tandi again took hold of the doorknob.

"Oh, you don't wanna hear the truth? But then, maybe you can't handle the truth."

"The question is, Evonne, can you tell the truth?"

"I can tell you Jared hadn't even started drinking when he asked me if I wanted him since you didn't. He started kissing on me before we even got to the bar."

That stopped Tandi from turning the knob to open the door. Those words were biting. She wanted to dismiss them and throw them upon the same pile of garbage as the *we were drunk* crap, but the *we were drunk* crap was easier to take than dealing with Jared lusting after Evonne sober. She didn't want to believe Jared had asked Evonne if she wanted him, but he had cheated on her before and maybe he thought this was a way to get back at her for walking out on him.

"And it wasn't the first time he propositioned me."

For the second time, Tandi released the doorknob. She faced Evonne although inside her heart quivered. She couldn't believe at one time she blindly trusted Jared.

"Now do I have your attention?" Evonne asked.

"So if Jared propositioned you before either one of you was drunk, how did *you* let it happen?"

Evonne let out a long, forlorn sigh. "Tandi, I didn't just *let* it happen. I guess once I got drunk, I got weak . . ."

"Or stupid."

". . . Nothing serious happened before that."

Disgusted, Tandi shook her head. "This is too unreal. I just can't believe you let—"

"But I didn't! I was drunk."

"Evonne, you're supposed to be my friend. Drunk or sober, you're not supposed to sleep with my husband."

"Tandi, I'm owning up to my part in this. I'm human. Jared was coming on to me. I got weak. I didn't rape him. He played a major role in this."

"I'm sure he did."

"Tandi, from the moment you talked about leaving Jared, I was trying to get you to stay and you know that. I talked to Jared. I told him where he had gone wrong. He wanted to talk to you but you wouldn't talk to him. You left him out there for any woman to take."

"Not you! Not my so-called best friend. You're not supposed—" Again Tandi went to pacing. With all that was going on in her life, she wasn't supposed to be dealing with this crap.

"Tandi, I'm sorry. I—"

"You know what, Evonne?" Tandi pulled up close to her. "Don't be sorry. It's no big deal. Look, I have a sense of humor, and maybe one day—maybe not today—I might find this whole thing funny. But for right now, I'm a good sport. You can have Jared. You have my blessing. I hope you both enjoy each other."

Evonne sat back. "Tandi, I am *not* with Jared. I wouldn't do that to you."

"But you already have."

"Just that one time. It hasn't happened since. Haven't you spoken to Jared? Didn't he tell you? It's the truth."

Sitting because she was literally drained of her strength, Tandi didn't know what to believe. "I'm not speaking to Jared."

Evonne breathed a soft sigh of relief. "I guess I can't blame you, but, Tandi, I need to tell you this also. Jared called me last night, three times, and asked me to come over."

That bastard! Tandi fixed her eyes on a single square of dull, badly scratched parquet flooring in the center of the room. For the life of her, she couldn't understand why hearing that upset her. She didn't want Jared anymore. She had Brent. What Jared and Evonne did together or apart shouldn't still be annoying her.

A fleeting self-satisfied smirk touched Evonne's lips. "Jared said he had tried to talk to you, but since you had closed him out altogether, he saw no reason to hold back his feelings for me any longer."

Tandi felt like a deer caught in the hypnotic light of an oncoming car. As much as she didn't want to listen to another ugly thing about what Jared was doing, she felt like she had to. She stared at the square, unable to blink.

"I told Jared I couldn't have anything with him because you were more important to me."

Tandi looked up. "That's almost funny. Evonne, no one is as important to you as you, yourself. That I'm sure of."

"I won't dispute that. I like me, but, Tandi, you've been like a sister to me. There isn't anything I wouldn't do for you . . ."

Tandi privately smirked.

". . . When Jared cheated on you, I'm the one who talked you into giving him another chance. Would I do that if I wanted him for myself? And what about that day when we met at the restaurant? Didn't I try to make you see what you were doing? I didn't want you to leave Jared, remember?"

All of that was true. Evonne had always tried to keep her and Jared together.

"I would never knowingly betray you, Tandi. You have to know that about me. Think about how Jared betrayed you in the past. I swear, I didn't know he had any feelings for me, and I, certainly, have never encouraged those feelings."

Fighting back tears, Tandi sniffled. How had she been so fooled by Jared?

Evonne went and sat next to Tandi, taking her hand. "I am your friend, Tandi. I told Jared I could never be with him, that you meant more to me than anyone on this earth, more than my own sisters. What happened really was a mistake. I was drunk. I was weak. But I'm not now. I turned Jared down because I don't want him. I want our friendship back. Can't you try to forgive me?"

Tandi's resolve to hate Evonne seemed to dissolve. Evonne wasn't totally blameless, but she had gotten caught up in Jared's web of charm and persuasiveness. Hadn't Jared, with that same charm and persuasiveness, gotten her into bed on their first date? Like Evonne, she had been weak. She wanted Jared the minute she laid eyes on him. Maybe Evonne had wanted him like that when the alcohol weakened her sense of right and wrong. Maybe it wasn't fair to shut Evonne out of her life when, ultimately, it was Jared's betrayal. He was the one who had taken a vow of fidelity to her, not Evonne.

"Tandi, I'm here for you. I will always be here for you."

Wanting to believe Evonne meant what she was saying, Tandi was willing to forgive Evonne but she wasn't altogether sure she would ever trust her around Brent or any other man who might enter her life. At this moment though, with all that was going on in her life, she needed a friend and next to Daina, Evonne was it.

33

Whatever his role as father had been before, Jared realized it was minimal compared to what it was now that he had MJ three days a week while Tandi dealt with her father's illness. As strange as it was, in the past month, he felt more like a daddy and not just a father or breadwinner. Getting MJ ready for school, making sure he was fed, making sure his homework was done, and checking his clothes was the new job Jared found himself immersed in. It was a lot to contend with, but he was learning. He had assumed that taking care of MJ would be a breeze; after all, MJ was potty trained. Not so. He was responsible for MJ's every need, and that was substantial. Belatedly, he could see why Tandi had been asking him to help her. If she were speaking to him, he would humbly apologize to her.

Tandi called the house on the days MJ stayed with him, but she'd only speak to MJ. If he answered the telephone she'd say, "May I speak to my son." After the second time, he simply called MJ to the telephone and after a while, he left the phone answering to MJ when he thought it might be Tandi. After talking to Glynn, he finally accepted that there was nothing he could say or do to make things right with her. Her anger was too deep. And he couldn't blame her. Sleeping with Evonne was unforgivable. Hell, he was disgusted with himself. He could only imagine how bad it was for Tandi, and he was just beginning to see how badly their breakup was for MJ who was always worried about Tandi if she was late calling him. No longer was MJ interested in playing with his PlayStation. He didn't want to go over to any of his friends' houses, he refused to go to karate practice, he only wanted to stay home. MJ's appetite had increased and knew no bounds, yet he gained no weight. Jared didn't know if it was growing pains or stress.

The days he picked up MJ after school should have been fun, but MJ was often sullen.

"What's up, buddy? You feel okay?"

He shrugged.

Jared nudged him. "What's wrong?"

"Sean told everybody in class that Mommy don't live with us anymore." MJ turned his face toward the window. He was quiet.

"MJ, don't worry about what other people say. You know and I know that your mother loves you no matter where she lives." He continued driving toward his office, but he kept glancing over at MJ. He saw the tears streaming down his face onto his jacket. While he felt badly for him, he didn't know what to say to make him feel better. Maybe the office was the last place either of them needed to be. Using his cell phone, he called Marci.

"Hey, it's me. Anything I need to know about?"

"Mrs. Glautman just called saying she wants to accept the settlement offer Coles Pharmaceuticals made. She said she doesn't want to stay in court for the next three years. I told her she needed to talk to you. I know how you feel about settling so low, Jared."

Again, Jared glanced at MJ. His tears weren't letting up. "Marci, call Mrs. Glautman back. Tell her that I'll wrap up her case by the end of next week."

"Jared, are you sure?"

"It's a good offer. Anything else?"

"Well, you had a few other calls, and I told them you'd be back by three-thirty."

"I won't be back today," he said, glimpsing MJ as he lay his head on top of his backpack sitting in his lap. His crying was silent but no less disturbing. "Marci, I'll be in first thing in the morning. Take care of those calls for me. Have Raoul call Coles and get them started on the paperwork."

"But, Jared—"

"I have to go," he said, ending the call. Making a right turn, he headed for home, all the while trying to figure out what he could do to comfort his boy. That was something he never really had to do. That was Tandi's job. He thought hard about what she would do, but he couldn't call to mind any occasion since MJ was past the toddler stage where he saw her comfort him. That's because he hadn't been around. Unsure as to what to do, he lay his hand on MJ's head to let him know he was there for him.

Once home, MJ raced up to his room and, again, because he still didn't know what to do, Jared sat, helplessly, at the top of the stairs, listening to MJ cry until he cried himself out. After a while, in the silence, Jared dozed off.

"Dad."

Jared awakened immediately. "Yeah, MJ."

"Dad, if you and Mommy never get back together, we'll never all live together again, will we?"

"No."

"Will you get another wife?"

"I can't say, but I don't think so."

"But you might?"

"Right now, I don't see it."

MJ seemed to visibly relax. Jared slid over and patted the empty spot next to him on the step. Once MJ was seated, he slid closer to him until they were touching along their thighs and sides. He put his arm around MJ's shoulder and held him.

"Are you all right?"

"I miss Mommy being here."

"Me, too."

"She won't marry somebody else, will she?"

"I don't know."

They sat quietly, each with his thoughts.

"Dad, is there something we can do to make Mommy wanna come back home?"

"MJ, I wish I knew."

After a moment's thought, MJ said, "I know. Tell Mommy I'm sick. She'll come home."

"Your mother would be mad at us if we lied to her about you being sick."

"It's not really a lie; I do feel sick. My stomach hurts."

"That's not really being sick, MJ. When I think about how unhappy I made your mother, mine hurts sometimes, too."

"It does?"

"Yes, but after a while, maybe yours won't hurt so bad."

"Do you love Mommy?"

He squeezed MJ. "With all my heart."

"Me, too."

They sat thus in their silent thoughts. Jared about Tandi, the wife and lover he had hurt and lost; MJ about the best mother in the world.

Jared had an idea. "What say we go out for cheeseburgers?"

"Okay."

"How about afterward we go to the movies?"

MJ perked up. "Can we?"

"Sure, why not?"

"It's a school night. Mommy—"

"We won't tell her. It's a special night—boys' night out. We need to unwind. You with me?"

"Yes!"

"Good. Go change into a pair of jeans. I'm gonna put on a pair myself, and don't forget your denim jacket."

Buzzzz!

"Who could that be?" Jared asked, looking down at the front door.

MJ jumped up. "Want me to get it?"

"I'll get it," he said, standing. "You go change."

"What we gonna see?"

"Whatever you want, as long as it's not violent or full of sex."

Buzzzz!

"What I want to see is scary," MJ said, running off to his room.

"Make sure you hang up your clothes and turn off the light," Jared said, going down to see who was at the door.

34

Jared's first instinct was to slam the door in Evonne's face.

"I just wanna talk to you for a minute, Jared. That's all. One minute of your time."

"No," he said, closing the door.

"Please, Jared." Evonne quickly put her hand up to stop the door from closing. "I'll only take a minute."

Jared glanced behind him up the stairs. If he didn't hear Evonne out, she would take up more time begging him to. Jared stepped outside, pulling the door up behind him. "Make it short."

"Jared, I know I was very blunt about my feelings, and I'm sorry if I shocked you, but I had to let you know how I felt. I thought we—"

"There is no *we,* Evonne. I want nothing to do with you."

"Okay, I understand that."

"Good, then there's nothing else to say." Behind his back, Jared turned the doorknob.

"Okay, but please. Just give me one more minute. I'm sorry if I made you feel uncomfortable. I want you to forget what I said. I'd like to still be your friend."

"We're not friends, Evonne. We've never been friends. Now, I have more important things to deal with." He started back inside and was about to close the door.

"I spoke to Tandi," Evonne blurted, stopping Jared.

Jared stepped outside again. "When?"

"I went to see her the other day."

"She actually listened to you?"

"Yes, but she was very unforgiving. I tried to get her to at least forgive you, even if she could never forgive me. I told her you loved her, that you would do anything to get her back."

He was skeptical, but asked, "What did she say?"

"She said she wants nothing to do with either one of us. She . . ."

Jared closed the door.

" . . . said that we deserved each other and that she would never forgive us."

If only he could talk to Tandi himself.

"Jared, Tandi said she didn't love you anymore and that as soon as she could, she was filing for a divorce."

What was he, stupid? He was wasting his time listening to a woman who had tricked him into making love to her, and who couldn't keep her lies straight. "Remember your lie, Evonne. You told me weeks ago Tandi had already filed for a divorce."

"But that's what she told me. I was only repeating what she said. Look, I tried hard to get her to give you another chance, but she wasn't interested."

"I have to go. MJ's waiting for me."

"Oh, he's here? I'd like to see him," Evonne said eagerly.

"I don't think so."

The door suddenly opened. "I'm ready, Dad."

"Good. We're out of here." Jared patted his pocket for his house keys. They weren't on him.

"Hi, Michael Jared," Evonne said cheerfully.

"Hi, Miss Evonne. We're going to the movies. It's boys' night out."

"Oh, that's nice. What're you going to see?"

"Evonne, I'm sure you have somewhere else to be. Don't let me keep you," Jared said. "MJ, I have to get my keys. I'll be right back." He rushed back into the house, snatched his keys off the hall table then, feeling the urge to go to the bathroom, raced to the back of the house. He wasn't going to change his clothes as he had planned, not with Evonne lurking about.

Evonne saw Jared go to the back of the house. She pulled the door up. "So, Michael Jared, how are you? Are you okay?"

"Uh-huh," he answered as he walked toward the SUV.

"A night out with your dad," Evonne said, walking along with MJ. "That's gonna be great fun,

"Uh-huh."

At the front of the SUV they stopped. Evonne glanced back at the front door. She lowered her voice. "I can't remember the last time I went to the movies. I don't have anyone to go with, and I hate going alone. I would love to go with you and your dad. Would that be all right with you?"

"It's boys' night out, Miss Evonne."

"That's cool. I'd love to go with you guys. Wouldn't that be cool, Michael Jared? Wouldn't you like that?"

Uncertain, MJ glanced back at the door.

"See, Michael Jared, it could still be boys' night out. If I went, I would just watch the movie and not say a thing. You wouldn't mind that, would you?"

MJ dropped his eyes. "Um, I guess not."

"Michael Jared, you want me to come, don't you?"

MJ again glanced back at the front door. "I guess. You should ask my dad though."

Evonne, too, glanced furtively back at the door. "Maybe," she said in a hushed voice, "if you ask your dad if I could come along, it'll be okay."

Anxiously looking at the door, MJ bit down on his lower lip.

"All three of us could have a lot of fun, MJ."

"You really wanna come?"

"I'd like to, but only if you want me to."

MJ lightly kicked the front tire of the SUV. "I guess."

"Michael Jared, I won't come if you *really* don't want me to. Do you want me to?"

MJ shrugged.

"Are you sure?"

"I guess."

"Let's get going, MJ." Jared quickly locked the front door and bounded over to the SUV. Unlocking it with his remote, he pulled the door open for MJ. "Good-bye, Evonne."

Evonne quickly put her arm around MJ's shoulders, holding him back from climbing up into the SUV. With a single finger, she tapped him firmly on the upper arm.

MJ lowered his eyes. "Dad," he said, softly, "can Miss Evonne go with us?"

It wasn't hard for Jared to read MJ—he was avoiding looking him in the eye and the earlier excitement was gone from his voice. "Not tonight, son, it's *our* night."

MJ started to smile but Evonne, smiling herself, tapped him again. "He wants me to come, Jared. Right, Michael Jared?"

MJ, his eyes again lowered, said nothing.

If he hadn't already been a victim of Evonne's scheming, Jared would not have believed what she was doing with MJ right before his eyes.

"MJ, get in," Jared ordered.

"Jared, I would love to come. It would be fun."

MJ quickly slipped from under Evonne's arm and climbed up into the SUV. He scooted across to the passenger seat, claiming his place.

As he closed the door, Jared glimpsed MJ's furrowed brow. Without a doubt, it was Evonne's idea to come with them. She was disgustingly conniving.

Jared grabbed Evonne and pulled her away from his SUV, out of earshot of MJ. He squeezed her arm. "Don't you ever try to use my son again. In fact, you stay your conniving ass away from him and away from me."

Evonne tried to pull her arm free. Jared was hurting her. "I don't know what you're talking about. Michael Jared asked me to come. Ask him." She called out, "Michael Jared, didn't—"

Jared snatched Evonne hard. "Leave him alone!"

"Jared, please let me come. I'll see the movie and you can bring me back here to my car afterward. Then I'll go home."

"You listen to me, Evonne. Stay the hell away from me and my son. Stop calling my house, stop showing up at my door. You call or come around here again, I'll get a restraining order so fast, you'll get whiplash from being served. And if I have to file charges against you, I will do it gladly. Now, get the hell out of here." Jared punctuated his threat with a light shove.

"Jared, please."

Jared climbed up into his SUV and slammed the door.

"Okay, Jared," Evonne said pleasantly, forcing herself to smile. "Maybe next time."

Jared backed quickly out of the driveway.

Evonne waved. "Bye, Michael Jared. Enjoy the movie."

Through the rearview mirror, Jared watched Evonne wave. The

woman had to be out of her damn mind. She was trying to insinuate herself into his life and mess with his head. She had played him that night he slept with her, and for all he knew, she was playing Tandi, too. The woman was a snake and, apparently, Tandi never suspected.

"Dad."

"Yeah, MJ."

"I didn't want her to come with us."

"Don't worry about it, son. I got your back."

35

In four days, Sporty was coming home. After two weeks in the hospital flat on his back and six weeks more in a rehabilitation center getting speech and physical therapy so he could at least learn to turn over on his own and get himself up off the bed and into his wheelchair. He was coming home with the blessing of all who had worked with him. He had been a terror.

For two nights Tandi had been unable to sleep. She dreaded Sporty's return and hated she had to be there for it. Sporty was not going to be able to live alone; he needed constant care. He couldn't cook for himself, he couldn't dress himself, he couldn't get in and out of the tub by himself, and, as yet, he couldn't go to the bathroom by himself. For the time being, she was forced to stay because Glynn wasn't going to. He was bringing Sporty home but she doubted he'd do much more. In fact, it was surprising he had found time to visit Sporty nearly every day, even if it was but a quick minute; minutes more than she did. She had refused to go see him after the first three weeks. She had grown tired of seeing the angry, accusatory look in his eyes. If Sporty could have spoken coherently and not made the gobbled grunting sounds he'd been making since he woke up, he would have cursed her for sure. As it was, he glared at her constantly, and with the right side of his mouth drooping, he appeared to be sneering at her.

For sure, Sporty was angry at her and about his situation, but she was angry, too. Her new life had to be put on hold. She had to give up her new apartment, she had to delay adding more hours to her work schedule, and she had to give up Michael Jared. The more time he spent with Jared, the more he wanted to be with him. He asked to go live with Jared full time once he learned Sporty was coming home, and although Sporty wasn't going to be home for a while when Michael Jared asked, he still didn't want to be in Sporty's house. With a heavy heart, she let him go. She didn't want to make his life any more difficult than it was. The irony of it was, she was now spending less time with him than Jared used to.

God, her life was miserable. Not only couldn't she be with Michael Jared, things weren't what she had hoped they would be with Brent. Something wasn't right. She couldn't figure out what it was, she just felt that something wasn't. She spent a lot of time with him, mostly making passionate love that left her sexually sated for the moment, but that seemed to be all there was between them. They didn't go out much nor did they talk much about anything of consequence. She couldn't say she was happy about that, especially since she had begun to notice Brent was all about himself. He no longer indulged in the foreplay that fed her carnal senses like he did the first weeks they were together. Instead, he wanted her to constantly massage his naked body until her fingers cramped, and she was tired of touching him. Oh, Brent still said the right things to keep her coming back, but he, at times, when she couldn't come, pouted and held back from making love to her the next time they got together.

Like that evening, Brent was acting like a spoiled child. "I'm just a little tired tonight," he said, yawning.

Yet, for all his so-called tiredness, Tandi saw that Brent was as naked as a hairless cat with an erection as big as a Polish kielbasa. Apparently, his tiredness was only a state of mind. She watched him lay on top of the bed on his back with his arms straight out from his body. She knew immediately what he wanted—he wanted her to work for his loving. He wanted her to massage his body by rubbing her oil-covered body all over him, slithering over him like she was a snake, while he lay prostrate, outstretched with his eyes closed, relishing the smooth, erotic feel of her body on his tantalized skin. Then he wanted her to kiss him anywhere and everywhere her lips and tongue dared. Oh yes, he made her work for the loving he now knew she craved, and that was sad. She had come to realize she needed to get lost in an orgasmic session of lovemaking so she could forget, for a little while anyway, that her life wasn't turning out like she had envisioned. All that, Brent was aware of, which was why he smiled as she took off her clothes, but she had no intention of doing any of what he wanted tonight.

Brent made love to her anyway, and as soon as he grunted his last thrust, he leaped off her, unceremoniously uncorking her like she was a wine bottle. She felt like a hooker. Brent had never done that to her before. He bound across the room to his bureau and pulled out the bottom drawer. From it, he took out a round, royal blue tin, the kind that fancy candy or nuts came in. He brought it back to the bed.

Tandi could see it wasn't a new tin—it had a few dents in it. Curious, she sat up.

"I got us something to enhance that good feeling we got going on between us," he said, pulling off the top and holding the tin out for Tandi to see.

Her jaw dropped. There was no candy, there were no nuts. There were three small, clear plastic snack bags—one held what had to be marijuana, another had two tiny vials of white looking rocks, and the third had about a tablespoon of white powder Tandi assumed was cocaine. Brent was smiling at her like he had shown her his secret cache of gold coins. This, Tandi didn't need, and Brent didn't seem to notice her pulling back from him as he was busy putting two thin sheets of bamboo paper together. That's when she saw the small glass pipe. She had heard and read enough to know this tin of contraband wasn't for an anti-drug using naysayer like herself.

Tandi wrapped the sheet around her body. "I don't like this. I don't do drugs."

Brent gingerly sprinkled marijuana onto the paper held between his fingers. "Baby, this is purely recreational—it's like an aphrodisiac. I don't do hard drugs."

She looked at him like he was stupid. "Crack? Cocaine? The last time I heard, those were hard drugs."

Brent opened the bag with the cocaine in it. "Baby, I use only a little of this stuff when I'm stressed out. It mellows me out. If you had seen me when I got home this afternoon, you wouldn't've wanted to be around me."

"What? Are you saying you're high now?"

"Baby, relax. We only have to smoke one joint to get a nice buzz." He sprinkled a pinch of cocaine over the marijuana.

"*We* won't be smoking a joint."

Brent looked at her. "Don't tell me you don't smoke once in a while."

"I have never smoked. The question is, why didn't you tell me that you did?"

"It's no big deal," he replied, rolling the joint between his thumbs and forefingers.

She could not believe how delusional Brent was. Suddenly, she did not want to be there. Now she knew what she had only sensed when she felt something wasn't right. Brent was a drug user. Was this something Glynn also knew about him way back in high school?

"Baby, this is light stuff. I smoked my first joint when I was fourteen years old. I never smoked around you—you were so sweet and innocent." He leaned in to kiss Tandi.

She pulled back. "Well, don't do it around me now. I'm still innocent—or should I say naive?"

Brent stroked Tandi's cheek with the back of his hand. "Baby, you're not naive. You're sweet."

His touch left her cold. What she was, was blind. How had she not seen the signs? And now that she was thinking about it, there had been signs. Brent's eyes were always glassy, and there were times she smelled something and couldn't quite put her finger on what it was because there was always incense burning. Now that he told her, she knew the smell. When she was younger she had gone to parties and sat in movie theaters where the smoke hovered and drifted, giving nonsmokers contact highs. One time she had zonked out and bumped her head on the back of her seat. She never did get to see the movie. She didn't like it then, no way was she going to like it now.

Brent ran his tongue along the edge of the paper. "C'mon, baby," he said, quickly sealing the joint. "Don't tell me your husband never took an occasional hit."

"No, he never did," she said indignantly. She watched Brent slip the whole joint into his mouth and out again, wetting it. "Brent, I'm not comfortable with this. I don't like you doing this."

"Chill, baby. I told you it's no big deal."

"Chill? I will not chill out. Brent, I am against illegal drugs. You smoke crack, too, don't you?"

He glimpsed the glass pipe and the crack vials. "Oh, that? A friend gave me that. It's nothing. I don't mess with crack."

"Then why would your friend give you that stuff?"

"Why would anyone give me argyle socks or a red bow tie for Christmas? I have no use for them either, but I don't throw them away. Look, baby, I'm the same person I was a few minutes ago before you saw my stash. This is nothing," he said, easing the whole joint into his mouth and out again.

"You can go to jail for this."

Brent clicked his teeth. "Baby, everybody and their mamas got a stash in their house."

"I don't."

"Well, you don't count."

"I beg to differ. I do count when it comes to drugs—I'm against it, Brent. Don't you get it? This is illegal. You can be arrested for this."

"Baby, they can't lock up everybody. There would be no one left to run the country." Winking, he flicked his lighter and lit the joint.

Tandi couldn't believe Brent was smoking a joint in front of her and not caring how she felt about it. The smell was pungent. How had he kept this from her over the past four months?

Sucking hard on the joint and then holding his breath, Brent held the joint out to Tandi.

She pulled back. "No!"

Brent blew the smoke out in Tandi's direction. She covered her nose and mouth. "Come on, baby, take a drag. You can't get lung cancer from marijuana."

Turning her head, she put up her hand to ward him off. "I said no."

"This is seis, the good stuff. No seeds. Baby, take just a little one. Do it for me."

Tandi angrily shoved Brent's hand away. "I said no!"

"Damn, baby. You almost made me drop it." Brent saw that the fire had gone out. He relit the joint.

Tandi frowned at the pungent odor and the cloud of smoke surrounding her. She covered her mouth. "Put it out."

"Just a minute." He took a deeper drag. The tip burned bright.

Totally disgusted, Tandi watched as Brent sucked in the smoke, held it, puffing out his cheeks. Suddenly he leaned forward and blew the smoke right into her face.

"Brent!" she screamed, shoving him hard.

He laughed.

"Damn, Brent! This isn't funny."

"Okay, baby. I'm sorry. I just wanted you to get high with me. Sex will be even better if we're both high."

"Are you saying you're usually high when you make love to me?"

"Hell yes. That's why our sex is so damn good."

Tearing the sheet from around her body, Tandi almost fell trying to get off the bed. "I'm going home."

"Okay. Baby, damn. I'll put it out." He drew on the joint long and deep, like he was about to go under water.

Totally disgusted, Tandi began grabbing up her clothes. "I'm never coming back here!"

Brent still had not put out the joint. "Baby, c'mon." His voice was low and mellow. "Calm down. You're gonna blow my high."

Tandi ran out of the room into the bathroom across the hall. She began to immediately pull on her clothes. She could not believe Brent used drugs. Drugs never crossed her mind. If she let Brent around Michael Jared, she'd never be able to lay her head down again without worrying about whether he would expose Michael Jared to drugs.

"Okay, baby, I put it away," Brent said from the other side of the bathroom door. "I'm sorry."

Fully dressed though not feeling exactly fresh, she opened the door and pushed past him. "I have to go."

"I said I was sorry. I didn't know you didn't do a little something."

"Yes, you did," she said, slipping her feet into her shoes, "or else you would have let on months ago that you did drugs."

"Yeah, well, I tell you what. Let's make a deal. I won't do any drugs around you, and you—"

"No deal. It's no better if you're doing it behind my back."

"Baby, it doesn't affect me. You didn't even know I smoked, and I do it every day."

She was appalled. "You're absolutely right. I really didn't know, so I wonder what the real Brent Rodgers is like. The one who doesn't use drugs to bring himself down or to get it up in order to make love to me."

"Baby, I am the real Brent Rodgers. I told you, drugs don't affect who I am."

Tandi couldn't believe what he was saying. "It saddens me, Brent, that you believe your own lie. I'm leaving." She started past Brent.

He took hold of her by the waist and pulled her up against his body. "Baby, why are you so upset? It's not like I'm a junkie."

"I really hope you're not, Brent, for your sake and mine because I can't be in a relationship with you if you are."

"Baby, I'm not." He began to grind himself on Tandi's thighs. He whispered in her ear, "You feel that? That's all yours." He tongued her ear, tantalizing Tandi. "Baby, let me . . ." He began kissing her neck while he shoved his hand in between her thighs and grabbed her. ". . . put my Johnson in your sweet hot box."

She would be lying if she said Brent's hot kisses, that his hand, that his hardness against her thigh didn't feel good. Her libido had a mind of its own as she felt herself throbbing in Brent's hand. She could feel herself sinking into the asylum of sexual fantasy that she had lived in for so long. But in those fantasies she had been with another Brent Rodgers, not this drug-using liar. Not this man who could do harm to her son.

"No!" She pulled herself out of Brent's tangled embrace. She looked at the drug-induced sick little smile on his lips. "Look, I can't do this knowing you're on something."

Brent cupped himself. "You want this, don't you, baby?"

Tandi glanced at what she was giving up. She shook her head. "Not like this."

"Okay. If the smoke bothers you that much, I won't smoke around you."

"That's just it, Brent. I don't want you to smoke or do any drugs at all—whether I'm here or not." She started for the door. He followed her.

"Okay, no drugs at all—after tonight. Tomorrow, I'll be clean. You'll see."

"I will, won't I?"

She slammed the door behind her knowing she probably wouldn't be seeing him the next day.

36

For two days Brent called, leaving messages on Tandi's voice mail. He begged, he pleaded, he apologized. He swore on his soul he'd given up drugs—"I want you more than I want to get high." Tandi doubted Brent had or could give up drugs that quickly, but she wanted to believe he was trying. She could only hope he was telling the truth, but his secret drug use only made her wonder what else there was about him she didn't know about and probably couldn't handle. She stayed away from him for two days and then because she was feeling unusually tense with Sporty due home, she went back to him. She needed some release. True to his word Brent didn't bring his drugs out in front of her, but the stale, sickening smell of smoke rose above the floral room freshener he tried to mask it with. Despite that, his glistening eyes told on him, not to mention that he was overly eager to make love to her. All this time she thought he was naturally hot for her. Boy, was her ego bruised. Still, she needed to feel him inside her, filling the void that her life was so full of. She cleaved to Brent like her life depended on it. Maybe she was making a big deal out of nothing. Plenty of people used marijuana and cocaine socially and carried on productive lives, just as Brent was obviously doing.

Truth to tell, if either one of them was a junkie, it was probably her. She needed him to satisfy her emotional needs as much as her sexual ones. At times, she felt like she had to get a fix, and like a junkie, hours after she had been with Brent, that fix would wear off and her body would quiver with a yearning so powerful it would awaken her out of a deep sleep and she'd have to go back for more. Like a junkie fighting her demons, she was beginning to not feel good about what she was doing. In her weakness, she was addicted to the sex Brent temptingly held out to her. The only time the shame she felt for her weakness dissipated was when she erupted into a gloriously orgasmic release of the pent-up frustration she was feeling about having to stay in Sporty's house. Too bad that release was short-lived. Afterward, the tension returned.

What Tandi had become aware of, was that when she wasn't being made love to by Brent, thoughts of him no longer occupied her mind like they once did. In fact, the odd thing was, of late, disturbing thoughts of being made love to by Jared crept in and confused her. Where was that coming from? Such thoughts were supposed to be forever scrubbed from her mind, but they weren't. Each and every day since she discovered Brent's secret, thoughts of Jared making love to her took over where thoughts of Brent used to be. And that was weird since it had been a long, long time since they had even made love, not to mention that she didn't want Jared after what he'd done and said to Evonne.

But, Jared wasn't letting Tandi's mind rest. She was reminded that a good part of what she had known her true happiness to be had been with Jared. She could remember, oh so long ago, that their lovemaking never left her feeling empty. She would be full of him for days afterward. Just brushing up against him was enough to ignite her senses, and he used to know that. He'd touch her intimately and smile, apparently enjoying the feeling himself. That's why it hurt all the more that he had stopped making love to her and had his affairs, including the one with Evonne. The fact that he had been lusting for Evonne was hard to take and all the harder to forgive.

Evonne, on the other hand, after some soul searching, she partially forgave. A part of her would never forgive her for sleeping with Jared, while a part of her forgave her because she had been Jared's victim. Since their talk, Evonne had become annoyingly contrite. She called every day to see how she was doing, and to see if there was anything she could do to help her prepare for Sporty's homecoming. The answer was always no because she didn't want to give Evonne an excuse to come over. She wasn't ready yet to hang out with her like nothing had ever happened.

On the telephone, she did tell Evonne about Brent. Later when she

37

The walls were closing in on Tandi. Her throat was tight. It was hard to breathe. Sporty was sitting in his wheelchair across the room, ten feet away, yet Tandi felt like he was up in her face. Everything about him choked her. His gauntness was stifling. His right hand, bony and long, lay limply on his right thigh; his droopy, saliva-shiny lips were nauseating to look at; and his hair was shades grayer. For Sporty this had to be a horrible nightmare—a nightmare of his own making—but for Tandi it was horribly unfair.

Sporty glared hatefully at Tandi.

She stared at him lamely, unable to say "welcome home," unable to kiss him like a dutiful daughter, worse still, unable to feel remorse or pity for him. His angry eyes made her feel cold, inside and out. This was a mistake. She wasn't going to be able to do this. Staring at him, she hugged herself protectively.

"Dong stand thar look' at ma lack tha!" Sporty breathlessly jabbered.

"Dad, don't get excited. Calm down," Glynn said, solicitously patting him on the shoulder.

Breathing laboriously loud, Sporty's chest rose and fell like he had been running hard. A stream of saliva ran from in between his drooping lips onto his chin.

Glynn pulled his handkerchief from his pants pocket. "Tandi, don't just stare at him. Say something."

She cut her eyes at Glynn. "What do you want me to say? Welcome home, Dad?"

"Go ta hell!" Sporty spat.

"Damn, Tandi, watch what you're saying. Dad's speech is impaired, not his hearing." Glynn dabbed at Sporty's chin.

Tandi felt nauseous. "Let's be real, Glynn. He couldn't care less what I say. In fact, he'd rather I get the hell out of his house."

"Gat damn right! Get out!"

"See what I mean?"

"Well, you made him say it."

"I guess I'm the one who made him as ornery as he is, too."

"Tandi, can't we just do what we have to do?"

"Glynn, I'm going upstairs." She started out of the room, skirting Sporty's wheelchair, going behind him, out of his line of vision.

"Tandi, wait a minute." Glynn lay the soiled handkerchief on Sporty's good hand. "There are things you need to know."

"Didn't you tell me everything yesterday?"

"No, I didn't. Tandi, this isn't easy for him either. I wish you'd try getting along with him."

"Glynn, I gave up that masochistic vocation years ago."

Sporty hit the armrest of the wheelchair with his good left hand. "She dan't got ta do nuthin' fa me!" Saying that, Sporty slumped from the effort.

"God, Tandi, have a heart. You can't be getting him upset. The doctor said no stress. Look at how hard he's breathing. Can't you try and put the bad stuff between you two behind you and help him get better?"

"Look," she snapped, "don't put that burden on me. I told you, I'll stay for one month, long enough for him to begin to make progress and until he's comfortable with his health aide, who, by the way, should be here. Where is she?"

Glynn glanced at his watch. "She'll be here any minute. Her name is Rose Montero."

"Hispanic?"

"Do you have a problem with that?"

"No," she said, looking at Sporty, "but he might. You know how much of a bigot he is."

Glynn sighed. "Are you getting some sort of sick pleasure out of making this situation more difficult than it has to be?"

"If I am, I'm not enjoying it. Glynn, I just don't wanna be here."

"Look, sis, I really do understand where you're coming from, but there's only you and me. Dad can't count on anyone else but us."

"I wonder why?"

"Tandi, you don't stop, do you? Just tell me, if you need to be here past a month, will you stay?"

"Do I have a choice?" She wanted to scream. She felt trapped. "Glynn, I don't know if I can do this. You need to be more involved in overseeing his rehabilitation."

"I'm gonna try to be here as much as I can, but you know my schedule."

"You're a liar, Glynn. You're putting it all off on me."

"Damnit, Tandi! Why are you so goddamn contentious? He's your damn father, too."

She wasn't intimidated by his closeness but she stepped back anyway, out into the hall. "You can't prove that by me," she said, rubbing the back side of her neck as she turned away from Glynn.

Sporty placed his left hand behind the left wheel of his wheelchair. Straining, he slowly pulled the wheel forward, repeatedly, until he was able to turn the chair around to face Tandi and Glynn.

"Don't start, Tandi," Glynn warned in a hushed voice. "He raised us alone. He did his best."

"Well, it wasn't good enough."

"Damnit, what's wrong with you?"

Sporty glared at Tandi.

"Tell you what, Glynn. Why don't you just figure out when you can be here to relieve me."

"You know I have to travel for my job. I can't stay here."

"I'll work around your schedule."

"I don't know when I might have to leave town."

"It seems to me, Glynn, you're not willing to help your father because you're not willing to put him first."

"I won't be of any help to Dad or my family if I'm unemployed. I have to make a living."

Sporty's eyes darted from one to the other.

"And I don't?"

"You wouldn't have to if you went back home to your husband."

Tandi felt her cheeks warm. "Then I wouldn't have all this time to be here for your father, would I?"

"Aa don't nee non of yaw!" Sporty babbled.

"I've been in on his recuperation from the start. That's why I was at the hospital a hell of a lot more than you. Where were you, Tandi?"

"Aa dadn't vant har thar!"

Tandi ignored Sporty. "You want a pat on the back, Glynn? Here," she said, reaching around Glynn to pat him on the back.

Glynn pushed her hand away. "Stop it."

"No, I won't stop. You act like you should be applauded for the things you've done. Well, bully for you. It's about time you did something around here. I've been doing around this house and for him all of my life, and for what? Not an ounce of gratitude from him ever."

"I can't deal with this crap," Glynn said, walking away from Tandi.

Tandi wouldn't let up. She followed Glynn back into the living room. "Does anyone care how I feel and what I've had to do around this house? No. It was expected of me, just like now. Glynn, tell me, why have we been treated so differently by this man we both know as our father? Why does he love you and treat me like something stuck to the bottom of his miserable life?"

Sporty strained in his efforts to turn his wheelchair back around.

"Maybe if you'd ever shown him some love, he might have reciprocated."

"He's incapable of showing love to anyone, except maybe you."

Glynn scowled. "You're getting real bitter, Tandi. You better—"

"Stop! Stop!" Sporty shouted breathlessly. He angrily brought his left fist down repeatedly on the armrest of the wheelchair.

"Dad, everything's fine," Glynn said. "Take it easy. My sister and I are relating."

"Says you." Tandi cut her eyes from Glynn and narrowed her gaze on Sporty. He was wheezing. Each difficult breath gave her goose bumps. What if he stopped breathing while she was there with him alone? Glynn would blame her. Oh, God, why did she have to come back here? She should have gone to a hotel in Manhattan or even in another state. Thank God Sporty didn't have a stroke when she was a child. She might have never escaped this house. If taking care of Sporty had been her fate back then, she would have never married Jared nor would she have ever had Michael Jared. No matter that Jared had let her down, she would never trade the life she once had with him for a minute of taking care of Sporty. As soon as this Rose Montero person was settled in, she was out of there.

Glynn was patting Sporty on the back. "Okay, Dad, it's all right. Tandi and I are through relating. Aren't we, sis?"

"If you say so, brother of mine."

Sporty shook his head. So did Glynn.

"Tandi, can we please call a truce? Can we end this?"

For Tandi it would never end, but she was tired of fighting. In the end, she was going to have to be in the house anyway, so what the hell. At least she let Glynn know what she thought of his pushing Sporty off on her.

Buzzzz!

"I have nothing more to say," she said, starting for the door. "Oh, by the way, Dad. Iona Lewis keeps calling. She wants to come by to see you."

"No!" Sporty exclaimed.

Tandi stopped moving toward the door. "Why not? She could be a big help to you." *And me!*

"No!"

"He doesn't want her over, Tandi, and you know that. Leave it alone."

"This is a fine time for him to break up with her."

Buzzzz!

"Tandi, it's his decision. Let it go. Are you gonna open the damn door or not?"

Tandi opened the door. It was the health aide, and Tandi could not have been happier. "Miss Montero?"

"Yes."

"Please, come in. I'm Tandi Crawford."

Rose Montero gave a little nod as she went past Tandi.

"Hello, Rose," Glynn said, rushing over and shaking her hand. "It's good to see you again."

"Thank you," she said, her accent evident. She swiftly scanned the room before looking at Sporty.

Glynn led Rose over to him. "Rose, this is your patient, Glynn Belson."

Rose put her hand out to Sporty.

He sneered at her and turned his head.

Sporty's rudeness irked Tandi. She huffed and turned away.

Rose lowered her hand to her oversized tote bag.

"Don't mind him," Glynn said. "This is his first day home so he's not in the best of moods."

"Yeah, right," Tandi mumbled.

"Aa dong nee . . . nobody!"

Tandi was biting at the bit, trying hard to not say anything.

Again, Glynn put his hand on Sporty's shoulder. "Dad, Rose is here to help you. She—"

"No!" Again Sporty brought his left hand down hard on the arm of the wheelchair. "Out ma house!"

"Glynn," Tandi said, "I think you should tell your father to calm down and be nice before he ends up here by himself. No one has to put up with his shit."

Sporty hit the arm of the wheelchair again, making it rattle. "Gatdamnit!"

Glynn rubbed Sporty's shoulder. "Tandi, you're not helping the situation. It's going to take time for Dad to get used to the idea that he needs help. It's up to us to help him even though he doesn't want our help."

Tandi smirked. "You want my help? Fine. I'll help." She turned to Rose. "Rose, it's nearly time for lunch. I'll show you the kitchen. I bought some soup so you don't have to cook today. If you want to put your things down, there is a small room down the hall on the left."

"Thank you," Rose said, uncertain if she should go off alone.

"Come," Tandi said, "I'll show you the way." As she left the room, Tandi said to Glynn, "Why don't you take your father—"

"Tandi!" Glynn exclaimed.

Sporty glared angrily at Tandi. His bottom lip trembled.

Tandi knew she was being childish, but she felt like the angry child who lived inside her for so many years was screaming to get out and confront Sporty while he was weak and unable to silence her voice. The whole time she was bitching with Glynn, she was aware of the angry glint in Sporty's eyes. There never seemed to be a time when it wasn't there. His stroke had not put that glint there; it had been there for years. As a child, it frightened her. He frightened her. Now that look angered her. It made her want to lash out at him, no matter what his condition.

"Glynn, why don't you get *our* father settled in his bedroom." She strutted off down the hall, taking Rose along with her. "Rose, I hope you're made of strong stock."

38

"Yo no necesito esto!" I do not need this!

"Rose! Rose! Hold still!" Tandi trotted alongside Rose swiping at her white blouse with a bunch of paper towels trying to sop up the chicken broth and noodles sticking to her, but it was like chasing behind a two-year-old. She couldn't get Rose to stand still long enough to clean her up.

"Rose, I have a T-shirt you can wear."

"No!" Rose angrily tried to pull her jacket on over her soiled blouse. *"Yo no soy un animal!"* I am not an animal!

The word *animal* Tandi understood. Whatever else Rose was saying Tandi didn't have a clue, but it was clear Rose didn't like it one bit that Sporty had knocked the bowl of hot chicken noodle soup off the tray onto the floor. If Rose had not jumped back, all of it would have been all over her instead of the few strings of noodles and splatterings of broth that landed on the front of her white cotton blouse. Thank God she was fast on her feet or else she could have been burned.

"Yo no necesito esto!"

Tandi continued to swipe at Rose's blouse while Rose, fumbling with her buttons, tried to button her polyester jacket. When she was done, the jacket was buttoned wrong—the right side at the bottom was longer than the left.

"Let me help you," Tandi said, trying to rebutton the jacket.

Rose slapped at her hands. "No!"

"I'm trying to help."

"Yo no soy un animal!" Rose said again. Grabbing up her tote bag,

Rose stomped out of the back room. At Sporty's bedroom door she stopped and pointed at him. *"El es muy malo!"* He is very bad!

"I know, I know," Tandi said, though she wasn't sure what she was agreeing to. She tried to hold Rose still. "Rose, please stay. Don't go. I'll make it up to you."

"No!"

Tandi glanced fleetingly into Sporty's bedroom. He was still sitting on the side of the bed facing the door, but he wasn't looking out into the hall. He was staring straight at the wall. Etched into his face was an extremely bitter glower. Oh, God. Rose had to stay. Tandi did not want to be alone with that look.

"Rose, I promise, I won't let him do that to you again. I promise."

Rose shrugged Tandi's arm off of her. "No! *Voy a casa!*" I am going home! she said, stalking off.

"See what you did!" Tandi shouted at Sporty as she started off after Rose. "Please, Rose, I need you."

"Malo, malo! Él es un hombre muy malo!" Bad, bad! He is a very bad man! Rose yanked open the front door.

"Rose, if you stay, I'll give you a raise."

Stopping outside the door, Rose turned back. *"No! No trabajare para un tan mal hombre!"* No! I will not work for such a bad man!

"I don't understand. Speak English."

"No!"

"Oh, God, Rose. Please stay."

"No trabajare aquí." I will not work here! she said, flipping her hand at Tandi as she turned and stalked off. *"Voy a casa!"* I am going home!

Tandi watched helplessly as Rose bustled angrily down the street. Rose hadn't lasted two hours. What in the world was she going to do? Who was going to clean up that mess? Who was going to tend to Sporty until the evening attendant came? Going back inside the house, Tandi slammed the door, shaking the two chrome picture frames on the wall on either side of the door. It was no surprise that Sporty had acted out—that was his raison d'être. His anger was all that was driving him. This time he was angry because while he struggled to feed himself with his left hand, soup spilled from his open mouth, which he could not as yet close all the way. Tandi had seen that. She had stood outside his room peeking in at him. She wanted to see for herself what he could or could not do for himself. She saw that he grew more agitated as he kept spilling the soup on the tray, on himself. Very little got into his mouth. The more Rose tried to help him, the angrier he became. When Sporty caught her watching, he knocked the bowl over and started ranting in that garbled way of his. He quieted down only when he got what he wanted—Rose bailing out.

And now, Tandi had visions of putting her hands around Sporty's neck and choking the meanness out of him. She was itching to get at him. She started back to his room, stopped halfway there, turned abruptly and went instead into the living room and snatched up the telephone.

As soon as Glynn came on the line, she said, "Your father just dumped his soup all over Rose."

"Aw, man. How is she?"

"Gone. She quit."

"Aw, damn."

"Glynn, you had better get someone over here, right now."

"Tandi, I can't guarantee—"

"I don't wanna hear it, Glynn. I will leave this old man in this house by himself in a heartbeat."

"You wouldn't do that."

"Try me." Slamming down the receiver, Tandi angrily thrust her hand on her hip and began to pace. She went out into the hallway and stood looking down the hall at the bedroom door. "You old fart." She wanted to burst into Sporty's bedroom and tell him in no uncertain terms what she thought about him. However, one stroke on her watch was one stroke too many. She stayed where she was, listening. She was expecting to hear Sporty spouting some unintelligible nonsense but he was eerily quiet and that irritated her even more. She wanted him to bitch, to raise holy hell. She wanted him to be his usual mean, old cantankerous self, bitching just for the hell of hearing himself make a fuss, so she'd have an excuse to rush screaming out of his house just as Rose had. The question was, why wasn't he bitching?

Curious, Tandi began tiptoeing down the hall.

Riiing!

She rushed back into the living room and snatched up the receiver. "Yes!"

"The agency said it's impossible to—"

"I don't wanna hear the word *impossible*, Glynn. I can't do this alone. If you can't get someone over here, I suggest you get over here yourself."

"I can't."

"But you will."

"Tandi, be reasonable. I have to work this afternoon. I took off this morning. Someone will be there tomorrow morning. Elise Gary will be there at six this evening. Can't you just—"

"No, I can't!" Tandi's fist was balled up tight. "Listen to me, Glynn. If I am left alone with that man, I will either ignore him and forget he's even in that room, or I will kill him the first time he looks at me crooked."

"Oh, man. Tandi, please—"

"Glynn! I am going to kick your ass . . . no. I am going to kick my own ass for letting you talk be into staying here."

"Tandi, I—"

Slam!

She couldn't stand to hear another word out of Glynn's mouth. She was so angry, she wanted to scream. How had it all gone so wrong so fast? Maybe leaving Jared hadn't been such a good idea after all; nothing had been right since. At least with Jared, there had been some order in her life. Maybe, in hindsight, there was more she could have done to reignite the passion of her failing marriage. Now it was too late. She had destroyed everything. The tears that filled her eyes were not for the dissipation of her marriage alone, but for the demise of who she used to be—a woman with a map of the roads her life was supposed to travel. All of those roads had success along the way in the early years of her marriage, in her career, and in her role as mother. Somewhere along the way, she went off track. None of those roads were supposed to lead back to Sporty's house where she found herself not liking the person she had become—angry and bitter just like Sporty. Maybe like him she had begun to wallow in self-pity. If she didn't stop, she could kiss the person she longed to recognize in her mirror good-bye.

"I cannot let this setback break me," she said to herself, squaring her shoulders. She had work to do. The sooner Sporty was mobile or at least capable of doing for himself, the sooner she could get on with her own life.

She collected the plastic garbage container and a long length of damp paper towels from the kitchen and headed for Sporty's bedroom. At his door she was met with an amazing sight: Sporty had gotten himself into his wheelchair. He was slumped awkwardly over the arm of the wheelchair and was trying to clean up the noodles and greasy broth off the floor with a handful of bunched-up tissues. The tissues were soaked and wadded up in his left hand. His right arm dangled lamely at his side a few inches from the floor. His left foot was on the floor while his right foot was still on the foot rest. Tandi was amazed that Sporty would even try to clean up his own mess. It was the last thing she expected.

"I'll get that," she said, entering the room, though not looking at him. She set the open garbage container down on the floor.

Sporty let the wet tissues drop to the floor.

Tandi looked at the messy tissues. If this had been another time, Sporty would have tossed the tissues into the container—always going for a three-point shot. Tandi picked up the tissues and tossed them in herself. Then, squatting, she began to quickly sop up the mess.

"You can sit up," she said. "I'll finish it."

Sporty said nothing at first. Several seconds later, he grunted.

Without looking at him directly, Tandi saw Sporty hadn't moved. She continued to wipe only inches from his foot.

He grunted again.

Now she did look. Sporty's head was cocked to his left shoulder, his face was strained, veins popped at his temples and on his neck. His and Tandi's eyes met. What she saw, fleetingly, in his eyes was sadness. He couldn't sit up. He was paralyzed on the right side of his body and had no muscle strength to pull himself upright. His eyes closed, but Tandi continued to look at him and was stunned to see a tear bead up between his lids. What she felt at that moment surprised even her—pity.

Dropping the paper towels into the garbage container, she got up off the floor. She knew what had to be done and so did Sporty. Neither said anything when she took hold of his shoulders and pulled him upright in his chair.

"Daddy, do you need anything?"

Sporty held his head high. His eyes remained closed, his face remained unchanged. He had shut down.

It was just as well. Tandi knew Sporty hated that she had seen how helpless he was. He had shut down because he did not want her to also see the helplessness in his eyes or hear it in his voice. Respecting Sporty's withdrawal, Tandi picked up the garbage container, and leaving the room, pulled the door up behind her. Outside his room, unbeckoned tears fell. Tandi stomped her foot.

I won't shed a single tear for him. I won't feel sorry for him.

That helpless old man was the same man who, months ago, said she was some bastard's child. He was the same man who made her life miserable from the time she could first remember being pushed away from climbing up onto his lap. No, she would not cry for him. No.

The tears came anyway.

39

Dropping his cue stick, MJ scampered up the basement stairs to the kitchen. He picked up the ringing telephone on the fourth ring. "Hi, Mommy!"

"Hey, son. How's my boy? Did you miss me?"

MJ quickly realized that the person on the other end wasn't Tandi. "Daina! Hi. I thought you were my mother."

"Well, aren't I? I'm your godmother. That doesn't count?"

"Yeah. Did you bring me a souvenir from Africa?"

"Kid, I better get a big hug and a kiss for what I brought you. It weighs more than I do and cost dearly to bring back."

Excited, MJ jumped. "It's big? What did you bring me?"

"It's a surprise."

"When am I gonna get it?"

"Whenever I get over there."

"Come tonight. I can stay up late on Friday nights."

"Lucky you," Daina said. "Where's your mother?"

"At Granddad's house."

"This late? Is he sick?"

"Uh-huh. He had a stroke."

"My God. How bad is it?"

"He can't walk."

"Geez. What time is your mother coming home?"

"She don't live here no more."

"What? What do you mean, 'She don't live here no more?'"

"She don't," MJ said, lowering his voice. He glanced over at the open basement door.

"Is this just until your granddad gets better?"

"No. She's getting us an apartment, and me and her are gonna live by ourselves. Daina, can me and my dad come and get my souvenir?"

"Michael Jared, wait a minute. I'm not getting this. Tandi doesn't live with you and Jared anymore?"

"No. They separated."

"What?"

"Mommy don't like my dad no more."

"Geez. I go away and my friends lose their ever-loving minds. Michael Jared, what's your—"

"Everybody calls me MJ now."

"Is that so? MJ, huh? Well, MJ, what else don't I know? Are you still a kid or have you graduated college and gotten married since I've been gone?"

"How I'm gonna go to college and get married when I'm only eleven years old?"

"Hey, seems to me anything can happen," Daina said. "Michael Jared, what's the telephone number at your Granddad's house?"

"If you're gonna call Mommy, she's not back yet."

"Back from where?"

"She went to visit a friend. She said she'd call me when she got back. She hasn't called yet."

"Where's your father?"

"He's down in the basement. He's teaching me to play pool. We got a new pool table. It's real cool."

"Tell your father that Herb and I . . . no, that I'll be over there in forty-five minutes. We have to talk."

"Are you gonna bring my souvenir?"

"Maybe. If there's a big kiss in it for me."

"A real big kiss."

"Hang up the phone, little man. I'm on my way."

Smiling broadly, MJ hurried back down to the basement. "Dad, Daina's coming over, and she got me a big souvenir."

40

Daina had said, "I don't believe this," no more times than Jared had said it to himself over the past five months. Time, however, made a believer out of him. He was now used to Tandi not living there. She still came to the house three times a week when he wasn't home to cook dinner for MJ and wash and iron his clothes. As for his own clothes, Jared had long since discovered the Chinese laundry and the cleaners near his job. What he couldn't take care of as easily was his mind. Tandi was forever on his mind. Every time he looked at the chaise longue in the bedroom where she liked to sit and read or watch television, he thought about her. It was her chair. To this day he had never sat on it. It was an antique that she paid fifteen hundred dollars for. Most likely she'd be taking the chaise with her when she moved into her own place. The bedroom still held so many of Tandi's personal items. Some of her clothes and shoes were still in the closet. There were perfumes on the dresser, and stray pieces of jewelry lay there just as she had left them, like she would return at any minute. He left her things as they were simply because he felt they were in the place they were supposed to be and saw no reason to move them.

In the distance, far up on the top floor, came a rapid tapping on the murumbu drum Daina had brought for MJ. The pot-shaped drum was bigger than he was, yet MJ managed to drag it up the stairs to his room himself and had been beating on it ever since, leaving Jared and Daina to talk.

"Jared, how in the world did you let that she-wolf manipulate you like that?"

"I didn't let her do anything. If I did anything at all, I let myself get drunk."

"That was stupid."

Like he needed to be told that. With no defense to argue, Jared held his tongue. Daina was going to speak her mind anyway.

"Okay, I'm not gonna get hysterical here. It happened, it's done. The question is, Jared, what are you going to do to get your wife back?"

"Daina, Tandi won't talk to me. In fact, I haven't seen her for more than a hot minute in two months. MJ tells me that as soon as Tandi can get away from her father, she's getting her own place. It's her decision. There's nothing I can do."

Tilting her head slightly, Daina peered at Jared. "Do I know you?"

Hell, he didn't know if he knew himself anymore, but still he didn't like the way Daina was looking at him. He had expected that she would be disgusted with him for sleeping with Evonne and even for taking his marriage for granted, but he didn't expect her to look at him like he had drowned a bag of kittens. Besides Tandi, Daina was the only other person who knew him better than he knew himself.

He and Daina had known each other since junior high and had tried to date once in their sophomore year in high school. However, they learned pretty quickly they were better off being friends than boyfriend and girlfriend. They couldn't get the hang of kissing and holding hands after having told each other for years about their romantic encounters—good and bad—with other people. They knew each other too well. There was no mystery, there was no excitement. But they did know what each liked in a partner. When Daina met Tandi, she called him right away.

"Have I got the girl for you."

And she did. He and Tandi hit it off right away. They were magic together. On their wedding day, Daina told the two of them, "Make me proud." The fact that he had let Daina down only added to his guilt.

"Okay, Daina, enough with the look. Say what's on your mind," he said, wanting to get the scolding over with.

"Right now, I'm thinking about your parents, especially your mother."

"And what does my mother have to do with this?"

"If she were alive, she'd be ashamed of you."

"Well, damn! Thanks a lot."

"Jared, wake up, man!" Daina said, rapidly popping her fingers.

"You're like a fat old frog sitting on a lily pad waiting for a fly to happen by. Did Evonne's caustic juices fry your brain?"

"Don't mess with my head, Daina. I've been having a hard enough time as it is."

"I bet you have," she agreed, "but let me see if I understand this. Tandi leaves you, you sleep with Evonne, Tandi says don't talk to her, you do as she says then you hide here in the house like a schoolboy who got caught with one hand in the cookie jar and the other in his pants, and do nothing to get her back. Is that what's been going on around here?"

"I'm not hiding."

"Then what are you doing? Jared, this isn't you. The Jared I know never waited to be chosen for anything. My Jared stepped up and demanded a spot on the track team even though he had failed the qualifying meet and went on to become the school's track star. My Jared demanded to be heard by the principal when the school cut back on funds for musical instruments. That Jared organized the students and raised money for new instruments and you couldn't play a lick on anything. Jared, do you remember that fighter? The guy you used to act like?"

Jared sat resting his chin on his fist.

"Come on, Jared. Take a memory pill. I remember when you wanted to start your own practice a year out of law school because you didn't like being an associate. You said associates were underpaid research flunkies for the partners of that Wall Street law firm you worked for. You went out on a limb and started a practice in a storefront on Hillside Avenue the size of a closet. Jared, you forged ahead against all odds of pulling in clients, most of whom were older than you were. That Jared? I admired his tenacity. What in the world happened to him?"

Sitting back, letting his body go limp, Jared returned Daina's questioning gaze. Maybe she was right. Somewhere in all this mess he had lost himself.

"Look at you, Jared. You look like a wet washcloth. Since when do you give up on something you want? Oh, but maybe I'm wrong. Maybe it isn't Tandi you want."

That was never a question in his mind, but there was a truth to be faced. "Daina, I deal with tangibles. Tandi hasn't given me any tangible signs that she will ever forgive me."

"You see, that's part of your problem. You've been a wuss ever since you cheated on Tandi the first time."

"What did you say? A wooze?"

"Did I stutter? I said wuss or would you prefer punk? Jared, you had so much guilt from that affair, you tiptoed around Tandi, afraid to even sneeze in her direction. Personally, I think that's why you had a problem getting it up for her."

The nape of Jared's neck warmed. "Damn. Who didn't Tandi tell?"

"Obviously, just you. So when are you gonna do something about that problem?"

Jared felt like two cents. Of course Daina would know everything about he and Tandi's marriage, but he wasn't about to talk to her about his inadequacy.

"I'm not discussing that." He got up from his chair.

"I don't see why not. That's part of the problem. Jared, you did what you did, get over it and give Tandi a reason to get over it."

"How can I? She won't talk to me, remember? And she is planning to divorce me."

Daina leaped to her feet and rushed at Jared, punching him hard in the stomach, knocking the wind out of him. He fell back down in his chair.

Bent over, Jared clutched his stomach. "Damn, Daina! Why are you so angry with me?"

"Because you're making me sick!" Daina began to pace. "Jared, I don't like seeing you like this. I don't blame Tandi; I wouldn't want your wussy ass back either."

Jared sat up. "Can you make me feel any better about myself?"

"I'm not trying to make you feel better about yourself. Personally . . ."

"Here we go."

". . . I wanna set a cherry bomb off under your ass."

"Why are you putting this all off on me?"

"Because you dropped the ball. I told you that three years ago. But did you listen to me? No, you didn't. Jared, my brother, you know I love you. I stood by you when you did Tandi wrong the first time."

"That's not what I recall. You stopped speaking to me for about two months."

"Let's not split hairs. Of course I was pissed with you, but I stood by both you and Tandi. While I wasn't speaking to you, I was pleading your case to Tandi even though I wanted to kick your ass. If you're gonna screw around, you should make it your business to not get caught."

"Humph, humph, humph," Jared said, shaking his head. "You have some nerve to beat up on me when you have such a warped sense of fidelity."

"Excuse me, but I'm no hypocrite—I know whereof I speak. Yes, Herb is my husband, but Herb, as you know, has problems that Viagra can't fix, and I'm far from closing up shop."

"But how can you look Herb in the face after you've been with someone else?"

"Because I'm not throwing what I do in his face. I love Herb, Jared. He's a great person and we're fabulous together. Why should I divorce Herb because he can't do anything for me sexually? If sex was what our marriage was based on, then it would have ended after his surgery for testicular cancer. Herb never recovered from that surgery or the radiation treatments. His doctors said that he should have, but he didn't. It was bad enough that we would never be able to have children together, but it was even worse when his desire to have sex was prematurely cut off with his balls. And since I didn't hold Herb's balls in my hands at the altar, I wasn't about to desert the man. Therefore, I know how to be discreet. I respect Herb by making sure he never knows if or when I do anything extracurricular."

"And that makes it right?"

"It makes it respectable, but I'm not the one on the hot seat, you are. Tandi forgave you your indiscretion because you made her believe you were sorry and that she was the most important person in the world to you."

"And it was the truth, except Tandi didn't really forgive me. That indiscretion, as you call it, is what she holds over my head."

"That's because you wounded that part of her that made her believe in you. Wounds like that are hard to heal, Jared, and usually never close completely. There is always a scab. And when the one who caused that scab in the first place picks at it, it bleeds all over again."

"I don't see where I did anything wrong after that affair. When Tandi left me, I hadn't done anything. Hell, Evonne hadn't even happened yet."

"Don't even mention that skank's name with her messy self. What you did wrong, Jared, was that you stopped paying Tandi, the woman, any attention. And I guarantee you, she associated that with your cheating on her."

Jared's hand dropped from his stomach. "How many times was I supposed to tell Tandi I was working, trying to make a good living for her? Why can't she understand that?"

"Jared, Tandi's not stupid. She understood that," Daina said, mo-seying over to her chair and sitting down. "What she probably couldn't understand is why you let your work form a wedge between you two. On some level, she sees your work, your career, as a mistress that you see every day, which means you're cheating her out of the love and af-fection you promised when you married her."

"Oh, that's bull."

"Okay, Mr. Stubborn, Mr. Hardhead. Don't tell me later that I didn't explain this to you, but we can stop talking about this. The pro-blem you have to deal with now is saving your marriage."

"I don't think it's salvageable."

"Geez, Jared, do try to grab onto an ounce of optimism, please."

Dropping his head back, Jared chuckled. It was all too funny. Maybe that was it. He hadn't allowed himself the luxury of being op-timistic. At this point, he was enjoying being with MJ and for the mo-ment, that was all he could handle.

"I'll admit that I do want Tandi back, but . . ."

"But?"

". . . but I'm no longer up to scraping my knees raw to get her to give me the time of day."

"Jared, you don't have to crawl. In fact, Tandi wouldn't want you to crawl. Hell, she's like me. She likes strong men, men who take charge, men who are decision makers, men who know what they want. You are one of those men, Jared—that is when you're yourself. Look at you, you look like you're about to cry."

Jared closed his eyes. He could hear MJ pounding away on his drum. At least he was enjoying himself, while the pounding was be-ginning to give him a headache. Daina was wrong. He wasn't even close to crying. He was all cried out. Of course he wouldn't dare tell Daina that he had already cried, more than once. She'd have a fit. Yes, he wanted Tandi back so badly that it hurt to even think about it at times. More importantly, their breakup was hurting his practice. And wasn't that ironic? One of the issues that had come between them, he had lost interest in. He worked the cases that demanded his attention, but most afternoons he left the office in Raoul's and Marci's capable hands while he went off with MJ. He would check in before closing just to make sure that everything was all right, but if he didn't get it to-gether soon, his practice would suffer.

"Jared, if you want Tandi back, you're going to have to pull yourself out of this deep funk."

"Actually," he said, settling back, "I've gotten to be quite comfortable in this funk. It feels like a big old easy chair cradling me in the midst of the mess I've made."

"That frog on the lily pad again," Daina said. "Damn, Jared, you might be a lost cause."

MJ's pounding was beginning to sound more rhythmic, but Jared wished he'd put it away for the night an hour ago. It was getting to be nine-thirty.

"Where's your sense of humor, Daina? I'm no more comfortable in this funk than I am sitting here listening to you harangue me."

"Thank God. Because you don't have time for self-pity, brother. You scared me. I was worried about you."

"So what do you propose I do?"

"First of all, I propose that I go see Tandi."

That got Jared's attention. "When?"

"Tonight, tomorrow, as soon as I speak to her. I'm gonna get on her behind for not doing what I told her to do."

"And what was that?"

Daina smiled devilishly.

"What?" Jared asked.

"Now, don't be mad, but I told Tandi—mind you this was three years ago when you cheated on her—to go out and get herself a man packing one the size of a horse and ride his ass to death."

Forgetting that his stomach was sore, Jared jumped right out of his chair. "How could you tell her that? You're supposed to be my friend."

"I'm Tandi's friend, too."

"That's what Evonne said just before she betrayed her."

"Boy, don't make me come over there and show you what I learned in that self-defense class," Daina warned seriously. "For your information, I told Tandi that to keep her from leaving you."

"Was that advice supposed to make her stay? I'm glad you're not a lawyer."

"Hey, if getting laid by another man would have kept your 'happy' home intact, I was all for it. You weren't taking care of Tandi, Jared. Tandi was love deprived and sexually frustrated. An affair might've put a smile on her face and some excitement in her life."

"Daina, does your brain know what's coming out of your mouth? I'm in this mess in the first place because of an affair."

"And that's because you got caught, stupid."

"That's it. I'm through talking to you." Jared went to the liquor cabinet. "I don't think I ever realized how warped your thinking was." He poured himself a glass of warm sparkling seltzer water.

"My thinking might be warped to you but the French and the Italians can vouch for it. But I'm telling you, Jared. Get your ass in gear and figure out what you really want, because, if I know Tandi, she isn't sitting in her father's house twiddling her thumbs."

Jared gulped down his water.

"Yuck. At least put some ice in it."

"Yeah, it was nasty," he admitted.

"I bet it was. By the way, Michael Jared—"

"MJ."

"Yeah, him," Daina said. "He said Tandi went out tonight. I wonder with whom. Jared, aren't you curious?"

"No," he lied.

"Well, I am."

Jared tried to be cool. "So you're going to try to see her tonight?"

"You bet your ass I am. Tandi knew how to reach me and didn't call me one time to let me know what was going on back here. And neither did you, by the way."

"Could it be that neither one of us wanted to spoil your vacation?"

"How considerate of you both. Spoiling my homecoming is so much better."

"Daina, you're too full of yourself. As awesome as you are, there was nothing you could have done for me or Tandi."

"I'm gonna make you eat your words."

"Okay, we'll see."

MJ was pounding off beat again. Jared glanced up at the ceiling. He glanced at the wall clock. It was nine-forty. "It's time for the drummer boy to cut it out."

"He just needs lessons."

"Daina, would you do something for me?"

"Of course."

"When you see Tandi, don't shove me down her throat."

"I hadn't intended to. My goal is to find out who she's seeing," Daina teased. "It might be someone I can play with."

"Daina, you have problems."

"Not me, brother." Daina stood. "You. If you get your head straight, and if Tandi is playing around, she'll put her play toy aside like a pair of snagged panty hose."

"You're not leaving, are you?"

"Actually, I'm staying until Tandi calls. Right now, I'm going upstairs to show Michael Jared—"

"MJ," Jared corrected.

"He's serious about that MJ thing, huh?"

"Very."

"Well, I am going up to show *MJ* how to beat on that thing."

"It's late, Daina, and I don't know if the neighbors can hear the noise or not. Besides, I have a headache, and you don't know how to play that thing anyway."

"I beg your pardon. I was shown by a tribesman, personally."

"Where was Herb while you were getting personal instructions?"

"Boy, get your mind out of the gutter. Herb took pictures of me getting real drumming lessons. I'll show them to you as soon as they're developed."

Jared rolled his eyes. "I can't wait."

MJ's pounding escalated.

"MJ!" Jared shouted up the stairs. "That's enough! Put it away."

MJ shouted back, "Five more minutes, okay?"

"No! Not one more second. Put it away or I'll take it away. It's time for bed anyway."

"Aw, Dad. And Mommy didn't call yet."

"Aw, Dad," Daina mimicked, sticking out her lower lip.

"Don't start, Daina. I'm tired of you, too."

"Yes, but you can't do anything to me. In fact, you need me." She playfully punched Jared in the arm.

"Unfortunately."

"Hey, show some gratitude. I'm about to single-handedly save your marriage. How do you like me now, brother man? Don't you just love me?"

"Not as much as you love yourself."

"Oh, but you will. Now, what do you have to drink around here besides hot seltzer water?"

"Ginger ale, fruit punch, orange juice."

Daina reclined on the sofa. She reached for the remote control. "Nothing for adults, huh?"

"I thought you weren't drinking anything stronger than ginger ale since Herb stopped drinking."

"Remember, I don't drink around him—don't wanna tempt the boy—but I do have a taste when he's not around, and tonight, he's not around."

"It's getting late. Shouldn't you call him?"

"He knows I'm here. He told me to tell you he'll stop by tomorrow."

"Tell him to bring his best chess game. I've been practicing."

Daina chuckled softly. "Like that'll make a difference."

"Thanks a lot." Jared stood at the bottom of the basement stairs. "When does Herb go back to work?"

"Monday."

"What about you? Are you done traveling for a while?"

"Until August. After I turn in my article, I'm taking a break. I'm tired of traveling."

"As a senior travel editor, Daina, I don't know how you can say that."

"Easy. I'm tired of lugging suitcases and sleeping in everybody else's bed but my own. And believe me, I'm beginning to hate fancy hotel food."

"So are you gonna eventually stop traveling?"

"I'm thinking about it. I mean really, where haven't I been?"

"What will you do?"

Daina shrugged. "Try my hand at my first love."

"Ahh." Jared smiled. He nodded. "I think you should. You'd be a great writer."

Daina took the compliment with a smile. "Imagine the tales I could create using all the exotic places I've been to as backdrops."

"I can imagine them banning your titles from public schools."

"Oh, they wouldn't do that. I'm a good girl," Daina said coyly, fluttering her lashes.

"Yeah, right—good and nasty. I'm going out to get you your Remy Martin," Jared said, stretching, "before I change my mind." He was tired but he could use the fresh air.

Feeling weary from her flight, Daina yawned and stretched also. "Is anything open this late around here?"

"There's a liquor store down on Hillside near Francis Lewis Boulevard that's usually open. I'll be back in a few.

Jared took his time driving down to Hillside Avenue. Daina had given him a lot to think about. He'd never tell Daina—her head was big enough—but he felt infinitely better now that she was back. If anyone in the world could get Tandi to talk to him again, it would be Daina. At least he prayed that she could.

41

The magic was gone. Brent had made love to Tandi, and she hadn't felt a thing beyond the assault on her body. She didn't throb, her skin didn't tingle, no beads of sweat rolled down between her breasts, and the orgasmic release that she had counted on to sustain her sanity hadn't been achieved. Brent had worked hard on top of her, yet it wasn't the magic he had performed so many times before, satisfying her, making her feel, at least for a little while, that she was loved. She had selfishly turned a blind eye to his drug use because he was taking care of the bothersome itch that had to be satisfied, but it seemed of late she wasn't itching anymore. Maybe hating Brent's drug use was putting a damper on enjoying sex with him as well as being with him. Even now she watched as he went off into the bathroom, knowing full well that he was cloistering himself away in there to smoke. That was his routine—before they made love and after they made love.

Tandi turned her back to the door and drew her body up tight. The realization that Brent needed to get high before he could make love to her did very little for her self-esteem. It wasn't Brent who desired her, it was the drugs.

The bathroom door opened. Brent came out and immediately closed the door behind him. He lay down next to Tandi, snuggling up close to her back. His hand moved slowly up and down the side of her body from her waist to her thigh.

"I can't get enough of you," he said.

She could feel him. He was ready to make love to her again. The problem was, she wasn't ready. She pulled away. "You're high."

"No, baby," he said, drawing Tandi back up against his body, holding her while planting wet kisses on her neck and shoulder.

She cringed, tightening her muscles.

"C'mon, baby, relax. I got something real good for you."

What Brent had for her was pressed against her behind. She shifted her body a few inches away.

Brent moved with Tandi. He continued kissing her on the neck while rubbing himself on Tandi's naked behind in areas that made her squeeze her buttocks tight.

"No, Brent, I don't take it that way."

"Aw, baby, we should try new things."

Tandi hooked her legs over the side of the bed and pulled herself out of Brent's embrace. She sat up. "I said no," she said, twisting sideways to look at him.

He rolled onto his back. "Damn, you're in a bad mood. What's your problem?"

"Frankly, Brent, I still don't like that you're using drugs. You promised me that you'd quit."

"I did."

"Don't do that, Brent. Don't lie to my face. I know what you've been doing."

Brent fixed his eyes on the ceiling. "Okay. I won't do it again. You satisfied?"

"No, because you've said that before."

Brent's eyes were slowly closing and opening. "I mean it this time."

Tandi got off the bed and stood naked before Brent. She thought she could deal with him using drugs, but she was wrong. She worried constantly that she would not be able to keep him from meeting MJ. She could not take that chance.

"Brent, I think we should stop seeing each other for a while."

"Baby, when you see me tomorrow, I won't smoke anything."

"You're not listening to me, Brent. I won't be coming tomorrow." When she saw that his eyes were closed, she realized he really wasn't listening. She began snatching up her bra and panties. "I'm going to take a shower."

A strong pungent smell hit Tandi in the face when she opened the bathroom door. Her breath caught in her throat as she tried to not inhale. She quickly closed the door back.

"That's it. I'm done."

"Baby, what's wrong?" Brent asked from the bedroom.

"I can't take a shower because the bathroom smells like . . . like toxic smoke."

Brent came to the door. "Sorry, baby. I don't have a window in there so I can't air it out."

"It wouldn't matter if you did." She stomped off toward the kitchen where she'd have to wash up in the sink.

"Baby, I'm sorry." Brent waited until Tandi was in the kitchen, out of sight, before he rushed back into the bedroom and closed the door.

In the kitchen Tandi used paper towels to wash herself down, roughly drawing the cheap, flimsy wet towels across her skin, growing more irritable because they were shredding.

"He's a damn drug addict," she said under her breath. "I'm not doing this anymore."

Brent reopened the bedroom door. "Baby, what did you say?" He walked casually into the kitchen, still naked, as he rubbed his hands together.

"I said I'm not doing this anymore!" She yanked on her panties.

"Baby, I won't do it again," he said, trying to take Tandi into his arms.

"No, Brent." She pulled herself free of him. "I'm through asking you to give up drugs."

"I told you I would. I promise."

Tandi pulled on her bra. "Don't make promises you can't keep," she said, realizing she had said the very same thing to Jared. Boy, how funny was that? While she was hooking her bra in the back, Brent slipped his arms around her waist. He lay his head on her shoulder, trying to nestle in the crook of her neck. She felt like her skin was crawling. She pulled her head back. When Michael Jared was a baby, he had lain on her like that but he had been her baby and on the rare occasion he did it now, he was sick, and still she was his mother. She enjoyed comforting him. Brent's mother, she was not. She could feel his weakness. It disgusted her.

"Baby, I don't wanna lose you," he whined.

Tandi peeled Brent's arms from around her and stepped back. "Then take several months to clean yourself up. Get some help."

"It won't take but a week, but I'll do it for you, baby," he said, again trying to pull Tandi into his arms.

"Do it for yourself, Brent."

"I will, baby, I promise."

That word again. Out of Brent's mouth, it meant just the opposite. He may as well had said, "Hell no. I'm gonna keep doing what I damn well please."

Tandi checked her watch. It was almost midnight. "Darn it. I have to call my son. Do you mind if I use the phone?"

"Baby, you don't have to ask."

"Fine. I have to finish dressing. I'll use the telephone in the bedroom." Tandi hurried away from Brent's dolefully droopy eyes.

"I'm gonna fix something to eat," he said. "You want something?"

Tandi didn't want a damn thing. She continued out of the kitchen.

"Baby, you're not mad at me, are you?"

Pissed was more like it. Brent had decimated her fantasy. He was nothing like Tandi remembered and nothing like she had hoped. That old adage, "Be careful what you wish for," came to mind. Boy, was she regretting what she had wished for. Brent was a drug addict. He needed help, and she wasn't up to it. Her plate was full to spilling over, and mothering a grown man was something she was not equipped to do. Their relationship had to end. She saw no future.

Dressed and about ready to walk out the door Tandi remembered her call to Michael Jared. Knowing him, he was fighting Jared about going to bed and was waiting for her, especially since she had promised to spend the whole weekend doing whatever he wanted. This morning he had decided on horseback riding, a movie, in-line skating, and the amusement park. Very ambitious itinerary, but she'd do at least two things on his list. Still, no telling what else Michael Jared might talk her into doing, which was why she had gone to the bank and withdrawn four hundred dollars. It was a lot, but making sure that Michael Jared was happy was all that mattered. Tandi made her call.

42

*S*eeing Daina was like seeing the sun rise after a dark stormy night. At Daina's car Tandi welcomed the embrace of a friend she was sure of.

"I love your hair," Tandi said, touching Daina's intricately twisted braids.

"A woman in Somalia did it. I feel like African royalty."

"You look it. So it was a good trip?"

"It was a long trip. Fifteen countries on the continent. My God. The foods, the people, the music, the climates, the languages, the religions, the arts . . . I could go on."

"It's gonna take you a month just to decipher your notes."

"No it won't. I slept with my laptop. I left nothing to chance. I input everything I saw and did the minute I saw and did it. It was just too overwhelming to scribble notes on paper or put on a recorder. I'll get it done. The South African Department of Environmental Affairs and Tourism paid me well . . . but enough about me." Daina sized Tandi up. "Did you lose weight?"

"A pound or two."

"Looks more like ten."

Locking arms, they began to walk toward the house. "I needed to lose some weight."

"You always looked good, Tandi. The excess weight you should have lost years ago was your pal Evonne."

Tandi came to an abrupt halt, stopping Daina just as abruptly. "Evonne didn't go after Jared, Jared—"

"Hold up!" Daina said, unlocking arms with Tandi. "You're not about to tell me that you blame Jared for that whole ugly mess?"

"Well, a good part of it anyway." She continued up the walkway to the house.

Daina rushed to catch up. "Tandi, you can't be serious. Evonne is a manipulator. Whatever she told you about what happened between her and Jared is a lie. I'd bet my life on it."

At the door, Tandi looked back at Daina. "You never did like Evonne."

"And she never liked me. She hated when I was around because I know a messy ass, conniving tramp when I see one."

"Daina, that's pretty rough. I don't want you to talk—"

"You haven't heard all that I will be saying about that tramp. Tandi, I warned you about her a long time ago. I told you she couldn't be trusted."

"Yes, but you were talking about her being my competition in the real estate market, not with my husband."

"Duh," Daina said, looking at Tandi like she was stupid. "Tandi, if you can't trust a person in business, you certainly can't trust them in your personal life. I can't believe you let that she-devil breech the inner-most sanctum of your personal life, allowing her to get next to your man."

That good feeling she had when she saw Daina vanished. "For one thing, Daina, Jared is no longer my man, and secondly, Evonne has always been a good friend. Until that incident, she had never given me reason to suspect her of wanting Jared."

"That's because she beguiled you. I always said you were naive when it came to people."

"Stop calling me naive!"

"Well, then you're too trusting."

"In that case, Miss Know-it-all, I shouldn't be trusting you. I should have never trusted Evonne, and I certainly should not have trusted Jared. He's a man, remember?"

"And he's no saint, but neither are you or I. Evonne? She's the devil's own."

Tandi put her hands on her hips. "Did you come over here to make my life even more miserable?"

"If that's the way you wanna look at it, yeah," Daina replied, not giving an inch. "Let me remind you of an incident you seem to have forgotten. Do you remember the night of the Mason and Eastern Star fund-raising event for that women's abuse center over in Rego Park four years ago?"

"And?"

"Do you remember me telling you that Evonne kept rubbing up against Jared every chance she got, and you kept telling me I was imagining things?"

"You were because nothing happened."

"That's because Jared was so busy managing the donation collection and so many people were around him that he didn't notice and didn't give Evonne the attention she wanted."

Tandi had forgotten all about that because she hadn't seen anything suspicious herself. Like Evonne and Jared, she was busy, but she did remember Daina telling her what she had seen.

"Tandi, I've suspected Evonne of wanting Jared for a long time. She never did anything that you could put your finger on, but when you weren't watching, I'd catch the bitch looking at Jared like he was a tub of chocolate. You know, in that yearning kind of way that we women have."

"You never mentioned any of that to me," Tandi said, not feeling especially good about what Daina was saying. She started to turn the knob to open the door.

"Let's sit out here for a minute," Daina said.

"Fine." They sat on the stoop. It was a cool May night, but it was bearable.

"Tandi, Jared is like a brother to me, but you, you're like a sister, and the bond between sisters is stronger. We have to look out for each other. We have to protect each other from she-devils and lowlife men. Jared has made mistakes—poor baby. But, I love him anyway. Of course, I would disown him in a heartbeat if I thought, even for a second, that he was in his right mind when he slept with that tramp. I would never speak to him again in life for hurting you like that."

Tandi was impressed. Daina did truly love Jared. He really was the brother she never had, and they were closer than most siblings, certainly closer than she and Glynn. Daina had no living siblings—her two sisters were long gone. Stella had died of breast cancer five years ago, and Janeen's life was taken in an automobile accident a year ago.

For Daina to say that she would disown Jared, her life-long friend, was an awesome thing to say. It made Tandi think hard about everything that had happened since she left Jared. Could Evonne have viciously lied to her on purpose?

Daina took Tandi's hand. "You know I'm right about Evonne."

"Maybe, but—"

"The girl is telling you one thing and Jared another. She's playing you against each other."

That really sickened Tandi. "But why?"

"For the grand prize—Jared," Daina said. "Listen, I told you when I introduced you to Jared that if he and I could have had that special thing, you know, that *umph*, that thing that makes a relationship a storybook romance, you would have never gotten within handshaking distance of him."

Tandi had no doubt about that.

"But I'm not a selfish person. There was no magic between me and Jared, but there was for you and Jared. The two of you are great together, and—"

"*Were* great together."

"Well, you can be again. Tandi, Jared is a great guy and like most of us, he's flawed. He's not perfect. He trips and falls sometimes, too. The man is a hard worker. He's a good father—"

"Now he is."

"He always was. He loves his son. He was just busy—busy making a living—and you know that. Jared works hard for his money and, unlike some men, he's no miser with the money he puts in your pockets."

"Yes, but he became quite stingy when it came to loving me, being with me."

"Okay, so we all know Jared messed up, including Jared himself, but I assure you, Tandi, if you open up even a little bit to him, you'll never regret it."

"Daina, I don't know how you can say that with such authority. I'm still regretting staying in the marriage after he had that first affair. Three years later, an affair with Evonne. Who knows what went on in between."

"Nothing. The client? A colossal mistake. Evonne? He took leave of his damn mind, and you're partly to blame for that."

"What?"

"Tandi, you left Jared wide open for Evonne to set a trap for him. She laid it, he stumbled in. If indeed he was drunk, the man didn't have a chance. Therefore, he didn't cheat on you on purpose."

"Come on, Daina. You can't expect me to believe Jared had no will of his own, that he was so drunk Evonne could manipulate him into screwing her."

"If he was drunk like he said, I do. Tandi, a man's mind and body together have to want sex from a person in order to call it cheating, and Jared was out of his mind."

"I don't wanna hear it. A screw is a screw. It went in, it came out."

"Oh," Daina said, chuckling, "is that how it works?"

Tandi couldn't help but snicker herself. "That's what I hear."

They fell against each other, giggling like two schoolgirls.

"This isn't funny," Daina said, getting control of herself. "The bottom line is Jared doesn't want Evonne. He never has."

"Says you."

"Says Jared. He hasn't had sex with her again, and according to him, she's been calling him like crazy and popping up at the house . . ."

Tandi's jaw dropped.

". . . trying her best to insinuate her messy self into his life."

"Are you serious?"

"Am I Black?"

That fact was as clear to Tandi as the moon in the sky. She felt like such a fool.

"Jared said Evonne told him that she always wanted him, that you didn't deserve him."

Tandi clenched her jaw and glared out at the street. She should have kicked Evonne's ass when she had the chance. The woman had looked her dead in the eye and lied like a rattler in the shade. The bitch!

"The skank played you and Jared both," Daina said. "She's really low."

Tandi's leg went to shaking. "That bitch told me Jared was dead sober when he came on to her. That he initiated the affair. That he was calling her."

"She was lying. Tandi, if you don't believe Jared, ask your son. He's witnessed Evonne in action."

"What? What has he seen?"

"He's seen Evonne come to the house and try to get with Jared . . ."

"Oh, shhhit."

". . . And, he's answered the phone when she's called trying to talk to Jared."

Tandi suddenly stood and walked off the stoop. "I'm gonna kill her!"

"I'll help you, but right now, calm yourself. Save the anger for when you see her."

"She better pray I never see her face again in life."

"I know that's right."

"I can't believe I fell for her lies."

"Tandi, you believed her because you didn't wanna believe Jared."

"That's not true."

"Isn't it?" Daina asked. "Tandi, you were already angry with Jared. You probably would've believed that he was a serial killer if—"

"I would never! I know Jared. I know what not to believe."

"Then why did you believe he slept with Evonne on purpose?"

"Because I saw her in my bed with him!"

"Fair, but seeing isn't everything. You should have listened to Jared's side of the story. And, actually, you should hear the terrible things that your *friend* has said about you."

Tandi drew back. "Like what?"

"That you had been sleeping around way before you left Jared, and—"

"That's a lie! I didn't even meet up with Brent until weeks after I left Jared."

"Brent? Mm. I want the four-one-one on this Brent, but first, your *friend* told Jared that he could have never satisfied you because you were an habitual malcontent."

Tandi sucked in her breath. Evonne had been stabbing her in the back, and she hadn't even felt the blade going in.

"I knew there was a reason why I couldn't stand to be around Evonne," Daina said, standing and kneading her sore behind. "Evonne is sneaky, she's a liar, and she's messy. And that's the worst kind of person to let in your house. Which is why I believe Jared, Tandi. He would never lie to me. We know each other too damn well to play games. And that's what Evonne is about, role playing. Tandi, Evonne didn't just want your man, she wanted your lifestyle. Haven't you ever noticed how she was always looking around your house like she wished it was hers?"

That Tandi had seen Evonne do, but she had thought nothing of it since they were both in real estate. That was something she did also, look around houses she was in. If it were true that Evonne wanted Jared all along, how was it that she had not sensed it, felt it, known it?

"In my opinion," Daina was saying, "especially since you now know where Evonne is coming from, I think Jared deserves a chance to be heard."

Tandi wiped at her eyes before a single tear spilled over. "Yeah, but even before this mess with Evonne, I left Jared because I no longer wanted the loveless life we had together."

"Tandi, Jared knows that he let you down. He's willing to do anything to make it up to you."

"I don't think he can."

"It won't kill you to let him try."

Not convinced that giving Jared another chance would make things right, Tandi lazily looked up at the full moon suspended high up in the sky over Queens. It was the brightest thing in the sky, yet it was unattainable, unreachable. Maybe that's how Jared saw her—unattainable, unreachable. Maybe that's why he wanted her back. But what if she went back and discovered that she couldn't forgive him? She would hate herself for putting herself through that torment all over again. Her life and Michael Jared's would be worse than before she left. She couldn't do that to either one of them.

"Daina, I know you believe in Jared, but at this time in my life, I just don't."

"Understandable, but it's not like you can't get back to believing in him," Daina said. "Tell me about Brent."

Tandi dusted off the back of her pants. "Nothing much to tell."

"That, I don't believe. You wouldn't be seeing him otherwise, so spill."

Tandi was pensive. What she needed to tell she couldn't. "Okay, nosy. Brent was my first love."

"Nice."

"It could have been."

"Oh, it's not going well? Do tell," Daina asked, her eyes gleeful with anticipation.

"Don't sound so pleased."

"Oh, but I am. Jared could use a break."

"It's not all about Jared, Daina. After being back in my father's house, I'm beginning to realize that I have a whole lot of issues to deal with. There's something in me that I need to figure out, something that I need to discover that will give meaning to my life."

"You didn't find that something in being with your first love?"

"Hell no."

"Why not? You'd been wondering about this guy for a while. In fact, I remember you mentioning a first love quite a while ago, but I don't remember you saying his name was Brent. Did thoughts of Brent come between you and Jared? I mean like, did you—"

"Haven't you ever wondered what it would be like if you had gotten together with your first love?"

"No! My first love was a jerk with zits the size of acorns on his nose and forehead that I'd known since junior high school. His big dream was to become an exterminator—a bug killer. I had a crush on him because he wore these tight, show-the-world-what-you-got dungarees, and I was a virgin looking for my first tumble with someone I figured was safe."

"How old were you?"

"Eighteen and ready, but I had to turn the bug man loose real quick."

"What happened?"

"When it was time to get busy, what he pulled out of his pants was smaller than the zits on his nose."

Tandi laughed. "How was that?"

"He'd been wearing a stuffed sock in his pants."

Tandi doubled over laughing while Daina, trying not to laugh, quickly broke down and did the same. Standing out front of Sporty's door, Tandi enjoyed the first laugh she'd had in months. She didn't care if her laughter carried in the still of the night to every house on the block. It felt really good to laugh with Daina. Wiping her eyes, she climbed the stairs and hugged her good friend.

"I'm so glad you're home."

"Thank you very much," Daina said, mimicking Elvis Presley, keeping the smile on Tandi's face. "Now tell me about Brent."

"I'll tell you inside," Tandi said, pushing open the front door. "Brent—"

"You a hateful old man!" a woman's voice shouted.

Tandi froze.

"Aa don't nee uneducated, wanna be nurse messin' over me!" Sporty shouted back. "Get da hell out!"

"Oh, God," Tandi moaned. "Not again."

43

"*M*r. Belson, just 'cause I empty your filth, you do not have to treat me like scum! I just as good as you. In fact, I better than you. I never be nasty to a people who help me."

"You a lazy woman. Get out my house!"

"I go gladly!"

Tandi rushed into Sporty's bedroom and bumped chest to chest with Elise on her way out of the room. They both grabbed onto each other to steady the other.

"Elise! What's going on?"

Sporty answered, "I want her outta my damn house!"

"This mon, here!" Elise shouted, pointing at Sporty. "Him a proud mon. Him will not use the bedpan. Him want to go to the toilet. If him sit up in he wheelchair more, it be easy to go to the toilet. I tell he him no need to use toilet just to water . . . him must use the bottle."

"You use it, goddamnit! I ain't never gonna, you stupid woman!"

"Daddy!"

"Mon, you stupid."

"Stupid bitch!"

"Stop it!" Tandi screamed. "Both of you!"

"Him call me a bitch. I not a bitch!"

"You are!" Sporty shouted. Saliva trickled out of the right side of his mouth.

"Look at he," Elise said, pointing. "God give he back him tongue and him use he words to be hateful."

"Go ta hell!"

"This has got to stop," Tandi said, looking to Daina for support.

Daina was looking amusingly at Sporty. "Having a stroke didn't humble him a bit, did it?"

"It made him meaner," Tandi replied, wishing she could twitch her nose and vanish into thin air.

"Get her fat ass outta my house!"

"Fat ass! You fat mouth!"

"You're a ugly—"

"Daddy! Stop it! That's enough!" Shouting like that gave Tandi an instant headache. "Elise, please, ignore him! Don't play his game."

"Humph!" Sporty said. "She better not ignore me. She can't tell me I can't use the goddamn toilet. I been using the toilet since before she was born."

"You was not born of a woman," Elise said. "You was spit from a rabid dog."

Daina giggled behind her hand.

"You witch!" Sporty boomed, breathing hard. "You wasn't born either. You was dug outta the ground."

"Oh, God," Tandi said, "I can't take this."

"You nasty old mon. You—"

"Elise, please. Please go and wait for me in the front."

"Mrs. Crawford, him act up when you not home. Him hold he water a long time till him 'bout bust then him want to make me rush he to the bathroom. Then when I make he use the bottle, him make me go out the room."

"Whatcha wanna do? Stay and look at my dick?"

Daina doubled over with laughter. Tandi hit her, but Daina couldn't stop laughing.

"I really can't take another minute of this," Tandi said, feeling a vicious headache coming on.

"See! Him dirty, dirty man, Mrs. Crawford. When I come back to he room, him done spilt he water on the bed and him cuss me like it be my wrong."

"It is, you ugly woman! I told you—"

"Who you call ugly? You ugly! Inside you self and out."

"Go ta hell!" Sporty shouted. He started trying to pull himself off the bed. He failed, falling onto his left arm.

"See, look at he. He cannot get up and he cuss the hand that help he."

"Bitch!"

Hearing it all, seeing it all, Tandi wanted to scream. She wanted to turn on her heels and run out of the room, out of the house and never look back.

"Mon, you lame like a old dog!" Elise said, taking one step toward the bed. "I can hurt you bad and you not be able to defend yaself."

Daina howled with laughter.

Tandi hit her harder. "This isn't funny."

Nodding repeatedly, Daina began coughing with laughter.

Sporty tried again to get up. "You threatenin' me? I'll get up out this bed and knock you out!"

"Stop this," Tandi ordered. She went to the bed and pushed Sporty back down.

Elise had her fist balled up. "I get you first!"

Standing between Elise and the bed, Tandi put out her arm to stop Elise from getting closer to Sporty. "I said stop! Elise, please go into the living room."

"This is getting ugly," Daina said, no longer laughing. She said in a hushed voice behind Elise's back to Tandi, "Let her kick his ass."

"Daina, this is serious. You're not helping me one bit."

"This is not funny," Elise said angrily.

"You're right, Elise, I'm sorry," Daina said, now in control of herself.

Tandi eased Elise away from the bed. "Please go into the living room and wait for me."

Sporty wasn't through. "You need to go back to whatever island you come from. I don't want you in my house cooking no goat."

"You evil, evil mon!"

"Okay!" Tandi shouted, putting up her hands. "Enough!"

Elise pointed a shaky finger at Sporty. "You will never get out that chair. You a nasty mon. God's punishin' you."

"You ugly witch!" Sporty shouted, his jaw shaking.

"You toad!" Elise shouted back. She started for the bed.

Daina caught Elise by the arm, holding her back. "Elise, he's not worth it. Let's get out of here."

"Who the hell is she?" Sporty asked, noticing Daina for the first time. "What's she doing in my house?"

Daina smiled prettily. "It's so good to see you again, Mr. Belson."

"I don't know you."

"Maybe that's a good thing," Daina said, ushering Elise out of the room. "Elise, wouldn't you like something to drink?"

"I will not drink nothin' from this house—it will be bitter."

"Get her out my house!"

"I go on my own!" Elise shouted from the hallway.

Tandi slammed the bedroom door shut. She rushed back over to the bed. "What's wrong with you?" She wanted to slap Sporty hard across the face. He must have sensed that; he looked at Tandi as if to dare her. She clamped her jaw tight to keep from saying she wished he had died.

"Elise, forget about him," Daina could be heard saying outside the bedroom door.

"I will never come back to this evil house!"

Sporty shouted at the door, "Go to hell!"

"You be there first!" Elise shouted back, her voice farther away down the hall.

"I'll send you there tonight!"

Tandi hit the bed hard with her open hand. "Daddy!"

"That woman don't know me! I'll—"

"Daddy, stop it! What's wrong with you? Have you lost your mind?"

"I don't need her," he snarled, and then as an afterthought, "Who's that other woman?"

"She's not your concern."

"She is if she's in my house. She could be a thief."

"You would think like that, wouldn't you?" Tandi said, her patience completely shot. "Daddy, if you know like I know, you best be worrying about whether or not Elise walks out of here."

"The hell with her!"

"No, it's going to be the hell with you, you crotchety old man. You can't do a damn thing for yourself. You need someone here. This is the fifth home health aide you've run out of here in three weeks."

"I can take care of myself."

"You can, huh?" Tandi stepped back from the bed. "Show me what you can do."

Sporty scowled at Tandi. His chest was heaving, but he didn't attempt to move.

Tandi was nauseated by the saliva that dribbled down his chin onto his T-shirt. But she was not about to clean him up. "Daddy, I've had enough of your tantrums. If you could do anything for yourself, you would have gotten up off that damn bed and gone to the bathroom your damn self. That's why Elise is here. She is supposed to be helping you. Would you please let her?"

"You stood by and let that woman talk to me like I was an idiot."

"No, I stood by and let both of you give me a goddamn headache. Daddy, the agency is getting tired of having to replace health aides that you've abused. I'm telling you right now, if Elise leaves and the agency can't replace her, I'm leaving you in this damn house by yourself to rot."

"Go ahead," Sporty said, turning his head toward the window. "I don't care."

"Oh, you care. That's why you're more bitter than ever," she said, moving to the foot of his bed. "Daddy, here are the facts. You had a stroke. It disabled you. It partially paralyzed you. Well, too bad. Shit happens. Get over it. Whether you accept it or not, it's your own fault. You never stopped smoking, you never stopped drinking, you—"

"I did!"

Tandi gripped the heavy wooden footboard. "For how long? A minute?"

Clenching his jaw, Sporty glared at her.

"You never took your pressure pills like you were supposed to, you ate what you wanted, and in the end, you played with a loaded gun and shot yourself. And now, you have the nerve to be angry at everyone who tries to help you because you hate that you can't do for yourself. You give the physical therapist a hard time, you give the health aides a hard time, and you give me a hard time. The only person you didn't abuse was the speech therapist, and that was because you wanted to speak again so that you could be nasty to the rest of us. But I got news for you, damnit, I am not putting up with your nastiness anymore. I am not letting you abuse the people who are here to help you. And understand this, old man, if I leave, Glynn is not going to come and take care of you. You will be put in a nursing home so fast you'll think yesterday is today."

Sporty mumbled, "I ain't going into no damn nursing home, and you can't put me in one without my consent."

"You wanna put a bet on that?" Tandi leaned toward Sporty. She waited for him to retort. He didn't. "If you make one more health aide run out of this house, you will be put in the worse nursing home I can find. And there are plenty of those out there where you will be strapped in your bed, twenty-four-seven, fed through a rubber tube up your nose, and by the time someone changes your diaper, trees will have taken root."

"You can't do that."

"Oh yes, I can. Try me. It would give me great pleasure to make that call." She could see the defiance in Sporty's eyes wavering.

"Glynn . . . Glynn will never let you put me away. I know he won't."

Tandi heard the uncertainty in his voice. "You must be trying to convince yourself because I know different."

Closing his eyes, his tongue mute, Sporty lifted his wet chin slightly. He was trying to shut Tandi out, but she knew his ears were wide open. "Look, old man, all of the health aides have told me you're worse when I'm not here. You better get over yourself because I'm tired of you acting like a tantrum-throwing two-year-old who acts up when Mommy's not home. I plan not to be around here much longer, so you had better get your act together and learn to behave."

Sporty's eyelashes didn't flutter nor did a muscle in his face twitch.

"Now, once again, if Elise quits, I am going to have to beg, shame-lessly, for another health aide. When that one comes, you had better kiss her ass and pray she's not offended by the feel of your lips. Because if she is, you're out of here. Do you understand me?"

Sporty continued to hold his eyes closed, which was just fine with Tandi. Stubborn, hateful old man. He wouldn't give an inch to a run-away train if it meant he had to lose ground. For sanity's sake, she had to get away from him once and for all.

She looked at the large wet spot on the bed. This she was not going to clean up. Maybe if he lay in his own pee the rest of the night, he'd take her threats seriously. Looking again at his face, she knew that wasn't likely. Disgusted, she flipped her hand hard at him and stomped out of the room.

44

Tandi found Daina sitting with Elise in the kitchen over a cup of tea, which she hadn't touched. "Elise, I am so sorry my father said those terrible things to you."

"I never work with such a mean mon," Elise said through her weak sobs. "How can a sick mon be so mean?"

"Humph," Daina said. "You think he's mean now, you should have seen him when he was well. He used to scare away flies, and you know how hard it is to get rid of flies."

That frightened Elise. "I will not work here."

"Daina, you're not helping."

"I was just trying to lighten it up around here. My goodness, it's so tense in here."

"Don't help me that way," Tandi said, pulling a chair closer to Elise and sitting. "Elise, please, could you stay tonight—"

"No! I will not!" Elise exclaimed. "I cannot."

"I don't blame you," Daina said.

Tandi pointed a warning finger at Daina like she was a naughty child. She looked back into Elise's angry, teary eyes. She took Elise's hand and held on to it tightly.

"Elise, it is true that my father has never been a very nice man, and it's also true that he is a very proud man. My father is angry because he's sick and can't do for himself. Believe me, I know it isn't easy to work with him, but I need you, please, to stay and help me."

Shaking her head, Elise dabbed at her eyes with a crumpled paper towel.

"Please, Elise, just until I can find a replacement."

Elise pulled her hand free of Tandi's grasp. "No. I tell all me friends not to work here."

"Oh, God, please, don't do that."

"Him will insult my friends, so I will tell."

"Elise, I promise you, my father will not insult another living soul. Look, if you'll stay until I get someone else, I'll pay you a bonus for every day you're here."

Elise's tears dried up instantly. She looked at Tandi guardedly. "How much bonus?"

Tandi glanced uncertainly at Daina.

Daina mouthed, "Fifty."

Tandi went with that. "Fifty."

"One hundred dollars," Elise stated.

Tandi glanced again at Daina who shrugged.

"That's a lot," Tandi said.

"Not to work for such a mean mon," Elise said coolly.

"Can't argue that," Daina conceded.

"Whose side are you on?" Tandi asked.

"Yours of course, but the woman already knows how difficult your father is to work with. She deserves the money."

"I'm not saying she doesn't."

"I do," Elise said.

"You certainly do," Daina said, "but, Tandi, you should not have to pay Elise from your pocket. Your father caused the problem, let him pay for it."

Tandi wasn't about to dispute that. "Glynn has power of attorney, but he's in Albany. I'll speak to him in the morning."

"I'm going home," Elise said, starting to push away from the table.

"Elise, wait a minute," Tandi said. "I have access to my father's checkbook. I will pay you an additional one hundred dollars a day until I get someone else."

Elise eyed Tandi suspiciously. "I don't—"

"Please, Elise."

"You will make him not talk to me?"

"He will not talk to you. I promise."

"Good, 'cause I will leave if he talk one word to me."

"I understand," Tandi said, standing. "You will finish out the night, right?"

Elise stood also. "Yes, but I want my hundred dollar before I go back to that mon."

"No problem. I'll write you a check."

"No. I want cash money."

Daina coughed softly into her hand. She had to, to keep from laughing.

Tandi began to feel anxious again. "We don't keep very much cash in the house."

"I must have cash money. It will make me feel better when I work with that mon."

Daina coughed twice more, making Tandi look at her. Daina quickly cut her eyes away.

"Okay, Elise, that's fair." Tandi felt like she was negotiating a house sale. "I will go to the bank tomorrow and have two hundred dollars in cash for you when you get here in the evening."

"I need one hundred dollars tonight. I—"

"Elise," Daina chimed in, "you can trust Mrs. Crawford for the money."

"You can," Tandi said.

"I trust Mrs. Crawford," Elise said. "I don't trust that mon's mouth. Cash money make it a lot easier to do my job."

"I know that's right," Daina said.

Tandi couldn't argue Elise's reasoning. It was sound, and she was desperate. "Okay, cash," she said. "I'll be right back."

She rushed out of the kitchen to the living room where she had tossed her pocketbook onto the chair when she raced through the house. Luckily, she had taken four hundred dollars from the bank earlier. She dug down inside her pocketbook for her checkbook. What she expected to see even before opening the checkbook—a wad of twenty and fifty dollar bills—she didn't see. Flipping back and forth between the blank checks and the check register, then looking inside the side pockets, she searched anxiously for the money she knew had to be there, but wasn't. Not a single bill was there.

"Where is my money?" she asked aloud, dropping the checkbook onto the chair. She pulled out her wallet. Again she turned the wallet inside out. There was thirty-one dollars in all. She began pulling everything out of her pocketbook. Then turning it upside down, emptied it of everything—her lipstick tube rolled off the chair onto the floor. There was no money anywhere. There was a frightful pounding in Tandi's chest. Her hands began to tremble. She grabbed up her checkbook, again searching through it as if she were searching it for the first time. The money just wasn't there.

"Where the hell is my money?"

"What's wrong?" Daina asked from the archway.

Tandi sank down onto the edge of the chair, sitting on the contents of her pocketbook. "I can't find my money."

"Did you lose your wallet?"

Reaching behind her, Tandi felt for her wallet and checkbook. She held both out to Daina.

Daina came closer. "There's no money in them?"

"Thirty-one dollars. I went to the bank today. I had four hundred dollars in my checkbook."

"I don't understand. You have your wallet and checkbook. Are you saying that—"

"I'm saying someone stole my money."

"Who? Did you leave your pocketbook somewhere unattended?"

Starting to shake her head no, Tandi stopped instantly. Her eyes widened as she saw in her mind's eye, her pocketbook sitting on the chair in Brent's bedroom. She had left it there when she went out to the kitchen to wash up. It was the only time it was out of her sight. She had gone to Brent's after leaving the bank. But what was she thinking? Brent wouldn't steal from her, at least she hoped that he wouldn't. He wasn't a thief. He had a good job and plenty of money.

"Tandi, retrace your steps from the time you left the bank. Did you—"

"Someone must have picked my pocketbook," she said, standing. She began stuffing everything back inside.

"But how did they get the money and not the—"

"I have thirty-one dollars. What do you have?"

Eyeing Tandi suspiciously, Daina opened the flap of her pocketbook slung across her shoulder. She took out her wallet. "You know I live and breathe by the almighty plastic," she said, opening the wallet and counting what cash she had. "Twenty-six dollars."

Tandi threw her pocketbook back down onto the chair. "I need one hundred dollars."

"Call Jared."

"No."

"Then you're not desperate."

"Mrs. Crawford," Elise said from the hall. She wouldn't even come into the living room. "You do not have cash money?"

Quickly stepping around Daina, Tandi rushed to Elise. "I have it. I just don't have all of it, right now. I can give you fifty-seven dollars now and tomorrow I—"

"No," Elise said, starting to turn toward the back of the house where she kept her coat and oversized pocketbook.

"Wait! Elise, I can go to the bank."

Elise turned back. "The bank is closed."

"Banks are never closed in New York City," Daina said. "ATMs, honey."

"That's right," Tandi agreed. "Look, I have a bank card. I'll run to the bank and—"

"I cannot wait."

Daina went over to Elise. "You can wait a half hour, can't you?"

"No."

"Okay, I have an idea," Tandi said. "Elise, you can come with me to the bank. I can get the money and then we can stop off and get some burgers at White Castle or McDonald's, whichever you prefer. They're open twenty-four hours. You must be hungry."

The sound of Sporty coughing made Elise look back at his room. "I change my mind. The spirits no good here. Money cannot change that. It be best I leave."

"That's nonsense," Daina said. "Spirits. Please."

"Miss, be careful what you mock," Elise warned haughtily.

Arching her brow, Daina sidled smoothly away from Elise and stood behind Tandi. "Your father is in trouble," Daina whispered.

Tandi could see Elise was dead serious and realized money was not going to sway her. "It's all right, Elise. I'm sorry it was such a bad experience for you."

"Very bad," Elise affirmed. She walked away.

Daina slid even closer to Tandi as Elise passed. "What island is she from?"

"Does it matter?" Tandi went back into the living room. "She believes in spirits, and if the ones here are bad, no amount of money will make her stay. Asking for a hundred dollars was just a way out."

"I bet if you had it, she would have stayed."

"Maybe, maybe not."

"If you had called Jared, like I told you to, he would have brought you a thousand dollars, and we would have found out. I should have called him myself."

"No, you shouldn't have." Tandi eased her weary body onto the sofa. The truth was, she was too ashamed to ask Jared for money, especially suspecting—no, knowing, as a fact—that Brent had to be the one who took the money. Did he think she wouldn't miss it? Did he think she wouldn't suspect him? How could he do that to her?

"Good-bye, Mrs. Crawford," Elise said.

Tandi gave Elise a limp wave of her hand.

"I'll show her out," Daina volunteered. She scooted around Elise to get to the door.

Elise started out but stopped and looked back at Tandi. "Mrs. Crawford, burn white candles and pray the evil leave that man's black soul."

Tandi mouthed, "Yeah, right." White candles? What was that supposed to do? Sure, Sporty was evil to the core, but a wispy flame from a white candle would never reach deep enough to exorcise his soul. He was a lost cause. She was wiped out from dealing with Sporty and his mess. Every muscle across her upper back ached, but the biggest ache was her pride. She had continued to see Brent even after she saw what he was, a drug addict. And more than likely, he took the money for drugs. Damn. Jared had never even taken a quarter from her and certainly he had never put her through anything as bad as drugs and bold-faced lies.

Daina sat next to Tandi. "You know what happened to your money, don't you?"

"If you're my friend, Daina, you won't ask me about the money. I can't talk about it."

"Okay. I'll respect that. So, what about this Brent? If you're my friend, you'll tell me about him. In detail."

"If you're my friend, you'll wait until I feel like talking about him."

"Touché," Daina said. "Okay. So. Back to the bad boy of the geriatric set. What do we do about the super grouch back there?"

"As far as I'm concerned, he can pickle in his own piss. I'm not touching him."

Daina suddenly stood. "Where're the rubber gloves?"

"What? Daina, why—"

"Let's just get this over with. We're only gonna have to clean him up later. We may as well do it now before he starts stinking. Where's your room? Upstairs? I'll find it. I need something to work in." Daina marched out of the room. She shouted back, "Get me a pail of water, some ammonia, a sponge, some rubber gloves, a change of sheets, oh, and a face mask, if you have one."

Amazed, Tandi sat staring at the empty archway. Daina had never been one to sit back and wait to be told what to do. She always took charge. She was all about action. But this? Cleaning up after Sporty was the last thing she expected to see Daina do. When Michael Jared was a baby, Daina wouldn't even change his diaper. Hell, she didn't even clean her own house—she had a woman come in once a week. God bless her. Daina proved always to be a better friend than she had ever been to her. How lucky for her.

On her way to the stairs, Daina stopped at Sporty's door. "Mr. Belson, I am not Tandi. If you bat an eye at me, I will shove that foul-smelling sheet down your throat so fast you won't even know it happened. And that's after I hog-tie your ass with dental floss."

45

Brent's answering machine at home repeatedly told Tandi to leave a message. That she had done twice asking him to call her—immediately. He never did. The third time she threatened, "If you don't return every penny of my damn money, I'm going to the police." No return call came even then. Days passed. She kept calling but slammed down the receiver the second the answering machine picked up.

Only once had she called his office. It made no sense to call again after she was told he had not worked there in well over a month. Brent had never said a word. Wasn't that just like him? No one in his office would tell her why he had left or if there was a forwarding address. Twice she went by his apartment. There was no answer to the ringing of his bell. It was all so insane. She wanted her money but she also wanted to know how he could steal from her. If it was for drugs, then there was no question that four hundred dollars was a small price to pay to get out of the relationship. She could have lost a whole lot more in the long run.

Still, her anger with Brent never abated. When she was alone, she found herself talking to herself about what she'd say to Brent if and when she ever saw him again. "You lowlife drug-abusing bastard. How dare you steal from me. I never want to see you again in life." Yeah, big words, a bit late.

It was one thing talking to herself, but Tandi was still too embarrassed to talk to Daina about Brent. True to her word, Daina continued to respect her privacy while continuing to stand by her. In fact, if it hadn't been for Daina, Sporty would have pickled in his own piss every one of the three days it took to beg up another evening health aide.

The agency manager, Mrs. Rothman, did not mince her words. "This is Mr. Belson's last chance. I have found him one last aide, and I mean his very last aide. Carline Hughes is very good with difficult patients. She is very patient. If Mr. Belson runs her out, this agency is through placing aides in his home."

"I understand," Tandi had said.

"I hope you do, Mrs. Crawford. Your father's illness is no excuse for his abusive behavior."

"Mrs. Rothman, I assure you my father will behave from now on." When Tandi said that, she had her fingers crossed.

Since that conversation the day before, Tandi had been praying that Carline Hughes was six feet tall and weighed two hundred and fifty pounds. Thankfully, that day she would be finding out. The previous night, Daina had all but pulled out pom-poms and turned somersaults. Daina hadn't complained one time about taking care of Sporty, but she was tired of the menial labor. The only thing she didn't do for Sporty was cook, which was Tandi's job.

To say the least, Tandi was truly grateful to Daina, which was why she decided to tell Daina about Brent—albeit what she told wasn't as important as what she didn't tell. Brent's drug use and his stealing her money was best left unsaid as she was sure Daina would share that information with Jared. Lord knows what he'd think of her, and for the first time in a long while, she cared about what he might think. She told Daina that she had ended the relationship with Brent because she wasn't quite sure she and Jared were through. Daina took that tidbit and ran with it. Daina began working overtime to convince her to at least talk to Jared. While she was steadfast in her decision to stay away from Jared, Tandi was beginning to feel that maybe she was the one who didn't deserve a second chance. She was guilty of spending valuable time fantasizing about Brent when maybe there was something she could have been doing to save her marriage. No, she couldn't talk to Jared just yet. She had her own demons with which to wrestle.

Besides, she had more pressing matters to address. She had to stay close to the house to make sure Sporty didn't send another home health aide packing. Oh, he had not flapped his lips at Daina, and that was because Daina's threats carried weight, but with anyone else, he might not be so inclined to back down.

The bell rang. It was six o'clock straight up.

Opening the door for the new health aide, Tandi almost said out loud, "I hope you're not the home health aide." This little five feet four, one hundred and forty pound, fifty-ish something woman was the last person Tandi wanted to see standing in front of her.

"Mrs. Carline Hughes?"

"Yes," she replied in a low, soft voice.

Oh, God. Sporty was going to eat this little woman alive. Where the hell were the big Berthas of the world? "I'm Tandi Crawford. Come in," she said, stepping aside to let in the attractive older woman. Mrs. Hughes slipped past Tandi with her hands stuffed down in her coat pockets. Unlike some of the other health aides who boldly looked around the living room, Mrs. Hughes, her eyes lowered, didn't look around. She seemed to be nibbling on her lower lip, and, if Tandi wasn't mistaken, the woman was trembling.

What had Mrs. Rothman said about this woman handling difficult patients? That couldn't be possible. No way was she going to be able to stand up to Sporty. The agency apparently had to scrape her off the bottom of the barrel to get her to come to the house because surely the word was out. Oh, well, a nursing home was only a phone call away.

"Mrs. Hughes, my father is recovering from a stroke. Have you worked with stroke patients before?"

A timid nod was Mrs. Hughes's response.

Tandi wanted to ask, "And?" but saw that was a waste of breath. Mrs. Hughes wasn't giving her any eye contact, which meant she wasn't interested in conversing. Well, beggars couldn't be choosers.

"Okay. Mrs. Hughes, why don't I tell you about my father's evening routine. He watches television until about midnight, which is when he drops off to sleep. I plan and cook his meals—he won't eat anyone else's cooking. Whatever is on the menu that evening will be on the second shelf in the refrigerator. He likes to eat at seven. He gets a bath every morning so all you have to do is give him a light sponge bath before his bedtime. Other than for doctor's appointments and to go to the bathroom, he never leaves his room. Oh, and just so you know, he does not like to be drawn into conversation. It makes him extremely grouchy, but you don't look like you like to talk very much yourself. Am I right?"

A timid shrug was as much of an answer that Mrs. Hughes was willingly offering.

"Well, be forewarned. Mr. Belson has a terrible temper. Please do not let him bully you. And please, do not take any verbal abuse from him whatsoever. If he gives you a hard time, let me know right away. I will take care of him. Okay?"

A simple little nod.

"Do you have any questions?"

Mrs. Hughes shook her head.

Already Tandi could see the woman running for the door. "Okay, then, let me show you back to your patient's room. It's this way."

Buzzzz!

"Just a minute." Tandi turned back to the door.

"Mrs. Crawford," Mrs. Hughes said, "I'll find the room myself."

"If you'll wait, I'll go with you." But Mrs. Hughes had already started off down the hall."

"Okay, you go right ahead." Tandi opened the door. It was Daina.

"I feel like I'm reporting to work."

"For the last day, hopefully. The new health aide is here."

"Thank God." Daina came inside. "I was thinking about telling Glynn he had to pay me."

"You and me both." Tandi glanced down the hall toward Sporty's bedroom. Mrs. Hughes was nowhere in sight. "As timid as this new woman is, Glynn will be paying a nursing home by Monday morning."

"Oh, damn, that bad?"

"Girl, please, I think the woman was trembling."

"Oh no."

"If she makes it through the next hour, I'd be very surprised. Although it is strange that my father hasn't said anything about Mrs. Hughes entering his room."

Daina pulled the sleeves of her shirt up to her elbows. "You need to let me tie that old man to his bed and strap a bedpan to his ass. We could tape his mouth shut with a straw sticking out and feed him that way. I promise you, he won't be a problem ever again."

"It won't work. He could still breathe and burn off any restraints," Tandi said, tiptoeing down the hall. She was really curious. It had been quiet, too quiet.

Sporty's mouth was closed but his eyes were ablaze with anger so intense that Tandi was surprised Mrs. Hughes hadn't run from the room.

"Boy," Daina whispered, "he certainly is afraid of that nursing home, isn't he?"

"Thank God he's afraid of something," Tandi whispered back.

Mrs. Hughes, with her hands still in her pockets, stood at the foot of the bed looking down at Sporty. Her face was unreadable.

"Did he say anything to you?" Tandi asked.

"No, but I told him I was his new health aide."

"And he said nothing?"

"No."

Daina whispered, "Could this be love at first sight?"

"Oh, please," Tandi said. "More like a lion sizing up his prey."

Mrs. Hughes unbuttoned her light jacket.

"Mrs. Hughes, this is my friend, Daina Harding."

"You can call me Carline," Mrs. Hughes said, slipping out of her jacket.

Tandi noticed that Sporty's eyes never left the spot where Carline had stood. A gully of creases lined his forehead.

"I'll take your jacket," Tandi said.

Carline handed her jacket and her large tote to Tandi. She then began picking up the balled-up tissues that Sporty had dropped onto the floor.

Sporty's eyes suddenly began to follow Carline around the room. He still had not said a word.

Daina and Tandi looked at each other. "I think your dad is smitten," Daina said.

"Shhh." Whatever it was, Tandi didn't care. As long as Sporty didn't open his mouth.

"Carline, if you need my help," Daina said, tugging on Tandi's arm, "just give a yell."

"I'll be fine," Carline said, getting down on her knees to reach tissues that had rolled under the bed.

Tandi liked that Carline wasted no time getting to work. "Carline, the bathroom is across the hall and the kitchen is on the other side of the house to the right. I'll put your things in the closet out in the hallway. If you need me, I'll be in the living room. Thank you for coming." Tandi let Daina pull her out of the room.

Carline seemed to not notice Tandi's and Daina's exit. She was busy stretching to reach farther under the bed for a wadded-up tissue.

46

Sporty's silence was eerie, but most welcomed. Tandi could not believe it took a woman as timid as Carline to tame the mighty beast. Then again, maybe tame wasn't altogether right. Sporty's silence had to have something to do with his fear of being put away in a nursing home. But, hey, if that was what it took to shut his mouth, then so be it. Carline reaped the benefits of that threat. Sporty didn't bother Carline as she went about cleaning up his room. Within days Carline had even, miraculously, cleaned him up. Sporty was no longer unkempt, unshaven, or glued to his bed. Somehow, Carline got him to get out of bed and sit in his wheelchair.

How Carline accomplished that miraculous feat Tandi didn't know, but it was clear by the scowl on Sporty's face the first time she saw him out of bed he wasn't a happy camper. Not that anyone cared. What Tandi did care about was the fact that they had gone three weeks without a major temper tantrum. Only once had he bitched, and that was over not being able to find the remote control. Small matter. His real anger was at her. That was quite evident in the way he glared unceasingly at her. But that was all right, too. She didn't care about that either. On the occasional sojourn she made into his room, Sporty kept his mouth shut. He'd clench his jaw and stare intently at the television the whole time she was in his room. It had to be killing him to not speak his mind, but that was too bad. It was about time he learned to keep his mouth shut, especially since he never had anything pleasant to say anyway.

What was unusual was Sporty's tolerance of Carline sitting in his room when she wasn't actually doing something for him. Normally, he would have been spitting nails. He never let any of the other health aides sit idle in his room. He made them go out into the kitchen. If he wanted them, he bellowed for them. Maybe it was like Daina said. Maybe Sporty was smitten with Carline. She wasn't bad to look at. In fact, she was better looking than Iona Lewis and all the other women Sporty had bedded. Her gray-streaked hair was always pulled up on top of her head in an array of soft curls at the crown. It was quite becoming. In fact, Carline had a figure. Surely, Sporty noticed that although he went through great pains to not pay attention to Carline sitting in the corner of the room near the window, her head down, her fingers nimbly working her crochet needle like a well-oiled machine.

Tandi admired the intricately designed turquoise square fanned out over Carline's lap. "That's beautiful."

"Thank you."

"I always wanted to learn to crochet."

Carline's fingers quickly twiddled the needle rhythmically as if a fast, upbeat tune played in her head.

"What are you making?" Tandi asked.

Carline didn't look up. "A bedspread."

"It's beautiful."

"Thank you."

Tandi was used to Carline not looking at her or having very much to say. She liked it that way. She looked around the clean room. She was satisfied. What magic this woman had worked on Sporty needed to be bottled. Sporty was even working with the physical therapist without argument and most days used the urinal bottle without fuss. Strangest of all, he was eating Carline's cooking. When he first came home, unless Tandi cooked for him, he would eat only crackers.

Right from the start, Carline insisted on cooking.

At the time, Tandi was sprinkling black pepper on chicken cutlets. "Carline, I would love to let you cook, but he won't eat anyone else's cooking."

"I assure you, he'll eat my cooking."

Tandi was taken with Carline's self-assuredness. "Do you know something I don't?"

"You give in to his demands too much."

"Oh, really? Not hardly."

"You must tell your father what you expect of him and if he does not like it, he gets nothing."

"That's how I handle my son. My father acts worse than any child I know."

"Your father is misunderstood," Carline said casually.

"Oh, so that's what it is? I just don't understand him."

"I'm not saying you in particular," Carline said. "I think your father has probably been misunderstood by most people, as a whole, all of his life. That can make a man appear angry at the world when he's not."

"Well, maybe he should explain himself so people don't get the wrong impression. And it would help if he wasn't so damn mean."

If Carline had more to say in defense of Sporty, she didn't venture to, but that's when Tandi gladly handed the chicken cutlets over to Carline to finish preparing.

An hour and a half later, from the hallway, Tandi had watched Sporty eat his dinner. He didn't question who had cooked it. From that moment on, she let Carline plan and cook his meals. That was one more step toward her being able to leave. The apartment Tandi had originally applied for was gone, but she reapplied for an apartment in the same building. Hopefully, one would come available soon. A huge weight was slowly being lifted off her shoulders by Carline's presence, and that feeling of dread that Sporty would have another stroke was no longer her constant, uneasy companion.

Tandi watched Carline crocheting a few minutes more. The awkwardness of nothing being said by either of them was Tandi's cue that it was time for her to leave.

"I think I'll go and fix myself a salad."

"I'll go with you," Carline said, laying her work down. "I have to fix his dinner."

Together they left the room, neither acknowledging Sporty. What they didn't see was Sporty watching them leave. They didn't see him drop his head to his chest as tears rolled down his cheeks.

In the kitchen, Carline sat at the table and began peeling potatoes. Tandi went to the refrigerator. "He seems to be coming along."

"He's making progress."

"I just hope he's able to walk again," Tandi said, looking into the refrigerator. She saw what she wanted.

"Your father's illness is not fair to you."

Kicking the door closed with her foot, Tandi carried her armload of lettuce, tomato, cucumber, French dressing, and square of cheddar to the table.

"Let's just say his illness has put a serious hold on my life."

"That shouldn't be anymore," Carline said, letting the skin of the potatoes drop into a plastic bag on the table. "That's why the other health aide and I are here."

"Which I am very grateful for. Hopefully, I'll be able to move out soon."

"That should make your son happy."

Tandi had taken a knife and was about to cut into the cucumber. "You know about my son?"

Carline began peeling a third potato. "I saw the picture you have of him up in your room."

Tandi slowly cut her eyes at Carline. "Why were you in my room?"

"I was doing laundry."

She hadn't even noticed that her laundry had been done. "Not my laundry."

"I'm sorry. I thought I'd help you out since you were working and getting in late some evenings."

Tandi didn't know if she should thank Carline or be upset. Her room was off limits.

Carline never stopped peeling potatoes. "I hope you don't mind that I went into your room to get your clothes."

"Carline, you shouldn't be doing my laundry. It's my father you're here to take care of. I'd rather you save your energy for him."

"I was just trying to keep busy."

"That's fine, but I'll do my own laundry. Thank you anyway."

"It was no trouble."

Tandi began cutting the cucumber into thin slices. "You mentioned my son. Did I tell you about him?" She knew she hadn't.

"Actually, your son called here a few times. He called yesterday. I gave you the message. Remember?"

"Sure, I remember."

Dropping the last peeled potato into the pot, Carline carried it over to the sink. She ran cold water over the potatoes to rinse them.

"Are you making mashed potatoes?"

"Yes." Carline began cutting the white potatoes into bite-size cubes. "Is your husband a good father?"

That was an odd question but Tandi answered, "He is now, now that I'm not around to do everything."

"Men are like that. When they are alone, they are not as helpless around the house as they want us to think when they are with us."

Wasn't that the truth? Jared was darn near domesticated according to Daina. Now he perked his own coffee and made his own breakfast. When she was home, he wouldn't lift a finger to toast a slice of bread.

"Mrs. Crawford, may I cook enough chicken for you?"

"No, thank you, Carline. I'm fine, but let me help you. I'll get the vegetables."

Tandi took an inventory of the bags of frozen vegetables. There were string beans, broccoli, and carrots. The day before, she had made carrots for MJ, which she knew he would eat because it was his favorite vegetable. She had also made enough chicken and rice for Jared if he wanted some, but she didn't leave a hint she had done that.

From the freezer, Tandi took a bag of string beans. She fingered the hard, lumpy, frozen cut beans through the cold plastic. Her fingers were chilled but she wasn't bothered by that. She was bothered by thoughts of Jared, which were starting to sneak into her head, just as thoughts of Brent had for all those years. For the first time she felt like she might be ready to see Jared again.

Carline took the bag of string beans from Tandi. "The potatoes are on. Why don't you sit and let me make you a cup of hot chocolate."

"Carline, please call me Tandi. That Mrs. thing makes me feel so old."

Carline acknowledged with a slight nod.

"And, I only like hot chocolate in the winter," she said, although she did sit.

"Not me," Carline said. "I drink hot chocolate like most people drink coffee. Hot chocolate goes a long way in helping to solve one's problems."

"I don't know about that. In my lifetime, I've drank hot chocolate aplenty and I have a lifetime of unsolved problems."

"I guess nothing works for everyone." Carline took two small pots from the cabinet alongside the stove. "Would you drink a little hot chocolate with me anyway?"

Tandi watched Carline move around the kitchen with ease. "Sure, why not."

Carline filled one of the pots with milk.

"Are you married, Carline? Do you have children?"

Carline went about placing the pot on top of the stove over a lit burner. She stood staring down into the pot of dense whiteness.

"Carline?"

Carline kept her back to Tandi. "Would you like marshmallows?"

"No, thank you."

Quietly, Carline went to the sink. She began pulling and tugging on a corner of the bag of string beans, trying to open it. The plastic gave a little but it wouldn't tear.

Tandi was reminded of what her aunt Gert used to say. *Don't be nosy. People will tell you what they want you to know. And what they don't want you to know, they'll keep to themselves.* Obviously, Carline was keeping her personal life to herself.

"I'm sorry, Carline. I didn't mean to pry."

"I love marshmallows," Carline said, taking a fork and sticking it into the bag.

Okay, so she had really stepped out of line, but a simple yes or no would have sufficed. "My son fills his cup halfway up with marshmallows first then he pours in the hot chocolate."

"That's a lot of sugar. You allow that?"

"On occasion. What can it hurt?"

"I guess nothing." Carline ripped a small jagged hole in the bag with the fork. She tugged at the hole. It widened. A few of the string beans popped out into the sink. Those, Carline picked up, rinsed off and dropped into the pot. She then emptied the whole bag of string beans into the pot. She turned back to Tandi.

"I've been married, but, unfortunately, I've never had children to call my own."

"I'm—"

"Please, don't be. The path I walk in life is the one I've chosen. No use crying over it now."

Tandi understood what Carline was saying. Hadn't she taken a path with Brent that led places she wasn't prepared to go? There was no use crying over that either.

"I'll get you that hot chocolate," Carline said, lighting the burner under the string beans.

"Can I help?"

"No . . . no. Sit. I'm here to help you."

47

Five months ago, five days ago, no one could have told Tandi she would be going out to dinner with Jared. She still didn't believe it herself. She felt like a nervous teenager getting ready for her first date. Although she had told herself she wasn't dressing for Jared, but for herself, she had changed her outfit no less than four times and still she wasn't satisfied with the way she looked. Jared used to like her in straight skirts because he liked to see the sensuous curve of her hips and the definite roundness of her behind. Jared also liked her in red. Like most men, he liked the spiciness of red, and the straight skirt Tandi had on was cherry red and hit her just above the knees, just enough to show off her shapely legs. Of course, the sexy red ankle-strap high heels were kicking. They made her legs appear longer and shapelier. Tandi looked hot. The mirror told her so, but even if she didn't have a mirror, she felt hot.

Tandi stood looking at herself. "Stop lying. You know, you're dressing to please Jared." Maybe that wasn't such a good idea. Jared might get the wrong message.

She took off the red skirt, kept on the black silk shell and put on a straight black skirt. Again in the full-length mirror Tandi looked at herself. The ten pounds she'd lost was in all the right places. She looked good. That outfit, too, would please Jared. But what the hell, why not?

Tandi fell back onto the bed. "Damn you, Daina." She should not have let Daina talk her into going out to dinner with Jared. She told herself it was for MJ's sake. It was important that she keep a line of communication open since MJ was living with him—temporarily. They had to be, at the very least, cordial. But, as much as Tandi hated to admit it, she was looking forward to seeing Jared, and not just for MJ's sake. After all those years of comparing Jared with the Brent of her dreams and then comparing the Brent of her reality with the Jared she gave up, she saw that Jared had been the better man and the better father all along. And if she were to be honest with herself, for a very long time, Jared had been the better lover.

Everything had been fine between her and Jared up until she found out about his affair. That's when he seemed to have forgotten about her. That's when she couldn't help but wonder if the other woman was on his mind. That's when she began to doubt herself—her attractiveness and her worth to Jared who never understood that. At least not while they were still together. Daina swore that he did now. Did it really matter anymore? This was why she explained to Daina that she wasn't going out with Jared with the intention of getting back with him. She was going out with him out of curiosity. She wanted to know how it would feel to be out with him again, which was why she didn't know what to put on her body to make herself feel attractive, yet not predatory.

Buzzz!

Tandi's heart raced as she sprang off the bed. She looked at the alarm clock. If that was Jared, he was early—twenty minutes early to be exact. She wasn't ready. Her makeup wasn't done and her hair was messed up from laying back on the bed. She quickly pulled her robe on over her clothes.

Buzzz!

She went to the top of the stairs. "Carline!"

Carline was already on her way to the door. "I'll get it."

"Thank you." If that was Jared, she wasn't the only anxious one. She started looking for her comb.

"Tandi, it's a friend of yours, Evonne Fulton."

Tandi couldn't believe the audacity of the woman. She had not seen or spoken to Evonne since Daina returned, and she had no intention of speaking to her tonight of all nights.

"Carline, would you tell—"

Evonne suddenly appeared alongside Carline. "Hey, girl, it's Friday night. I thought you and I could do some hanging. We haven't done that in a while."

Carline slipped away.

Tandi was floored by Evonne's facade of cheeriness, which obviously belied the deceit in her heart. It was no wonder she had been so fooled by Evonne's lies.

"Come on, Tandi. Don't just stand there. Go get dressed." Evonne started up the stairs. "I feel like partying. We're going into Manhattan tonight. Queens is too dead."

You have a whole lot of nerve! Tandi told herself. *Be cool.*

"What's wrong with you?" Evonne asked, still climbing the stairs.

Stay cool. "Evonne, you should've called before coming over."

"I did call. In fact, I've been calling, but you're never home."

Tandi cringed as Evonne came closer. If Evonne made it all the way up into the bedroom, she might get too comfortable, and Tandi certainly didn't want that. She started down the stairs, meeting Evonne halfway.

Stay cool. "I have other plans for tonight, and I'm running late. I'll walk you back down."

"Well. I guess I'm being put out," Evonne said as she pivoted on the step and started back down. Walking ahead of Tandi, Evonne did not go to the front door, but into the living room.

Stay cool. Tandi stayed out in the hall. "Evonne, I have to finish getting dressed."

"Where's your date taking you?"

Tandi held her robe close to her body. "Did I say anything about a date?"

"Oh, it's a date, all right. I see those red heels." Evonne started lowering herself to sit.

Stay cool. "Don't sit."

Stopping halfway down, Evonne arched her brows. "You're kidding, right?"

Stay cool. "I don't have time."

Evonne sat anyway. "Damn, I'm not staying long. Why are you acting so funny?"

Tandi was losing it. She was at the breaking point. Her breath was coming in short, shallow gasps. She wanted to blast Evonne about all the lies she told, but not in Sporty's house, and certainly not in earshot of his bedroom. She closed her eyes.

"Evonne, I need for you to leave—now."

"Are you upset with me about something?"

Tandi hugged her robe to her body as her foot went to tapping.

"Well, say something. Did I do something to you I don't know about?"

"You have a whole lot of damn nerve."

"What? What did I do? I—"

"Cut it out! You know, I was hoping you'd take a big-ass clue and leave, but since you didn't, let me clue you in to what I know."

"What the hell are you talking about?"

Tandi balled up her fist. "Stop bullshitting me, Evonne!"

"Honest to God, Tandi. I don't know what you're talking about."

Tandi charged into the living room. "You pathetic liar!"

Gasping, Evonne brought her hand to her heart. "What am I lying about? I've told you the truth about everything that happened with Jared."

"Liar! You've lied about everything. You've lied about being my friend, you've lied about Jared."

"No, I didn't!"

"Liar! You hovered around me like a hungry-ass vulture waiting for the opportunity to pounce on my husband, for how long? Years?"

"That's not true!" Evonne suddenly stood. "I told you what happened between me and Jared was an accident. If Jared said anything else, he's the liar."

"No, Evonne, you're the liar. You lied your way . . ."

"I did not!"

". . . into my bed because you've always wanted Jared . . ."

"That's a lie!"

". . . and maybe even the life I had with him."

"That's a lie! I never—"

"Don't waste your breath or my time, Evonne. Just get the hell out!"

"I think Jared is the one who cheated on you, not just with me, but with other women."

Tandi glanced down the hall toward Sporty's bedroom. The door was ajar.

"Evonne," Tandi said, lowering her voice, "I know every lie you told Jared before you went out to the bar, every lie you told while you were at the bar, and every lie you told after you screwed Jared."

"Wrong again. Jared screwed me. Whatever he told you to the contrary is a lie. He's trying to—"

"Shut up!" Tandi screamed, forgetting about Sporty.

Evonne froze.

"What you told Jared about me was calculated to make him want to get drunk so he'd be so wasted he wouldn't know you had slithered into his bed."

"You're way off. Think about it. Jared wants you back. Don't you think he'd make up lies about me to make himself look good?"

"Did Jared lie about you coming back over there a second time begging to get with him?"

Evonne put her hands on her hips indignantly. "Yes the hell he did! I never went back over there."

"Are you calling my son a liar?"

"Well . . . well, I—"

"I my ass! I asked my son. He told me about how you tried to finagle your way into going to the movies with them."

"That's not true. He misunderstood me, and so did Jared. I did go over there one time to see what I could do to help you and Jared settle your differences, but I—"

"Liar!"

"Stop calling me a liar! Tandi, you're my best friend. I wouldn't go after Jared. He's lying to you."

Tandi marched to the front door. "Not according to my son and Daina." She opened the door.

Evonne stayed put. "Oh, now this all makes sense. Daina is behind this."

"No, Daina pulled my coattail." Tandi held the door open.

Evonne was not leaving. "So you believe her over me?"

"I'd believe Clinton over you." Tandi caught a glimpse of Carline pulling her head back into Sporty's room. "Leave, Evonne."

"So, you're gonna throw our friendship away just like that?"

Tandi couldn't believe Evonne was that psychotic. "You know what my aunt used to say about friendship? She said, 'Some friendships are like autumn leaves. Their colors change, they fall by the wayside, they get ugly, and eventually they disappear into the earth.' Do you understand that, Evonne? You changed, you got ugly, and I want you to disappear. So please, go."

Evonne shook her head. "No, I'm not gonna let you blame me because you couldn't hold on to your man."

"Just leave, Evonne! Get out," Tandi said, pointing out the door.

Evonne strolled to the door but she didn't step outside. "He didn't want you, he wanted me."

"Oh, did he tell you that when he told you he'd file a restraining order against you if you kept bothering him?"

Evonne glared bullets at Tandi. "I hate you."

"It's good to know we have the same feelings for each other, so get the hell out."

Evonne still wasn't ready to leave. "You're so full of yourself. You were always throwing what you had up in my face, showing off your jewelry, your house, your car, your man. And then you had the nerve to whine and complain about everything he didn't do for you."

Evonne's contempt washed over Tandi like a freezing rain. "That's right, Evonne, show your true face. Let me see who you really are."

"I'm really someone who can't stand the sight of you. You don't know how many times I wanted to smash you in the face."

"Perhaps you should've, then you wouldn't've had to pretend all these years to be my friend when what you really wanted, you couldn't have."

"Bitch, if I really wanted your husband, I would have had him. And if he was mine, I would have treated him a whole lot better than you did. You can believe that. I would not have sat on my fat ass and whined like a helpless bitch."

"I've been one too many of your damn bitches. You can go to hell. But let me tell you about this whining fat ass of mine. Jared is taking it out tonight. He's my date, and if I want him to be, he'll be my man—again. Now get the hell out!"

"Fu—"

Tandi snatched Evonne! She yanked her around! She shoved her hard out the door and immediately slammed the door behind her.

Defiant, Evonne pushed back against the door but the slam lock held it strong. "Bitch, your man fucked me! He couldn't even get it up for you!"

Tandi put her shoulder against the door and double bolted it. "Yeah, but he had to be tore down drunk to get it up for you."

"Bitch!" Evonne shouted through the door. "You're nothing! You can kiss my ass."

Breathing hard, Tandi stood staring at the door, not believing what had just happened. She clasped her shaking hands together tightly. Hearing how Evonne felt about her secondhand had hurt, but hearing it firsthand was worse by far. Had Evonne always hated her, even from the beginning of their so-called friendship? If not from the beginning, when did she start? Did it start when she stupidly spilled her guts about the sweet pleasure of Jared's lovemaking or when she complained about him no longer making love to her? Had she been bragging when she talked about her life or had Evonne, in her own jealous mind, perceived it that way? In her ignorance, she thought she had been simply sharing her life with a friend just as that so-called friend shared hers. Had she been so naive that she hadn't even suspected she had been keeping company with the enemy? How had that happened? Had she herself been so needy that she closed her eyes to Evonne's deception so that she could say she had someone besides Daina to call friend? The question was, why had she allowed herself for years to wallow in self-doubt and pity that she would even need anyone at all to make her feel like she mattered?

Buzzz!

Tandi stepped back from the door. If Evonne was still out there, she was going to kick her ass. She peeked out through the blinds.

"Oh, God." It was Jared. She wasn't ready and now she didn't know if she was up to going out with him at all.

"May I get the door?"

She whirled around and found herself face-to-face with Carline.

"Why don't you go up and finish dressing. I'll have your guest wait in the living room."

"It's my husband, but I don't think I can—"

"Of course you can. Go on, finish dressing," Carline nudged Tandi away from the door. I think you'll enjoy a night out. Stay as long as you like. I'll stay with Mr. Belson."

"Are you sure?" Tandi asked, wondering what Carline thought of the argument she'd obviously overheard.

Buzzz!

"Go on."

Tandi touched her hair. She hadn't combed it yet. "Give me a minute to get up the stairs." She ran off down the hall.

Carline watched Tandi race off, her robe flying behind her. She waited until she heard Tandi run up the stairs before she opened the door.

Expecting to see Tandi, Jared had been about to present the dozen red roses to Carline.

"Good evening, Mr. Crawford," Carline said.

"Good evening. You are?"

"Carline. Mr. Belson's home health aide. Mrs. Crawford will be down in ten minutes. Come in."

Jared stepped warily inside the house he had not been in in more than ten years. The last time he was there, he and Sporty Belson had almost come to blows over Sporty calling him a second-rate ambulance chaser. That day Jared swore he would never step foot in there again. Boy, did circumstances have a way of making one eat one's words.

"May I get you something to drink?" Carline asked.

"No thanks." Jared went on into the living room. He didn't sit as he looked around the room. Nothing had changed, but it didn't smell as old and as stale as MJ had described.

"Can I put the flowers in a vase for you?"

"No. I'd like to hand them to my wife."

"That's nice. Would you like to sit down?"

"Please, don't worry about me. I'm fine."

Nodding, Carline left Jared and went back to her charge.

Upstairs, Tandi had stripped the black skirt and shell off and had pulled on the short, tight-fitting, low-cut, spaghetti-strapped black dress she had bought to wear out with Brent but never did. She kicked off her red heels and slipped on a pair of vampy, black high-heeled sandals. Evonne didn't know with whom she was messing. Up against her, Evonne didn't have a chance with Jared. As before, Tandi's full-length mirror told her she was hot. The fire was coming from her aura and not from the color of her dress. Tonight, anything that touched her that wasn't sanctioned was going to get burned. The only thing missing was the black shawl she'd bought to wear with her dress, and that was in one of her two suitcases in the attic. Fortunately, the finished attic was on the same floor a door away.

Tandi hurried into the attic. She went straight to the pullman-sized suitcase sitting alongside the old dining room chair she had sat in months ago, reminiscing about the games of hide-and-seek she and Glynn used to play in there when Sporty wasn't home. Opening the suitcase right away, she took the black fringed shawl from its protective plastic bag. Quickly rezipping her suitcase, she hurried out of the attic and had turned off the light when her mind told her that she had seen something that was out of place. Something that was different. She switched the light back on and scanned the attic until her eyes came to rest on the steamer trunk. The padlock was on the floor. The trunk was wide open.

"Oh, my God." Tandi went to the trunk. It was empty.

"Tandi!" Carline called. "Tandi, your husband is waiting for you."

48

*S*eething out in her car, Evonne kept pounding on her steering wheel, unable to stop hurting her hand, but it was the only thing she could do to keep from screaming like a woman who had lost her ever-loving mind. Like a fool she had sat and watched Jared, looking finer than she had ever seen him before, carry an armful of roses into the house for Tandi. It had sickened her. She had almost thrown up. Those roses should have been for her. She was the one who loved him. She was the one who could make him happy, not that malcontent who would never be satisfied.

Tandi had turned on her. She couldn't believe it. Tandi was supposed to be her best friend. It wasn't fair. Jared lied. She hated them both. No, not Jared. Tandi. She hated Tandi.

Unable to drive away, Evonne waited for Jared and Tandi to come outside. She watched as Jared chivalrously held his car door open for Tandi like she was a queen. It should have been her. Even now, Tandi wasn't appreciating Jared—she wasn't smiling. Her face was cold, just like her. She thought she hated Tandi before, but seeing the smug, cold look on her face, she absolutely despised her.

She watched Jared and Tandi drive off, neither giving a thought to her, neither thinking about how they had hurt her.

"I hope you both drop dead!"

Evonne's hand ached horribly. Yet, ignoring her pain, she put the car in gear and peeled off. She didn't need Tandi, she didn't need Jared. She hated them both. The hell with them. She was better than both of them.

49

The blood-red roses paled next to the rich mocha glow of Tandi's skin when she slipped her shawl off her shoulders. She smelled of Oriental Musk, her favorite body splash. To Jared, Tandi looked as good as she smelled. She had lost a little weight but the loss had been in all the right places—her smaller waist made her hips seem even broader as they curved down into her shapely thighs. She was wearing that black dress like it was painted on her body. God, she was beautiful. He had known all along that she was, but it had been a long time since he was struck by her beauty and that was his own fault—he had stopped noticing. Tonight, however, he was. He would never make that mistake again.

But something was wrong. Tandi wasn't talking, and that bothered him. He didn't know what was on her mind. Unless Tandi opened up, he wouldn't know if he had a chance. He had noticed when she came into the living room back at the house, that she didn't look too happy. Had she changed her mind and not wanted to come out with him tonight?

Whenever she could, without being obvious, Tandi stole a look at Jared. How long had it been since she had seen him looking this good? Hell, how long had it been since she'd seen him at all? Jared always wore a suit, and he was always groomed, but there was something different about the way he looked tonight. His hair was cut close the way she liked it. His mustache was smaller but impeccably trimmed. In fact, other than being older, he looked as he did the day they married, and like the day they married, she felt weak every time he touched her. When he put his hand on the small of her back as he took her to their table, she thought, how right this was. And it was. This was all she had been asking him for, a little romance, a little attention. She should not have had to leave him to get this.

"You seem so far away," Jared said. "A penny for your thoughts."

She smiled timidly.

"I know, it's corny."

Tandi nodded.

Jared picked up his fork and put it down again. "I'm glad you came out with me tonight."

"I'm glad you asked me," she said, meaning it. Despite her bitter feelings about Evonne and the memory of her laying in bed with Jared, she was determined that those feelings and memories would not spoil her evening. Tandi began eating her dinner of grilled salmon and asparagus as Jared put two roasted mushrooms from his plate onto hers. She looked at him.

Belatedly realizing what he had done, Jared blanched. "I'm sorry. I guess old habits are hard to break." He reached across with his fork to take them back.

Tandi blocked her plate with her hand. "I still like mushrooms."

"Good."

They finished their meal in silence as words were yet to be found that would easily flow between them.

"Michael Jared would have loved this," Tandi said, setting her spoon down in her empty glacé dish.

"MJ."

"Yes, I know. I'm still trying to get used to it."

"You will. But you know he eats ice cream every night."

"Jared," Tandi said reproachfully.

"I don't let him take much," he defended. "Besides, he said you would let him have it."

"Not every night, and he knows that."

Jared smiled. "He's slick."

"He's spoiled. He's been getting away with a lot—lately."

Jared slid his half-eaten strawberry glace a few inches away. He was never one for desserts.

As if on cue, the waiter appeared and collected both their dishes. "Would you like anything else? A demitasse perhaps, or a glass of wine?"

"Two demitasses," Jared said without consulting Tandi. He dared because he didn't want the evening to end.

Tandi smiled in a secret way. She didn't mind that Jared ordered for her. It was like old times, but she didn't dwell on that. Those days were behind them. But Jared drinking a demitasse? That was a new one on her. He drank black coffee, but he used to say that a demitasse was a joke. But she understood what he was doing and didn't remind him that he once said that the cup belonged in a doll's house.

"Daina must have promised MJ something to get him to stay over at her house," she said.

"Actually, they're not at her house. They're up in the Catskills."

"Daina didn't tell me she was going up there."

"It was a last-minute decision. She and Herb went up there to get the house ready for summer."

"But tomorrow's Saturday. I told Michael—MJ—we'd do something together."

"I know. He said to tell you to have a good time tonight, and that he'll see you early Sunday morning. That's when Daina's bringing him back."

Tandi gave Jared a knowing look.

He knew what she was thinking, and she was right. He, Daina, and MJ had planned the evening. It had even been MJ's idea that he kiss Tandi when he gave her the roses. He had kissed her on the cheek and not on the mouth as MJ had instructed. He didn't want to start the evening off wrong.

The waiter returned.

Jared watched as Tandi accepted her demitasse. She thanked the waiter with a gracious nod. He still liked her style, and he still enjoyed being with her. Why hadn't he done this for her all along without feeling like she was putting too much demand on his time? It wasn't like he had to dig ditches. Simply sitting and eating and talking to his wife was as easy as breathing. Looking back, he had been overly selfish with his time while Tandi had always been so selfless in her giving of her time and all that she did for him. She had every right to walk out. Acknowledging that truth saddened him. He began slowly turning his demitasse cup in a circle.

This time it was Tandi who asked, "Private thought?"

He stopped turning his cup. "I was thinking about MJ," he lied.

"He gave up his weekend with you because he thought it best we go out together. He thinks we should date."

Musingly, Tandi sipped her demitasse. What she had been afraid of was happening. Michael Jared was growing up without her. His outlook on life was changing. Apparently, he had gotten over his angst about his parents being sexual beings.

"I told MJ to not worry about us," Jared said, picking up his cup. His hand and his lips practically swallowed his cup when he turned it up to his mouth.

Tandi smiled to herself when Jared looked as if he was going to swallow the tiny cup. He quietly set his cup down in its saucer. It made not a clank. He watched her. He could see that Tandi's eyes were twinkling. Something was making her smile. He wondered if it were him. He wondered if this was a sign that she might forgive him.

"Tandi, I know I promised I wouldn't talk about certain things, but do you think you'll be moving out of your father's house soon? MJ hates that you're there."

"Actually, I'm waiting for an apartment to come through."

Jared's heart sank.

"The health aides that are with us now seem to have Daddy pretty much tamed, especially Carline. How she's doing it, I don't know, but he hasn't gone off on her. So, it's a matter of time."

"You don't have to look for an apartment. You have a home."

There was no mistaking what Jared meant, but for Tandi, going back home wasn't just going back to a house. It meant going back to Jared, and at this point, she didn't know if that was what she wanted.

"Tandi, I'm sorry I said the house was mine. It's ours."

"Jared, you promised we wouldn't talk tonight about us. You—"

"I said I wouldn't pressure you and I won't, but, Tandi, it's killing me to not talk about what went wrong. You left me. You cut me off. You didn't give me one opportunity to tell you how I felt about that."

"That's not true. Months and months before I tried to talk to you, but you weren't listening."

"Looking back, perhaps I wasn't. Did you read any of my letters?"

Tandi's silence was her answer.

Feeling badly, Jared refrained from asking why not. "Look, my need to talk to you is stronger than my promise to not pressure you. What I've been telling you in those letters is that I realize that I've been wrong."

"Jared, to be fair, there's more to my leaving home than you and me or even the mistakes we made. To tell you the truth, I hadn't been happy for a very long time with my life, period."

"So why didn't you tell me that? Or maybe you did and I didn't hear you. Did you?"

"No. I don't think I knew at the time that I was unhappy with my life. I was too busy blaming you. Since I left home, I've been doing a lot of thinking and . . . re-evaluating."

"What have you come up with?"

"For one, I was bored—for years. Jared, I don't like selling real estate."

"You did in the beginning. What changed it for you?"

"I don't know. I guess brick and wood just don't do it for me. Don't get me wrong, some of the homes are architecturally beautiful, but I think I need to be doing something that I like that I can make a living at. And right now, I just don't know what that is."

"Sure you do."

She arched her brow. "I do?"

"Yes, and it still has to do with houses."

"Then, I don't know—"

"Tandi, when we first met, there was only one kind of magazine you'd buy, and you bought every one of that type on the market. Do you need any more of a clue?"

No she didn't. Home decorating and interior design were her passion. "Wow. I forgot all about that."

"As I see it, you got into the wrong area of real estate. Your heart is in interior design. You used to want to be an interior decorator, remember?"

Tandi hadn't thought about that in years. An interior decorator was what she wanted to be from the time she was a teenager rearranging her bedroom every other month. She had planned on going to the Fashion Institute of Technology for interior design when she graduated high school. She had a flair for colors and a taste for fine furniture. It had been her dream to decorate the homes of the rich and famous so that the lack of money would not stymie her artistic expression. That dream was set aside when she first moved out of Sporty's house on her own and she had to make a living. Then along came Jared and Michael Jared, and that dream was forgotten. Now that Jared had reminded her that she once had a passion at all, Tandi began to feel it in her soul.

Jared saw the twinkle of inspiration in Tandi's eyes. "You can still follow that dream, you know."

She felt invigorated. She was excited. "But I'll have to go back to school."

"That's a good idea. I'll support you in whatever it takes to get you there," Jared said, daring to hope she would allow him to do that for her. Even more than that, he didn't want her to become any more ensconced into the arms of the man she was seeing than she already was.

"Jared, I can do this on my own. I don't need your money."

"I know you can. I just want you to know that I'm here for you. I'll help out in any way I can."

"Thank you, but I'll be all right."

Tandi was pushing him away. He was afraid she would. It could only mean that she wasn't going to let him back into her life. "Can I ask you a question?"

She automatically put up her defenses. Whenever that question was asked, the question that followed was often loaded.

"Are you serious about the guy you're seeing?"

Loaded and fired. "What did Daina tell you?"

"Just that you had a friend."

Big mouth.

"So, is he just a friend?"

"Jared, we're not having this discussion."

He sat back. Maybe it was just as well. He really didn't want to know all the details anyway. Besides there was something he needed to say. "I never wanted to sleep with Evonne."

The mere mention of Evonne's name put a sour taste in Tandi's mouth.

"I won't make excuses, I won't play it down. I just want you to know I recognize that I made a mistake. What I want is for you to forgive me, so that—"

"Jared, I didn't come out with you tonight to put you on any guilt trips or to strip you of your pride. I—"

"You're not. It's just that I know how much I hurt you."

"Jared, I've totally forgiven you for Evonne."

Amazed, he could only look at Tandi and wonder how.

"Ironically, it was something Evonne said that got me to forgive you."

"What was that?"

"She said if you were hers, she would have treated you a whole lot better than I did. And it made me think about our life together and how I treated you."

"You weren't so bad."

"I could have done better."

"And so could I. Many times I wasn't there for you."

"Jared, would you please let me shoulder my share of the blame?" Tandi asked, tearing. "We were in this marriage together, good or bad. We both had something to do with the outcome; however, I know what my faults were and so do you probably. I—"

"Tandi, but you did the best you could when I—"

"Okay. You want some blame? Well, Jared, I do blame you for one thing."

He was taken aback but hadn't he asked for it? He waited.

"I blame you for making me feel so unloved, so unwanted."

"Tandi, I swear to God, I didn't know I was doing that. I thought if my practice was a success, then everything else in our lives was okay. Obviously, I got that wrong. I hope you'll let me make it up to you."

"I don't know if you can. It may be too late for us."

"It's never too late. We can start over. We can date if you want, whatever it takes."

From the moment Jared gave her the roses earlier, Tandi was close to crying. Daina had said Jared wanted her back with a passion. This she could see and feel all evening, and she couldn't say that knowing this didn't make her feel good.

Jared wanted to hold Tandi. "It's a beautiful night. Would you like to walk a little?"

She nodded.

Again, Jared was hopeful that all wasn't lost. He signaled the waiter for the bill. If God was watching, this evening would never end.

50

Jared was feeling good. The evening was turning out better than he had hoped and what's more, the weather was cooperating. Rain had been predicted. As yet, not a drop had fallen. The night was refreshingly crisp and picture postcard clear. Only the brilliance of street lights and spotlights in Rockefeller Center outshone the full moon high above St. Patrick's Cathedral. It had been a tepid spring and now that it was the middle of June, it was finally beginning to feel like summer was on its way. It was a perfect night for strolling in Manhattan. In fact, Jared had forgotten that he liked strolling in the city after the maddening work crowd had fled and left the sidewalks to tourists, native strollers, entertainment seekers, and to diners hungry for tasty treats of every nation.

Side by side Jared and Tandi strolled up Fifth Avenue, neither their shoulders nor their hands touching, although Jared itched to take her hand in his but dared not presume she wanted him to. As they started across Fiftieth Street, he put his hand on her arm just under her elbow.

Tandi liked that Jared was being the perfect gentleman. His touch was nice. It was familiar.

They continued, not talking, just enjoying the walk. From time to time their arms brushed against each other, making each aware that the other's touch was electric. If Jared had only known that if he slipped his arm around Tandi like he used to so many years ago, that her wall of determination to not give in to him was in jeopardy of crumbling like dried out toast. And that made Tandi mad. She wasn't ready to step back into a marriage that frustrated her and made her feel empty inside. She couldn't believe how comfortable she was being with Jared. Emotionally, she felt herself seesawing between being guarded and wanting to feel his arms around her. Coming out with Jared tonight was supposed to get them talking again. That's all. She wasn't supposed to be falling back in love with him. Wrapping her shawl more snug around her shoulders, Tandi picked up her pace.

Jared quickly matched Tandi's stride. "What's wrong?" He had sensed her attitude change ever since he touched her.

"Nothing."

"Are you angry with me?"

"I wish I were."

"Why?"

"Ah, it's not worth talking about."

"Isn't not talking where our problems started?"

Tandi stopped. "Can we please not try and drag all of my demons out tonight? There is only so much I can handle right now." She zipped off again.

Again, Jared matched Tandi's stride, all the while glimpsing the confusion in her face—the way she rolled her lips inward, the way she kept frowning. They continued in silence. After a block Tandi slowed down. Jared followed her lead. Although they still walked side by side, they walked more than a foot apart. Jared felt that his arm should have been around Tandi's waist. She should have been nestled deep in the crook of his arm, by now he should have kissed her at least once. What they should have been doing, they couldn't, not when there was a strained awkwardness between them still. Maybe it was up to him to make the first move.

"It's almost ten-thirty," he said. "We could catch a jam session uptown at The Blue Note. You game?" They started across the street.

No was what she was supposed to be saying, but, "Sure. Why not?" was what Tandi heard herself say.

"Good. Let's go back for the car," he said, pleased she hadn't turned him down.

A few feet from the curb, together, Jared and Tandi about-faced and started back across the street. Without warning, a yellow taxi cut around the corner . . .

"Watch out!" someone shouted.

. . . coming close enough to Tandi to swipe the lower fringes of her long shawl with its rear side panel as it speedily glided past her.

"Hey!" Jared snatched Tandi back. His heart was racing.

Tandi gasped, "Oh, my God." She fell back against Jared.

Jared wrapped his arms around her, holding her protectively against his body. Tandi's legs felt wobbly. She clung to Jared.

Several people gathered around as the taxi sped on, its motor roaring as it cut in and out of traffic going down Fifth Avenue.

"Did you see that?" a man asked excitedly.

"Yeah. That maniac could have killed you, lady!"

"Miss, are you all right?" a woman asked Tandi.

She really wasn't. She shuddered.

Jared tightened his embrace, trying to still Tandi's trembling. He could almost feel her heart pounding in unison with his own. "Are you hurt?"

Closing her eyes, Tandi lay her head against Jared's chest. She slipped her arms around his waist and grabbed fistfuls of his jacket.

"That bastard," he said. "He could have killed you."

Suddenly, there was a loud thunderous crash.

A chorus of gasps came up from the few people still standing around. They all turned in the direction of the crash farther down Fifth Avenue.

"Oh, my God," a short gray-haired woman said. "I wonder if it was that taxi."

"If it is," Jared said, "it would be just desserts."

"Jared!" Tandi exclaimed. "Some innocent person may have gotten hurt."

"Or killed," a man said.

"That would be unfortunate," Jared said, "but that maniac could have killed you."

"That's true," the short gray-haired woman said.

"Did anyone get the license plate in case it was that taxi?" a man asked.

"Man, it happened so fast," a teenager replied, "I didn't catch one digit. Did somebody peep who was driving?"

"It was a man," a woman said behind Jared and Tandi, "but that's not saying much."

"I'm gonna go see if it was that taxi," the teenager said. He and the girl he was with took off running toward the accident.

"People drive crazy in this city," the short gray-haired woman said.

"That's because everyone's always in a hurry," another woman said.

"Yes," the short gray-haired woman agreed. "You have to be careful walking out here. Miss, maybe you should go see if it's the same car that almost hit you."

"I don't wanna know," Tandi said, beginning to feel her heartbeat slow. She let go of her hold on Jared, but he didn't let go of his hold on her. "I wasn't hit, and if the accident is bad, I definitely don't wanna see it."

"I think we should go down there," Jared said. "If it's that taxi, we should report it to the police."

"Jared, you're probably right, but I'm just not up to dealing with it."

"Are you sure you're not hurt?"

"Yes."

"Okay, then, I'll go get the car. You wait inside that restaurant on the corner."

"I'm okay. I'll walk with you."

"Tandi, are you sure you're up to it?"

"Jared, I didn't get hit."

"Mister," the short gray-haired woman said to Jared, "that taxi came mighty close. You should get her checked out anyway." She walked off.

"Yeah, Tandi, we—"

"No," Tandi said, "I'm fine. Can we go?"

Jared glanced up at the light. It was green. He checked for oncoming traffic anyway. All was clear. With his arm still around Tandi, he started across. She always fit just right in the crook of his arm, and he always liked the feel of her hips swaying against him. But she wasn't walking her usual hip-swaying way, she was limping. Once across the street, he stopped again.

"You are hurt. You're limping. Are you hurt?"

"No," she said with a chuckle. "These heels are killing my feet."

He looked down at Tandi's three-inch heels. "If I had to wear those things, I'd sue somebody, but I have to tell you, you do look good in them."

"I'd better. They cost enough."

"I tell you what. You stay here. I'll go get the car."

"Jared, I said I can walk."

"You're a stubborn woman. Your feet are killing you, you were almost run down, and still you insist that you're okay."

"I am. Don't get me wrong, I do feel a little shaky, but isn't that to be expected? It was kind of scary."

"Yeah, it was."

"But the truth is, I'm not in a hurry to get back to my father. He's in quite capable hands."

Reading between the lines, Jared took that to mean that Tandi didn't mind being with him. "Then—" A man suddenly brushed roughly against Jared, pushing him into Tandi.

"Hey!" Jared shouted after the man.

The man didn't stop or turn around.

Jared started after him. "Hey, you!"

Tandi quickly pulled Jared back. "Let it go. We *are* standing in the middle of the sidewalk."

"Yeah, but he could've walked around us. There's plenty of space out here."

"Jared, haven't we had enough excitement for one night?"

"Yeah, but—"

"It's not important. Why are you so upset?"

Jared couldn't let go of his anger. "I guess I'm still pissed about that fool almost hitting you."

"I'm okay. Let it go."

Jared loudly exhaled his frustration. He told himself to calm down. He didn't want his being upset to upset Tandi, and most definitely, he didn't want to ruin a promising evening. He eased his arm back around Tandi. She didn't seem to mind as they continued toward the underground garage on Forty-seventh Street where they left the car.

Beginning to feel better, Tandi relaxed against Jared. The close call had shaken her, but she had to admit being with Jared at that moment reminded her that she felt safe with his arms around her. What she found interesting was that Jared was his usual calm self when she was almost struck by that car, but he had lost his cool when that man bumped into them. That wasn't like him. She didn't think much of anything could get him excited.

"Don't take this wrong, Jared, but you're usually so mild-mannered, I'm surprised you let an accidental bump tick you off."

"Now that's interesting. I'd think you'd be upset if I didn't say anything to that guy. You always seemed to think my mild-manneredness was a bad thing."

Tandi stopped in front of a storefront illuminated in blue light, closed up for the night. "Actually, that wasn't the problem. Not getting a reaction out of you when I tried to talk to you is what annoyed me."

"Why, because I didn't rant and rave? Being calm didn't mean I had no emotions, that I didn't care."

"That's just it, Jared. I didn't think you cared about anything. Maybe once in a while you should've shown me that you were upset about something I said or did. Then I would've known you were alive. You were always so monotone in your emotions, I never knew where I stood with you."

"But I was that way when we met, when we were dating, and before we got married. I didn't change, Tandi."

"It seemed to me that you did. About six years after we got married, you seemed to shut down emotionally. It was as if you were angry at me because you married me."

"Tandi, how could you say that or even think it? That's not how I felt."

"But, Jared, I wouldn't have known that by the way you were acting, and the longer we were married, the more you seemed to close yourself off from me."

Jared couldn't argue that this was the first time she had told him this. She had told him a number of times over the years that he was emotionally distant. He just never allowed himself to address it. He had dismissed Tandi and her complaints as hormonal and went on about his business. He couldn't do that anymore. His marriage was on the line.

"Tandi, this might sound cold, but I have no excuse for my aloofness, except to say, I saw no reason to sweat the small stuff."

Tandi's mouth fell open.

"Before you get excited, hear me out."

Tandi started to walk away.

Jared pulled her back, ignoring the single couple who curiously glanced their way on the quiet street. "Listen to me. As I saw it, we weren't having major problems involving our health, our finances, or our lives. I felt everything was as it should be. We had each other, we had MJ. I didn't think I needed to reaffirm my love for you—"

"In word or deed," Tandi interjected.

"I thought I was doing it in deed."

"Okay, I'll give you that. You probably thought the lifestyle you provided for me and Michael Jared expressed the love you had for us, but a woman—me—I needed more than materialism, Jared. I needed to feel you, to be with you emotionally. And the more I needed that from you, the more you pulled away."

"I know," he said, remembering not wanting to come home some nights because he didn't want to hear her complain. "I knew something wasn't right, Tandi, but I didn't know what it was or what to do about it. When you'd want to talk and our talks became arguments, I'd pull back. To be honest, distance was safe. I figured we couldn't argue if I didn't allow myself to get caught up in the huddle with you."

"Well, Jared, that distance is what hurt me, what hurt us."

"I understand that now, and I'm sorry."

They fell silent then, looking into each other's eyes. In Tandi's eyes Jared saw a cautiousness that she was not fully committed to trusting him. In Jared's eyes, Tandi saw that he was hungry for her, a look she hadn't seen in years, and it excited her and scared her all at once. Again, she walked off. Again, Jared caught up with her and again, he took a chance. He slipped his arm around her waist, and again she let him. It seemed right. Jared liked the feel of Tandi's now swaying hips against his body. She liked the feel of him drawing her close and wondered what it would be like to be made love to by him again, but so much more had to be said before she could find that out.

"I have to tell you something," she said.

He wondered if it was about the man she was seeing.

"Jared, after you cheated on me, I couldn't stop hating you. I hated everything about you. Everything you did irritated me. Even the calmness that was so a part of you grated on me. I started equating that calmness with weakness. Forgive me, but I thought you had no balls. That you weren't man enough for me anymore."

That was not news to him. He had known she was feeling that way for a long time. It was the look of disgust he'd seen so often on her face that gave her away. If he could have taken hold of Tandi and shaken her until she saw him for the man he was, he would have, except it would have made him an abuser, something he wasn't. He let that disgusted look stay because again he didn't know what to do to make it disappear.

"I was wrong," Tandi said. "I'm sorry."

"It's not all your fault." He let his arm drop from Tandi's waist. "I guess I let you down."

Tandi stopped walking. She tried to not notice the people who eyed them as they walked past. She took Jared's hand and made him stop also. "Look, I knew you weren't weak. I mean, I thought you were weak to indulge in an affair, but I knew that as a man you stood heads above so many others. You really are a good man, Jared, and I know that. Maybe all that anger I had inside was partly at myself for not satisfying you, and . . ."

"But you did, I—"

". . . partly at my father. I just found myself angry all the time. And then when you became so distant, you were the one I took it out on. It was wrong, but all I could think about was hurting you so that you could experience the same pain, the same loneliness I did."

"Well, I think you accomplished that. When you left, I wasn't feeling the best."

Good. It was good to know he felt something.

"But I found I had plenty of time to think about my life with you and without you. I wasn't liking the latter. And the funny thing is, all that time I took from you to invest in my practice, when you left, I took that same time away from my practice to give to MJ. I mean, I will have to reinvest some of that time back into my practice, but it won't have to be as much as I was putting in before. When I realized this, I understood that it was me and not the practice who was destroying our marriage. That's when I discovered that I'm strongest with you in my life."

Tandi felt vindicated. "That's probably one of the nicest thing you've ever said to me. Thank you."

Jared didn't need to say "you're welcome" because he was obliged to Tandi for giving him the chance to let her know how he felt. He held his hand out to her. "Friends?"

Misty-eyed, Tandi let out all the pent-up pain she'd been holding on to with a single breath. She lay her hand in Jared's, and for a minute they stood smiling at each other. Then, hand in hand, shoulder to shoulder, they continued down Fifth Avenue.

"Tandi, did I ever tell you about my grandfather? My mother's father?"

"Just that he went to school only two days in his life, and that he was a truck driver. You said he did well in his life."

"Yes, but did I tell you that he made more of an impression on me than my own father?"

"No. How?"

"By giving me confidence. When I was twelve and had gotten my butt kicked for the third time by Horace, the school bully, my grandfather told me that I was beat before I was even hit. He told me that after I was beat up by Horace the first time, that Horace knew that he could always pick on me, and he was right. My grandfather said, like animals, people can smell fear. Which meant Horace could smell how afraid I was of him."

"So Horace kept picking on you?"

"Relentlessly, but I wasn't the only kid he beat on. I was the one who wouldn't fight back, and I think that pissed him off even more. He probably thought I was a little punk."

"But, Jared, why didn't you at least try to fight back?"

"Because my father said he'd beat my ass if I fought in school. Believe me, I was more afraid of my father than Horace, and besides, I was a skinny kid. I didn't think I could beat Horace. He was one of those big, beefy kids with hooves for fists. It was my grandfather who said that I could beat Horace, that I had to fight back or all the kids would think I was weak. But he also said because I was quiet and easygoing, I had an advantage over Horace. He said Horace had no idea what I could do because I wasn't wolfing. My grandfather said a man's strength wasn't in his blustering, but in the firm set of his jaw, the quiet of his demeanor, the fire in his eyes, and the power behind his convictions."

"Smart man. I'm sorry I never got to meet him."

"You would have liked him. Granddad put me in karate classes where I learned discipline first and how to fight second. The next time Horace got up in my face, even before I knew any serious karate, I put him on his ass with one punch. The boy was shocked. Afterward, I didn't boast that I'd finally beat Horace, I went back to being my mild-mannered self. I liked myself that way. It was me. I had no more trouble from Horace or anyone else in school."

Tandi realized what she had mistaken for Jared's weakness was his strength. "Why didn't you ever tell me this story before?"

"I didn't think I had to."

51

Tandi changed her mind about going uptown to The Blue Note. Walking in the fresh, crisp night air with Jared at her side had done her a world of good. Without saying so, Jared was thinking the same. He didn't need music to set the mood with Tandi. It had been set the minute she fell into his arms after that near miss, and now as they stood, shoulder to shoulder, leaning against the railing high above the skating rink in Rockefeller Center in the shadows of dazzling sky- scrapers, he could not have been happier. It was after midnight and the streets of New York were still aglow with headlights. There were quite a few people, mostly couples meandering through Rockefeller Center enjoying the solitude of their own company. It was blissfully quiet and Jared gave it not a thought when he slipped his arm around Tandi's waist.

"Are you cold?" he asked, his lips only inches from Tandi's cheek.

Her shawl was wrapped snugly around her shoulders, but that wasn't what was keeping Tandi warm. It was Jared. Not just his body. Him. Just being the Jared she had fallen in love with had warmed her to her core. No, she wasn't cold. Not in the least. She answered him by resting her head on his shoulder.

Jared savored the moment until MJ came to mind. MJ would love to see them like this. "You know what I've noticed about MJ?" Jared asked.

"What?"

"When he's happy, he laughs like you and cocks his head like me."

"I know," she said.

"The other day when he was kinda down, I asked him to tell me funny stories about you. That always makes him laugh."

"I beg your pardon. What's funny about me?"

"Believe me, according to MJ, plenty. He told me about the time you took him to Fresh Meadow Park and fell asleep on the grass, and ants crawled all over your legs and you woke up screaming."

"That wasn't funny. There must've been a thousand ants on me."

"He said you were jumping around and screaming like a crazed clown and that you took his soda and poured it all over your legs. He said you were really funny."

"Instead of helping me, the little monster laughed at me."

"He's still laughing at you," Jared said, laughing at her himself. He could imagine how frantic she must have been, but his laugh was bittersweet. He stopped. "You never told me about that day."

"By the time you got home, it was late."

He deserved that. He could say nothing, and "I'm sorry" had worn thin.

Tandi looked out over the empty skating rink at the bigger-than-life golden statue of Prometheus, the Titan who stole skills and fire from Olympus and gave them to human beings. Tandi enjoyed reading Greek mythology in high school and used to wonder how man came up with such tales.

Another couple passed along the railing, but for Jared they didn't exist. "Tandi, I want us back."

Those words, this whole scene, Tandi never dreamed or fantasized about. Jared had always been her reality, never her fantasy. It had been up to the two of them to make their lives a dream. She wondered if it were possible for them to get back together to do just that.

Jared sensed that Tandi was standing with her toes at the line that she herself had drawn in the sand. He could see that she was afraid, but he wanted her to trust him. He wanted her to step over that line. He wanted to let her know that it was safe. He kissed her lightly on the lips. She let him, allowing him to think that she wanted what he wanted. He went to kiss her again—with more passion.

She turned her head aside. His lips touched her cheeks. He kissed her there.

"It's too soon," she said.

"It's not too soon, if we both want the same thing."

Maybe they did, but Tandi wasn't about to let herself be rushed.

Silent, she looked steadily at Jared as she eased along the railing, away from him. He got the message and following her, took his time closing the distance between them.

"I should be getting back."

"I thought you said you weren't in a hurry."

"Carline gets off duty soon. I should be there."

"Why don't we call the house and ask her to stay a little longer? I'll pay her overtime."

"She offered to stay longer, but her day is pretty long as it is. I should get home."

Now he felt let down. They were so close, but he didn't want to show his disappointment by sulking. "I heard your father was giving the attendants a hard time."

"Not Carline Hughes."

"I met her tonight. She seems nice."

"The others were nice, too, but my father sent them all packing posthaste."

"So why is Carline still around? You think he likes her?"

"I doubt it. He doesn't want any home health aide around him, but he knows I'll kill him if he acts out again."

"So he's been behaving? He must really be scared of you," Jared teased.

"He better be, but it's really weird how well-behaved he's been. He hasn't talked back to me or Carline. In fact, he doesn't say anything against Carline at all, and that's surprising. He usually sees only the bad in everyone."

"That's the Glynn Belson I know."

"Yes, but in her own quiet way, Carline seems to know how to handle him."

"In other words, she has that outer calm and that inner strength?"

"Touché," she said. "Maybe that's why my father doesn't mess with her."

"That plus the fact that you threatened to put him in a nursing home."

"Geez, I'm gonna have to have a talk with Miss Big-Mouth Daina." She wondered what else Daina might've told Jared.

"Daina wants to see us back together."

Tandi started walking faster. Jared quickly pulled her to a stop.

"Don't run from us, Tandi."

"I'm not. Jared, I have to get home."

"Your father can hold his own for five minutes, it's me who can't. What Daina didn't tell me was whether you still loved me. Do you?"

Tandi looked across the street at the traffic light. It was red. Now that she knew the truth, she couldn't hold what Evonne did against Jared, and she couldn't, in good conscience, blame everything that went wrong in their marriage on him. The traffic light flashed bright green.

Jared waited anxiously for Tandi's answer. He remembered being this anxious when he asked her to marry him.

Tandi felt compelled to say what was in her heart. "Jared, I have never stopped loving you."

Jared didn't break into a smile, he didn't shout out in his glee, and he didn't grab Tandi and embrace her. What he did was gently lift her hand to his lips and kiss the soft warm center of her palm. The irony of it all was that he felt like he should be thanking the reckless driver who pushed Tandi back into his arms, back into his life.

52

There was something truly romantic about a date coming to an end at the front door. A sweet embrace, a soulful kiss was always expected, which was why Tandi would not let Jared walk her up to the house. Standing at his car, she committed herself to kissing him chastely on the cheek although it was obvious by the way he was looking at her that he wanted more. She didn't pull away when he parted her lips with his tongue and kissed her deep and long. All the while she was kissing him back, Tandi told herself she could not let Jared's words of love seduce her into making a hasty decision that she might regret. She ended their kiss long before he wanted it to end, and just in time to stop herself from surrendering to the magnetic pull between their bodies. Every inch of her tingled.

"I better go in," she said.

"May I call you tomorrow?"

"I'm going into my office tomorrow morning. I'm meeting a client. Call me there."

"I will," he said. "Tandi, it was nice."

"It was," she said coyly. It had been a whole lot nicer than she expected.

Jared slid behind the wheel of his car a happy man. He waited until Tandi was safely inside the house before driving off. He turned the sound up on his stereo—he felt like singing.

From behind the blinds, Tandi watched Jared leave. She liked that he didn't pressure her into making a decision about coming back to him, but that was like him, he never pushed. She could appreciate that now. Perhaps she had been overly—

Tandi's ears perked. She heard a noise. Was it crying? Was someone crying? Releasing the blind, Tandi stood stark still and listened intently, her breath hushed. Someone was crying. Damnit! Sporty had done it again. He had finally said or done something to hurt Carline. Why the hell couldn't she leave the house one time and come back without there being a problem waiting for her? Sporty's ass was in trouble for damn sure!

Not bothering to take off her shawl, and with the thin straps of her evening bag gathered and held in her hand like a whip, Tandi marched angrily down the hall to Sporty's bedroom. The door was closed, which was odd. Since his stroke, the door was never closed all the way. She put her ear to the door. Yep, someone was definitely crying.

Tandi barged into the room. The crying stopped instantly! There was a flurry of disentanglement on the bed between Carline and Sporty. Carline almost fell off the bed in her haste to get up. She had been laying on top of the covers alongside Sporty. Tandi almost didn't want to know what she had walked in on.

Carline quickly adjusted her skirt and blouse. She looked flustered, yet Tandi could see that Carline was not the one who had been crying.

Lying on his back, Sporty fixed his watery gaze up on the ceiling.

Tandi did not recognize the anguished man before her. Sporty's cheeks were wet, his lips trembled, and through the wall of water in his red eyes, she saw the pain of a hurting man. Gone was the haughty glare, the angry glint, the accusatory stare.

Tandi watched Carline settle stiffly into the chair that usually sat in the far corner of the room near the window. It was now alongside Sporty's bed close to the head.

"Someone had better explain what I just walked in on."

Carline picked up her crochet work. Her fingers began flapping like the wings of a hummingbird.

"Ignoring me won't work," Tandi said, speaking to both of them, but it was Carline she was looking at. "What's going on here?"

"Leave her alone," Sporty said, barely above a whisper.

Carline glanced up at Sporty but immediately dropped her eyes.

Tandi caught the anxious glance Carline shot at Sporty, just as she also glimpsed the same anxiousness he sent Carline's way. When

Sporty began wiping at his eyes and cheeks with his pajama sleeve, Tandi didn't know what to think. The whole scene was too bazaar. The two of them in an embrace, and Sporty crying? It just didn't make sense. She never imagined that she'd ever see a day when Sporty would shed a single tear. She never believed him capable of such a show of emotion. Stranger still, he was still tearing. Something was very, very wrong.

"Daddy, why are you so upset?"

Sporty swiped his sleeve brusquely across his eyes, drying them completely. His lips were a thin line.

That hard, callous look Tandi was accustomed to returned as Sporty stared at an invisible spot on the wall over her head. The silence was earsplitting. She watched them both in their struggle to not look at each other and give anything away. If this was about a patient/caretaker romance, Tandi could accept it, but her intuition told her that this was not what was going on. Sporty would not have been crying. If anything, he would have been scolding her for interrupting his game. No, there was something more.

"Somebody had better tell me something! What the hell did I walk in on?"

Neither answered her. Neither appeared to have even heard her.

Sporty, Tandi knew, would not answer her, and she wasn't about to wear herself out trying to make him. "Carline, may I speak with you out in the kitchen?"

Carline's needle slowly stopped flapping. She lay her crochet work down across the large canvas tote she carried it in alongside her chair. She got up and went, unhurriedly, toward the door. She stopped at the foot of the bed.

"I'm sorry," she said to Sporty.

Tandi was puzzled. "For what?"

Without responding or looking at Tandi, Carline went on out the room.

Lagging behind, Tandi saw that Sporty was steadfast in looking at that invisible spot on the wall. Dismissing him with a roll of her eyes, she left the room.

Left alone, Sporty pursed his lips tightly to stifle the cry that strained to burst from him. He began to shake as a dam of tears washed over his lids.

53

"Carline, what happened in there? Why was my father crying? Why were you laying on his bed?"

Carline was standing at the open refrigerator door. "Why don't you take off your shawl and sit down? I'll get you something to drink."

Tandi's hand flew to her hip. "Don't patronize me. I do not want to sit down, and I do not want anything to drink. What I want is for you to tell me why my father is crying."

Taking out a bottle of apple juice, Carline closed the refrigerator door. "Depression and tears are common when a patient is recovering from such a debilitating stroke. Patients often cry when they feel that all is lost."

"I'd believe that if it were someone other than my father. Something else happened. What was it?"

"Nothing," Carline replied, taking a clean glass from the dish drain. "Little things that you and I take for granted your father can no longer do, like picking up a fork with his right hand or dressing himself or walking, can make a grown man cry like a baby."

"And I'm supposed to believe he let you comfort him?"

"When a person is feeling that low, comfort from a stranger is sometimes better tolerated than from a loved one." Carline poured herself a glass of juice.

"Loved one, I am not."

"Of course you are. Tandi, your father is a man who has a hard time expressing his feelings, but you should never take it personal."

"Oh, I take it very personal that my father takes to you like I've never seen him take to another living soul. Are you having an affair with him?"

"No," Carline said barely above a whisper.

"If that's the truth, you're sending conflicting messages. While you speak very professionally, the position I found you in on my father's bed was not."

With her glass to her mouth, Carline took in just enough juice to wet her tongue. "We weren't doing anything inappropriate. I was comforting him."

"Do you comfort all of your patients in that manner?"

"Of course not!"

"Well, if you and my father like each other, that's all well and good, you're both adults. Just be forewarned, my father has—or rather he used to have—quite a sexual appetite. And that appetite has nothing to do with love. He's incapable of loving anyone."

Carline set her glass on the counter. "He loves you."

"Excuse me?"

"Your father loves you—in his own way."

"How would you know, and more importantly, why would you care?"

"I'm just trying to help. I'm sure your father had his reasons for whatever he may have done to make you feel unloved."

Uneasiness had been steadily building inside of Tandi. Something wasn't right. "Carline, you speak as if you know those reasons."

"I didn't say I did," she said, putting the bottle of juice back in the refrigerator.

Tandi was struck with the realization that Carline seemed right at home. She had become, disconcertingly, familiar with the house and with Sporty from the very first day. She never asked where anything was, nor did she waste time opening cabinet after cabinet looking for anything; she already seemed to know. Which reminded Tandi.

"Carline, have you been up in the attic?"

"Why would I go up to the attic?" Carline asked. "I have no reason to go up there."

Tandi wasn't buying that. "Earlier tonight, I went into the attic to get this shawl out of my suitcase. While I was there, I noticed that the old black steamer trunk my father kept locked for years was un-locked."

Carline carried her glass to the table. She sat. She drank a little more of her juice, yet, she didn't swallow it right away. Musingly, she let the nectar flow over her tongue, tasting its sweetness before letting it slip down her throat.

"Well?" Tandi hooked the strap of her evening bag over the back of the chair. That feeling of uneasiness was full blown. "Carline, were you up in the attic?"

"I told you—"

"And I'm telling you that that trunk has always been locked. My father is the only one who has the key. Now suddenly it's open and there's nothing inside."

"Perhaps there never was—"

"Don't even try it," Tandi said, aggravated with the woman she had thought her own personal angel.

Carline fell silent.

Tandi noticed Carline was avoiding looking at her. "My father can't climb stairs, so surely he was not up in the attic. In the past month, my brother hasn't stayed in this house long enough to leave his footprint in the carpet, and he could care less about what's supposed to be in that trunk. So, I'm asking you for the last time, Mrs. Hughes, were you up in the attic?"

Carline musingly rubbed her fingertips together. They were wet from the tiny beads of sweat on the cold glass of juice.

Tandi slammed her hand down on the table. "I swear to God, I will have you locked up, if—"

"Yes!" Carline said. "Yes, I was in the attic."

Turning abruptly, Tandi stormed away from the table and just as abruptly, she about-faced and charged at the table, her finger pointing threateningly at Carline. "You're fired! I want you out of this house. But first you had better return everything you stole or I will call the police."

Carline was unfazed.

"I trusted you! How dare you go through this house foraging and pillaging like a lowlife thief."

"I took what was mine," Carline whispered.

"Why would you steal—" Tandi's mind had been slow in assimilating what her ears had barely heard. "What did you say?"

"I took what was mine."

"Yours? What the hell does that mean, yours? What was yours? That makes no damn sense."

"I claimed what was mine."

That uneasy feeling was stifling her. What Carline said made no sense. "I didn't know you had a mental problem, lady. This is my father's house. You don't live here. So there's nothing stored up in this house that belongs to you. So you claim nothing."

"You were a headstrong little girl," Carline said, "but you were also a really curious child."

"What the hell are you talking about? You didn't know me as a child."

"I knew you very well."

"You're crazy." Tandi could not fathom what Carline was talking about. She didn't know her and had never before seen her. Surely she'd remember if Carline had ever been in her life.

"Tandi, what I took from the trunk were my things, things that were symbols of a life I felt, at the time, I had to give up."

Tandi's eyes widened.

"I know it makes no sense to you, but—"

"You're sick!" Tandi felt lightheaded. "I want you out of here. I want you out of my father's life."

For Carline, there was no turning back. "I left his house when you were three years old. It was the biggest mistake of my life."

Tandi's shawl slipped from her shoulders. It slumped to the floor like a bird shot out of the sky. It lay gathered at her feet, no longer graceful and flowing.

"My God. What are you saying?"

"Tandi, I'm your mother."

54

Carline had said, "I'm your mother," as casually as if she had said "good morning," yet the words slammed into Tandi like a ton of bricks, knocking her off her feet. Her legs gave way and her body fell heavily into the chair because her mind's wires were jumbled and rendered incapable of telling it to do otherwise. Her tongue felt thick and heavy in her mouth. She could only stare at the woman across the table. What Carline claimed was impossible. Tandi's mother was long ago dead.

"I'm sorry you had to find out like this."

Struck silent, in total disbelief, Tandi felt like she was waiting, waiting for the punch line, but she could clearly see that there was not the tiniest flicker of a humorous glint in Carline's eyes, so Carline could not have been joking.

As if waking from a deep sleep, Tandi said, "My mother's name is Lorraine, Lorraine Belson. She's been dead more than thirty years. You're not her."

Carline began lifting her glass to take another drink. The only sign that she was feeling anything was her shaky hand. She couldn't steady her hand so she set the glass down, though she continued to hold it in a two-handed grip.

Tandi was unable to continue sitting and was unable to stand still. "I get it," she said. "You think my father has a lot of money. Is that what you're after? Well, you're wasting your time. He's not a rich man."

"Carline is my middle name. Hughes is my late husband's name. If

I had walked through the door as Lorraine Belson, you would not have let me in."

"No matter what your name is, I don't believe you. I want you out of this house."

Carline closed her eyes. "You have a crescent-shaped birthmark high up on the inside of your right thigh and a beauty mark about an inch above your belly button."

Tandi gasped. "My . . . my father could have—"

"Why would your father tell me such a personal thing?"

"Because . . . because—"

"I have a similar beauty mark on my stomach. Would you like to see mine?" Carline stood and began pulling her tucked blouse out of her skirt. She exposed a tiny black beauty mark above her belly button.

Seeing it, as plainly as she had seen her own beauty mark so many times, Tandi was taken aback although not convinced.

Retucking her blouse, Carline sat down again. She said nothing as she waited for Tandi to get over her shock.

"My mother is dead."

"For a long time, I was."

"You're not my mother. How could you be? Anyone can have a beauty mark on their stomach—it's not an anomaly."

"No, it's not, but it could be hereditary."

That word stopped Tandi. She stared disbelievingly at Carline. "Lady, if you're my mother, which I most definitely do not believe, then why would you let Glynn and me think you were dead? Tell me that, Mrs. Hughes."

Tears sprang into Carline's eyes. She lowered her head.

The fake tears irritated Tandi. "Answer the damn question!"

Carline raised her head. "I am your mother."

Every time Carline said the word *mother*, Tandi's heart fluttered while her anger intensified. Could it be true? No, it couldn't be true. If it were, how could it possibly be?

"I don't believe you. You're trying to pull a scam."

"No, I'm telling the truth. I would have never left you, if I had been strong, if I had not been so afraid."

Tandi stopped abruptly at the head of the table. "Afraid of what? Responsibility? Yes, that must be it, responsibility—the biggest part of being a parent is being there for one's children to make sure all their needs are taken care of. Obviously, you couldn't do that. The question is why."

Carline couldn't bring herself to say what needed to be said.

"That's what I thought. You have no answer, but fuck it! I don't believe you anyway. You're sick. I want you out of this house."

Carline began wringing her hands. "The truth is never easy. I could've made it easy on myself and never said a word, but I would have only prolonged the lie. I can't live out the rest of my life with this lie over my head. God would—"

"Oh, so now you bring God into it. Is the mention of God supposed to make me believe your lie? Okay, Mrs. Hughes, if what you're saying is true—you swear before God, right? Then nothing you could say in the way of explanation would justify what you did. I can understand a woman leaving her man, but I will never understand a woman who deserts her children, her own flesh and blood."

"So you do believe me?"

"No, I don't believe you! I'm standing here trying to figure out why you would mess with me like this."

"I'm not messing with you, Tandi. When I left you back then, my mind, my life was so messed up, I didn't have many choices. It was either leave you or kill you and myself."

"Stop it!" Tandi was incredulous. "I don't wanna hear any more of your lies."

"I'm not lying! Tandi, I gave you life. I named you. You're my flesh and blood."

Tandi gasped. "No, no. You're lying." She couldn't believe. It was too far out there to be true.

"I know I told you I never had any children. I had to tell you that because that's what I've been telling myself for the past thirty-four years. It was the only way I could try and forget about you and Glynn. I told you I was weak. It's true, I was. For years I was strung out on drugs. By the time I had the strength to withstand—"

"Withstand what?" Tandi asked, glaring at Carline. "The hard work associated with being a mother?"

"No. The criticism of others."

"Oh, please! Tell me something that makes sense, which none of this does."

Carline rubbed her hands hard. "I was too ashamed to face you and Glynn."

"That's bull! We were children."

"Yes, but years were slipping by. You were smart. I didn't wanna see you hurt the way you are right now. I didn't want you to hate me."

Tandi's cheeks were tight, her throat was scratchy; she wasn't sure anymore what to believe. "Oh, you think I'm hurt now? The hurt you hear in my voice, that you see on my face, that's part of my soul, Mrs. Hughes; it's been with me all my life, it's never left me, it's been my constant companion. That hurt has made my life miserable."

"And I'm so sorry. I never intended for you to suffer. I—"

"You're not my mother, so why are we still discussing this? I don't even know why you're still in this house."

Carline gave up on drying her tears; they wouldn't stop coming. "When you were a little girl, Tandi, you had a one-eyed baby doll with one leg. Its hair was scraggly and matted and you used to tie a few strands of it in a pigtail with a dirty white shoestring."

Tandi felt sick. "My-my father told you about that doll."

"No, I found that doll under a park bench. It was the only toy I could afford to give you. You loved that doll. You never let anyone take that doll out of your arms. "You named that doll Candy."

The room was spinning. Tandi stepped back from the table. There was something soft under her feet. Looking down, she saw she was standing on her shawl.

Getting up quickly, Carline went to pick the shawl up from the floor.

Tandi quickly snatched it up before Carline could touch it. "I don't need you to pick anything up for me!" She tossed it across the back of the kitchen chair closest to her.

Carline went back to her chair and sat.

Tandi turned first one way then abruptly turned back the other way. This was all so insane. Her mother was dead. This woman was an imposter. "I have to talk to my father."

"Tandi, no! You and I need to keep talking. We have to—"

"You and I have nothing to talk about. I don't want you here."

"I can't deny what I did was wrong, but I was—"

"Lady, I'm not buying any of this. I want you gone."

"I made some bad decisions, Tandi, and I'm sorry."

"Oh, please. Parents make bad decisions every day. We send the kids out without a raincoat when we see the sky is cloudy, or we send them to the corner store forgetting that they have to cross a busy street. I know, I'm a parent. But we do not just up and leave our children."

"I didn't have a choice. Once I left, I couldn't come back."

"Well, maybe you should have tried. In case you didn't know, a child who cries itself to sleep for its mother would rejoice if that mother miraculously returned, not caring what the reason was for her leaving. All would be forgiven. A child's love for its mother does not wash away with its tears. That love is like a tattoo on the soul. And just in case you hadn't noticed, Mrs. Hughes, I am not a child. I am a woman who is angry as hell that you dare to show up now and drop this bomb on me and expect that I am mature enough to not be hurt by your revelation."

"So you do believe me?" Carline asked again.

"Do I look like I believe you?" Tandi snapped. "No, I don't believe you. I can't believe you. I know you're lying."

"Tandi—"

"Mrs. Crawford to you!"

Carline pushed a stray curl off her face. "I didn't expect that you'd forgive me, but—"

"You're dead! How can you expect anything?"

Lowering her head, Carline let her hands settle onto her lap.

Tandi began to trudge around the kitchen, circling the table, circling Carline. If what Carline said was true, then she should have been embracing Carline, but with her whole being, Tandi wanted to rail against this woman with a mighty truculent roar! It was all too much. It had to be a lie, a lie that was weighing her down, draining her, making her weary. She slowed her pace. She dragged herself to the other side of the table across from Carline. She felt no better with the kitchen table between them.

Carline shied away from looking at Tandi. She was looking at the ring of water at the base of her glass.

"Why did you come to this house?"

"For years I used a private investigator. He told me about Sporty's illness."

"Oh, my God. You've been spying on us? You—"

"I had to know that you were all okay. Tandi, I really do work for the agency. I asked to be assigned to this case. I figured it was time to face my past."

"Did my father know you were alive?"

"No."

"Liar! He had to know. There's no way he didn't, but you know something? I don't believe anything you're saying."

"Tandi, I know this is difficult for you to understand."

"Well, bully for you for understanding that."

"Okay, if you don't believe me, believe your own eyes. Take a good look at me. Tell me if you don't see yourself."

Instead of looking at Carline, Tandi turned away from her. She couldn't look. She didn't want to see anything. She had to keep telling herself, *My mother is dead!* Wasn't that one of the first things she ever remembered Sporty telling her?

"Your mother is dead," he had said. "She won't be coming back." Tandi didn't remember crying that night, but she remembered crying many nights after that.

And that was just it. Lorraine Belson was dead, but how did Carline Hughes know about her doll, Candy? Why did Sporty give her the key to the trunk when he himself hadn't opened it in all these years? And Sporty? Did he stop being a pain in the ass because he was afraid of being put in a nursing home, or did he calm down the day Carline Hughes walked in the door because she was his dead wife come to life? Was it possible? Was Carline Hughes, Lorraine Belson?

Tandi started across the kitchen. "I have to talk to my father."

"No, Tandi! This is between us. I'm the only person who can answer your questions. I'm the only one you need to talk to. Are you afraid of me? Are you afraid to face me?"

"No, I'm not afraid to face you. I'm not afraid of anything." She glowered at Carline. Staring intently, studying her face. What she saw there weakened her knees. She saw her own eyes looking back at her. Carline's nose, Carline's lips were so much like her own nose and lips. How had those obvious likenesses gotten past her? But of course, she would not have been looking for her dead mother in Sporty's home health aide, not when she was supposed to be dead.

"Then stay and bitch at me if you have to, but listen to me."

Tandi felt sick. She wanted desperately to run from the kitchen, from Sporty's house altogether, but she needed to stay just as desperately.

"Tandi, I have always known how you were getting on."

"Isn't it a shame I can't say likewise? There were no messages from the other side."

"I know I've overwhelmed you when you already have so much going on in your life. I—"

"You don't know anything about my life."

"I know that this has been a rough time for you. I'm sorry that—"

"Save it!"

"I'm sorry that I've never been here for you, but . . ."

"I said save it."

". . . but it was best that I be thought dead."

"Best for whom? You? What about me? What about Glynn? What about my father? That is, if he didn't know. Is that what I came in on, him crying because you were alive? Oh, but he's known for weeks that you're alive, hasn't he?"

"Sporty didn't know, not until I walked into this house. Please don't blame him. I take sole responsibility for my absence. Thirty-four years ago, I had word get back to Sporty that I was dead. I wanted him to get on with his life."

"Oh, he did that just fine. Sporty became the most bitter man I've ever known. He treated me worse than a one-legged stepchild, but that wasn't your problem, was it?"

"I didn't know that he was in such pain that he took it out on you."

"Of course you knew. I thought you knew how we were getting on. That private detective didn't tell you?"

Carline fell silent. With trembling fingers, she wiped her face.

Tandi saw that Carline's hands were trembling, but she didn't care. She did care that she was beginning to lose her own battle against breaking down—her voice was cracking, her throat was tight, and her heart was crumbling.

"You say what you've told me is all true? If it is, then you and my father are despicable beings. I wish you were both dead!"

"Tandida!" Sporty bellowed.

Tandi froze, her heart about stopped.

Sporty slowly wheeled himself into the kitchen. "Don't ever talk to your mother in that way again."

Tandi dissolved into a torrent of painful sobs.

55

When Carline couldn't bear Tandi's woeful sobs any longer, she went to her and tried to wrap her up in a motherly embrace.

Tandi's arms shot out, thrusting Carline back, slamming her back into the kitchen counter. "Get away from me! Don't touch me!"

"Tandida!" Sporty shouted. "Don't take your anger out on her."

Tandi sucked her lungs full as she turned on Sporty. "Don't you say a damn thing to me! You're no better than she is."

"I should have told you about Lorraine the first day she came here. It was my decision to not tell you who she was. Tandida, you want to be angry at somebody, be angry with me." Sporty wheeled himself over to Carline and took her hand. "Are you all right?"

Carline nodded, though she herself couldn't stem her own tears.

The strangest feeling swept over Tandi when Sporty took Carline's hand. She was angry that he had lied by his silence, and she felt chastened by the harsh way he had spoken to her; those feelings she was familiar with, but this new feeling—jealousy—she wasn't. He had never been this concerned or gentle with her.

"Come sit down," Sporty said to Carline. Using the control lever on his chair, he wheeled alongside Carline to her chair. He then swivelled around so that they were seated side by side.

Tandi was disgusted with the two of them. "You're both liars. You deserve each other. I'm leaving this house. I never wanna see either of you again in life."

"Tandi, please!" Carline stood. "Don't go. You need to hear the whole story."

Tandi's legs were rubbery, but she forced them onward.

"Tandida, now is your chance to get answers to all those questions you've asked of me over the years. Are you now too afraid, or are you too stubborn to hear the truth?"

That stopped Tandi from taking another step.

"We owe you the truth," Carline said.

"Do either of you even know what the truth is?"

"Yes," Carline answered, looking at Sporty. She lightly touched her hand to his cheek. "I'm so sorry."

Tandi watched Sporty's eyes mellow, his face relax. A strange glow of what? Love? Is that what was in his eyes as he gazed at Carline? The sight amazed Tandi. In all her life she had never seen him seduced by the single touch of a woman. With Iona Lewis and others, he had always been so gruff, so harsh, so controlling. This was not the same man. This man was gentle, caring, and had shown that he could cry. Did he still love this woman risen from the dead?

Sporty turned his head so that his mouth was in Carline's hand. He tenderly kissed her palm.

Completely mesmerized, Tandi gawked as Carline, moving her hand, leaned in and kissed Sporty tenderly on the lips. Reveling in that kiss, Sporty closed his eyes. A tear beaded up in the corner of his eye.

Tandi was awestruck. Who was this woman?

It was Sporty who Carline looked at and not Tandi. "I knew this day would come," she said. "I used to have nightmares about it. In my dreams, I've seen us all, including Glynn, talking, but I could never picture in my head, asleep or awake, what the outcome would be."

"The truth would be a nice outcome," Tandi said.

"Sit down, Tandida. See if the truth is really what you've wanted all these years."

Tandi pulled the chair with her shawl on it back from the table. She sat, although she felt like she was waiting for her own execution. "Go ahead, Daddy. For the first time in your life, tell me the truth."

"Tandi, this is not your father's truth to tell. I'll tell you everything you need to know," Carline said, holding on to Sporty's good hand. Although his hand gave her strength, Carline knew she was in this alone. She kept giving Sporty anxious sidelong glances but he wasn't looking at her; he was looking stoically at Tandi.

Tandi crossed her legs and folded her arms high across her chest.

She began shaking her foot impatiently. "Any day now," she said, not liking this woman one little bit.

Leaning closer to Sporty, Carline again spoke to him. "I want you to know if I had it to do over again, I would never have left you. I would have stayed by your side and raised our children together."

The only sign that Sporty was feeling anything was in the sad stare he fixed on Tandi. She didn't like that Sporty was staring at her, nor was she comfortable with what she saw in his eyes—tears. They frightened her. While it was all so surreal, the reality was, if the truth could reduce him to tears, she didn't know what it could do to her.

"Tandi, long before I came back here," Carline began, "I used to look in my mirror and pretend I was talking to you and Glynn, but especially to you."

"Trying to get your story straight?"

"Yes, you could say that I rehearsed my story. I wanted to be able to say the right thing to make you understand why I did what I did. Of course, now that we're only a few feet apart, I don't know what to say."

Tandi didn't want to hear that. "Ad-lib."

"Fine," Carline said. Tandi's coldness was expected but she didn't think it would bother her as much as it did. "I'll start at the beginning. It wasn't so painful then. I was seventeen when I met Sporty. He was twenty-one. I lived in Richmond, but I was here, in New York, visiting my cousins on my mother's side of the family."

"I know nothing of your cousins."

"There's a reason."

"And that would be?"

"I'll get to that," Carline said, "but . . ."

Rolling her eyes, Tandi huffed.

". . . first, about me and your father. It was summer. It was my older cousin, Melvin, who introduced me to Sporty. He didn't want me to be the fifth wheel at a party a group of us were going to that night. Sporty and I fell in love the moment we met. We were inseparable the rest of the summer, and we did a lot more than hold hands. At the end of the summer, after crying my heart out, I went back to Richmond and Sporty went back to college—Wilberforce, I believe."

Sporty nodded.

"And?" Tandi asked.

Carline looked to Sporty. "We wrote each other, we called back and forth. I lived each day waiting for Sporty to visit me in Richmond for Christmas."

"So your mother allowed you to see a college man?"

"She didn't like it at first, but after she spoke to him on the telephone, she warmed up to him and said it was okay . . ."

"What a trusting mother you had."

". . . as long as we didn't have sex." Carline ignored Tandi's remark. "Of course, I couldn't tell her that we had already had sex, and stupid me, I hadn't realized that I had been missing my period. I never thought about the possibility of getting pregnant. I hid my pregnancy from my parents for months."

Tandi rolled her eyes.

Carline saw her. "I know. Suffice it to say I was almost three months along before I knew. I was scared out of my mind, and Sporty was devastated. He had only one more year to do at Wilberforce."

Sporty sniffled. Carline ran her thumb across the back of his hand.

Tandi sucked her teeth. This story was no different than the story of so many young people whose lives were changed because of unwanted pregnancies. "So, you got married. You had Glynn and me, and then what?"

"Actually, we didn't get married."

"Not then."

"Not ever."

That surprised Tandi. "You were never married?"

"No."

Tandi's arms fell onto her lap. She looked at Sporty. Hanging his head is what he should have been doing.

"Why didn't you marry her?"

"He wanted to marry me," Carline said, jumping to his defense.

"Then why didn't he?"

"There was college, and—"

"Wait a darn minute." Tandi wasn't letting that college bit get by her. "My father didn't get his degree from Wilberforce, he got it from Queens College when I was twelve years old, so, unless I'm wrong, he came back home while you were pregnant. Why didn't you marry?"

Carline looked down at Sporty's hand. "When I was six months pregnant, my parents brought me back to New York to meet Sporty's parents."

"In other words, there was a demand, marry my daughter or—"

"Or go to jail for statutory rape. There were angry words and threats from both families and a lot of crying from me. Sporty wanted to finish school first, but my father was adamant. I guess because he loved me and, in an effort to bring peace, Sporty said he'd marry me right away, but—" Carline said, looking painfully at Sporty. His lashes were wet. His shoulders began to shake. She put her arm around him.

Tandi looked away. She couldn't bear seeing Sporty like this. It unnerved her, while Carline's mothering him made her uneasy. "For God's sake! Would you go on!"

Carline removed her arm from around Sporty, while he struggled to still himself. "It all went wrong when Sporty's mother asked my parents where they were from, who their people were."

"So? Were there horrible secrets about some uncle who was taken by aliens with four eyes and was himself pregnant or something?" Tandi wasn't trying to be funny, but she was half expecting Carline's explanation to be outrageously stupid.

"If it were as outrageous as that, we would have been okay, but it was what we didn't know that destroyed us." Carline again sought the courage to go on by looking to Sporty. He couldn't help her. He was again looking at Tandi. "Tandi, Sporty and I are first cousins on my father's side."

Tandi didn't blink once. She couldn't, she was stunned. Sporty and Carline both waited anxiously for her to say something, but she couldn't speak.

"I swear to God," Carline said, "we didn't know that my father and Sporty's father were brothers."

Tandi looked from one to the other. "That's insane."

"But true," Carline said.

"How do you *not* know something like that? You're blood!" Tandi went back to trudging around the kitchen. "Your fathers were brothers. You said yourself that your parents met. Were they blind? Did they not see each other?"

"They—"

"Were there no family reunions? Picnics? Christmas gatherings?"

"Never," Carline answered. "My father was nine when he lost touch with his brother. They were separated when their mother died. My father moved with an aunt to Baltimore. My uncle, Sporty's father who was seven at the time, stayed with his grandmother—his mother's mother—who lived alone. She died a few years later. No one informed my great-aunt. Sporty's father was put into a foster home and was eventually adopted. The brothers never saw each other again in life."

Tandi gasped. "Oh, my God. Daddy, please tell me this isn't true."

Sporty's answer was the tears that rolled down his cheeks.

"It wasn't until I got pregnant that they came together and started talking and comparing notes about their childhood. It was when they told each other that their original surname was Masterson that they realized who they were and what Sporty and I had done—unknowingly."

Tandi stared at Sporty. "This is incredible. Daddy, how could you not tell me and Glynn about this?"

Sporty shielded his eyes with his good hand.

"Back then I thought, we all thought, it was incest," Carline explained, "but that's—"

"Back then?" Tandi asked. "Oh, you don't think so now? What's different?"

Carline glanced at Sporty. "We're not sister and brother."

"No, but you are first cousins."

"Yes, but we *are not* sister and brother," Carline stressed. "The bloodline is thinner with cousins. We're like distant relatives."

Tandi couldn't believe what she was hearing. "I think a lot of people and biologists will disagree with you. Let me enlighten you both: You are *not* distant enough."

Another awkward moment of silence filled the room. Carline and Sporty could look at each other, but they couldn't look at Tandi.

"Yeah, and?" Tandi asked impatiently. "What did your families do?"

"Our families," Carline resumed, "argued a lot back then, which is why marriage between me and Sporty was out of the question. Sporty and I were forbidden to see each other, and both of our parents demanded that I have an abortion."

"Needless to say, you didn't. What if Glynn or I had been born deformed or insane or something?"

"Let me ask you one, Tandi. Do you understand abortion and how it brutally rips a baby from the womb?"

"Yes, I do, but the circumstances . . ."

". . . were extenuating," Carline said, finishing Tandi's sentence. "I loved Sporty and he loved me. We didn't know who we were until it was too late. Our parents scared us to death with stories of what could happen to our baby—like you said, retardation and such. On top of that, they pounded into our heads that we had sinned, that we would burn in hell. I couldn't accept that. I didn't want to believe any of what they were saying. I wanted our baby. I didn't care how he came out, as long as he was alive. Thank God, nothing was wrong with Glynn."

"But didn't you even, for a minute, consider the other consequences of your union?"

"Tandi, if Sporty and I had known that we were cousins the day we met, we would have never gotten together."

"Ignorance is no excuse! Once you were told, you could have made other choices. Daddy, you had to know differently. You were older. I can't believe—"

"It was too late!" Sporty shouted. "Can't you understand that?"

Tandi glared at Sporty. His trembling chin unnerved her. Even when he had his stroke, he didn't seem to suffer such deep abiding anguish. He didn't cry one time that she knew of. All these years, was this the pain that festered in his soul and made him so bitter, so cruel? Was this why he put her through hell? His hell? Was that why he was looking at her now like he could, through the power of telekinesis, make her understand what he had gone through?

"Your father didn't think we should have the baby," Carline said, speaking for Sporty. "He was afraid it might be retarded, too."

"Oh, so one of you did have a little sense. I'm not surprised he wouldn't want such a child, but was it okay with him that the two of you were together at all?"

"Yes," Sporty answered for himself.

"My God, that's a sin."

"No," Sporty croaked. "How could it be a sin when we didn't know in the beginning that we were related?"

"But you found out before it was too late. You could have altered the course of all of our lives."

"No, Tandida, it really was too late. What Carline and I were feeling, we couldn't just shut off like a faucet. Don't you understand that? Everything in life doesn't go by rules. We should have been able to get married." Sporty began to weep.

Tandi could sit no longer. She didn't know this man who spoke of a forbidden love with a woman he had cloistered away in his soul. This man, this emotional man, should have been her father.

Gently patting Sporty's hand, Carline consoled him. "When my parents took me back to Richmond," she began to explain, "they set up an appointment for an abortion and even took me to the hospital, but I ran away when they weren't looking. I hid out at a friend's house, and Sporty met me there. With his college money, we ran off to Los Angeles, had our baby, and lived together as husband and wife. No one questioned us, no one cared."

Tandi was more confused than ever. "So if you both defied your parents and you made a life together, how is it that you ended up leaving us and we all ended up back in New York?"

"I-I couldn't—" Carline brought her hand to her mouth.

"Don't stop now. What happened?"

Carline wept into her hand.

"Tandida, it's been hard for Lorraine," Sporty explained.

"And it hasn't been hard for me? Do you think my life was a lark growing up?"

Sporty didn't back down from Tandi's anger. "None of us had it easy."

"You know something, Daddy? I really don't wanna hear from you. You've had thirty-four years to tell me about this, but never did. I want to hear from her, *Mrs. Hughes,* about that part of my life that is so secret. You can do that for me, can't you, *Mrs. Hughes?*"

Carline couldn't answer. She was too upset.

"Okay," Tandi said, "I guess I have to figure this one out myself. Let's see." She put her finger to her lip in an exaggerated motion to show that she was thinking. "I know I was born in California, because that's on my birth certificate, but that's about all I know. How old was I when I was brought to New York? What happened in California?"

Sporty answered, "A year and a half after we were in California, Lorraine's father found us through a girlfriend of hers where we lived. He came to tell us that Lorraine's mother had died of a heart attack. He said our sin had killed her."

Carline stifled her urge to cry aloud.

"He told Lorraine to never come back home, that she was no longer his daughter, and that I was nothing to him. He made Lorraine feel so guilty, so bad, that she ran away from me and Glynn. I came home one day and she was gone. A single line written on a piece of paper taped to the door of our apartment said, 'I can't. I'm sorry.' "

Carline gave in to her anguish. Her shoulders shook with her weeping.

Tandi wasn't about to let either Carline or Sporty's anguish deter her from finally learning the truth. "Where was Glynn?"

"Lorraine had left him with the lady on the first floor. I waited, hoping, praying that she'd come back. I looked for her for six months."

"I'm so sorry I put you through that," Carline said. "I wasn't strong."

"God, I wish you'd stop saying that. It's really annoying me." It seemed that neither Sporty nor Carline heard her. Sporty was looking at Carline in such a way, it was clear he was still in love with her. When Sporty realized Tandi was watching him, he quickly dropped his eyes, but Tandi cared not at all that revealing their past was shaming him or tearing him up inside. She had to know more.

"Mrs. Hughes, where did you go?"

Carline stuck her finger under her nose and inhaled deeply through her mouth, trying to pull herself together.

"Your mother was alone," Sporty said. "She—"

"I ended up on the street, in the gutter. I was on drugs," Carline said flatly. "I had to prostitute myself to get what I needed."

"Oh, God," Tandi said, going back to pacing. "This goes from bad to horrific. So I'm a crack baby or something?"

Neither Carline nor Sporty sought comfort or support from each other either by a glance or the touch of a hand. Both their eyes were downcast.

"God, help me," Tandi said. "So at what point in all of this was I born? You must have gotten back together."

Still Carline and Sporty didn't look at each other. After a tense heartbeat, Sporty tore his gaze from the floor. "We never got back together."

Carline shrank inside herself. She closed her eyes.

"What are you saying?" Tandi asked incredulously. "Was I fucking hatched?"

Carline covered her face completely, which scared Tandi even more. "Tell me!"

Tears rolled down Sporty's face. "Before I left California, I told a neighbor if she should ever see Lorraine again, to tell her that I had taken Glynn back to New York. If it wasn't for Gert, the only friend I had in the world, I don't know what I would have done. She let me stay with her. After some months went by, I settled in my own place. I sent my address to the neighbor in case Lorraine wanted to come to me."

Sporty was dancing around Tandi's question, and it was irritating her. She grabbed a pot top out of the dish rack and banged it twice on the counter, making a crashing, earsplitting racket.

Both Carline and Sporty jumped, both stared wide-eyed at Tandi.

"Look! I'm getting tired of this bullshit. I don't care which one of you tells me, but right now, one of you had better tell me, this instant, about my birth."

Carline didn't respond. Her stooped shoulders, her bowed head told Tandi she was trying to hide inside herself.

"Tandida, my family wanted nothing to do with me or Carline."

"Oh, big surprise. Finally I understand why we never had family around."

"That's right. I was all alone, except for Gert. I got myself a job, and went on with my life without my family."

"I got that. But is it that simple? You went on *smoothly* with your life? I don't think so, Daddy. Somewhere along the line I was born. Somewhere, somehow you decided to keep this incredible story to yourself. And somewhere along the way, you became a very bitter, ugly man, and at some point, you chose to be mad at me."

Carline raised her head. "He wasn't mad at you. It was me he was angry with."

"Apparently so, but I'm the one who lived with him, which brings me back to the question, how did I get into this blissful picture?"

"Your mother—"

"I'll tell her," Carline said, placing her hand on Sporty's arm. "I owe her—no, I owe you—that."

"Is this man, Glynn Belson, Senior, my father or not?"

56

"No. Sporty is not your father."

There, it was said. Tandi had at first held her breath, but then she let out the breath that for so long had been cramping her heart. She didn't know if she should laugh or cry. She felt like doing both, but she couldn't get her face to crack an expression. Calmly, she stood and went over to the window and looked out onto the backyard. It was really late. The curtains and shades were drawn at the back windows in the house across the way. Who's to say that some deep, dark secrets were not rearing their ugly heads, in otherwise unwitting lives, in that house, secrets that may forever remain behind those drawn shades, perhaps as they should be? Tandi drew the curtain closed and turned back to face the woman who had risen from the dead to give her answers to questions that hurt more than the not knowing.

"I know we've hurt you," Carline said.

Tandi simply looked at Carline. That was an understatement. Suddenly, she felt as if she was plucked from a sauna and shoved into an ice chest packed with dry ice that chilled and burned her all at once.

"Why is his name on my birth certificate?" she asked, indicating Sporty.

"I put Sporty's name on your birth certificate because I wanted him to be your father, and I didn't want you to have no one to turn to."

Tandi raised her eyes upward. "Oh, God, will I ever wake up from this nightmare?"

"Tandi, I understand how you must feel. I—"

"You don't know how I feel. You were never kept in the dark about your identity. You always knew, without a doubt, who your parents were."

"Yes, but—"

"There is no but! You just told me I have no father. That—"

"Sporty is your—"

"He is not, damnit! You just said so," Tandi cried.

Sporty shielded the tears that rolled down his cheeks.

Tandi hugged herself. "Jesus. This is so weird. I'm relieved to finally . . . finally know for sure what I've always suspected—I have no father. I feel oddly vindicated for questioning that all these years, but damn, I don't feel good about it." She was tearing. "I feel terrible. I feel sick. Oh, my God, I feel sick. My life has been a lie from the day I took my first breath."

"Tandi, I never meant to hurt you."

"Of course not. Why would you, my dear mother, intentionally hurt me, your own flesh and blood? So you are my real mother, huh?"

Carline pursed her lips as her eyes filled with fresh tears.

"Then tell me, Mrs. Hughes. How is it that I ended up in this house without you?"

Carline rubbed Sporty's hand as if for good luck. "When I found myself pregnant with you, I went back to the apartment in Los Angeles but Sporty had already gone back to New York. I didn't blame him for leaving—he had every right to hate me."

"But, I didn't hate you," Sporty said.

"I know that now," Carline said, patting his hand. "I wanted so badly to get in touch with you, but I thought you would hate me even more for having another man's baby on top of leaving you."

"Lorraine, I told you, I would've taken you back."

"I didn't deserve you."

"Spare me!" Tandi wanted to scream to relieve the tension in her chest. "I don't care to hear what you felt for each other, I need to know how I got in this goddamn house."

"Tandida, take it easy."

"Did you ever take it easy on me, *Daddy?*"

Sporty could hold Tandi's angry glare but a mere second. He dropped his eyes.

"It's all right," Carline said, assuring Sporty. "Tandi's anger belongs on my shoulders."

"No truer words," Tandi said.

This time, Carline wasn't fazed. "After I had you, I didn't have a place to live. I didn't have any real friends, and there were times when I wasn't lucky enough to shack up with acquaintances or get a cot in a shelter. Many a night I slept on the street or in an alley on a cardboard box with you in my arms. It wasn't a good life for you. I thought of giving you up for adoption but I was afraid I'd never know anything about you. I couldn't go back to my family, so I took a chance that Sporty wouldn't turn his back on me. You were three years old when I made my way back to New York. I knew where Sporty was because he had sent the address to our old neighbor, and I kept that address with me always. It was one of the hardest things I ever did, but I got up the courage to show up at Sporty's apartment. I waited outside for hours for him to come home. All the while, I was praying he wouldn't turn me away. When he came home, he had Glynn with him, and I wanted so badly to go up to him, to beg him to take me back, but I knew it was asking too much. I—"

"Excuse me," Tandi interrupted. "Let me understand this. You say that asking him to take you back would have been asking too much?"

"Yes."

"Oh, but asking him to take me, another man's child, was a breeze?"

"No-no, it wasn't easy, but Sporty was the only person on earth that I could turn to. I knew he wouldn't turn his back on my child. He always had a kind heart."

Tandi turned her back on both of them.

"Tandida," Sporty said softly, "I know what you're thinking."

It struck Tandi that she had never heard Sporty say her name so softly before. She fought hard against the urge to cry.

"I know I was never kind to you. I'm sorry."

"Sorry just isn't enough." Tandi began to feel a soreness in her shoulders. She began kneading the hard, tight muscle in her left shoulder. "Sorry can't erase thirty-four years of sadness."

"Please, don't blame your father. He—"

Tandi whipped around. "My father? I thought you just said he wasn't my father."

"He's the only father you've ever known, Tandi. Don't blame him for what I did."

"Oh, don't worry. I have enough blame for you, too. I've always blamed you for leaving me, for dying. Oh, but you're alive, aren't you? Well, I—"

"Tandi, I hated that I couldn't keep you with me," Carline said quickly. "The first years of your life, I tried dragging you behind me, leaving you in places with people I didn't know, but there were too many occasions when I had to run out in the middle of the night because someone had reported me to some child protective agency.

"Tandi, your life with me was hell on earth. I couldn't raise you on the street never knowing if and when you would eat; not knowing where you would sleep, sometimes, from day to day. When I was in the gutter, used up and on drugs, I was afraid in my desperate hours I would sell you for a hit. A stupid hit, damnit!" Carline sobbed hard while Sporty tried to console her.

Tandi didn't feel her heart beating; she didn't feel herself breathing. She felt nothing, yet she knew she was wide awake because why else would such words shock her? She remembered none of those horrors of her early years, which was, perhaps, fortunate; it might have been one more scar on her psyche to contend with.

"Tandi, you can't begin to imagine how low a life I was living. I didn't want that life for you. Every day I was amazed that, somehow, with God's help, I survived to see another morning. Every day I thanked God he gave me presence of mind to bring you to Sporty, and I thank God, too, that no matter how angry Sporty was at me for walking away without even the courtesy of a good-bye, he loved me enough to save your life."

Carline gave up trying to dry her face.

"God knows, if Sporty didn't take you, Tandi, you might have died on the streets; or if you had survived, you never would have grown up to be the woman you are today. And you are a strong woman, Tandi. I've seen that."

"You don't know anything about me!" Tandi's stomach was as tight as a drum. She felt like she had to go to the bathroom. She sat again because she didn't have the strength to stand. "I just can't believe all these years of lies."

"Tandida," Sporty said, barely above a whisper, "when Lorraine left the first time, I was scared because I was alone with a baby to raise. When she left the second time, I was angry. I was really angry. I was angry because she wouldn't stay, I was angry because now I had two children to take care of, and I was angry because I didn't think I could do it alone. I had thought about getting with a woman, any woman, just so she could help me take care of you and Glynn, but I couldn't be with anyone long enough to want to marry her or wake up with her every morning. I was so damn mad, I hated the world. I wanted Lorraine back, but she was too ashamed to be with me. I was even angrier with her for that. She was supposed to stand by me. She never called or sent a single postcard. I couldn't forgive her for walking away and began to feel resentful. And, yes, every time I looked at you, I got even madder. I was wrong to make you the brunt of my anger."

Tandi wouldn't look at Sporty. With all her might she willed a shield of iron around her heart. She did not want to warm up to him. She did not want to be grateful to him for saving her life. She wanted to keep her anger with him burning like brilliant embers. She did not want his apology or his tears to mean anything to her, and mostly, she wasn't comfortable with him being this humble. She preferred him bitter and mean. It was easier to hate him and Carline.

"Sporty," Carline said sadly, "I'm so sorry."

Although his chin was quivering, Sporty went on. "I grew more angry as each year you grew to look more and more like your mother. You were always a reminder that I still loved her, but couldn't be with her. My life wasn't any easier having to live with the secret of who my children were. That's why I said Lorraine was dead. Her death was easier to explain. Tandida, I hope you can forgive us for the lies."

Tandi made herself look at Sporty. With all that he put her through, she never would have imagined he had taken her in and raised her when she wasn't even his own child. And no way would she have ever comprehended the depth of his suffering.

Sporty and Carline watched and waited for Tandi to say something, anything.

Rubbing her forehead in a slow circular motion, Tandi closed her eyes. If only when she opened them, she was sitting on a beach somewhere in the Caribbean with the sun and nothing else beating down on her head.

"Can I get you something?" Carline offered, starting to get up, snapping Tandi out of her wishful thoughts.

"No," she said, looking at the sad, anxious faces in front of her. "So tell me. What am I supposed to do now?" She wasn't expecting an answer. "Should I be thanking you for taking me in, or should I be thanking you for giving me up, or should I be saying 'I hate you' to both of you for doing what you did?" Tandi shrugged hopelessly. "Damn, I don't know what to do."

"You don't have to do anything," Carline said. "I'm the one who needs to ask your forgiveness."

"That goes for me, too," Sporty said.

The tears came again, betraying Tandi. "Forgiveness can only go so far," she said. "It doesn't erase the hurt. It only makes it bearable. Right now, I don't know if I can forgive either of you. I mean, Dad . . . Sporty, you could've told me this years ago when I was ten years old and first questioned you as to whether you were my father. Who knows what a conversation like that could've done for our relationship?"

"I didn't know how to tell you. I was afraid."

"You? Afraid?"

"Yes, me! I've been afraid for years that you and Glynn would find out about me and your mother. I didn't want you running away and ending up on the street."

"Like I did," Carline added.

Tandi went to pacing again. "I still can't believe this."

"After my stroke, and certainly before Lorraine came through that door, while I was scared you'd see right through me, I was terrified I'd die and you'd never know the truth."

"You're a coward! You should have told me and Glynn anyway!"

"I know, but I didn't want you to know that you and your brother were all I had in the whole damn world. All I had to live for."

Tandi drew her hand to her heart and let it lay there. "Don't talk to me like that," she cried. "I don't wanna know about your fears, and I damn well don't wanna know how you supposedly needed me. I know it's all a lie."

"It's not. I should have shown you how much I really loved you, but—"

"Stop it!" she shrieked, slamming her hand down on the table. "I don't wanna hear this!"

"Don't blame Sporty for—"

"I'm not talking to you! I'm talking to him," she said, pointing an accusatory finger at Sporty.

Carline clamped her mouth shut.

Tandi continued her attack. "Do you have any idea how badly I felt all of my life because you were so mean to me, or how much of an out-sider I felt I was with you and Glynn?"

"Tandida, it's not like I set out—"

"Mrs. Hughes," she said, dismissing Sporty's lame attempt to ex-orcise himself of any blame, "I have a question for you." She waited until Carline looked at her.

"Who is my real father?"

Carline's mouth started to move but it closed without a word being spoken.

Sporty tightened his hold on Carline's hand.

"Do you even know? Can you venture a guess?"

Quiet tears eased over Carline's lids and slipped down her cheeks. She whispered, "I don't know."

Tandi shook her head in despair. "This is such a cruel joke, but I don't get the punch line. Aren't I supposed to be laughing about now?"

Neither Carline nor Sporty had the courage to answer Tandi.

Tandi felt like her heart was caught in a vise, squeezing it, keeping it from pumping. "Oh, but I shouldn't be so upset. I'm no one special. I'm not the first, and I certainly won't be the last person born who will never know the identity of the man who donated his sperm."

"I'm sorry, Tandi. I made some very bad choices that—"

"We both did," Sporty said. "It's not all your fault. I should have stayed in California and waited for you."

"No, I—"

"Lorraine, I knew the stress you were under. I should have been there for you when you came back. I deserted you."

Tandi was nauseated by their magnanimous gesture to shoulder the blame for each other. From her perspective, they were equally at fault.

"Sporty, I deserted you. I should have been stronger."

"I wasn't that strong myself or—"

"Oh, please!" Tandi shouted irritably. "Do this on your own time."

Carline and Sporty both hushed up instantly.

"The truth is, neither of you did what you should have. Fine, you were pregnant before you learned that you were cousins, and fine, you didn't want to abort Glynn, but you should have kept your commit-ment to raise him together, no matter the consequences. And when you saw that you couldn't stand united and strong, you should have given him away."

"We couldn't," Carline said while Sporty agreed with her by shaking his head.

"Oh, yes, you could've. You defied your parents, you defied the world, but neither of you honored your so-called commitment to each other. And look at you, both of you ended up alone—one as a bitter old man and the other, a woman hiding in the shadows, stealing peeks at the family she threw away. You know what you should have done when you realized you couldn't raise me, Mrs. Hughes? You should have given me up to strangers. I would have been treated better."

"Please, Tandi, don't say that. I just didn't know what else to do. I was—"

"Tandida, your mother was hurt when she—"

"She gave up her right to be called my mother. Glynn and I—Oh, Lord. Glynn. How will he take this God-awful revelation?"

Carline and Sporty looked fearfully into each other's eyes.

Struck by the look that passed between them, Tandi gasped. "You hadn't planned on telling him or me, had you? If I hadn't happened upon the scene in the bedroom and questioned it, you would have never told me a damn thing."

"We were waiting for the right time," Carline said.

"Wasn't that more than thirty years ago?"

Neither answered her.

"You people are heartless. Hasn't the festering of your sordid secret tale taught you anything? Don't you understand that all of what we're dealing with now could have been avoided?"

When her eyes were awash with tears, Carline closed them.

"Tandida, please, you have to understand—"

"No, I don't, but I have a big question for you both."

They both looked like they were waiting for an earthquake to open up a gaping hole under them.

"Now that you've supposedly spoken your truth, what are you expecting from me? From Glynn? And, tell me, please, with our skeletons rattling out in the open, are we supposed to be the happy family that we never were and have picnics in the park and sing carols around the Christmas tree?"

Carline and Sporty looked to each other to answer. Tandi waited while they seemed to be searching for the answer in each other's face.

"Can't answer that, can you? I didn't think so. This is all the more reason why you should have thought about me and Glynn, and not just about what you wanted for yourselves. And, dare I ask, what is the relationship between the two of you supposed to be now?"

Carline and Sporty continued holding each other's gaze and in that gaze, they saw the answer, and so did Tandi.

57

Tandi could only guess that Carline had stayed the night in Sporty's bedroom, the two of them—cousins, distant relatives/distant lovers—whispering about their past and speaking with high hopes and mild trepidations about their future. They were old and couldn't care less anymore about what people would think—that is if people ever knew. Perhaps, years ago they had been too young to anticipate the consequences of their actions, but Tandi didn't see where their maturity was working to their advantage. Their coming together would solve nothing. If anything, it would complicate her and Glynn's lives more, that is if Glynn was ever told. She had decided against calling him the previous night. Such horrific news of his parentage should come from Carline and Sporty—they owed him that. However, if they didn't voluntarily tell him real soon, like within the next forty-eight hours, she would force their hand and have Glynn come over and introduce Carline to him as his mother. He hadn't even laid eyes on her yet.

The night before, she left Carline and Sporty in the kitchen without a backward glance. She went up to her childhood bedroom. It was where she needed to be—alone with the childhood doubts and memories that she could finally put to rest. After a sleepless night, she had left the house early without saying good-bye, without having seen or heard either Carline or Sporty stir on the other side of the bedroom door. God, how strange to know that her mother was alive and just on the other side of a piece of wood an inch and a half thick. All her life she had craved to know her mother, and now that she did, she wished she didn't. God, how awful it was to feel that way. Tandi never imagined she could feel such anger or be in such pain, such confusion.

With nothing else on her mind, being at work was the last place she should have been but she had nowhere else to go, which was the story of her life, which was why she was in the quandary she was in in the first place. She felt like she would burst wide open if she didn't tell someone about Sporty and Carline. She didn't want their secret to fester in her mind and destroy her and make her bitter like it did Sporty. She needed to talk to someone. The problem was to whom? At another time, right away, she would have called Evonne with such juicy gossip, especially if it was about someone else, but she was no longer speaking to Evonne, and this juicy gossip wasn't about someone else. It was about her, and she was brimming with shame. She couldn't confide in Daina as confiding in Daina was like confiding in Jared, and she just wasn't ready to tell him about the mess of a family he had married into. The irony of it all wasn't lost on her. By the time her date with Jared ended last night, she was no longer eager to end their marriage, but once he found out about Carline, he might want to end it himself, and without him and Michael Jared, she had no family. Suddenly the possibility of losing Jared scared her. Then again, if she went back to him now and never told him about Carline and Sporty and he later learned about them, he might not believe that she came back to him because she loved him. Oh, God, what was she supposed to do? The pain of discovery and potential loss was rendering her helpless as well as hopeless. Why did she have to demand the truth? Why was she so bullheaded? She didn't see a glimmer of a way out of this black hole of deceit and confusion.

Miraculously, Tandi was able to get through showing a house to her client, but she couldn't remember for the life of her how the client felt about the house. Back in her office, her tiredness came down on her. She put her arms on her desk and rested her weary head. While she was able to shut out the ringing telephone right on her desk, she could not shut out all that she'd learned about Carline and Sporty.

"Tandi."

Slowly opening her eyes, she looked groggily at Joan, the office assistant, who had slipped into her office.

"You have a phone call on two."

Tandi sat up and glanced down at the flashing button on two. "A client?" she asked.

58

Tandi and Jared lay facing each other, inhaling each other's breath. They had slept only briefly, but they had slept in each other's arms. Well into the early morning hours, Jared had gotten his fill of Tandi more than once and wanted her yet again now that he was awake. All was, also, well with Tandi. She was supremely serene. After they had made love the first two times, at one-thirty in the morning, she told Jared everything about Carline and Sporty. Jared was just as shocked as she had been, but he put it all in perspective.

"That would have been a heavy burden for either of them to deal with if they had stayed together. I can't begin to imagine how difficult it must have been for them apart and alone in this world."

"How can you sympathize with them?"

"I'm not trying to sympathize with them, but because I'm not as close to it as you are, I can see how bad it must have been for them. This is an amazing story, and I'm . . ." Jared searched for a word. "I'm flabbergasted."

"Imagine what I am," she said.

"I know. Tandi, I don't have to tell you how I feel about your father, but this explains so damn much about him. Maybe he's not as bad a man as we thought."

"He's not my father."

"Oh, he is your father, whether you can accept it or not, but I'm appalled that he kept this secret to the detriment of your relationship, and I'm upset that your mother took herself out of the equation completely, leaving you all to think she was deceased. Unfortunately, they made choices that will forever haunt them with guilt and shame. Especially your mother, with her own mother's death on her conscience. Your father had to be feeling some responsibility for that death, too. It had to be rough for both of them."

Unexpectedly, the tiniest tinge of pity for Sporty and Carline snuck up on Tandi and saddened her. Maybe Jared was right—it had to be rough for both Sporty and Carline. They were star-crossed lovers whose love for each other was forbidden by society and God. Neither had lived happy lives, and who was to say whether their twilight years together would be any happier? But how sad it would be for them to leave this earth and to have never known true happiness. Just thinking about that brought tears to Tandi's eyes. Nestled up against Jared, she talked until the first ray of dawn peeked through the window. She was a bit more understanding about how she came into the world, and a whole lot less bitter about the man who raised her when he didn't have to. It was his anger at her that she was having a hard time forgiving. In fact, she didn't know if she'd ever be able to forgive him or Carline for not standing strong.

"Forgiveness takes time," Jared said. "When the time's right, you'll know."

By the time she stopped talking, Tandi was mentally exhausted, but her body was eager to be made love to by Jared. She wasn't too tired for that. After they made love, no more words were needed. They let the warmth of their naked bodies speak for them.

Knock . . . knock . . . knock.

Tandi covered her breasts. They hadn't heard Michael Jared come into the house or come up the stairs. Now that Jared had given him his own house key, Michael Jared never again had to ring the bell.

"Come in," Jared said.

The door swung open. In pranced a smiling, bright-eyed MJ. "Good morning," he said cheerfully. At the foot of the bed, he climbed up onto the trunk and knelt down.

"Well, hello my beautiful son," Tandi said, pleased to see the broad smile on MJ's face.

"Hi, Mommy. Hi, Dad."

"Good morning," Jared said. "Are Daina and Herb downstairs?"

"No, they left," MJ said. "Daina said she'll call later. Her and Herb were going to church and I didn't wanna go. I wanted to see Mommy."

"How did you know I was here?"

"Daina called Granddad's house last night and that lady said you didn't come home, so Daina said you were probably here."

"Trust Miss Daina to know," Tandi said, thinking how good a friend she had been to both her and Jared.

"Mommy, what's for breakfast?"

"Didn't Daina feed you?"

"Yeah, but I'm still hungry."

"No surprise," Tandi said. "What do you want?"

"Pancakes and sausages and scrambled eggs with cheese and orange juice."

"You're not real hungry, are you?"

"I'm starving."

"Boy, I told you you have a tapeworm living in your body," Jared said, looking at how beautiful Tandi was. For months he had longed to have her here, and it was a dream come true that she finally was.

"Dad, stop saying that 'cause I don't believe you."

Jared laughed.

"Don't worry, honey. I'm going to make the biggest stack of pancakes you've ever seen."

"Mommy, that's fine for me, but what're you and Dad gonna eat?"

"We're gonna eat you," Tandi said.

Jared laughed heartily. He couldn't've asked for a better start to his day. He had his family back.

Playful, MJ tweaked Tandi's big toe through the covers. "Mommy, you used to always say that when I was little. You can't really eat me. I'm not food."

Giggling, Tandi pulled her foot out of MJ's reach. "No, but you certainly feed my pride. So, what did you do up in the Catskills?"

"I went row boating. It was fun. Can you, me, and Dad go up to the Catskills? Daina says we can stay in her house."

Tandi deferred to Jared. She didn't want to make a promise that Jared wasn't going to be able to keep.

"We can go at the end of July."

"But, Jared, you—"

"We'll go," Jared said.

MJ bounced up off the trunk and back down again. "All right!"

Secretly Tandi was praying that when the time came, Jared would not back out because the sparkle in Michael Jared's eyes would surely dim.

Seeing how happy Tandi and MJ were filled Jared with a full, well-fed comfortable feeling in his gut. It reminded him of the long ago early mornings they used to spend together as a family. He should have never let those little things that made Tandi happy slip away.

"Dad, Daina said in the winter that I could go skiing up there. Can I get my own skis?"

"I don't see why not. But, first, I think we should go away for a few weeks this summer. We need to practice being a family on vacation."

MJ's eyes widened. He leaped onto the bed. "Where?"

"A cruise would be nice," he said, looking at Tandi who was smiling pleasantly.

"On a boat?" MJ asked.

"On a big boat. A ship."

Tandi got up on her elbow and kissed Jared. They kissed full and long.

"Mommy! Dad!"

Chuckling, Tandi laid back. "Disgusting, huh?"

"No. I just don't wanna watch y'all getting mushy."

"We don't want you to watch," Jared said. "Hey, I have an idea. MJ, instead of making your mother cook, why don't we go out for breakfast."

"Oh, boy!" MJ exclaimed. "The Pancake Hut."

For Tandi, this was getting to be too good to be true. "But, Jared, don't you have to rest up for the week?"

"I'll rest tonight. Sunday is family day. I plan to spend the day with my wife and son. And before I forget, I've hired another attorney."

"Really?"

"Yes. He's going to lighten my load quite a bit. I had Marci hire a secretary to help her out."

"Can I come in to work to help out, too?" MJ asked.

"Sure, on Saturday mornings. Why not?"

"All right."

That feeling of being let down began to creep up on Tandi. "You're going to still open the office up on Saturdays?"

"One Saturday a month to take care of administrative work for the month. I can never seem to get that done on weekdays. Don't worry. It's going to work out just fine."

He could see Tandi was worried. "I promise," he said.

MJ grinned from ear to ear.

"The other three Saturdays belong to you, Tandi. Whatever you want to do, it's up to you. Saturday nights will be our date nights."

"Jared, don't make—"

"I made you a promise to put you and MJ first in my life. I will keep that promise."

She wanted to believe him.

"What will I do on Saturday nights?" MJ asked.

"We'll find something for you to do," Jared said.

"I could go with y'all."

"Once in a while," Tandi said.

"Maybe," Jared said. "The funny thing is, MJ, in time, you'll be begging us to stop dragging you along. Until then, Saturday afternoon, you can hang, but Saturday night, you gotta go. I'm taking my girl out."

"Jared, we can't leave him home alone. We—" Tandi saw that they were both smiling at her.

"Gotcha," Jared said.

"Mommy, we're playing with you. I'm gonna go stay with Daina or Uncle Glynn. We already asked them."

Jared smiled smugly. Under the covers, she kicked him. He laughed.

"Dad said we can do whatever I want on Sunday."

"I agree," she said, feeling love for them both.

Jared squeezed Tandi's side.

Turning to face him again, she touched his cheek. His prickly stubble tickled her hand. She had never loved him more, except maybe on the day they wed and the day Michael Jared was born. Last night Jared had asked her once again about Brent, and she had answered, "He was but a memory that I should have left buried. He is no one to me or us." He didn't question her any further.

MJ screwed up his face. "What we gonna do after we eat?"

"Since it's a special Sunday, we do whatever your mother wants to do," Jared said.

"Mommy, you wanna go to the movies?"

She couldn't stop looking at Jared. She nodded.

"So, when're y'all getting up?"

"Soon as you let us," Jared replied.

"Y'all can get up now. I'm not stopping y'all."

Jared held Tandi closer. "Yes, you are."

"You want me to go out the room, right?"

"That would get me going faster," Jared said, smiling a secret smile at Tandi.

Looking from Tandi to Jared, MJ continued to sit, not moving an inch.

"Michael Jared, would you do me a favor?" Tandi asked.

"MJ," Jared reminded her.

"Oh, excuse me. MJ—"

"Mommy, you can call me Michael Jared, if you want."

"Thank you, honey, but I'll call you MJ since you prefer that."

"But I don't mind if you wanna call me Michael Jared. I'm used to you calling me that."

"Thank you, that's so sweet of you."

"That's my boy," Jared said proudly.

"Honey, would you do me a favor?"

"Yes."

"Go downstairs and turn on the television to the Weather Channel. We need to know what the weather is so we'll know how to dress."

"It's hot, like it was yesterday."

"MJ," Tandi and Jared both said in unison.

"Okay, but I know y'all just wanna get rid of me."

"You're right," Jared said. "Close the door behind you."

Nimbly springing up off his knees, MJ landed hard on the floor. "When I get older, I'm gonna go out whenever I want and leave y'all in bed all day," he said, moseying over to the door.

"Until then, go downstairs," Jared said. "We'll be down in a little while."

"I might starve by then."

"MJ," Jared said, "the longer you take to leave, the longer—"

"I'm going. Man." MJ started slowly pulling the door up behind him, but then he stopped.

They both saw the worried look on his face. "Honey, what's wrong?" Tandi asked.

"Mommy, you're not gonna leave again, are you?"

Leaving them was the furthest thing from her mind. Her family was here, not in Sporty's house where he and Carline would be making a new life for themselves, and not in an apartment with barren walls that had not heard Jared's passion or Michael Jared's laughter. Last night after she couldn't get Sporty and Carline off her mind, she called Glynn's house and left a message for him to go see his father—immediately—because he and Carline, his home health aide, had something vitally important to tell him that would forever change his life. If Glynn got the message, he'd beat a path to Sporty's door, especially if he thought Sporty's money was involved. Who knows? She hadn't yet heard from Glynn, so all she could do was wait. In the meantime, she was grateful that she was in the loving arms of her man, where she should be.

Jared, too, waited anxiously for Tandi to answer. He had been too afraid to ask that question himself.

"I'm home to stay," she said finally.

"All right!" MJ shouted.

Jared inched even closer to Tandi. They both felt that sweet intense pull between their bodies and were impatient to satisfy their yearning. They began to kiss.

Although he was smiling, MJ said, "Yuck."

They heard the door close just as their lips parted. Last night their bodies had come together in a familiar rhythm of passion, their souls had come together in remembrance of times when they shared the same dreams, but, now, their minds, too, came together out of desire. They were in love again.

Sweaty and out of breath, Jared lay on top of Tandi completely satisfied. She lay under him a very happy woman.

Riiing!

"Let it ring," Jared said, kissing Tandi on the neck. He didn't want to let the world in just yet.

Riiing!

To Tandi, the ringing was like the calling of her name. "I have to get that." With Jared still on top of her, she answered, "Hello?"

A long, drawn breathless wheezing filled Tandi's ear, disturbing her. She pressed the phone to her ear. "Who is this?"

"Tandi. Oh, God—" the hoarse voice croaked before it broke into deep, painful sobs.

Tandi's nose began to sting. "Glynn?" She started to raise up with Jared still on top of her. He immediately rolled aside.

"Glynn!" she said loudly, trying to get him to hear her through his crying, while tears rushed to her own eyes. "Glynn, talk to me."

DISTANT LOVER

GLORIA MALLETTE

ABOUT THIS GUIDE

The suggested questions are intended to enhance
your group's reading of this book.

DISCUSSION QUESTIONS

1. Since her husband Jared's affair three years before, Tandi Crawford felt trapped in their sexless, non-communicative marriage. Could Tandi's simmering anger, together with the fact that she never forgave Jared, be the impetus behind her fantasizing about her first love, Brent Rodgers? Did this contribute to the widening gulf between them?

2. It was obvious Jared was sincerely regretful of indulging in an affair on Tandi. What could Jared have done differently to convince Tandi of his sincerity?

3. Brent Rodgers was Tandi's fantasy. Most people often wonder what happened to their first love and wonder, what if? Brent turned out to be not all that Tandi dreamed of. Did Tandi's fantasy of Brent make it impossible for him to live up to who she imagined him to be? Was the better man for Tandi, the man she had all along?

4. Most women have best girlfriends—they need each other to pour their hearts out to, to gossip with, to share their ups and downs with, to shop with. Evonne was Tandi's best friend. Did Evonne betray the friendship way before she slept with Tandi's husband, Jared, when she began to envy what Tandi had? Are there ever signs that a friend can and will betray the friendship? Do women tell their girlfriends too much about their relationships with their significant others?

5. Tandi was willing to continue trusting Evonne even after Evonne betrayed her, yet she was unwilling to trust her husband, Jared, after he had an affair on her the first time. Why is that?

6. Tandi most definitely had issues with her father, Sporty, for never showing her love, and for always appearing to be angry with her. Could Tandi's lack of love from her father, and loss of her mother at such a young age, affect her relationship with her

brother, Glynn; her husband, Jared; and her father himself now that he's older and needs to depend on her?

7. Sporty was a bitter, crotchety old man. He never spoke about his past and lied to Glynn and Tandi about the mother they never got to know. Once Mr. Belson's past was revealed, was his bitterness understood and/or justified? Was he wrong to keep the past secret from Glynn and Tandi? Could revealing the past earlier have made a difference in the hostile relationship Tandi and her father shared?

8. It could be argued that Tandi was fated to return to her father's house, as it was only in his house that the truth about the past could possibly be revealed. In returning home, although she protested, was Tandi subconsciously hoping to get closer to her father?

9. Tandi's long lost mother, Carlene, couldn't face what her intimate relationship with her cousin did to her family. She turned to drugs to numb her pain, and eventually deserted Sporty, Glynn and Tandi. Is the stigma of marrying a cousin just as strong today as it was in the past? Once Glynn was born to Carlene and Sporty, despite their familial connection should they have stayed together to face the world as a couple? Could they have stayed together and never exposed themselves? Will they stay together now?

10. Now that Tandi knows the truth about her parentage, do you think she'll ever see her father, Sporty, in a different light? Do you think she'll ever get over her anger with him? Will she ever be able to open her heart to him?

The following is a sample chapter from
Gloria Mallette's eagerly anticipated
upcoming novel
WHAT'S DONE IN THE DARK.

It will be available in January 2006
wherever books are sold.

ENJOY!

PROLOGUE

Celeste was miserable. The muscles in her behind were burning, her legs were stiff and achy, and her back hurt. Listening to eight-and-a-half hours of taped hits from the sixties and seventies, and sitting in the backseat of her father's car was torture. Yawning, she arched her back, stiffened her body, tightened her buttocks, and stretched her arms high and wide, pressing the palms of her hands into the cushiony tan roof of the old green sedan, and while she stretched her left leg out across the seat, her right leg was only partially extended; her foot had gone under the front passenger seat only so far. In that front seat, her mother, Stella Reese, was asleep. She'd been sleeping since they left Warren, Ohio, and crossed the border into Pennsylvania, heading back across to New York City. Even when her father, Richard, pulled into a rest stop along Interstate 80 to use the rest room and to get something to eat, Stella had not awakened, she was that tired. They'd spent three days in Warren at Cousin Edith's wedding, her third, where Stella had been her favorite cousin's matron of honor—more like her gofer. All in all, it was a nice wedding, but it was for old folks and Celeste hated that her mother had made her go when she wanted to stay home and hang out with her boyfriend, Sean. He was her first real boyfriend that her parents allowed her to have, and they had been going together for only two months. And now that school was over for the summer, they could be together a whole lot more, but oh, no, her mother wouldn't let her stay home.

"I'm not leaving you and Katrina home alone together. The house might not be standing when your father and I get back."

"So why don't you make Katrina go. I'm always the one you make go somewhere."

"Because Katrina's older and more responsible. You're seventeen and with all those friends you have, and not to mention that little boyfriend of yours, Sean, no telling what kind of trouble you could end up in. Go pack. And I don't wanna hear any more lip."

Katrina was lucky. Although she was twenty and still lived at home, she was never forced to go anywhere with their parents. Of course, no one would ever say it out loud, but Stella and Richard both knew that Katrina would bitch every single mile going and coming like she did when they drove down to Atlanta back in 1983, five years ago, for a family reunion on Richard's side of the family. Celeste could tell by the way her father had gripped the steering wheel and squeezed his eyes shut that he was fighting against driving off and leaving Katrina behind at the rest stop. That was a miserable trip. Katrina never stopped whining and bitching, and seemed to take great pleasure in picking on her the whole way. Katrina was that much of a bitch, which is also why Celeste couldn't stay home like she wanted to. No matter how minor their disagreement, she and Katrina would inevitably end up screaming at each other, which within minutes would escalate into them going for each other's throats. Their last fight, two weeks ago, was over who would get the last banana. Katrina felt she should have the banana because she'd called for it first; "That banana is mine." Celeste felt she should have the banana because she hadn't had one in two days whereas Katrina had eaten a banana every day for the past week. After fighting and pulling on the banana, the banana was squeezed into mush by their grabbing hands so neither got to eat it. Boy, were Stella and Richard angry when they saw the scratches on their neck and arms, the broken coffee table, and the smashed banana and the mushy black banana skin smushed into the green carpet in the family room.

Stella and Richard blamed both her and Katrina, but if they really thought about it, they would have realized that it was Katrina who was at fault. Katrina couldn't stand the sight of her. For a long time, Celeste had tried to be friends with her one and only sibling, but Katrina wasn't having it. Katrina just didn't like her and never tried to hide it. Celeste could remember when she was three being pinched all the time by Katrina—always when her parents weren't in sight. When she was ten, Katrina cut the strings on her violin. "I'm tired of you giving me a damn headache every night. You sound like you're trying to kill a cat."

Celeste didn't think her playing was all that bad and cried pitifully.

Katrina got punished more for saying the word damn than for cutting the violin strings. The violin belonged to Celeste's school and her parents had to pay for replacing the strings but that was about all, which led Celeste to think her parents hated her playing as well. That was when she gave up trying to learn how to play the violin, and when she also gave up trying to be Katrina's friend. Since then, she'd told her parents often enough that she didn't like Katrina. "She's mean," she said every time Katrina did something vicious to her, which was quite frequent. They were older now, but nothing had changed. Other than Katrina constantly calling her a spoiled brat, Celeste still couldn't understand why Katrina didn't like her and didn't look forward to seeing her after being away for three days. Originally, they had planned on staying four days in Ohio, but they were coming home a day early because Richard couldn't stand sleeping another hot night on the old, wobbly army cot set up at the foot of the full-size bed that Celeste slept in with her mother. She got to sleep in the bed because she had horrible menstrual cramps and sleeping on the cot didn't help.

Richard didn't have a bit of fun and quite literally exhaled when he pulled up in the driveway of his own two-story, roomy Cape Cod house in Laurelton, Queens. "No place like home," he said, cutting the engine and turning on the dome light so that he could see all they had to gather up.

"The house is dark," Stella said, looking at all the windows on the front of the house, upstairs and down. "Katrina must be out, unless she's back in her bedroom."

Pulling on her leather thongs, Celeste was hopeful. *If she's out, I won't have to see her stupid face tonight. Thank God for small favors.*

"Where would she go on a Sunday night?" Richard asked.

"Somewhere with Damon," Celeste replied. "You know how tight they are."

"It's after ten. Doesn't she have to go to work tomorrow?"

Stella answered, "No, she took off."

"Again? That's not a good way to start out."

"Richard, it's only a summer job at Burger King," Stella said, picking up her pocketbook from the floor between her feet. "Katrina'll be fine once she finishes college and gets a regular job."

"Yeah, right, Ma. You know Katrina doesn't like to work. She said she's gonna marry somebody rich so she won't have to."

"Well, she better do it soon," Richard said. "She's not gonna make a living staying in bed all day or partying every night."

"Yes she can, Dad. She could become—"

"Celeste!" Stella said. "Don't you start. You, too, Richard. Both of you leave Katrina alone. She'll be fine."

Celeste snickered behind her hand. Her mother knew what she was about to say, and that's because Katrina thought she was the bomb and used her body to get any guy she wanted. What did that say about her?

Stella pushed open her door and again looked at the house. "I left a message for Katrina telling her that we would be coming in tonight. You'd think she'd be home."

"Where did you leave the message, Ma? On the house machine or the one in Katrina's room?"

"The house machine, I think."

"Ma, you know Katrina never checks that answering machine."

"Yeah, that's true, I forgot."

Again Richard yawned. "Man, I'm tired. The next time we go anywhere, I'm staying in a hotel."

"Me, too," Celeste agreed, as she collected the empty potato chip bag, candy wrappers, empty soda cans and plastic slushie cups tossed on the floor. "Ma, I don't like sleeping with you."

"I don't like sleeping with you either; you toss and turn too much, but you and your daddy are just spoiled."

Richard pushed a button under the dash and popped the car's trunk. "If you consider me spoiled because I like sleeping in a king-size bed and having my own damn bathroom to use when I need to, then so be it, I'm spoiled." Then opening the door he slowly pushed himself out of the car. "And another thing, I don't like being cornered by family with their hands out."

"Who asked you for money? You didn't tell me anything about that."

"Your nephew Joe, and your cousin Ralph."

"Did you give them anything?"

"Sure did—a handshake and a 'I'm broke' speech. What do they think, we're rich?" Stretching out fully, Richard walked stiffly to the trunk and grunting, started unloading the suitcases.

"I didn't know they'd asked you for money," Stella said, deciding to keep her mouth shut about giving Edith fifty dollars, Joe thirty dollars, and Ralph fifty dollars.

"I'm with Dad, Ma. I'm for staying in a hotel, and for flying the next time we have to go anywhere." Taking her bag of garbage and her small carry-on bag, Celeste got out of the car, glad to be able to fully stretch out her legs. "Dad, planes fly to Ohio, you know."

"Good, save your money. Next time we'll meet you there."

"I'm not going back to Ohio," Celeste said, meaning it, and she wasn't ever driving anywhere that took more than an hour to get to.

"That's your family, Celeste," Stella said.

"Your family first, Ma, and they're boring."

"Celeste—"

"Let her be, Stella. She's a teenager, everyone's boring to her."

"That's right. I'm going inside to call Sean."

"Before you do, miss, come get these bags," Richard said, indicating two large plastic shopping bags full of clothes that Stella and Celeste had shopped for in Ohio that were still in the trunk. "And hurry up and open up the door and get the lights on." Richard's hands were full and he didn't feel like digging into his pocket for his house keys. "I have to go to the bathroom."

Stella stayed behind. "And, Celeste, come back and help me get the rest of this stuff out of the back."

"I have to go to the bathroom, too," Celeste said, using her key to unlock the door.

"I bet you do," Stella said, knowing that Celeste was anxious to get her hands on the telephone.

"Dad, I'll use the upstairs bathroom." Dropping the bags in the front hall, Celeste quickly turned on the lights in the hallway and in the living room, and then taking the stairs two at a time, rushed up to the bathroom on the second floor. As soon as she took care of her business, she headed for her bedroom to cool out and call Sean, but just as she was passing Katrina's bedroom, she heard a noise coming from behind the closed door. She looked down at the bottom of the door and saw a thin line of light. Katrina was home. Celeste pressed her right ear to the door. She heard the sound of someone shushing someone. Normally, she would not go into Katrina's room uninvited, which was never, but she was intrigued. Celeste pushed open the door. Out of the corner of her eye, she saw the closet door as it was closing.

"Who told you to open my damn door?" Katrina was on the far side of her bed hurriedly trying to pull on her panties. Her hair was all over her head.

"I saw that," Celeste said, her eyes glued to the closet as she boldly stepped inside Katrina's room. "Who's in there?"

"Celeste, U'ma kick your ass." Katrina searched frantically for her bra. "Get outta my room!"

Teasingly, Celeste said in a hushed voice with her hand to her mouth, "Ma, Dad, Katrina's home. And she got company."

"U'm gonna kill you, Celeste. There's no one in my room. Get out and close the door."

"Is it Damon? Ooh, Ma and Dad are gonna kill you. You're not supposed to have him up in your room."

Katrina fumbled with her bra but couldn't get it untwisted to get it on right. She yanked it off her arm and threw it at Celeste. "Get out!" She took a step toward Celeste, but she glanced at the closet door and stopped. "Please, Celeste," she said in a softer voice, "just leave. I'll owe you."

"That's all right. This is payment enough. Damon, you better come out before my dad gets up here. The window's open."

"Celeste, stop talking crazy. There's no one in my closet."

"Then why do you look so scared." Celeste started for the closet.

Katrina rushed over and blocked Celeste, pushing her back toward the door. "Get out before I kick your ass."

Celeste was no longer seeing the humor of the situation. Katrina was caught and what better way to get back at her. "You better get dressed before Ma and Dad get up here."

"I hate you."

"What else is new? Ma! Dad! Y'all better get up here!"

Again, Katrina pushed Celeste. "I'm gonna beat your ass!"

"Let's see if you get yours beat first." She pushed Katrina back.

Richard and Stella rushed into the room. "What're you girls fighting about now?" Stella asked, out of breath. "Katrina, if you're home, why are all the lights out?"

Katrina stood bug-eyed, mouth open, staring at her parents.

"Girl, put your clothes on!" Richard said, standing behind Stella.

Katrina scurried back to her bed to search for her white tee shirt in the rumpled bedsheet and spread. Quickly finding her oversized tee shirt, she hurriedly tried to put it on but her head and arms got caught up in the shirt. She yanked irritably on it until she was able to pull it on right.

"Now, what's going on up here?" Richard asked.

"Celeste barged into my room without knocking."

"That's because I heard something."

"You heard me, stupid! I am in my own room, you know."

"Yes, and you're butt-naked. Dad, I heard another voice in here."

"That's a lie! Ain't nobody in my room but me."

Richard and Stella both glanced around the room. Seeing nothing but Katrina upset about Celeste barging into her room, they both looked at Celeste.

"Celeste, you know you girls are supposed to stay out of each other's rooms," Stella said. "It's ridiculous that you two can't get along."

"I'm sick of it myself," Richard said. "I want it to stop."

"I didn't do anything wrong," Celeste defended.

"You came into my room—uninvited!"

"Is that true, Celeste?" Stella asked.

"Yeah, but—"

"Celeste, we've only been home five minutes. I'm tired. Must you start up with Katrina the minute we step foot in the house?"

"I didn't—"

"Get out of my room!"

"Celeste, go to your room," Richard said. "Tomorrow—"

"Y'all always taking Katrina's side. Y'all never listen to me." Celeste charged at the closet door, getting there before Katrina could stop her. She yanked open the door exposing the half-naked man hiding there. But it wasn't Damon as Celeste had suspected, it was Sean—her own boyfriend. A boyfriend she had only kissed.

All hell broke loose. While her father was snatching Sean out of the closet and hauling him toward the door, Celeste, when she recovered from the shock, which was quite swiftly, charged—claws out, teeth bared—at Katrina. Before her mother could come between them, Celeste pulled a handful of Katrina's hair out of the top of her head. In that moment, she hated her sister.

1

Seven hours to flight time—12:15 P.M.

Celeste couldn't sleep—she was too excited. She had been up and moving about since four thirty, just minutes before Willie turned over and covered his head to block the harsh overhead light and long before the morning sun peeked into the bedroom window. For two weeks now, Celeste had been ticking off her list of things to pack. Her large suitcase was open on her side of the bed with everything neatly folded inside. The only things not packed were her toothbrush, her deodorant, and her comb. Oops. Scratch that. This trip, she didn't need a comb. Her hair was braided. This trip, she was being smart—her braided hairstyle was going to save her a lot of time and energy—no rollers, no blow drying, no combing. She was going to swim, air dry her braids in the hot Caribbean sun in the Bahamas and Bermuda, and dance the night away with nothing on her mind but a Sin on the Beach high and making love to her man.

For a year and a half Celeste had been looking forward to her first vacation in nine years. The last vacation had been on the occasion of her marriage to Willie. Then they had gone to Virginia Beach—the poor man's version of the Caribbean. Celeste glanced over at Willie on his back on the bed with nothing but a pair of black briefs to cover his fabulous nakedness. Yep, the boy still looked good. For sure, she was definitely going to revisit her honeymoon on this trip—she was going to wear Willie out. Since their honeymoon, they had not had the money nor the time to go on an extended vacation of any kind. All of their money had gone into buying and fixing up their brownstone—Celeste's pride, and now paying a babysitter five afternoons a week when Justine's second grade class let out. Justine was her joy, Justine was the reason Celeste's heart sang. Her brownstone, on the other hand, was her just reward for working hard all her life. While she had no regrets about all the money spent on the brownstone, she couldn't say the same about her family. From the start, her mother had been against her buying a house in Bedford Stuyvesant which was, once upon a time, one of the poorer sections of Brooklyn, but, shoot, she and Willie needed a place to live that wasn't going to gag them every time they had to cough up the monthly rent. Her father used to say, "A home is what goes on inside the walls, not what goes on outside the walls." But her mother would always retort, "Then let's see you make a home in a landfill." That pretty much summed up how Stella Reese felt about much of Brooklyn. She and Katrina both seemed to have forgotten that they had once lived in Bedford Stuyvesant for two years in the seventies after Dad lost his job and they were forced to go onto welfare. Katrina swears to this day that she was never on welfare, but at the time she had no memory lapses when it came to eating the food that those monopoly-looking food stamp dollars brought. That's because her ass was hungry and a hungry gut doesn't turn its nose up and question where the food came from.

Unlike Katrina, Celeste remembered the hard times and learned from them—nothing came easy—which is why she and Willie were able to move into a brownstone that had been all but abandoned. Right away they fixed up the master bedroom, the second floor bathroom, the kitchen, and slowly, over seven years, renovated one square foot at a time around them. They had no problem with moving into a community that had no where to go but up.

Just weeks after they returned from their honeymoon, she and Willie had driven up and down the brownstone-lined streets of Bed-Stuy, as the natives of the community called Bedford Stuyvesant, admiring and dreaming about one day owning one of the grand, ornately adorned turn-of-the-century row houses of brown slate. Between the two of them working—Willie as a communications specialist and she as a debt collection agent—they couldn't afford a house of any size, but they were looking anyway. Hey, one never knew. They had just gotten married and felt that the one bedroom apartment they lived in in Flatbush, which had been Willie's, was too small and, as far as Celeste was concerned, too full of lustful memories of lascivious romps for

Willie. She wanted her own place where neither had memories of past lovers, and just when it seemed like they would not luck up on a brownstone for, literally, a dream and a fistful of dollars, they did.

A brownstone on Macon Street was advertised in *The New York Times* "Classified Section," an unlikely place for a house in Bedford Stuyvesant, so it really stood out. The asking price was fifty thousand dollars. She and Willie were both skeptical. Anyone in the know knew that shells—brownstones with nothing inside them but the dust from wood eaten away by termites—in Prospect Heights, Fort Greene, and Clinton Hill were going for one and two hundred thousand dollars. The ad had to be wrong.

"Bedford Stuyvesant or not," Willie said, "what kind of house goes for fifty thousand dollars in New York City?"

Celeste was disheartened, yet curious anyway. She and Willie drove from Flatbush to take a curious gander at this fifty thousand dollar brownstone. Surprise, surprise, it was as advertised. It was a brownstone. The brown exterior slate was flawless—it wasn't flaking or cracked—it needed only to be steam cleaned. The house inside, however, needed a lot of tender loving care—hell, it needed a bulldozer, a sledgehammer and a barrelful of cash. Although, miraculously, the three-story building had sturdy wooden floors, working plumbing and electricity flowing through its wires. Every dark, opaque-colored wall of dark brown, deep avocado green or brazen hot pink in the twelve room house, was peeling or cracked, and the floors had to be stripped of the yards of corroded linoleum that was stacked five layers deep on every floor throughout, including the bathroom and kitchen floors. The three bedrooms and two kitchens still had huge, rusty cast iron claw feet sinks and tubs, and the light fixtures were all original two and three-socket metal hubcap-looking fixtures that looked as if they came off an old Cadillac. But Willie wasn't fazed. He saw the potential of the house and so did Celeste. Willie claimed, for an additional fifty thousand dollars and doing the work himself, he could, over time, make the house into a showpiece. That is, if they could come up with the purchase price, which they immediately had problems raising since the banks weren't willing to loan money for a house that, realistically, needed about a hundred thousand dollars' worth of work.

The twenty thousand dollars they were able to come up with on their own wasn't enough when the deceased owner's son, Joseph Ross, living in Virginia, wanted the entire fifty thousand in cash, up front. Thinking that they were defeated, Willie said, "This isn't the only house in the world. We could save up for a few years and get a better one." But Celeste wanted this house. She refused to accept defeat. She had already researched the house so she knew that Joseph Ross's sister, Barbara Walkins, was the person listed as the contact for the house. Using her skill as a collection agent for Akron Financial Collections, Celeste was able to do a skip trace and get the unlisted telephone number for Barbara Walkins down in Atlanta, Georgia. From the word "hello," Celeste poured on enough charm to make a horse drink from a Dixie cup. After a two and a half hour conversation about the house, her family's life in the house, and the neighborhood before the blackouts and destruction of 1967 and 1977, Barbara said, "I like you. I'm going to tell my brother to give you the house."

And, literally, Joseph Ross did. He dropped the asking price down to $30,000 and then turned around and asked for fifteen thousand in cash and took back a fifteen thousand dollar mortgage. Celeste and Willie paid off the house in two years and, finally, after nine years, the house was just about where Celeste wanted it to be. She and Willie had done much of the work themselves. Willie once said, "Who knew what these hands could do?" Boy was he proud and he had every right to be. Their house was beautiful. They had one more bathroom to renovate on the top floor. Then they were done. They were taking time out now to go on a much deserved vacation, and Willie, with his sleepyhead self, was going to get all the loving his beautiful body could handle.

Standing over Willie, Celeste smiled down on her man, her sweetie pie. Willie looked so good, she could eat him up—she glanced at the clock radio on the night stand: 5:20—no time, but she kissed Willie full on the mouth anyway, savoring the softness of his lips without the sourness of his morning breath. Willie didn't stir. Celeste pinched his left nipple.

Frowning, his eyes squeezed shut, Willie groaned.

"Wake up, sleepyhead."

Grunting, Willie turned over on his side away from Celeste.

She tapped him once on the behind. "Willie, get up. I don't wanna get to the airport late and have to wait forever and a day on those long-ass lines. You know security is tight since 911."

Willie muttered, "What time is it?"

"Five-twenty."

Willie still didn't bother to open his eyes. "Baby, we don't have to leave until nine o'clock and even that's too early. Will you let me sleep?"

"Willie, you didn't finish packing, and I'm telling you right now, I am not packing for you." Celeste glanced over at Willie's suitcase on the floor in the corner. The only things inside were two pair of swimming trunks and a pair of leather sandals. "Geez, Willie, do you think you'll be wearing a pair of swimming trunks everywhere we go?"

"If I feel like it."

"Willie!"

"Damn, baby, relax. I can finish packing in five minutes. So would you, please, let me get my sleep out." Willie grabbed Celeste's pillow and covered his head with it.

"Okay. Fine." It annoyed her that Willie's one major flaw was that unless he was going to work, he didn't think anything else in the world was worth being on time for. Back when they were fixing up the house, many a day he had gotten lazy and deemed the house "liveable," which meant that he was tired of spending his money and all of his spare time working on the house. He'd only go back to working on the house when he got tired of hearing her bitch at him, like she was doing now.

"Willie, if you wait till the very last minute to pack your bag and you can't find everything you need, you better not scream for me to help you find a damn thing, because I won't! I'm done."

"Damn, woman! It's too damn early for you to be bitching at me."

"Then get up and do what you need to do! Did you put gas in that gas guzzling SUV last night? You know we won't have time to stop and get gas if you're running late."

Willie held the pillow tighter to his head and ears. He was so tired of hearing Celeste bitch, just to spite her, he wasn't getting out of bed until eight thirty—he could do that because he had filled his tank last night after he'd gotten his fill of some good loving.

"Okay, Willie, don't answer me, but if that SUV doesn't have a full tank, I am going to pack all of my luggage on top of your hard-ass head and use a crop on your hard behind and ride you all the way out to LaGuardia."

When Willie didn't respond, Celeste went back to checking her list of things she needed for the trip. If she brushed her teeth, she could pack her toothbrush too. She went off into the bathroom to do just that.

It was early yet, but she may as well get her shower over and done with as well.

With the water running in the shower while she brushed her teeth, Celeste didn't hear the telephone ringing back in the bedroom.

Willie answered crabbily, "Who is it?"

"We need to talk," was the hasty reply.

Willie knew immediately who the caller was—Andrew Coleman, his supervisor at Dialacom. "Not right now, we don't. Do you know what time it is?"

"Sorry, Willie, but I had to try and catch you before you left."

"Well, I'm not up yet and I'm not on company time. I'll see you in two weeks."

"I can't wait two weeks, Willie. I need to know what you're going to do."

"Coleman, I haven't decided as yet what my course of action will be, but I can tell you this much, Tyrell Johnson's name will be cleared."

The other end of the line was silent in Willie's ear. "I'm hanging up."

"Wait, Willie. I need to explain some things to you. Let me come by and talk to you."

"No."

"Come on, man," Coleman said. *"I can meet you at your house or any-where you want. I'm already on the road. I can be at your place in ten min-utes. You're still over on Macon Street, right?"*

"Coleman, don't come to my house." Willie sat half way up in bed. "I'm not dealing with this shit before I leave town. If you wanna do anything, you need to right some wrongs before I get back, then I won't have to show my hand."

Again, there was an uncertain silence on the other end. "You hear what I'm saying Coleman? Do the right thing, man."

"Man, don't you think I wanna do that?" Coleman was shouting. *"It's not as cut and dry as you think. If I recant my story, reinstate Johnson, I'm the one—"*

"Yeah, you're the one that'll be brought up on charges." Willie could feel his stomach muscles tighten into knots. "Coleman, you got Tyrel Johnson fired and brought up on charges for something you did. The man is in jail because you stole fifteen laptops. If I hadn't secretly set up that video recorder in the supply room yesterday morning, I wouldn't be the wiser, would I? It's too damn bad I didn't get to see the damn tape until last night, after I left work, or you'd be sitting in jail instead of Tyrel."

"*Listen to me, Willie. I can straighten everything out for Johnson. I can get back most of the laptops. I put a computer back yesterday. I know you saw that.*"

"You got that right."

"*Look, Willie, I'll say that the computers were misplaced, that there was a mistake. I'll get Johnson reinstated and the charges will be dropped.*"

"You do that—first thing Monday morning." Willie wasn't fooled by the lie. Coleman was a thief, and by default a liar.

"*I will, Willie, I swear. Just don't turn the tape in. And you know what I'll do for you, Willie?*"

"Let me guess—get me fired?"

"*No, no, Willie, I swear, I'd never do that. I'll get you a raise, a promotion. That's right, you'll be Senior Communications Specialist. You'll get a $5,000.00 raise. What do you say, Willie? You keep quiet, I'll take care of you, I promise. We got a deal?*"

"No deal."

"*Shit, Willie! I can't afford to lose my job. I can't go to jail! I got a family.*"

"You should've thought about that when you were sneaking laptops out of the office in that big-ass briefcase of yours."

"*Goddammit, Willie, I made a mistake. I—*"

"Man, I ain't got time for this crap." Willie slammed the telephone down, and quickly turned over in the bed with his arms folded tight. He was going to get his nap out no matter how pissed off he was. He flopped over onto his back, and lay his arm across his eyes to shield them from the overhead light.

Damn it! If only he had viewed the tape before he left work. Then he could have turned it in, but oh no. He didn't see the tape until ten thirty last night. Clearly, Coleman could be seen taking a laptop from his briefcase and putting it back on the shelf in the supply room. Earlier in the morning, Tyrel had been arrested for stealing the fifteen laptops. Coleman, obviously, thought it best if he return the laptop he had already taken earlier that morning before anyone discovered it was missing. The man was low to steal from Dialacom but even dirtier to put the blame on Tyrel, who worked as the supply room clerk.

A few days ago when Willie first heard about the stolen computers, he knew immediately that Tyrel was blameless. Weeks before, he had been out to lunch with Tyrel when he found twenty dollars in the restaurant. Willie was speechless when Tyrel turned the money over to the manager. Hell, if it had been him, he would have wasted no time shoving that twenty deep into his pocket, but Tyrel said, "My gain is someone's loss. I wouldn't feel right." Tyrel taking that stance had particularly amazed Willie because Tyrel was only twenty-four years old and it wasn't like he was making a whole lot of money. He had come from the mean streets of the South Bronx and had run the streets as a gang banger in his teen years. It was while he was locked up in jail that Tyrel had found religion—the Muslim religion. Willie had to ask himself, would a man who turned in found money steal from a company that took a chance and gave him a paycheck? He didn't think so. When he return from vacation, he would turn in the tape if Colemen hadn't cleared Tyrel's name. For now, that tape was stuck down in the living room sofa between the arm and the cushion where he slipped it after watching it. It was just as safe there as anywhere else in the house. Willie turned onto his stomach. He was determined to sleep at least another hour.

Riiiiiig!

The telephone's ring screamed in Willie's ear. He snatched up the receiver. "Look, man! I told you—"

"Willie?" a young girl's hushed voice asked.

Willie immediately sat up. He glanced at the door. He could hear the shower water running halfway down the hall, but he covered the mouthpiece with his hand anyway. "Whata you doing calling me here?"

"Baby, I miss you."